Blind Side

Published by Kandi Steiner
Edited by Elaine York/Allusion Publishing
www.allusionpublishing.com
Cover Design by Kandi Steiner
Formatting by Elaine York/Allusion Publishing
www.allusionpublishing.com

Blind Side

KANDI STEINER

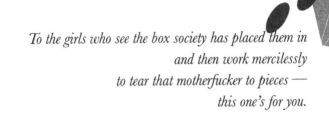

*To the girls who see the box society has placed them in
and then work mercilessly
to tear that motherfucker to pieces —
this one's for you.*

Chapter 1

GIANA

It was on the most beautiful day that I fell victim to Clay Johnson's post-breakup meltdown.

The summer sun was high and bright in the sky, warm on my skin as I bounced across the North Boston University football field with my iPad in tow, checking off the list of players I needed to pull over for interviews after the first day of fall camp. Fall was whispering on the cool breeze, the faint scent of apples and fresh turf promising another exciting year for the NBU Rebels.

This time last year, I had been an anxious mess — not that I didn't still shake like a leaf any time I tried to order a six-foot-three football player around. But now, I at least had the mediocre confidence of having an internship under my belt, of being hired on part time as the team's Public Relations Assistant Coordinator.

This was *my* team, my year to shine, and my time to step out of the shadows.

1

My caramel curls bounced as I swept across the field, tapping shoulders of the players I needed and directing them where to go. I only blushed three times, and I managed to speak just above mouse-level and keep eye contact with all of them.

Progress.

I'd earned my spot here, just like these players would fight for their spots on the team this season.

Confidence, I hoped, would come with time.

I smiled when I saw a request for Clay Johnson on my list, one of the easiest players to coach in the art of media relations. He was a natural, goofy and charismatic, and yet somehow eloquent and refined in his responses. He spoke on camera like he was a thirty-two-year-old professional rather than a nineteen-year-old student athlete, and he was *nice* to me — respectful, attentive. In fact, he was usually the one who would sock the other players in the arm to make them pay attention to me if my soft request for them to follow me didn't work.

Plus, he was the *definition* of man candy, and was absolutely irresistible no matter what gender or sexual orientation one identified with.

I spotted him easily among the sea of players, not just because of his height, but because he'd already stripped his practice jersey off and his muscles were gleaming in the New England sun. I tried my best not to drool over the smooth hills of his abdomen, not to trace the beads of sweat as they slicked over the swell of his pecs and ran down the length of him. Those broad shoulders were tan and tight, traps otherworldly, like he was an MMA fighter instead of a college safety.

It was only twenty seconds or so, the amount of time I allowed myself to marvel at the cutting edge of his jaw, the sharp bridge of his nose, the damp mop of coffee-brown hair that he absentmindedly ran a hand through. That motion had his bicep involuntarily flexing, and a flash of the cover of my current mafia romance read assaulted me at the sight.

I could picture it, Clay Johnson strangling a man with his bare hands, holding him off the ground with those biceps bulging, severe eyes promising death to the punk unless he told Clay what he needed to know.

A blink, and I was back on the field, professional as I approached him.

"Clay," I said, though I knew it was too quiet, especially when the guys around him broke out in a fit of laughter over something.

I smiled, tucking a wild curl behind one ear before I spoke up.

"Clay, I need you for media."

His whetted green eyes snapped to mine, effectively stealing my next breath with the gesture. Where those eyes were usually warm and crinkled at the edges, outlined in gold and underlined with a wide, infectious smile, today they were... lifeless.

Dull.

Frigid.

Almost... *mean*.

Before he had the chance to respond, I was swept off my feet in a sweaty hug from behind.

"Giana! My girl. Don't you mean it's *me* you're looking for?"

Leo Hernandez spun me around, and I knew better than to fight him. I simply waited until my feet were back on the ground before readjusting my glasses up the bridge my nose.

"You'll get your time in the spotlight, Leo. Don't worry."

"Never do," he said with a wink.

Leo Hernandez was a too-sexy-for-his-own-good running back, and a certified pain in my ass. It wasn't that he was bad on camera — quite the contrary, actually. It was his extracurricular activities *off* the field that kept me busy. The boy wouldn't know how to say no to a gorgeous blonde and a late night out, even if there was an NFL contract and a five-million-dollar signing bonus in the mix.

When I turned back to Clay, it was just in time to watch him as he brushed past me on his way to the locker room.

I scampered to catch up with him. "Uh, actually, the media is all lined up over *there*," I said, pointing to the other edge of the stadium.

"Don't care."

I stopped at the words, at how cold they were, shivering a bit and watching the muscles of his back ebb and flow before I shook my head and skipped to catch up to him again.

"It won't be long, just a quick five-minute interview."

"No."

I chuckled. "Look, I get it. First day of camp is tough. It's hot out here, you've got Coach watching, I—"

"No, you don't get it," he said, whipping around until I slammed right into his sweaty chest. He didn't attempt to catch me as I bounced back, but I righted myself, adjusting my glasses to look him in the eyes as he continued. "You're not a player. You're not part of the team. You're a part of the media. And I don't want to fucking talk to you, or them, or *anyone* right now."

Hurt flashed through me as he turned, but it only lingered a moment before I blew out a breath and let the pain go with it.

This was part of my job, dealing with athletic babies and they're mood swings.

I got this.

I cleared my throat as I caught up to him. "Well, I'm sorry you're having an off day, but unfortunately, this is part of your role as an athlete at North Boston University. So, you can either do this very short interview, or explain to Coach why you couldn't be bothered to."

That made him stop, and I watched his fists curl at his sides before he turned around, veins popping in his neck. He cracked said neck and then stormed right past me, on his way to the media line.

I smiled in victory.

At least, until I followed him to the perfectly nice female reporter from ESPN and watched in horror as he made an ass of himself, the team, and more importantly?

Me.

"Clay, after that bowl game last season that had us on the edge of our seat, we've all got big expectations for NBU football. How are you feeling about the season?"

Sarah Blackwell smiled a freshly whitened, toothy grin up at Clay, angling the microphone in her hand toward his beautiful mouth — which was currently in a flat, straight line.

"I feel like we could focus a lot more on football if we didn't have to waste our time talking to reporters like you."

My eyes shot open, heart catching in my chest as Sarah frowned, blinked, looked at me and back at the camera before lowering the mic.

"We know you're all excited about the season, I completely understand the desire to keep your focus locked in," she said with a forced laugh, trained and poised despite Clay's deadpan expression. "So, the hot news last season was about Riley Novo, the female kicker for NBU. She's back this season, and this time, dating a fellow teammate — Zeke Collins. Tell us, do you think that will be a distraction for the team?"

Clay was already speaking before she could lift her mic. "I think our dating lives shouldn't matter to anyone who isn't sad and lonely and desperate to have an opinion about someone else's relationships so they can avoid the shit show of their own."

Sarah tried to rip the microphone back down before he could curse, but I knew it was too late, and she chuckled through another forced joke with an awkward smile in place before dismissing us. Once the camera was off, she glared at Clay. "Real professional."

But Clay only looked down at me. "Anything else?"

I swore my eye twitched, but I smiled despite it, stomach in knots as I tried conjuring up excuses for the ass-skinning I already knew would be coming from my fire-breathing boss.

"We have a student here from the college news team," I said, guiding him along the fence behind reporters interviewing other teammates. "He's nice. And *fresh*," I said, stopping Clay short of where the young man waited. I lowered my voice. "Look, I don't know what's going on, but if you can't handle—"

6

Clay shook me off before I could finish, a head nod to the kid with the mic and the slighter larger one with the camera behind him his only greeting.

It wasn't *as bad* as the one before, but it was nowhere near the Clay Johnson I knew of last season.

He barely answered the questions, retorted with smartass remarks more than anything of context, and when the poor kid tried to grapple with his notes and figure out what else to ask him, Clay curtly said, "We done here?"

And then turned and left before the poor thing could answer.

After profusely apologizing, I called in a favor from Riley and Zeke, asking them to talk to both reporters about their summer together and how this year is different playing not only as teammates, but as a couple. They were hot news in college football, had been ever since they made Twitter meltdown after the bowl win last year by making out on the field.

Fortunately for me, *they* were in a happy mood and both very well-spoken on camera.

I smiled and gave them a thumbs up as I listened behind the camera operator, all the while burning holes into Clay's back as he stomped toward the locker room like a child.

When the interview was over, Riley thanked the reporters with me before pulling me to the side. Her long, chestnut hair was lined with golden streaks bleached from playing in the sun. She pulled it up into a high, tight ponytail, accepting a kiss on the cheek from Zeke and waiting until he was out of ear shot before she spoke.

"A word of advice," she said, lowering her voice as she looked around to make sure no one was listening.

"Might want to lay off Johnson for a while. Him and Maliyah just broke up."

I blanched. "What?!"

It was useless trying to keep the shock from my face. I didn't know Clay well, but I didn't *have to* to know that his high school sweetheart meant everything to him. He toted her around here every time she visited our campus last season, and I *distinctly* remembered having a hard time peeling him off her for an interview after our second home game win. He posted about her all the time on his Instagram, and the captions were always very clear about how he felt.

He was going to marry her.

But now, they were nothing.

Riley just nodded, brows bending together. "I know. Poor kid was talking to Zeke last semester about how he thought she was *the one*." She sighed, both of us watching Clay disappear into the stadium hall that led to the locker room. "He's been a mess."

My shoulders slumped. "I knew something had to have happened. He was always so happy last season, so… full of life."

"Well, I don't see him being that way for a while." Riley swallowed, still looking where Clay had vanished. "They were high school sweethearts."

I sighed, wishing I could find some empathy. *I* had never dated anyone, let alone been in love, and so the only thing I found simmering in my chest toward Clay in that moment was a distant sort of sympathy.

And a little frustration that I'd have to deal with the fallout.

"I'm going to have to set up a training with him," I said. "He'll still have to talk to the media, and Coach will have his ass *and* mine if he pulls something like that again."

Riley looked at me like she pitied me, reaching up to squeeze my shoulder. Before she could walk off, I called out.

"Any advice?"

She shrugged, a sad attempt at a smile on her face. "Make sure there's beer around."

Chapter 2

GIANA

Charlotte Banks was the canvas landscape picture of cool as she sat behind her desk the next afternoon, eyes on her computer screen while the tape of Clay's interview played back. That screen was angled toward me, too, so I could watch from where I sat opposite her — like I hadn't replayed it a hundred times already.

If I expected a blow out, I didn't know my boss. Mrs. Banks appeared almost bored as she watched the screen, occasionally looking down at her manicured nails and picking at the skin around them before she'd fold her arms over her chest once more. Her short copper hair was straightened and styled to perfection, the strands framing her sharp chin, not a strand out of place. Her lips were painted a muted red, and her wide, golden eyes were like that of a cat lazily watching a mouse struggle where she has it by the tail.

I swallowed when the video stopped, an image of Clay's uncharacteristic frown frozen in place. I chanced a look at my boss, who simply blinked and waited for me to speak.

"I'm sorry," I started, but she held up a hand, her voice warm and smooth like dripping hot fudge as she spoke.

"Not what I want to hear. Try again."

I closed my mouth, considering before I opened it once more. "Clay and his girlfriend broke up, which I was unaware of until after the interview. He's clearly in no headspace to be on camera, and I take full responsibility for not realizing that until it was too late."

Charlotte etched a brow, unfolding her arms and turning her computer screen back around before she was scribbling on a notepad on her desk.

"Good information to know," she said, not looking at me. "But still not what I wanted to hear."

I fought the urge to deflate, using every muscle lining my spine to keep it straight, my chin raised, eyes on her.

She glanced up at me before sighing. "Can you handle it or not?"

I bristled at the accusation, at the fact that she even had to *ask*. But then again, I couldn't blame her — not after what she'd had to work with since I first walked through her door. It had taken all my effort, every single day, just to look these guys in the eye and speak loud enough to direct them where they needed to be.

I'd come a long way, yes... but I certainly had a ways to go.

"Of course," I answered, hoping my confidence was convincing.

"Good, then we don't need to discuss it further." She took a sip of her room-temperature water — I knew it was room temp because it had been part of my job as intern last year to make sure it was. "I'm depending on you to handle this kind of work so I don't have to waste my time or energy. Use the intern if you need to."

The intern.

Charlotte couldn't even be bothered to call her by her name.

It was the same way for me, until I proved myself worthy last fall. Although I was in hot water before this season had even started, so I imagined *last year* didn't matter much. Still, Charlotte had to see something in me — potential, grit, tenacity — otherwise, I wouldn't be here.

I held onto that as she continued.

"Coach Sanders has informed me that he'd like the team to be more involved in giving back to the community," she said without waiting for a response from me, and I knew the quick change in subject meant that she expected me to take care of the Clay situation — whatever that looked like. "He gave some touching sob story for his reasoning, but I know without needing clarification that it will make the team look good — and him by proxy. So," she said, clicking her mouse a few times until my phone vibrated with a calendar alert. "Save the date for a team auction."

"What will we be auctioning off?" I asked, adding the event with a tap of my thumb.

"The players."

I coughed on a laugh, but covered it as clearing my throat when I saw Charlotte was serious.

"It will be a date auction, with the date activities donated by various people in the community who want to take part, and all the funds raised being given to charity."

"Which charity?"

She waved her hand. "I don't know, you pick one."

I smiled, adding the task to my to-do list.

"You can go," Charlotte said next, and then she balanced her dainty elbow on her desk, finger directed at me. "Get Johnson under control. I'm inviting Sarah Blackwell back for an exclusive on Chart Day and I want him happy as a clam to speak with her."

I nodded, excusing myself without any verbal confirmation because I knew none was needed. And as soon as I ducked out of her office and closed the door behind me, I took a long, sweet breath that didn't burn from the smoke my dragon of a boss loved to fill the room with.

In the next breath, determination sank in, and I set my stride toward the weight room.

All my life, I'd felt the desire to think differently, to *act* differently, to challenge myself *and* the world around me.

Growing up, I was left in the shadows, the unremarkable middle child in a stack of five annoyingly talented kids. I had two older sisters and two younger brothers, and as such, I slipped into the background of our family without much consequence.

I was the third girl, unremarkable in its own right, sentenced to wear hand-me-down clothes and never have the chance to form an identity of my own. Couple that with the fact that I had two brothers born not too long after me, the boys my parents had prayed for, and you could say I was as invisible as the dust collecting on the top of a ceiling fan. I only seemed to be noticed when I got in the way, when my presence became a nuisance or flared up someone's allergies.

Still, I didn't feel bitter growing up. The comparison game never really got to me. I thought it was spectacular that my oldest sister, Meghan, excelled at softball and went on to play in college, receiving a full-ride scholarship. I was in awe of my second oldest sister, Laura, getting into MIT. I knew without a doubt that she'd change the world with her passion for science engineering. And I had nothing but love for my younger brothers, Travis and Patrick, who were little inventors set to appear on *Shark Tank* once they got the right million-dollar idea hammered out.

If anything, I kind of loved existing in the forgotten space in-between. No one bothered me when I locked myself in my room for the weekend, reading and watching documentaries. With all my parents' attention on my siblings, I was free to use my time exploring the world and what makes it tick, which was my favorite thing to do — aside from getting lost in a smutty, taboo romance novel.

It drove my mom insane that I didn't have direction when I left for college. She also didn't particularly like that I'd pulled away from the church when I was in high school, thanks to my self-education in religion and newfound questions that neither she *nor* our pastor could answer. Add in the fact that she found a gritty motorcycle club romance stuffed under my pillow and read a scene that made her clutch her pearls before declaring I was *banned from reading anything like this ever again!* And I guess you could say we weren't exactly close.

But, to her credit, she didn't spend much effort on trying to steer me toward a career path or toward the church, not before she'd sigh and give up and turn her focus back to one of her God-fearing children who had a good head on their shoulders.

What she couldn't see, what *no one* could see, was that I didn't know what I wanted to do with my life yet because I didn't know enough *about* life itself.

I'd never traveled outside of New England, never had a boyfriend, and never even gotten close to second base, let alone to going all the way.

There was still so much of life I wanted to soak up and study before I committed to my role in it, which was a big reason why I pushed myself out of my comfort zone when I came to college and picked the major that was least suited for me.

Public Relations.

Putting me — the quiet, nerdy virgin — in charge of public perception just seemed like a disaster waiting to happen. But that's why I loved it. That's why it was important to me.

It was unexpected, and different, and challenging.

And I wouldn't stop until I'd mastered every aspect of it.

Chapter 3

CLAY

I had a lot of expectations for my sophomore year at North Boston University.

After winning our bowl game last season and having a winning record on top of it, I expected us to be *the* team to contend with in The Big North conference. And after having one of the best seasons of my life, I expected to make said team easily, to start every game, and to demolish the records I'd set last year. I also expected us to win, to get not just *a* bowl game this season, but one of *the* bowl games — the ones that would serve as semi-finals and take us to the National Championship Game.

What I had *not* expected was for my girlfriend of five years to dump me.

Any time I thought of it, my chest caved in on itself. It felt impossible, how the girl I loved, the girl I thought I would *marry,* could walk away from me so easily. It was like being safe onboard a cruise ship one moment, basking in the tropical sun, only to be thrown overboard the next — nothing to hold onto, no one to hear my screams as the ship continued on its course and left me behind in the unrelenting waters.

What was worse was that it wasn't just a breakup — not the way most of my friends knew them, anyway.

Maliyah Vail wasn't just my girlfriend, she was family.

We grew up together. Our families were close, weaved together in every way like a thick blanket. Her dad and my dad were best friends in college, and even after my parents split, her mom made sure to keep an eye on mine, to make sure she was okay.

Which she wasn't often.

What I once considered a fairytale childhood was demolished with just one decision — my father's. Overnight, we went from a happy family of three to a broken family that consisted of me and Mom, and every now and then, Dad.

When he wasn't busy with his *new* family, that is — the one he'd easily replaced us with.

Maliyah had been by my side through all of it. She was there through the episodes with my mom, who didn't know how to cope after the loss of her marriage and tried to find solace in the worst kind of men after. She understood the abandonment I felt from my dad, and her own father stepped in to take his place, teaching me all the things a father should have as I grew up. More than anything, she was there through all the ups and downs of playing football, reminding me every chance she had that I would make it one day, that I would go pro.

It didn't feel like losing my girlfriend.

It felt like losing my right arm.

It still hadn't sunk in that we'd *finally* made it through a grueling year of long-distance — her in California where we grew up, me here in Massachusetts — only for her to get into NBU, move across the country, and... break up with me.

Nothing about it made sense. I'd tried combing through every word of her breakup speech and had come up empty each time I tried to find reasoning.

"What we had was a great first love, Clay, but that's all it was — a first love."

Maliyah's face crumpled, but not in the way that said she was actually hurt by the statement. It was a collapse of pity, like she was telling a little kid why he couldn't ride the big boy rollercoaster.

"We made a promise," I said, thumbing the promise ring on my finger. We'd exchanged them at sixteen, a promise that we'd be together forever — a wedding band in everything but law.

But when I reached out for hers, her finger was bare, the gold band nowhere in sight, and I swallowed as she pulled away with a grimace.

"We were young," she said, as if that made her breaking my heart reasonable, as if our age somehow disillusioned the love I felt for her.

The love I thought she felt for me.

"But, you're finally here. You're at my *school."*

That made her frown. "It's my school, too, now. I'm on the cheerleading squad. And I have... goals. Things I want to accomplish."

She couldn't look at me when she said it, and my nose flared with emotion that I struggled to keep at bay. I knew that look. It was the same one she gave when I bought her a dress that she didn't really like, but didn't want to tell me so because it would hurt my feelings. It was the look she got from her father, Cory Vail, a powerful tech lawyer in Silicon Valley who was used to getting what he wanted.

And who expected his daughter to do the same.

It was easy enough to put the pieces together, and I sobered at the realization.

"I'm not good enough."

Maliyah just looked at the ground, unable to even deny it.

And in the blink of an eye, the girl I thought I'd marry and build a life with was abandoning me, just like my father had — even when they both had promised they'd stay.

I was the common denominator.

What I'd done hadn't been enough for either of them.

"We'll both be happier," she said, patronizing again as she rubbed my arm. "Trust me."

The memory was wiped from my mind with the hard snap of a damp towel against my thigh.

"Argh!"

I cried out, hissing at the sting it left behind as Kyle Robbins howled with laughter. He bent at the waist, the towel he'd wound up and whipped me with falling to the ground in the process.

"You were zoned *out* man," he said through the laughter. "Didn't see that shit coming at all." He popped up then, looking across the weight room at another teammate. "Did you get it?"

Before whoever he'd tasked with videotaping the prank could answer, I grabbed him by the neck of his tank top and ripped him down to eye level, holding him firm when he tried to squirm away.

"Delete that shit, or I swear to God, Robbins, I'll give you the biggest wedgie of your life and hang you from the rafters by your shit-streaked, shredding tightie whities."

He almost laughed, but when I twisted my fist more, intensifying the grip, his eyes flashed with terror before he smacked my arm and I released him. He and I both knew I could have held on longer if I'd wanted.

"Damn, *someone's* got their panties in a twist," he murmured.

One of our teammates returned his phone to him, and I snatched it out of his hand before he could walk away, deleting the video myself before I tossed it back to him.

"You used to be fun," he commented.

"And you used to have Novo's name shaved into the side of your head," I shot back, which made the guys around us break out in muffled laughter that they did a sorry job of hiding.

Kyle's face turned red, the memory of him losing a game of 500 to our kicker last season, and therefore having to do whatever the team decided as punishment washing over his narrowed gaze.

But he just sucked his teeth and waved me off, making his way over to the bench press, and it felt like a fly finally ditching my picnic for someone else's.

Kyle Robbins was a prick, and the fact that he'd cashed in on the whole Name, Image and Likeness thing any time he could meant he brought even more attention to the media circus we already had around us on any given day. I hated it, and only tolerated him because he was a damn good tight end and on the same team as me.

I cracked my neck when he was gone, catching the inquisitive gaze of our quarterback and team captain, Holden Moore, as I settled back in place on the squat press machine.

"You good?" he asked, racking the weights he'd been using like he wasn't all that interested in the answer. I knew better, though. Holden was a born leader, one of the few players on this team I actually looked up to. He was checking in not because he was nosy, but because he gave a damn.

"Good," was my only answer, and then I was back in position, kicking into the platform until my legs were straight. I released the latch on the weight, squatting my knees toward my chest on an inhale, and grunting as I extended to push the weight back up.

After another ten-rep set, I locked the weight once more, sitting up and wiping my forehead with a towel.

Just as a petite pair of saddle tan flats came to a stop between my Nikes.

My feet dwarfed those little shoes, at least twice the length and width, and I arched a brow as my gaze climbed up the legs they were attached to. Those legs were covered in black mesh tights, see-through but for the areas where the fabric was thicker, creating a polka-dot pattern. The corner of my mouth curled in amusement when those tights ended at the hem of a black skirt with a cat nose and whiskers stitched into the front.

I knew then that it was Giana Jones.

She was always dressed like a quirky librarian, like a mix between a nun and a naughty schoolgirl. For some reason, I'd always found it irresistibly adorable, how she mixed and matched modesty with a covert kind of sex appeal. I wasn't sure she even realized she did it, that she could catch more stares from wearing a turtleneck than some girls could in a bikini.

She folded her arms across her chest as I took my time bringing my gaze the rest of the way up, noting her pale pink sweater and the collared white shirt she wore beneath it. One finger pressed her oversized glasses up the bridge of her nose when I finally met her gaze, and I smirked even more at the curl that popped out of place where she'd piled her thick hair on top of her head in a braided bun.

"G," I mused, sitting back a little on the bench so I could appreciate the view more. "To what do we owe the pleasure?"

"Giana," she corrected, though her voice was soft as she did, almost so much so that I didn't hear her at all.

My eyes flicked down to the cat whiskers spreading the length of her hip bones. "Cute skirt."

She rolled her eyes. "Glad to see you're in a better mood today."

"Don't let him fool you," Holden piped in from his bench. "He had Robbins in a death grip two minutes before you walked in here."

Giana gave Holden a questioning glance before shaking her head and focusing on me again. "We need to talk."

"I'm all ears, Kitten."

Her cheeks flushed as pink as her sweater before she glared at me. It was as if that nickname snapped a new persona into place. I watched as she went from sort of cowering and shy to standing taller, shoulders back and chin up.

"After the stunt you pulled yesterday, my ass is in hot water, and we need to discuss media protocol and on-camera etiquette."

It was my turn to roll my eyes as I got back into position for another rep of squats.

"I did my time over the summer," I said, and then I pushed the weight up, beasting out my next ten reps with her still standing beside me. When I racked up the weight again, sitting up, she hit me with a patronizing smile.

"Well, clearly, you didn't comprehend any of it."

"I comprehended just fine."

"After yesterday, I beg to differ."

I shrugged. "So, I suck at being on camera. Just don't put me on. Simple as that."

"No, not simple. You're a star defensive player with a lot of media requests. And you *don't* suck on camera. You were like a fish in water any time I had you interviewed last season."

"Times change, Kitten."

She gritted her teeth. "Stop calling me that."

A teammate somewhere behind me let out a soft *meow* that made another bubble of laughter burst through the weight room, and I fought to hold back my own.

Giana sucked in a hot breath through her nose before pointing a finger at my chest. "You have a mandatory PR meeting with me tonight after team meetings. The coffee bar by the student union. Eight PM sharp. If you're late, you'll have Coach Sanders to answer to — understood?"

Appreciation simmered in my chest at the sight of her standing her ground, at how she raised her voice just a notch and tipped her chin at me while she waited for my response.

"Yes, ma'am," I purred, and I couldn't help it.

I glanced at her skirt again.

To her credit, she ignored me if she noticed at all, turning on her heel and sashaying a few steps before she was almost hit by Hernandez doing a tricep strap work-out. She dodged his fists just in time, nearly stumbling into a leg extension machine before she did a little spin and avoided that, too.

I watched her pinball the entire way out of the weight room, and didn't realize how much I liked the distraction of her until she was gone.

And the only thing left to think about was Maliyah.

Chapter 4

CLAY

"**Y**ou're just going to *love* him, Clay," Mom said through the phone, the sound of dishes clattering in the background telling me she was working on dinner.

I was on my way across campus after a grueling day of camp to meet with Giana for our little PR refresher, and I was not in the mood to hear about Mom's latest boyfriend.

But I didn't have a choice.

"He's a real gentleman. And he's serious about business." She paused. "And about me, which is refreshing."

I tried my best to harness a smile even though she couldn't see me, mostly so it would help me sound like I believed her. "He seems great, Mom."

"You'll see. When you come home for Christmas." There was a pause, and then, "So, tell me about you. How's football?"

I sighed before answering the question, which I really was grateful for. I knew Mom was in a good place because she asked, because she didn't spend the whole call wailing about herself and her problems. Not that I minded when she did that, either. I was there for her no matter what.

Still, after so many times repeating the same narrative, I had a hard time believing this man would be any different from the rest.

My poor mother was stuck on a spinning Ferris wheel of heartbreak she couldn't get off of ever since my dad left when I was eight.

The cycle went like this:

Mom would meet a new guy, usually at *Le Basier*, the ridiculously overpriced restaurant where she waited tables in Los Angeles. Mom was a looker — I got my sharp green eyes from her, and my naturally tanned olive skin — and she'd always bring home the kind of guys who were enamored by her beauty. She was charming on top of it, which usually meant the men slipped willingly into her web and were content to be consumed by her energy.

The problem was that once the relationship started getting real, once the shine wore off and they realized my mom could be a lot to handle, they left.

And they always left her with even more scars than she had before.

Dad leaving Mom messed her up. It messed *both* of us up — especially when he quickly moved on to another woman, had two kids with said woman, and built a completely new life that didn't include us. Add that to her already traumatic dating life *before* Dad, and you could say Mom had her reasons for acting a little... *much* at times.

Most men couldn't take it. They couldn't sit with her in the hard times, couldn't hold her hand through the panic attacks or give her words of affirmation when she so desperately needed them. When her jealousy and paranoia swept through her like a hurricane, they didn't batten down the hatches and ride out the storm alongside her.

They took the fastest escape route out of town, leaving her to manage the damage.

And in their parting words, they made sure to make her feel like the crazy one, the nag, the jealous bitch, the psychotic, untrusting woman. Never mind the fact that *they* gave her plenty of reasons to feel those emotions.

But in the end, it was always me there picking up the pieces.

And that was when I braced for the *other* side of my mom.

When she was happy, when things were good, Mom was the brightest light of sunshine. She was enigmatic and fun to be around, motivated and driven, passionate about everything. She'd be invested in my life, in keeping our home clean and put together, and most of all, in her relationship with whoever the guy was.

But when they left?

She was a disaster.

Mom had always been a drinker, ever since I could remember. The difference was that when I was younger, when it was her and dad, that drinking was usually a bottle of wine between them — one that led to them laughing and dancing in the kitchen.

But Mom drinking A.D. — after Dad — looked a little different.

It was entire cases of beer consumed on her own. It was crying and screaming and clinging to the toilet as I held her hair or pressed a cool washcloth to the back of her neck.

And that was another part of the cycle that repeated itself — happy drunk when she was with someone, and a drunken mess when they left her.

Sometimes, in the worst of the breakups, she'd turn to drugs. Sometimes, she'd let depression take her under. Sometimes she'd get so close to being fired that I wondered how she'd stayed with the same place all this time. She'd blow through her savings, get into so much trouble that she needed to ask her only son for money, and then make me feel guilty if I didn't give it to her.

And I would — every time.

It didn't matter if I had to clear out my savings, work a summer job, or sell my PlayStation.

I would never turn my back on my mom.

That was a given, something I'd felt strongly ever since *she* didn't turn her back on me when my father did. She wasn't perfect, but she'd always been there, and for that alone I'd give her the last penny in my bank and the shirt off my back, too.

But it didn't mean it didn't sting, that I didn't realize especially as I got older how much her cycle had fucked me up, too.

"Chart Day is just around the corner," I finished after filling her in on how camp had been going so far. "So, we'll see."

"You'll make the team, baby," she said without hesitation. "And you'll start, and before you know it, you'll be signing a multi-million-dollar NFL deal and buying your mom a big mansion on the beach."

I smiled, the vision she'd had for me one I'd heard a thousand times. It was born when I was young, from the time we realized I actually had some pretty decent talent in football. I could still remember her sitting me down after a game when I was twelve, still wearing my dirty uniform and cleats. She made me look in the mirror and she stood behind me, her hands on my shoulders and eyes locked on mine in the reflection as she said, *"You're never going to have the struggles I've had, Clay. You're going to be rich."*

"Speaking of football, did I tell you Brandon used to play?" Mom asked, jolting me from the memory. "He was the starting quarterback of his high school team."

My smile was flat, the sign for the coffee shop coming into view as I rounded the university courtyard where students were spread out on blankets, smoking vapes, laughing, and enjoying the evening.

I wondered what that felt like, to actually have time as a college student instead of having every waking moment consumed by a sport.

"I'm sure we'll talk all about it at Christmas," I said. "I gotta run, Mom. Another meeting."

"At this time of night? They keep you busy, don't they?" She chuckled. "Well, I love you, baby. Call me later this week to catch up." She paused. "Are you... have you seen Maliyah?"

Ice thickened in my veins at the sound of her name. "No."

It was salt in the wound, the reminder that it wasn't just me hurting from our breakup — but our families, too. We had been together so long, through so much, that I knew my mom viewed Maliyah like a daughter.

They were closer than we were sometimes, bonding over things I knew I'd never be able to because I wasn't a woman.

"Well," Mom started, but then she thought better of it, letting a long pause linger before she said. "Just stay focused on football. Everything else will work itself out."

"Love you, Mom," I managed.

"Love you. Oh, and—"

Before she could ask anything else, I ended the call, pausing for a brief moment of silence and relief outside the front door of the coffee shop. The evening breeze was warm and pleasant, the last bit of summer clinging to the still-green trees.

I took a deep breath, hating how anything more than a sip of oxygen anymore made my chest burn. It had ever since Maliyah walked away from me, after I'd realized that this was my new reality.

It had already been a long day. The absolute last thing I wanted to do was get an ass chewing for not being Mr. Sunshine on camera.

But if it was ordered by Coach Sanders? I didn't have the option to bail — not without endangering my starting position.

So, with a final sigh, I pushed through the glass door, a small bell above it chiming my entry.

Rum & Roasters was one of the only bars on campus, likely because it was civil and low key in comparison to the bars *off* campus. It was never crawling with wasted, underage college students toting their ridiculous fake IDs, but rather comfortably full of upperclassmen who were old enough to drink and preferred to have a quiet evening of conversation or live music rather than grind on the dance floor.

Their loss.

Still, there was something comforting about it as I pushed inside the dark space, the smell of old books and candles and coffee overpowering any alcohol being served. It was a lot more pleasant than the stench of the bars I preferred to frequent, and I had to admit it had a vibe.

Some guy played acoustic guitar on a small stage in the corner, singing softly along with the sound, but he kept the volume low enough that everyone seated at the dark booths and candle-lit tables could have conversation around it.

I stopped at the bar, scanning the tables in search of Giana. Something in my gut churned at the sight of a couple making out in one of the corner booths, but I skimmed past them quickly, eyes darting around until I found the person I was looking for.

Candlelight and shadows battled for territory on Giana's serene face, her eyes wide and soft, lips turned up into a crescent smile. She had a comically large mug of some sort of foamy coffee drink cupped between her small hands, and she sipped it from time to time as she listened to the music.

And she was *really* listening.

Her legs were crossed, still swathed in those modestly sexy tights she had on earlier, and her little foot bounced along with the tune. It wasn't one I recognized, but she quietly mouthed along with the lyrics, her eyes fixed on the musician.

And when he looked up from his guitar and caught her stare, she flushed so fiercely I could see the crimson even in the dim light of the bar. She quickly tore her gaze away, looking down at her coffee and biting back a smile. By the time she glanced back up at the guy on stage, he had moved on, winking at a couple girls seated close to the stage.

Curiosity had me smiling, and I strolled over to her table, not stopping until I was directly between her and the guy with the guitar.

She blinked when I interrupted her view, like she was surprised to see me, like she'd forgotten she'd even invited — no, *demanded* — me to come. She startled, nearly spilling her coffee as she sat it down on the table, adjusted her glasses, and stood.

"You're here."

I cocked a brow. "Wasn't I supposed to be?"

"Well, yes, but I—" She covered her surprise with a smile, waving her hand before she gestured to the chair opposite her. "Do you want a beer or something?"

The look I gave her was answer enough, and she tipped a finger up to the waitress walking through the crowd.

The waitress wasted no time in asking me for my ID, and fortunately, I had a pretty stellar fake — thanks to Kyle Robbins. That was about *all* he was good for outside of being too good of a tight end for me to hate him more than the amount you might hate an annoying little brother.

Once I had my IPA in hand, Giana propped her elbows on the table, steepling her fingertips together and facing me.

"Thank you for coming."

I nodded.

"Look, I don't want to be a nag, and I certainly don't want to be here, working after sunset, any more than you do." She paused to swipe a curl out of her face, and I realized then that she'd loosened the bun it had been tied up in all day, letting the wild gold and brown and blond strands frame her face like a halo. Her cheeks were peppered in freckles, her lips plump as she pursed them. "Can we just agree to go over this quickly, figure out the solution to our problem, and get some much-needed sleep?"

"What problem do we have, exactly?"

"Oh, other than you nearly biting the head off of an ESPN reporter?" She shrugged, pulling her laptop out of her bag and propping it on the table between us. "Not much."

"She was a nuisance. They all are."

"You didn't seem to care last season when they were running all your tape and talking about how you're the next Ronnie Lott."

"Yeah, well, a lot has changed since last season."

"Like your relationship status?"

The words were like a slap to the face, and I actually jerked my head back at them, surprised to hear the quick reply from the girl I'd always seen as a wallflower.

"I don't mean to be rude," she amended quickly, and just like that, the softness slipped over her again. Her voice was quieter, hesitant. "I know... well, I can *imagine* how difficult a breakup is, especially with your high school sweetheart."

"How do you know so much about it?"

She leveled me with a look. "It's my job to know. And it's also my job to make sure you're okay."

"Is that supposed to make me feel all warm and fuzzy, Kitten?"

She deflated, sitting back in her chair. "Quick and painless, remember? We can be out of here after you finish that beer if you cooperate."

I grumbled out an exhale, waving at her laptop and taking a long pull of my IPA while I waited for her to get out whatever she needed to.

"Ms. Banks has invited the reporter you refused to speak with back for Chart Day. She wants to give her an exclusive." Giana's eyes flicked to mine then. "I can leave you alone until then, if you promise to take these next couple of weeks to get your mind right and give a *proper* interview when she returns."

"Leave me alone... as in?"

"As in, I won't schedule any other media obligations. No interviews, no podcasts, not even a photo op until Chart Day." She typed something on her computer. "And I *know* you don't need coaching on how to act on camera. You're one of the easiest for me to rely on when it comes to this." She paused, fingers hovering over the keys as she glanced back at me, the white light of her screen reflecting on her face. "But I can tell you're not okay. And I don't want to add anything to your plate. So... does this sound like a fair deal?"

There was something about how she said it, that I'm not okay, that made my ribs tighten around my lungs.

I managed a nod.

"Good," she said, but before she could go back to typing, she glanced over my shoulder at where the musician had started playing again.

And right on cue, she blushed.

I narrowed my gaze, watching her tear her eyes away and back to her computer before I slung my arm over the back of my chair and twisted so I could get a good look at this guy.

"This is a special one I wrote for a pretty girl," he said softly into the microphone, smiling again at a different table of girls seated at his feet. They brightened at his attention, and then he started strumming and singing, his dark brown Chelsea boots tapping away on the bottom rung of the barstool he sat on.

He had dark, shaggy hair, an unkempt stubble on his chin, and dark bags under his eyes. He looked like he was hungover, but maybe it added to the whole tortured artist bit. He also wore a shirt smaller than the one Giana was wearing, if I were to wager, and skinny black jeans with holes ripped over the knees.

The sign above the tip jar next to him said *Shawn Stetson Music*, along with his Instagram and Venmo handle.

I had to fight not to scoff as I angled back toward Giana, crossing my arms over my chest and sinking back into my chair.

"What's up with you and the guitar dude?"

Giana had her coffee cup halfway to her lips when I said it, and the mug wavered dangerously in her hands afterward, a little bit spilling out and onto her laptop as she cursed and sat it back down. She quickly wiped where the foamy liquid had splashed her keys, shaking her head with another furious blush on her cheeks.

"What? What are you talking about? There's nothing *up* with me and Shawn Stetson."

A nervous laugh bubbled out of her, one that resulted in a weird snort thing that made my lowered eyebrow bounce up to join the one lifted.

Did she just refer to him by his first and *last name?*

"Convincing," was all I murmured in response.

She pursed her lips, sitting up straighter and pulling her shoulders back. "I don't know what you're getting at, but let's turn the conversation back to—"

"You like him."

She gaped, clamping her mouth shut once she realized it was hanging open. "I certainly do *no*—"

"You're crushing on him so bad you can't even stand to hold eye contact with him across a crowded bar."

I'd never seen Giana so frazzled, and she hastily snapped her laptop shut and tucked it into her messenger bag. "You don't know what you're talking about."

But I just smiled and leaned over the table, elbows on the cool wood as my chest squeezed with an entirely different kind of emotion than the one that had been occupying the space for weeks now. It was excitement, albeit muted, but that part of me that loved to help others thawed like a frozen tree shaking off the last icicles of the winter.

And underneath that thawing ice was a flutter of hope as fresh as spring, an idea sprouting in my mind like a flower.

Or perhaps a weed.

"I can help you."

"*Help* me?"

A curl fell over her left eye before she brushed it away, and when I leaned in even closer, she looked down at my chest, pulling her hands into her lap like she was afraid they'd brush mine if she left them on the table.

"Go out with me."

Her eyes snapped wide at that, locking on mine before that snort-laugh thing bubbled out of her again.

"Or at least, *pretend* to go out with me."

That made her laugh even harder. But when I didn't laugh with her, she paled, one hand holding onto the edge of the table as the other came to her forehead. "I think I'm going to pass out."

"Please don't. It would be an even rougher start to our journey of making *Shawn Stetson* your boyfriend."

And of *me* getting Maliyah back.

Chapter 5

GIANA

"**Y**ou're insane."

"Insanely genius," Clay argued, resting his elbows on the table between us as he leaned toward me even more. It was almost comical, how massive his arms were compared to the tiny table, which wobbled precariously on its thin legs as it took his weight.

"I... it's just... *absurd.*"

I pushed my glasses up the bridge of my nose, cold fingertips brushing my hot cheeks as I uncrossed my legs just to cross them the other way. I then crossed my arms over my chest, all body language pointing to how uncomfortable I was with this conversation and the proposal in it.

I was here to coach Clay Johnson how to be better with the media after his breakup — which had thus far been agonizing not only for him, but for the entire team.

I was *not* here for him to tease me about my crush on Shawn Stetson, or to con me into some ridiculous fake relationship to get his attention.

The fact that he'd even picked *up* on my crush was embarrassing enough. Here I thought I'd always been good at hiding it — mostly because, to Shawn, at least, I was invisible. Ever since the first time I heard him play last semester, I'd all but stalked him, listening to him play on campus any time I had the chance.

I blamed my fascination with him on one of my favorite books — *Thoughtless*.

S.C. Stephens made me fall in love with Kellan Kyle, and when I'd finished that book and been completely lost, in the worst book funk of my life, unable to function... I'd stumbled into *Rum & Roasters*.

And there he was, Shawn Stetson, broody and mysterious and dark and handsome.

"Look, G," Clay said.

"Giana," I corrected.

"Would you rather I call you Kitten again?"

My eyes were mere slits as he smirked at his own cute joke.

"I'm a guy, and as a guy, I know what guys want. At least — most, straight, sane guys. And I'm telling you. That guy?" He pointed a finger at where Shawn was playing his set on stage, the bar dim in comparison to where a soft spotlight illuminated him. "He wants a woman of mystery, one who can be his muse, who will be a little hard to get, a little out of his league."

My eyes nearly bulged out of my skull before I covered Clay's gargantuan finger with both my hands and shoved it down, quickly glancing at Shawn to make sure he hadn't seen.

"I can have him eating out of the palm of your hand by Thanksgiving."

My cheeks were so hot, I was worried they'd singe my hair as it fell over my face. "What makes you think I'd want that?"

Clay just cocked a brow.

Okay, so I'm about as easy to read as a billboard right now.

I chewed the inside of my lip, glancing at Shawn and then back at Clay before I lowered my voice to a whisper. "He barely knows I exist."

"Another thing I can help with," he said, sweeping a large hand over himself. "Do you think anyone on this campus could ignore the girl who has Clay Johnson's attention?"

I rolled my eyes at the cocky insinuation, but couldn't argue against his point.

It was true.

That massive hunk of muscle and those piercing green eyes had been off the market since Clay walked onto North Boston University's campus — much to every girl's dismay. And while he'd been a miserable prick since he and Maliyah broke up, the groupies that followed the team around like flies were begging for even a taste of his affection.

Still...

"He's a musician," I pointed out, folding my arms. "He probably couldn't care less about football."

And the universe loved to play jokes on me, because at that exact moment, Shawn finished the song he'd been playing, and after strumming his guitar a few times, he spoke right into the mic and said, "Ladies and gentlemen, we have a celebrity here with us tonight. Clay Johnson, NBU's best safety and a shoe-in for the NFL. Make sure to get your autographs while you can."

Clay held up a hand in a humble wave as every pair of eyes shot toward us. I ducked and tried to hide my face as Clay ate every second up, throwing a seductive smirk and a wink at a particular table of girls. They quietly whispered to one another with their eyes sweeping over Clay, their smiles eager, all nudging one another like they were picking straws over who would try to talk to him first. I rolled my eyes when one of them not-so-subtly took a video of him on her phone.

"Any requests, man?" Shawn asked next, and the fact that he was talking to Clay and Clay was at *my* table was about as close as I'd ever been to being in the same universe as my crush.

Clay eyed me with that damn smirk still securely in place. "How about 'Just Say Yes' by Snow Patrol?"

I rolled my eyes again, and as Shawn began to play, Clay leaned in even closer.

"Are you out of arguments yet?"

I sighed. "So, let me get this straight. We would be in a fake relationship, in which you, hypothetically, would help me get Shawn, and I..." I blinked, coming up blank. "Would do what, exactly? I mean... what's in this for you?"

A shadow of something washed over his face then, and he sat back, shrugging a bit before he drank half his beer in one gulp. "Maliyah."

I frowned. "I don't understand."

"I know my girl," he said, his eyes more determined than I'd ever seen — and that was saying something, because I'd seen this guy power down the field for an impossible interception more than a few times. "I know that she still loves me, still wants me, but she thinks there's something better out there. She's always wanted the best." He paused. "She's been brought up with that desire. It's just part of who she is."

I had to fight to keep my lip from curling at how he made all of that sound like a good quality.

"But when she sees me with someone else, when she thinks I've moved on?" He shook his head with a devilish smile. "That green monster will get her. She'll be begging to get me back."

I wrinkled my nose. "I don't know, Clay... I don't want to play those kinds of games."

"Trust me — everyone plays them. So, if you're not playing — no, if you're not *winning*?" He shrugged. "You're losing."

His words made something in my gut tighten, my eyes skirting to where Shawn strummed his guitar on stage. My heart did a backflip just like it always did when his gaze washed over me, even though it was so quick I barely registered the color of his golden eyes before they were gone again.

I was invisible to him. I always had been.

I would never admit out loud how many times I'd fantasized about him, particularly when I'd re-read *Thoughtless*. Every time he played at this bar and glanced my way, I wondered if it would be the night he'd end his set and walk right over to my table, demanding to know me, demanding to take me home. When would he suddenly realize the wallflower girl who watched every set, who knew every word to his original songs, who sat quietly in the corner while every other girl threw themselves at him?

The fantasies always got a little spicy after that.

Still, even when he *did* look at me, my instant reaction was to look away, to hide, to sink into the crowd and become invisible once more. Attention like that made me uncomfortable, made me self-conscious, made me wonder if I had something in my teeth rather than if I was desirable. I wasn't the kind of girl who could hold his stare once I had it, who could smirk and lift a brow or lick my lips or draw a seductive circle on the rim of my coffee.

I didn't have *main character energy*.

I was more of the quirky, cute best friend with all the sage advice.

I sighed, heart longing for something that seemed so out of reach. When Shawn glanced at me again, I hid my face just like always, cheeks burning, and then I peeked up at Clay, who just cocked a brow like he'd caught me red-handed.

Or in this case, red-faced.

All my life, I'd been too scared to go for what I wanted — I was the exact opposite of Maliyah, of Clay, of everyone I worked with on the team. I wasn't like my siblings, destined for greatness and like a magnet to anyone in my vicinity. I wasn't like my boss, who commanded attention in every room she graced.

I was the side kick, and I had always been content to be in the background.

But now, for the first time, I found myself yearning for the spotlight.

And for a freaking *boyfriend,* for science's sake.

Uncrossing my legs, I leaned forward, folding my hands together on the table. "We need terms. Conditions. Rules."

When a smooth tilt of Clay's lips was his only response, I wondered just how much trouble I was getting myself into.

I held up a finger. "The first one being that regardless of what you help me with Shawn-wise, you do whatever I need you to do for the media. I'll leave you alone for the next couple weeks like I promised, but come Chart Day, you play the perfect college athlete and make me look good."

"Sounds like a lopsided deal now."

"Is it really, if you can get Maliyah back?"

He tilted his head at my challenge, sitting back in his chair and crossing his ankle over the opposite knee. He had to back all the way up from under the table to do so. "Touché. What else?"

I sat back, tapping a finger against my chin as I tried to recall all the fake-dating tropes I'd read. The truth was I read about a book a day, so they all blurred together after a while. But one thing I knew about pretending to date someone was that you absolutely *needed* rules, or things got messy.

"No PDA," I finally said.

Clay made a buzzer sound, the noise so loud a few students at the tables around us looked over their shoulders. "Impossible. No one who's actually dating avoids PDA."

"Fine." I made a face. "Then we need a safe word."

"A *safe word*?" Clay chuckled. "Do you think I'm going to be tying you up, Kitten?"

Something wicked gleamed in his eyes, like he'd just thought about what that would entail, and once again, he leaned his large frame over the tiny table.

"I mean, that can be arranged," he added with a smirk. "If you'd like."

The way my lips parted at the invitation, how my heart skipped a beat before galloping a little quicker than before, was *not* okay. Fortunately, I covered it pretty well as I rolled my eyes.

At least, I *hoped* I did.

"I just mean that if you do something I'm uncomfortable with, I want a way to tell you."

"Why don't we just go through what *is* okay?" he suggested.

I tilted my head, considering, and then nodded.

"Holding hands?"

"Of course."

"Kiss on the cheek, forehead, etcetera?"

My cheeks warmed. "Yes."

Clay arched a brow. "Kiss on the mouth?"

Again, my heart was beating out of rhythm, but I tucked my hair behind my ear, lifting my coffee mug to my lips for a sip of the foam that had gone cold. "I suppose it would be weird if we didn't." I snapped my fingers, pinning him with a glare. "But no tongue."

"No tongue?" Clay sucked his teeth. "Who's going to be envious of a peck on the lips? Certainly not your boy Shawn over there, I can promise you that."

I grunted, and like a bucket of ice water being thrown over me, I realized how incredibly stupid the whole premise was. I didn't live in a freaking book — I lived in real life, where there was no plausible way *any* of this would turn out in our favor.

"This is absurd," I said. "It's not going to work. And it's weird and desperate, and we should just forget the whole thing."

I started gathering up my things, but Clay reached out, his hand folding over my wrist so softly it surprised me given the mass of that calloused hand.

I stilled, swallowing as my eyes crawled the length of his toned arm, finding him watching me with a deep sincerity. It unnerved me, that gaze, how steady and yet somehow... *terrifying* it was. I wondered if this was what his opponents felt on the field, fear spiking the hairs on the back of their necks.

"Meow."

I cracked a laugh. "Meow?"

"If I go too far, if you're uncomfortable and want me to back off, just meow."

"Oh, my God."

"But you won't have to," he added quickly. "Regardless of all the research you've done on me and what you think you know, I'm a gentleman." He sat back, finally removing his hand from where it held my wrist, and I didn't realize I wasn't breathing properly until him removing his hold on me brought a sharp inhale through my lips. "And I want to make Maliyah want me back, not you fall in love with me."

I snorted. "Trust me, no worries there."

"Okay, so," Clay said, sitting up and counting on each finger. "I behave on camera, guide you through all the steps to get Mr. Emo Guitar Guy to fall for you, and you play along as my fake girlfriend to make Maliyah jealous."

"And if I meow—"

Clay smirked. "Now I kind of want to make you uncomfortable just to hear it."

"Don't," I warned.

"Fine. If you meow, I back off."

I nodded, considering all the terms. "One more thing," I said, clearing my throat as I picked at the paper frills stuck in the spiral of my notebook from tearing pages out of it. "What if things get... messy."

"Meaning?"

I scratched the back of my neck on a shrug. "I've seen enough movies and read enough books to know that sometimes, these things can get... complicated." My eyes found his. "What if one of us wants out?"

"You can't just back out," he said, frowning. "That would be breaking the deal."

"But what if..."

I couldn't say it, not with my pulse hammering so loud in my ears it was like a whole drum line in there.

Clay smirked. "So you *are* worried about falling in love with me."

My face fell flat. "Ugh, thank you for reminding me how impossible that is."

A barrel laugh left his chest as he extended his hand over the table. "If at any point you want out, just say so. I'm not holding you hostage. But," he said, taking his hand back when I went to grab it. "Don't quit on me just because you feel like it. I'm committing to the cause. Are you?"

"Trust me — if helping you get Maliyah back means I don't have to deal with another disaster like yesterday, I'll do whatever it takes."

A satisfied smile curled on his lips, his hand back in place. "Then we've got a deal, Kitten."

I slid my palm into his, a hard steady shake sealing the ridiculous plan.

And up on the stage, Shawn Stetson watched us with a curious look on that beautiful face of his.

● ● ●

A week and a half later, I snuck Clay into my office, peeking down the hall to make sure no players or staff saw us. Not that it would matter — I could easily play it off as media prep — but something about the *real* reason we were alone together convinced me I wouldn't be able to sell the lie.

I clicked the door closed as softly as I could once he was inside, turning toward him with a relieved exhale that no one saw.

"Why are you acting like we're about to hijack a bank?"

"Honestly? That sounds less scary than why we're *actually* here," I admitted.

Clay smirked, folding his arms over his massive chest as he took a step toward me. He was still in his practice jersey and padded pants, both of which were stained and damp and clinging to him. The closer he got, the more I smelled him — and I *wished* I was disgusted by the mix of sweat and dirt and grass and something like teakwood, but the cocktail was like his own brand of pheromones, and I had to actively work to keep my eyes trained on his cocky face instead of trailing the length of all his glorious muscles.

"It's just a little kiss practice."

"Do you *hear* how ridiculous that sounds?"

He chuckled. "We haven't had time to talk much since we made the deal. I think it makes sense to go through the plan."

I swallowed. "Right. Which is… what again?"

"We'll make our big reveal on Chart Day. We'll start by walking into the stadium holding hands before practice, get the rumor mill going. The team will be buzzing with high energy since everyone finds out who makes the team and at what rank."

"And then, in the cafeteria after practice, we... make a scene."

He nodded. "We make a scene."

"Because I run over to you and... kiss you."

Clay's smirk was incorrigible, and I swatted his arm.

"I'm so glad this amuses you," I said with a glare.

"I just find humor in how you can barely say the word *kiss*."

I cracked my neck, holding my shoulders back and refusing to admit to him that I'd only had a couple of kisses in my life — none of which rocked my world — and that this entire thing made me want to crawl into a hole and hide.

I *could* do that. It was an option. I could call this whole thing off right now and save myself the embarrassment.

But something strange happened after I left Clay that night at the coffee shop.

I realized something I hated to admit.

I *wanted* this.

It was outrageous, and would likely fail, but even the *possibility* of it working in a way that got Shawn to not only notice me, but take an interest in me?

It was too intoxicating of a fantasy to pass up.

So, if my role in all this was to make a scene so Maliyah would notice Clay was moving on?

I'd play my part.

Although, the fact that he thought I could make a girl like *her* jealous was a little ridiculous in its own right.

"Okay, let's do this," I said, ignoring that bit of insecurity niggling at my chest. I'd have plenty of time to let it keep me awake later. "So, you stand over there, pretend like you're in line or whatever."

I pointed by my desk, and Clay took his position, watching me with curious eyes.

"Alright," I said, wringing my hands. "Here it goes."

"Okay."

Clay waited, and I just stood there, rolling my lips together and willing my feet to move.

"Here I come."

He chuckled. "Okay."

After another long hesitation, he opened his mouth to question me, and I launched before he had the chance.

It was a quick five strides before I leapt, and I squeezed my eyes shut tight at the prospect of him dropping me or being knocked off center by my clumsiness. But Clay caught me with ease, his arms coming around my waist as my legs locked around his. My breath caught with the force, hair falling into my face a bit and glasses sliding down the bridge of my nose.

I pushed them back up slowly, breathing heavily as I catalogued every place my body touched his — my arms around his neck, my chest pressed against his, my thighs squeezing at his hips.

And between my legs, something foreign tingled where his stomach rubbed against me.

Panic zipped through me as I scrambled out of his arms. "Okay. Got it."

"Don't you want to try the kiss?"

I narrowed my eyes. "Don't be a brat."

"What?" He feigned innocence, throwing his hands up. "I think you'd feel more comfortable if you tried it now, when no one is around."

"I'll give you a nice long peck and then scream *you made it!* to seal the proud girlfriend thing."

Clay held up a finger and waved it side to side. "Not just a peck. No one is going to be convinced by that. They'd be more apt to think we're brother and sister than a couple."

"Fine," I ground out. "A little tongue. But just a quick sweep, capisce?"

He cocked a brow. "What are you, an Italian mobster now?"

I waved him off. "I need to get back to work. And you need to get back to practice. I think we're fine here."

Clay smiled, conceding and heading for the door, but he paused at the frame, something slumping his shoulders before he turned back to me.

"Thank you," he said, something thick in his throat with the words. "For doing this."

The moment of softness from him caught me off guard, but I laughed it off, shrugging. "Hey, it'll be *me* thanking *you* when you land me my first real boyfriend."

The second the words left my lips, I balked — the shocked expression on my face mirroring Clay's.

"First boyfriend?" he echoed.

I didn't have the chance to answer before Charlotte swung through the door of her office, which was connected to mine, and started rambling off about twenty things she needed from me.

I shoved Clay the rest of the way out the door without acknowledging his question, and once the door was shut behind me, Charlotte swept in.

"Are you listening?"

I snapped up straight, grabbing my notebook off my desk. "Following. And I have an update on the auction, too."

She eyed me cautiously, lifting a brow at the door I had just been guarding before she shrugged like it wasn't worth her time to ask any questions. Then, she turned and slipped back into her office, me on her heels as she continued on with our list.

And I somehow managed to pay attention despite how my heart raced in my chest.

Chapter 6

CLAY

"You ready for this?"

Giana was wringing her hands together in front of the stadium, doe eyes shifty as they looked around us like she was worried someone would overhear. The morning sun illuminated all the different colors in those eyes, ones I'd never noticed before — a strange blend of turquoise and gold and green.

Her fear of being seen was unwarranted. Most everyone was already inside, getting warm and trying to work out the anxiety from what this day held for all of us.

Depth Chart Day.

"You can back out," I said.

"No." Giana answered as quickly as I'd suggested, shaking her head and steadying her shoulders. "I'm fine, I just…" She bit her lip. "Look, I believe you when you say you're going to help *me*. That makes sense. I don't know how to flirt, let alone date, or get a guy who doesn't even know I'm alive to want me."

She was all nerves, her hands trembling a bit as she stared down at the chipping polish on her nails.

"But me, helping *you*," she said, shaking her head. "Making someone like *Maliyah* jealous?"

She didn't finish the thought, just bit the inside of her cheek and looked up at me like it was obvious, like she couldn't possibly arouse jealousy in anyone.

I didn't bother to tame the smile that curved on my lips as I let my eyes run the length of her. She'd left her hair down, the tight curls still a little damp from her shower that morning, and whatever makeup she'd done was light enough that all the freckles speckling her cheeks shone through the foundation. Her glasses were red-framed, matching the plaid skirt she wore and the knee-high stockings she'd paired with it. She was completely oblivious to how sexy her legs were, to how seeing that little skirt contrasted with the modest button up fastened all the way to her neck would make any straight man long to undo her, make any woman long to be as effortlessly alluring.

"Trust me," I said, taking my time as my gaze crawled back up to meet hers. "Maliyah will lose her fucking mind when she sees us."

Giana shook her head, clasping her hands together as she turned to face me. "Can we just run through it one more time?"

"I told you we needed more practice."

She waved me off with a face that said *yeah, yeah* before waiting for my cue.

"We'll walk in together, holding hands, and get a little close. Start up the whispers," I reminded her. "After practice, you'll meet me in the cafeteria."

"And I'll make a big scene, running to you and congratulating you on making the team." She paused. "And you're *sure* you'll make it?"

I gave her a flat look.

"Fine," she waved me off. "And then… we… kiss."

Her cheeks tinged pink.

I smirked. "Then, we kiss." I paused, arching a brow. "You *sure* you don't want to practice that part?"

She rolled her eyes. "You wish."

"I'm just saying. Might ease the nerves."

Giana ignored me, blowing out a breath and rolling her lips together before she finally stopped wringing her hands and straightened her shoulders. "Okay. Let's do this before I pass out, or throw up, or change my mind, or all of the above."

Her hand shot out for mine, and I smiled, intertwining my fingers with hers. As soon as I did, her breath hitched, like even just holding hands was new to her.

I leaned in and whispered in her ear.

"Fake it til you make it, Kitten."

She flushed, looking down at the sidewalk as I tugged her toward the stadium doors. Something similar to nerves bubbled in my chest, too, as I scanned my ID badge, and then we both slipped into performance mode.

In the last two weeks, we'd been so busy we'd barely had time to sleep, let alone come up with a game plan for the little deal we made. Fall camp was brutal, a blur of daily practices that bled into weight training and meetings and watching film. Giana was caught up in her own busy season, fielding reporters and managing the media circus every day, which left only late at night before we both passed out for us to discuss what would come next.

I convinced her that Depth Chart Day would be the perfect day for our couple debut, and she agreed — but that was about it.

Other than her holding true on leaving me alone media-wise, and me holding true on getting myself together enough for the interview I knew I had waiting for me at the end of today, we hadn't discussed much. We'd planted seeds, sure — lingering in the locker room after practice, walking together on campus, but today...

Today, everyone would know, and the game would begin.

Giana's hand trembled a bit in mine as we pushed through the doors, the hallway that led to the locker room empty and quiet. I could hear the soft sounds of voices and the distinct clattering of pads and cleats down the hall, and I knew before we got there that everyone would be in their head today.

By the end of practice, we'd know who made the team, who was starting, who was backup, and who was gone.

Chart Day was huge. There would be coverage for it all day on every sports channel, everyone in the nation who gave a shit about college football watching and assessing. Even when I was in high school, my teammates and I would make bets and watch to see if we were right when it came to who started for our favorite teams.

We'd also dream about it being us one day with that number one spot.

Giana and I had made it all of fifteen steps when Leo Hernandez spilled out of the athletic cafeteria, a half-eaten muffin crumbling as he took a massive bite of it and hustled toward the locker room. But he stumbled, doing a double take when he saw me with Giana. He nearly crashed into the wall as he gaped over his shoulder, his eyes widening at where our hands were laced together before they glanced up at me.

But he just grinned, took another bite of his muffin, and jogged the rest of the way down without a word.

"Breathe," I told Giana, squeezing her hand as we approached the doorway.

I'd planned the set up just right, knowing there wouldn't be enough time for questions from the guys before we'd be called on the field. This was just a little taste to get them talking, to get the word back to Maliyah — who would be on the field with us and the rest of the cheerleading squad for the first time this season.

I hadn't seen her since the breakup.

My stomach lurched at the realization that *that* streak would end today. I'd have to face her while also holding my shit together on one of the most nerve-wracking days of the season. I had no doubt that I'd made the team, but that didn't make the nerves any less — especially when I knew my ex would be there watching when Coach hung the chart.

When Giana and I made it to the arch of the open locker room door, I lifted her hand to my lips, pressing a kiss to the back of her palm.

"See you after practice," I whispered against her skin, and I didn't know if she faked it or if it was real, but the shy, seductive smile she threw back at me was pure art. She ducked her chin, squeezing my hand once before she peeled hers away and jetted down the hall to where the admin offices were.

I watched her go, smiling, and when I turned to head into the locker room, at least a dozen eyes were watching me.

Some had the decency to look away when I realized they were staring, pretending to re-tie their cleats or stretch or whatever they were doing before I showed up. But others couldn't be bothered, like Zeke Collins and his girlfriend, Riley Novo, who were both watching me with mirrored expressions of concern. Holden was doing the same, and meanwhile, Kyle Robbins wore a shit-eating grin.

"Well, well," he said, popping over to throw his arm around my shoulder. "What's going on there, Big C? You going steady with the skirt now?"

I shrugged him off like I was annoyed, but also planted a sly smile on my face that only made him more eager to pry information out of me. Fortunately, my timing was spot on, and our assistant head coach gave a short blow of his whistle to let us know it was time to make our way out onto the field.

I was last out, letting everyone file past me as I quickly pulled on my practice jersey and cleats. Then, I jogged out with my helmet in hand.

And for the moment, Giana and Maliyah were the absolute last things on my mind.

I didn't even glance at the cheerleaders already warming up on the sideline as I jogged out with the rest of the team, all of us gathering in the center of the field where Coach Sanders was waiting to give his pre-practice speech. I slipped into the familiar, comfortable zone that only existed on a football field for mc. The smell of the turf invaded my senses, the feel of it beneath my cleats like coming home after a long day, and when I took a knee next to one of my fellow defensive backs, focused was all I felt.

Where Coach usually had to blow his whistle to get us all quiet before practice, no one was talking today. We kneeled around him, one hand on our knee and the other on our helmet as we waited.

Coach Sanders was one of the best in the nation. He'd made waves in his short tenure at NBU, turning a team around that had a consistent losing record and hadn't seen a bowl game in decades, to being a top contender again for the first time since the 90s. The fact that he was in his early thirties only added to how impressive that was, and the truth of the matter was that I didn't care that he was a dick most of the time, that he was severe and almost never gave out compliments.

I respected him, and I'd follow him into a burning building.

He hung his hands on his hips, brow furrowed as his eyes washed over all of us. "Most of you know the drill for today," he said, sniffing. "I usually like to wait until after practice to even talk about it, because we have work to do, but I know it's difficult for any of you to ignore what's waiting at the end of it."

He paused, glancing down at the clipboard in his hand before he thumped his fist against it.

"I didn't take any decisions with this lightly. And I want you all to remember that nothing's permanent. You might have a number one spot and then get taken out before our season opener next week. You might be slated number three and end up starting. So, no matter where you are, keep working hard, and keep your eye on the prize. Understood?"

"Yes, Coach," we all responded in sync.

He nodded. "I'll hang it outside my office after practice so you can see it first," he said. "At five this evening, it'll be released online for the rest of the nation to see. I expect you all to be ready for media after film meetings tonight."

My teammates varied in how they reacted to that, some of them shifting uncomfortably, while others sported cocky smiles like they weren't worried in the least.

Coach scanned all of us once more before his eyes locked on mine, and a subtle tilt of his chin told me it was my time to take over.

I jumped up, pulling on my helmet as I yelled, "Who are we?!"

One by one, my teammates followed, and a chorus sang back to me, "*NBU!*"

"What do we want?!"

"*What all champs do!*"

"How do we win?"

"*Fight with class!*"

"And if all else fails?"

"*KICK THEIR ASS!*"

I threw my fist out, swallowed up in the next moment by teammate after teammate piling theirs on top.

"Rebels on three. One, two—"

"*Rebels!*"

I high-fived my brothers as I passed them, knocked helmets, smacked their asses with words of encouragement, and lifted Riley up in a spinning hug before telling her to go give 'em hell.

And though I still didn't look where those pom poms waved on the sideline, I could feel an all-too-familiar pair of brown eyes watching me as I jogged to the end zone for our first set of drills.

Sweat dripped into my eyes by the end of practice, every muscle screaming for relief as I dragged my ass into the locker room. The heat was brutal, adding to the misery Coach Dawson, our Defensive End Coordinator, had dished out for nearly three hours. I'd run so many sprints and tackling drills I felt woozy, but I held my chin high as I marched side by side with the rest of my team.

Riley slowed down at my side, nudging me with an elbow. "You killed it out there today."

"I could say the same for you, miss forty-two-yard field goal." I arched a brow. "You know, the chart was already made. You didn't have to show out like that."

"Didn't I, though?" She grinned.

Riley Novo was the only girl on our team — the only female playing in college football at *all* at the present moment. She'd had to overcome a lot last season to gain the respect of the team, mine included, but it hadn't taken her long to win us all over. Now, we protected her like she was our little sister.

Well, except Zeke — who protected her like she was his whole damn life.

On cue, Zeke swept in behind her then, tucking her under his arm as he ran his knuckles over her already-frazzled hair. She swatted our kick returner away, but then she was back in his arms, leaning up for a kiss that made my heart ache as I tore my gaze away.

I used to have that, too.

Now that practice was over, I didn't have anything to focus on, no reason to keep my eyes from continuing to drift over to where the cheerleaders were wrapping up their own practice. They all wore matching brick-red shorts and small white crop tanks, and a short scan of them was all it took for me to find Maliyah.

Long, bright blonde hair swished behind her as she laughed and did a little kick, trying to hold her foot up above her head for some sort of stunt. She fell out of it, laughing with the girls around her, those strawberry-pink lips stretched over her wide smile. Even from here I could see how her curves stretched against the clothing she wore, curves that had driven me and every other boy at our high school absolutely mad.

Her brown eyes flicked to me, and the smile she wore faded instantly.

I allowed myself one long, torturous moment of holding her gaze, and then I sniffed, turning back to Zeke and Riley and pretending like I was engaged in whatever conversation they were having.

It was almost time.

When we all finally made it into the locker room, it was a pathetic show of acting like we were pre-occupied with our lockers or duffle bags or cleats until Coach tacked the chart to the board outside his office before ducking inside it and shutting the door behind him.

It was pure chaos after that.

Player after player shoved to get to the chart, some retreating with their fists thrown up in victory, while others hung their heads or kicked their lockers. I hung back, sitting on the wooden bench in front of my locker and watching as Leo jumped up and down on his way to Holden, ringing him around the neck.

"Another year dominating offense together, QB1," he said, crushing his head to Holden's like they were wearing helmets. "Let's fucking go!"

Holden grinned, letting Leo make a show before he gently shrugged him off and got back to the humble appearance he always wore.

Zeke had Riley on his shoulders within seconds after that, toting her around as they celebrated their spots being secured — which was a surprise to absolutely no one. And I didn't even have to move from my seat on the bench before I was joined by Reggie and Dane, two guys who had played in the secondary with me last season.

"Bout'ta be beast mode this season, boys!" Reggie said, bumping fists with Dane first and then me. Dane was a safety, too, and we were always in friendly competition to see who could get the most interceptions.

"I'm coming for your record this year, Johnson," he teased, holding his fists in front of his face and doing a little juke move like he was a boxer.

I sucked my teeth as I stood. "Fat chance, Daney Boy. You better make a comfortable home in that number two spot because you're going to be there a while."

The jokes and celebration continued until we all slowly meandered toward the cafeteria, where we had about an hour to eat, catch a power nap if we wanted, or do whatever else we needed to do before we reported for position meetings. This was the end of camp, the beginning of the season, and as grueling as it all was now, it was even worse once we were expected to do all this *and* pass our classes, too.

My chest tightened when I filed into the cafeteria flanked by Leo and Zeke and saw Maliyah in the food line with the rest of the cheerleaders.

I watched her as subtly as I could until she took a seat at one of the round tables near the windows facing campus. She'd let her hair down from the ponytail it was in outside, that thick blonde hair tumbling down over her shoulders. That sight tugged at my heart the way memories of California did, the way thoughts of Christmas with both my parents did. She reminded me of home, of my family and hers, of how we all melded together to form something I thought was unbreakable.

It was surreal, seeing her here, in *my* school, *my* stadium, with *my* school's emblem stretched across her chest.

But it was hers now, too.

Sour disposition settled like an anchor in my gut. It felt like a betrayal, how she could tell me all through us being long distance how much she loved me, how much she couldn't wait to be here *with me*, only to finally make it happen and then dump me like a bucket of dirty water.

Idly, I wondered if it was her father's doing.

Cory Vail was a man I couldn't help but respect. Not only had he stepped up and stepped in to help me and my mom when my dad left, but he was also one of the top lawyers in the state. He'd built everything on his own, and through that, he'd garnered a taste for the finest things.

He wanted the best — best cars, best wine, best seat at every show or game he attended.

And best prospect for his one and only daughter.

I always thought that was me.

Maybe it was, at one time. Maybe he saw my future and had faith in me going pro, in setting up his daughter with a future he found suitable. Or maybe he was just biding time, letting our young love run its course before he planted seeds in her head that she could do better.

Or maybe he had nothing to do with any of this at all.

Regardless, I knew my anxiety would never let it go. I'd toss and turn every night wondering why she so suddenly broke up with me.

But today, I needed my focus elsewhere.

It was an effort to peel my gaze from hers, and I schooled a breath, checking my watch.

Right on time, Giana walked in.

Her hair was completely dry now, those curls full of life and bouncing as she blew in through the door. She smoothed her hands over her skirt, righting her glasses as she scanned the room. When her eyes found mine, I saw the worry there, saw how her little hands curled into fists where she held her skirt, bunching the plaid fabric in their grips.

She was such a fascinating enigma to me, somehow shy and brave all at once. One moment she'd be having an anxious meltdown, and the next, she was all chin up, chest puffed, brow bent in determination like nothing could sway her.

I watched as it happened, as she sucked in a long breath, squaring her shoulders and setting her jaw. I wondered if she was giving herself a mental pep talk, but didn't have time to debate it.

She tilted her head, just a bit, asking without words if this was it, if this was the time.

I nodded.

And then she took off in a sprint.

It was quite possibly the cutest thing I'd ever seen in my life, how her hair and skirt bounced along in sync with every step on her way to me. I watched as heads popped up table after table, my teammates and the cheerleaders and training staff alike watching as she barreled toward me.

Leo turned when he heard the slapping of her flats against the tile. "What the—"

But before he could finish that question, Giana launched herself into my arms.

I caught her in a whoosh of air and hair and a sweet scent that washed over me like a baptism, ocean breeze and sunflowers. Her arms wrapped around my neck, mine wound around her hips, and I felt the lace of her stockings as she crossed her ankles where they hooked behind me, the smooth skin of her inner thigh brushing against my waist.

She'd run at me with pure excitement and confidence, but the moment she was in my arms, her smile faded, breaths quick and shallow.

Her wide eyes locked on mine, fell to my lips, and then slowly crawled their way back up.

I squeezed where I held her hips, focusing on everything we'd rehearsed and not on the fact that she had her legs wrapped around me in a skirt — which meant other than a scrap of panties, there was nothing between us.

"You made it," she breathed, her lips staying parted once the words left them.

When we'd practiced in her office a few days ago, we'd agreed she was supposed to say that louder, with glee and excitement. *You made it! You're on the team!* But now, she swallowed, strengthening her grip around my neck as I wrapped my arms full around her and closed every centimeter of space between us.

"Was there even a doubt that I wouldn't?"

I balanced her in one arm, freeing the opposite hand to trace the blush that crept along her cheeks. Then, I tilted her chin with my knuckles, watching those wide eyes of hers flutter shut.

And I kissed her.

I don't know what I expected when this harebrained idea first came to me in that coffee shop bar across campus, but whatever it was ceased to exist the moment my lips found hers.

I was surprised by the soft firmness she met me with, tentative, but seeking. She froze at first contact, an inhale trapped in her chest, but then she slowly exhaled, pulled me into her, and deepened the kiss like we'd shared a hundred before it.

A peck was all I'd expected. Even though she agreed when I said we'd need more to be convincing, I had a feeling once this moment came, she'd allow only a quick brush of my lips against hers. Then, I'd smile and drop her to her feet, tucking her under my arm and pretending like everything was normal while everyone *around* us freaked out. That's what I'd imagined.

I had *not* prepared for Giana to roll her hips, arching into me and breathing in another long kiss with a shockingly seductive moan before I had the chance to break contact. That little motion, how her ass poked out and I felt the heat of her against my lower abdomen made my cock twitch, and I groaned, squeezing her hip before I reluctantly pulled away.

I knew every pair of eyes in that cafeteria was on us, so I couldn't say a word. I simply arched a brow to let her know that was *quite* a surprise of a kiss, but she only flushed deeper, tucking her chin and making her curls waterfall over her face as I gently set her feet back on the ground.

Just like I'd planned, I tossed my arm around her, kissing her hair before I put my hand at the small of her back and guided her to take the spot in front of me in line.

"You breathing?" I whispered.

"Barely."

I smiled, taking the serving spoon out of her hand when we passed the mixed vegetables. "You seemed a little frazzled when you blew in here."

"It's been crazy all morning," she said on a heavy sigh, reaching out for a blueberry cake donut, but then pausing and moving on.

I plucked one as I passed and put it on her tray when she wasn't looking.

"How was it out there for you?" She nodded at a cut I had haphazardly cleaned on my forearm. "Looks like it was rough."

"It wasn't an easy one, but at least we weren't in pads," I said. "I'll take that any day."

We both kept our focus on filling our trays, Giana telling me about all the media lined up for tonight while I smiled and nodded and listened.

But when we had our trays full and turned to find a table, we were both frozen by the stares.

Giana swallowed, glancing up at me, and I just nodded toward the table where Holden, Zeke, and Riley were. She followed tentatively behind me, and while I ignored everyone staring, I saw her scanning the room out of my peripheral.

I took a seat next to Leo, but Giana was still standing, her little fingers clamped around the red tray in her hands.

"Actually, I think I'm going to take my lunch in the office," she said, forcing a smile that I knew was covering the fact that she was absolutely freaking out at how many people were still watching us. "The buzz of Chart Day doesn't stop. See you on the media line?"

I smiled, wrapping my hand gently around her forearm and guiding her down a bit so I could press a kiss to her cheek.

"Can't wait," I whispered.

She couldn't hide the shy smile as she gave a small wave to the rest of the table and ducked off, weaving through the tables until she was through the doors and down the hall.

I watched her go the entire way, and the smile I wore was one of genuine surprise as I finally turned back around, grabbing my knife and fork and cutting into the pound of grilled chicken I'd piled on my plate. I had my fork halfway lifted to my mouth when my arm was elbowed harshly, and the chicken went flying down to the table.

"Bro," Leo said, looking behind me where Giana had disappeared before he stared at me again. "What the fuck was *that*?"

I shrugged. "What?"

"What do you mean *what*?" Zeke chimed in from across the table. "Are you two... together?"

A sly smile was all I gave in answer, cutting a new bite of chicken and popping it into my mouth.

Zeke shook his head, Riley watching me cautiously from the seat beside him as Leo threw his arm around my shoulder.

"Hell fucking yeah, man. Giana is hot as fuck."

I told myself I was still in acting mode as I went rigid at his comment, turning slowly in my seat to face him. His smile slipped, and he coughed, removing his arm from my shoulders and readjusting in his seat.

"You know. Respectfully."

I gave him a wry smile before shaking my head and getting back to eating, and though they all waited for more details, I didn't give a single one, and they eventually let it go and moved on to other topics of conversation.

After a few moments, I casually stretched my back, arms reaching up overhead as I twisted left and right. My gaze caught on one of the tables of cheerleaders, on a pair of warm brown eyes that had once felt like home.

Maliyah watched me with a hundred questions brewing in those irises, her jaw tight, lips almost pursed before they spread into a hesitant smile. She lifted her hand, just an inch, a small wave at me from across that crowded cafeteria.

But I simply cracked my neck and turned back around, finishing my lunch without another glance in her direction.

I wore a smug smile on my way out of that room and down the hall to the defense meeting. At least, until Holden caught up to me, pulling me to a stop.

"That was quite a show," he commented.

"Glad you enjoyed it."

Holden shook his head, eyes narrowing like he was onto me. "Look, I'm all for you moving on. God knows you've been a miserable prick since…"

He didn't finish the sentence, probably because my glare had turned murderous daring him to.

"But... Giana is a sweet girl."

I crossed my arms. "And what, I don't deserve her?"

"I didn't say that."

"What exactly are you saying then?"

He sighed, scrubbing a hand over his chin before he looked back at me. "Just be careful, man. Okay? She's not a rebound. She's not the kind of girl you fool around with to make yourself feel better."

There was something in the sincerity of his voice, in the way he looked at me with that request that rendered me without a smartass remark to combat it. I just nodded, and he did, too, before clapping me on the shoulder and heading the opposite way toward his own meeting.

My phone buzzed in my pocket.

Giana: Well, how'd I do?

I smirked, continuing my walk down the hall as I typed back.

Me: A triumphant performance, Kitten. A+

Giana: I almost passed out when I saw everyone staring at us.

Me: I would have caught you.

She sent back an eyeroll emoji, and then the little bubbles popped up that signaled she was typing more.

Giana: So, when's my first lesson in seducing Shawn Stetson?

I couldn't contain the laugh that bubbled out of me.

Me: Eager much?

This time, it was a middle finger emoji that came through.

Me: Name the time and place.

Giana: Let's just get through Chart Day and go from there. I think I've had enough... excitement for one day.

Me: So kissing me was exciting, huh? I thought I felt a little wetness on my abs after I set you down...

Giana: CLAY!

Another laugh barreled out of me, and I tucked my phone back in my pocket, ducking into the meeting room. It buzzed again as soon as I sat down, and I was still wearing my cocky smirk when I pulled it back out, expecting a string of cursing texts from Giana.

But it wasn't Giana's name on my screen.

It was Maliyah's.

And the waiting text only said one thing.

Hi.

Chapter 7

GIANA

It was blissfully quiet in my bedroom two nights after Chart Day, the gentle hum of the ceiling fan and crackling of my wood-wick candle the only sound. I was propped up against the headboard, fuzzy sock-covered feet folded underneath me as my latest addiction sat spread like a map in my lap.

One hand held my book open, the other kept a consistent stream of crunchy Cheetos flowing from the bowl beside me into my mouth. My eyes raced across the pages, heart picking up its pace as Nino wrapped his hand around Francesca's throat and pinned her against the door to the room he was keeping her hostage in.

Having my own apartment had been absolutely crucial for me after the hellish experience of having a roommate my freshman year. I learned very quickly that growing up in a large family that mostly ignored me had made me value my personal space.

I could *not* say the same for my roommate.

Two semesters of her bounding in my room after midnight drunk as a skunk and either crying to me about a boy or squealing to me about a boy, and I'd had enough. Not to mention the amount of dishes that girl dirtied, or how she couldn't be bothered to clear her hair out of a sink or shower no matter how many times I'd asked.

The final straw had been when she'd taken a stack of my books without asking — and not even to *read* them, but to use them as a door stopper while she brought in groceries.

Fury snaked down my spine even at the memory.

I'd saved and saved and begged Mom and Dad to help fill the gaps so I could get this place, a tiny studio apartment just a few blocks from the NBU campus. It was small, old, and smelled a little like mothballs — but I loved it. And since I much preferred to be alone than to be in any sort of forced friendship, I was happy here.

And tonight, I was indulging in a self-care night, one I desperately needed after fielding the media circus that had been keeping me busy all week. Things would slow down a bit now that Chart Day was behind us — at least, until the season opener this weekend — and I was celebrating the fact that I survived rounding up more than two-dozen football players for interviews, social media stunts, and fan appearances.

Not to mention the fact that I'd survived kissing Clay Johnson.

Just like it had a hundred times since that day, the memory of it had my pulse racing, and I let my book flop against my chest as I reached for the glass of water on my bedside table and gulped half of it down. After, I just sat there, staring at my bookcase at the foot of my bed as I replayed it.

I'd been kissed before. I had.

There was Ricky in the fifth grade, who threw a dodgeball over the playground fence and then asked the teacher if we could go retrieve it together. He pressed his lips against mine and held them there for three seconds — ones he counted on his fingers — before running off laughing.

There was also Matthew, the closest thing I'd had to a boyfriend, who made out with me in a very slobbery way every chance he could get my entire sophomore year of high school. He was also the first one to stick his hand up my shirt, which deterred me from ever wanting that to happen again if all boys groped as hard as he did.

But other than that?

I was not well-versed in the subject.

Well, unless you counted my romance novels, which was about all I could think about the moment I leapt into Clay's arms at the cafeteria with every single person watching.

We'd practiced. We'd rehearsed. I knew exactly what to do, what to say, to make a scene and make it convincing. I felt like the main character in a cheesy rom com, caught up in a crazy scheme with a guy *way* out of my league. It was thrilling. It was *fun*.

Until the moment he caught me, and my legs wrapped around him, and I realized there was nothing between us but my cotton thong that said *Monday* on the crotch.

It had stolen my breath, that recognition, the way I'd felt his stone-hard abs brush against my center. But it was nothing compared to when he tilted my chin like a cinnamon roll hero would and kissed me.

I didn't *mean* to lean into it, to inhale that kiss and nonverbally ask for more when I arched into him.

But I also hadn't expected it to feel so *good*.

He held me like I weighed nothing, his knuckles still there under my chin as his lips pressed softly against my own. And when I'd deepened the kiss, when I'd wrapped my arms tighter around his neck? He'd only pulled me closer, a low groan rumbling out of his throat that made something... *different* happen to me. It sent a spark of fire roaring up my inner thighs, one that sparked at my core and had me flushing any time I thought about it since.

It *also* had me salivating at the thought of doing it with Shawn.

Sure, it was fun with Clay, but it was pretend. Having an *actual* boyfriend who would kiss me like that all the time? So long, I'd yearned for that.

And until Clay offered me this ridiculous fake-dating situation, I hadn't realized how desperate I was to get it, what lengths I would go.

Now?

I was all in.

My boss had been as surprised as that cafeteria full of football players, calling me into her office after the media had finally packed it in and crawled off campus that evening.

"So. I see you've figured out how to wrangle Clay Johnson," Charlotte had said, not so much as looking at me from where she was typing away on her computer.

I'd merely pushed my glasses up my nose, knowing a response wasn't warranted.

"Be careful," she'd warned, but then her lips had tilted into a smile as her eyes met mine. *"And have fun."*

That was it. Permission granted.

I had a feeling it had a lot more to do with the fantastic interview Clay had provided ESPN's Sarah Blackwell than anything else, but I didn't question it. He'd owed me that much, at the very least.

And now, he owed me his part of our little dating bargain, too.

I blinked, coming out of my thoughts as I settled deeper into my sheets and folded my book open again. Another handful of Cheetos went in my mouth, and then I propped my book on my chest and slipped back into another universe.

"You forget who makes the rules here, Francesca," Nino warned against Francesca's lips, his breath like the hot metal of a gun against her neck. *"And who hands out the punishment to those who break them."*

She pressed into him, not backing away from where his fingers wrapped around her throat. "You've been dying to punish me ever since you locked me down here," she spat. And in a move so bold she couldn't believe it was she who made it, Francesca wrapped her hand around the bulge protruding through Nino's expensive Boglioli slacks. *"What's stopping you?"*

His grip on her throat tightened, and in the next breath, she was thrown back on the bed, gasping as her airway finally cleared.

Nino towered over her, hands steadily unfastening his belt as his eyes raked over her lean frame.

I swallowed, heat creeping down my neck, my spine, all the way to my toes as I soaked in the scene. One hand held my book open while the other explored, touching my neck the way Nino touched Francesca's, following his lead as he tortured her slowly. I heaved a sigh as my hand trailed over my breasts, and then I tiptoed my way down, slipping my fingertips beneath the band of my sleep shorts.

"On your knees," he commanded.

I shuddered, licking my bottom lip as I rolled my hips, my hand sliding lower. I spread my legs, wanting more access...

And kicked the bowl of Cheetos off the bed in the process.

"Shit!" I cursed as the orange snack littered my floor, the metal bowl that held the crunchy nuggets clanging loudly against the old wood. I hastily rolled out of bed, smashing a few Cheetos to dust in the process, which made me curse again.

After a quick clean up, I flopped back into my bed, staring at where I'd left that scene bookmarked and closed in the center of the bed.

I wanted that so badly — the passion, the need, the heat. I wanted Shawn to look at me that way, with possessive desire rolling off him in plumes. I wanted him to kiss me the way Clay had, for it to not be a joke or a pretense, but *real*.

I chewed the inside of my cheek, considering whether or not I should just pick up where I left off in my *self-care*. But instead, I rolled over onto my stomach, reaching for where my phone rested on the wireless charger on my bedside table. A few taps later and it was ringing.

"Hello, Kitten," Clay's voice purred, deep and seductive in a way that made me believe he didn't even realize he was doing it.

I chewed my thumbnail, but before I could back out, I took a breath and spoke as confidently as I could.

"I think I'm ready for my first lesson."

Chapter 8

GIANA

"**C**an you focus?"

"Oh, trust me, I'm focusing," Clay said Friday night, licking the pad of his thumb as he swiped another page of one of my books.

I huffed, crossing my bedroom to swipe the book out of his hands and put it back on the shelf. I made sure it was in its right place before I held up the two dress options again.

"Which one?"

"That's what I want to know. Which one is Cheyanne going to choose?" He shook his head, thrusting a hand toward the bookshelf. "I mean, her husband who loves her and made vows, or her first love who's back in town and can't live without her?"

"Her husband is a cheating asshole and a narcissist, and Roland is God's gift to the Earth. So, spoiler alert, she runs off with him."

"Scandalous," Clay said, quirking a brow at the shelf.

I snapped my fingers. "*Focus.*"

I held up the hangers in each hand, and Clay folded one arm across his barrel of a chest, balancing the opposite elbow on his wrist as he smoothed a hand over his jaw in consideration.

After I'd called him the other night, we'd decided this was the best time for our first lesson. The season opener was tomorrow afternoon, which meant Coach gave the team the evening off to rest and get ready.

Of course, only about *half* the team would actually rest. The remaining half would be out partying and hoping like hell they weren't too hungover to play at their best tomorrow.

I imagined Clay would be in that latter group, had he not been saddled with me. But this was all his idea in the first place, and I reminded myself of that as I waited for him to tell me what the hell to wear.

"Neither one of them feels like you," he said after a long pause.

I sighed, the hangers dropping to my sides, dresses on the floor. "Of course not. I bought them today with that exact intention."

"Why?" Clay shook his head, taking the hangers out of my hands and crossing to my closet. He stuck the dresses in haphazardly and then started filtering through my clothes.

"Excuse me," I said, slipping between him and my twenty skirts before I pressed a hand to his chest and pushed him back. "A little privacy, please?"

"You asked for my help."

"Just... sit," I said, pointing to my bed as I turned back around. I hung my hands on my hips, not happy with anything staring back at me — at least, not for *this*.

There were no fashion guidebooks on *What to Wear to Seduce Your Crush by Using Your Fake Boyfriend.*

"Wear something you like," Clay said from behind me, kicking his sneakers off and lounging back on my bed like it was home.

It was unfair how enticing he looked in just black joggers and a gray NBU t-shirt that he'd ripped the arms off. But that rip had his bulging biceps and shoulder muscles on display, as well as his lats underneath, and my gaze lingered there for a moment too long before I brought my eyes to a more decent location. Of course, that decent location was his face, which was freshly shaven, his slightly damp boyish hair curling a bit around the flat-billed cap he wore.

Here I was stressing about what to wear, and meanwhile, Clay was practically in pajamas, yet looked ridiculously sexy and ready to take home three supermodels with one smirk and wink combination.

He started thumbing through his phone, oblivious to me checking him out. "You don't want to be uncomfortable. It'll show."

"But what if everything that's comfortable to me is boring?"

He stopped texting, arching a brow at me. "Trust me, *nothing* you wear is boring."

I gave him a flat look. "You know what I mean. You've seen the girls who salivate over him at the foot of the stage." I sighed, looking back at my closet. "I don't have anything like *that*."

"You don't need anything like that." Clay snapped his fingers. "Oh! Wear the kitten skirt. My favorite. Makes your ass look—"

"Don't finish that," I warned. "And I can't. I was wearing that last time he saw me."

Clay blinked when I stared at him like that was an obvious issue.

I groaned, waving my hand at him and turning back to the closet. "Just... be quiet so I can focus. And stay away from my books."

"Your porn? Sure thing."

I rolled my eyes, but didn't grace him with a response as I paged through my blouse options. I paused when I came to a simple, white, short-sleeved button up, plucking it out and laying it over the back of my desk chair before I started swiping through again.

"Did I tell you Maliyah texted me?"

I whipped around. "Already?"

Clay's smirk was that of the Cheshire Cat as he nodded. "Right after lunch on Chart Day."

"Wow," I mused, turning back to my closet. "That didn't take long."

"All she said was *hi*."

"What did you say back?"

"Nothing."

I whipped around again, holding a black skirt with little white hearts stitched all over it in one hand. "What do you mean, *nothing*?"

He shrugged. "I didn't answer."

"Why on Earth not?"

"Because that's what she wanted. If I would have answered, she would have known I'm not over her, and that whether or not you and I are together, she still has power over me." He held up his finger. "But by *not* answering her, I showed her I'm not bothered in the least by her being here, that I've moved on."

I blinked. "Okay…"

But as I turned back to find the right shoes, I found myself shaking my head and wondering if all these games would ever make sense to me.

"Trust me. I know what I'm doing," Clay said. "You'll see after tonight. That is, if you ever pick an outfit."

I was sifting through my drawer of socks and stockings, and I turned long enough to peg him with a bundled-up pair that made him chuckle.

"Be right back," I said, disappearing into my bathroom.

Ten minutes later, I came back out to find Clay propped against my headboard reading one of my motorcycle club romances.

"Am I going to have to put these under lock and key?" I plucked the book from his hands, holding it out of reach as he protested.

"With dirty scenes like *that*? Yeah. Probably." He waggled his brows. "I saw you put a highlighter tab on the soft choking part…"

My neck burned hotter than it had in my whole life as my eyes nearly popped out of my skull. Without thinking better of it, I reared that book in my hand back and promptly threw it at Clay, who dodged it only by a hair.

"Hey, no shame!" He laughed. "Just info I want to tuck away for later," he added, tapping his temple.

In a miraculous feat of strength, I sucked in a long breath before smoothly letting it go, holding out my arms. "How do I look?"

Clay swung his legs off the end of the bed and pulled on his sneakers as his eyes made a slow descent from where I'd put a simple black headband over the crown of my curls, to where I'd zipped up the four-inch chunky black boots around my ankles. The white blouse paired with the black skirt perfectly, the hearts a sweet touch, and I'd even been as bold as to tie the ends of the button up just under my chest to show a little midriff as opposed to tucking it in.

I did, however, grab my cream cardigan and throw it over the whole ensemble.

Clay's eyes lingered on the black knee-high stockings I'd grabbed in a last-minute decision, making me self-conscious enough that I bent my knees together.

Finally, he let out a low whistle, rising to his feet. "This is going to be fun."

I narrowed my eyes. "Why do I get the feeling I should be scared?"

But he only laughed, nodding toward the door. "Come on. We don't want to be late for your boyfriend's big show."

●●●

"So, what exactly is the plan here?" I asked Clay as he held the thick metal door open for me, every ounce of light instantly being snuffed out once we dipped inside the bar. It took a moment for my eyes to adjust and note the smiling hostess illuminated only by two small candles.

"Just follow my lead."

"But what ex—"

I couldn't get the question out before Clay was leaning his elbows on the hostess stand, offering the slim brunette beauty behind it his signature smirk.

"Good evening," he said. "Table for two, please. Booth, actually," he clarified, and winked back at me.

I just stared at him dumbfounded. What difference did it make?

"I'm sorry, sir, but we're booked solid tonight," the girl said, twirling a strand of hair between her long, onyx fingernails.

Clay sucked his teeth, glancing at me just as my shoulders slumped. But then, he grinned again, tapping on the wood of the stand. "Good thing I have a reservation."

She lit up then. "Oh! Wonderful. What's the name?"

"Johnson."

The woman slid her finger down a list, and then smiled broadly, gathering up two menus. "Right this way."

I had to admit I was shocked, so much so that Clay had to hold his arm out for mine to lure me from where I'd been rooted in place by the door. He curbed a grin as we followed the hostess through the dimly lit bar, one vastly different from the casual place on campus where Shawn usually played. This one was known for fancy cocktails that cost more than a full four-course dinner should.

Still, I marveled at the bizarre chandeliers and busy, yet not tacky, floral wallpaper as we wound our way through the tables. And we were deposited in a back corner booth.

Right near the stage.

My stomach flipped at the sight of Shawn's guitar case, of the long, charcoal gray bandana that hung off the mic. It was his signature, one I'd never seen him play without, and it held my attention as Clay slid into one side of the small booth and I took the other.

"Your mixologist will be right over," the hostess assured us, and her eyes lingered on Clay for longer than necessary — long enough that I cocked a brow like I was his actual girlfriend. She coughed when she saw me, gave a brief smile and exited stage right.

My face softened once she was gone, only to turn and find Clay watching me with an arched brow of amusement.

"What?"

"Nothing," he said, picking up the menu. "You just play your part well."

I picked mine up, too. "She might as well have left her number on a napkin."

"Coaster."

I blinked, but Clay just smiled, holding up a thin white coaster with the bar name between his fingers. I saw without having to inspect closer that she, in fact, *had* sprawled her name and number on it.

I rolled my eyes.

"Don't worry, Kitten," Clay said, scooting closer and putting his arm around the back of the booth and thus around me, too. "I'm all yours."

I fought the urge to roll my eyes again, mostly because our waitress came over. I ordered a grapefruit mocktail, because unlike Clay, *I* didn't have a fake I.D., and I wouldn't be twenty-one for another year and a half. Clay picked a whiskey drink that was so strong, I took a sip once it was delivered and felt like I was breathing fire.

"I'm impressed you made a reservation," I said.

"I didn't."

I frowned. "But, you just—"

"With a last name like Johnson, I took my shot."

"What if the *actual* Mr. Johnson shows up?"

He shrugged. "We'll cross that bridge when we get to it."

I gaped at him. "Clay!"

"Alright, so," he said, turning in the booth to face me. I was tucked into the far back corner of it, a perfect view of the stage. "First thing's first. Shawn's going to come out and play his opening song, and then you're going to go up there and drop a twenty in his tip jar."

"A *twenty*?!"

"Money talks, sweetheart," he said. "It'll get his attention. And in a dark bar like this, you need to grab him somehow. Most of the other girls will try to do it with their eyes, sucking on the cherries in their drinks while they wait for his gaze to land on them. We're taking a more direct tactic."

I snorted. "Okay. And then?"

Clay leaned back, crossing an ankle over the opposite knee before taking a long pull of his whiskey. "We'll cross that bridge when we get to it."

"Is that the phrase of the evening?" I asked flatly.

Before I could lure more information out of him, Shawn took the stage. And unlike the coffee bar at NBU where he would have had a round of applause from all the groupies that followed him around campus, he received only a courtesy glance up from where customers were conversing here. Most of them went right back to talking, not bothering to listen to his intro — though there were a few tables of girls right up by the stage who leaned in eagerly.

One of them popped a cherry in her mouth, her lush lips rolling over the swell of it until she plucked it free from the stem.

Clay gave me a look, and I shoved him under the table.

"Good evening. I'm Shawn Stetson, and I'm going to play a little music for you tonight." He smiled, running a hand back through his long hair as he settled on the barstool and propped one boot underneath him on the lower rung of it. I'd seen him do it a hundred times before, and yet I still found myself sighing, smiling, and leaning my chin into my hand as I dreamily watched him pull his guitar strap overhead.

Clay's brows bent together, gaze drifting from me to Shawn and back again before he shook his head.

"If there's anything you'd like to hear, I'm taking requests. But for now, let's start with a little Harry Styles."

Butterflies flitted in my stomach as the first chords of "Cherry" smoothed over the crowd, and I found myself singing along, feet bopping under the table. I traced the stubble on Shawn's chin, wandered over the silver of his lip piercing, and fell into his trance as he crooned the sad, somehow seductive song.

A flash of a scene from *Thoughtless* hit me out of nowhere, and my heart jumped with the memory, with the fantasy all of this could potentially unlock.

When the song was nearly over, Clay covertly slid a twenty-dollar bill flat on the table toward me, and I swallowed, staring at it like it was a bomb, instead.

"Come on. Lesson number one — make him notice you."

He all but shoved me out of the booth then, and I caught my balance just as Shawn finished playing. Again, where I was used to a full-on cheer after he ended a song on campus, here there were just a few tables that clapped before it was silent again, save for conversation that went on regardless of him playing.

I held my chin up, moving with as much feminine swagger as I could muster as I weaved in between the two tables separating our booth from the stage. Of course, my *swagger* was about as strong as my will to resist a good Hallmark movie, and so I tripped over a tablecloth and stumbled on my way up. I righted myself, though.

Just in time for him to look up.

My knees wobbled when Shawn's golden eyes flared at the sight of me, faint recognition at first, and then pleasant surprise as I dropped the twenty into his tip jar.

"Thank you," he said into the mic, and I watched curiosity dance in his eyes before he added, "Any request?"

For a split second, panic zipped through me. *We hadn't discussed what I was supposed to do if he asked if I had a request!* But somehow, I held it together, and surprised even myself as I offered a slight shrug of one shoulder and said, "Play one of your favorites."

Shawn's eyebrows rose a little higher at that, an appreciative smile on his lips as I turned and walked slowly, *so* slowly, back to the booth.

I managed to get there without tripping this time.

Shawn was still watching me when I sat down, something... *new* in his eyes. He started strumming out the first notes of his next song, and he was still watching me.

It felt like someone had cranked the heat up the longer he watched me, and I realized in that moment why it felt so intense.

Because he didn't just look at me and then look away. He didn't wink at me as his gaze swept over the rest of the crowd.

He *noticed* me.

I was still high on that thought when I felt a touch that stole my breath.

Under the table, a warm palm splayed the length of my thigh so fast I sucked in a sharp inhale at the contact. I jerked my head toward Clay, who met me with low, lazy eyes and a cocky curl of his lips that lit me on fire almost as much as his hand slipping a few more inches up did.

"Clay," I whispered, though I'd *intended* on it being a scold. It was more breathy and questioning than anything else.

He descended on me, one arm behind me along the back of the booth, and the other still on my thigh as he did. I instinctively backed away until his hand left my leg and reached up to cup my face and hold me still.

One touch.

One small, simple touch, but I burned beneath it.

My lips parted, Clay pressing in on me, his scent like teakwood and spice as he ran the pad of his thumb along my jaw. His thumb trailed up then, smoothing over my lower lip and dragging down the center of it. I tasted him, salt and whiskey, and then my lip popped free and he tilted my chin just like he had in the cafeteria.

"Good Kitten," he purred, and then his lips were on me.

Not on my lips, but on my chin, along my jaw, crawling slowly down the length of my neck as my eyes rolled back and I arched to give him better access. His lips were warm and soft, delicately pressing against my skin as his hand slowly slid down the length of my ribs and under the table once more. He rested that palm possessively on my knee, fingertips wrapping full around it and tickling the inside of my thigh.

I was intoxicated by the heady rush until he pulled back, and when I lifted my head, our noses met in the middle. My eyelids were heavy, breath shallow and slow.

For a moment, Clay seemed to forget what he was doing, his green eyes flicking between mine as his grip on my knee tightened. But then he swallowed, leaning his forehead against mine.

"Look at him," he whispered against my lips, and then he kissed a gentle trail along my jaw until he could nip at my earlobe with his teeth.

It was embarrassing, the little mewl that ripped from me when he did, my eyes closing automatically as I gasped and leaned into the touch. But I peeled them open in the next instant, and just like Clay said, I dragged my gaze toward the stage.

And found Shawn Stetson staring right back at me.

He was singing a song, one I didn't know or couldn't identify with Clay still nibbling on my earlobe and neck as his fingertips drew circles on my knee. My heart raced like a leopard, sleek leaps and bounds across the jungle of my relinquishing inhibition as I succumbed to how it felt to have a man touch me like that.

And have a *different* man watching.

There was something dark in Shawn's eyes as he did, his brows bent so fiercely the line between them formed a shadow. It was an effort to keep my eyes open and watching him in return with how hot my cheeks were, how my body trembled, how my nipples peaked and ached beneath my blouse.

"No matter what *I* do," Clay whispered in the shell of my ear. "Keep your eyes on *him*."

The song ended and another began, and I learned that *stamina* was another of Clay's attributes. He never tired of touching me, teasing me, kissing along every bit of exposed skin he could find. He even slid my blouse down off my shoulder, sucking and biting at the skin there while I watched him before he did a subtle nod for me to turn my gaze back to the stage.

I didn't know how long had passed before, suddenly, he stopped.

A gasp expelled from my chest when he did, and I lurched forward, toward the new, cold and empty space he left between us with the act.

"I'm going to go grab a drink," he said.

"What? We have a waitress. She'll be right—"

Clay stood, giving me a look before he mouthed, *trust me*.

I frowned, not understanding, not really *breathing* properly after however many songs of having his hands and mouth on me like that. But he just turned and walked away just as Shawn finished the last of his song, and I righted myself, fixing my glasses and hair and smoothing a hand over my blouse and skirt.

"I'm going to take a little break and then I'll be back to play for you beautiful people all night long. Don't forget to leave your requests," Shawn said, and then he propped his guitar on the stand, running his hands back

through his hair. He clicked a few buttons on the con-
troller next to him, making a soft song fill the speakers.

The next breath, his eyes were on me.

I blanched as he hopped off the stage, smiling at a
few girls at one of the tables close to him as he passed.
One of them reached out to hook his arm. He laughed at
something she said, and all I could make out was that he
promised he'd be right back.

Then, he was headed straight for me.

"Oh God," I murmured, sitting up straighter and
praying to whatever goddess was listening that I didn't
look half as much of a hot mess as I felt. I didn't have
time to check my appearance or fix a damn thing before
he was standing right there in front of me, a shy smirk
on his face and both hands in his pockets.

"Hi," he said.

I blinked. "Hi."

He watched me, his eyes floating over my blouse a
brief moment before they lifted again. He threw a thumb
over his shoulder. "Thanks again for that tip. It was very
generous."

I smiled, somehow holding in the snort-laugh that
threatened to bubble over. "Well, I love listening to you
play."

"You come to the bar on campus, don't you?" He
tucked his hand back in his pocket. "I've seen you there."

He has?

"You have?"

I wanted to smack myself for not keeping the in-
credulousness of that statement inside, but it only made
his smile quirk up more.

"How could I miss you?"

My brows shot up at that, and for what I was sure wouldn't be the last time around this man, I was speechless.

"I don't remember seeing you with Clay Johnson, though," he assessed carefully, coolly. "Is he your…"

It was endearing, how the words died on his lips, and he looked like he might be thinking better than to ask before I replied, "Boyfriend?"

Shawn grinned down at the floor before meeting my gaze again. "God, that was a cheap line, wasn't it?"

A line?

Was he… hitting on me?

"Well, he's a lucky guy," he said, and again I found my eyebrows hanging out somewhere near my hairline.

Shawn looked like he wanted to say something else, but he just grabbed the back of his neck before pointing back toward the stage.

"Alright, well, I should probably get some water and make the rounds before this next set. But I'm really glad you came tonight…"

He paused, waiting for me to fill in the blank.

"Giana."

"Giana," he repeated, smiling around the syllables of my name. "See you around soon, I hope?"

He didn't wait for an answer before he gave me a knowing wink, turned on his heels, and made his way through the crowd, stopping at the table of girls he promised to visit. He was laughing with them again, but his eyes flicked to me, and he held my gaze until Clay plopped down in the booth next to me with a fresh drink that he didn't really need, since most of his first one was still there.

For a long moment, I just sat there, stunned, staring at the sleek marble table as Clay took a long sip of his drink and sat back, casually crossing ankle over knee and tossing his arm around the back of the booth as he waited for me to say something.

I slowly lifted my gaze to his. "What the hell just happened?"

Clay chuckled. "I told you."

"He walked right over to me. He said he recognized me from campus. He... I think he was *flirting* with me."

Clay cocked a brow, lifting his whiskey toward me with a knowing smirk like he wasn't the least bit surprised.

I gaped at him, then at Shawn — who was getting settled on stage again — before I shook my head and found a way to zip my lips together. I smacked a hand on the table, grabbing my mocktail and sucking half of it down in one gulp. I slammed it on the table with more force than I intended, turning to face Clay head on.

"I need more lessons. *Stat.*"

An amused laugh was my only reply.

Chapter 9

CLAY

I could still remember my first football game.

I was a little tyke, five years old and just shy of four-feet tall. I remembered the smell of the turf, the way the helmet and pads felt a little too big on me as I jogged out onto the field. I remembered that I didn't know a single thing about what I was supposed to be doing, but it was fun to run and catch the ball and get grass stains on my white football pants.

And I remembered both my parents were there.

I could still close my eyes and see their faces — Dad's severe as he yelled out ways to be better, while Mom was on the verge of crying tears of joy and pride the entire game. I remembered them holding hands.

I remembered them happy.

It was one of the last times I remembered them that way.

Everything changed after that — slowly at first, and then all at once, like a single book falling from a shelf before you realized it was an earthquake that would eventually take down your entire house.

They started by just separating, explaining to me that they were just going to live in different houses for a while. *"Mom and Dad just need a little space," Dad had said. "It's good for parents to have a little space."*

But a little space turned into not seeing my dad for weeks, and then months, until one day he came by with a stack of papers in his hands. I remember he rolled them into a tube, and I stole them from him and was pretending that tube was a telescope, and the ceiling was a sky full of stars. It wasn't until Mom asked if she could look through the telescope, and then unfolded those papers as she started to cry, that I realized something fundamental in my life had shifted.

Dad sat me down at our kitchen table and told me we were still a family, even if we weren't going to live together anymore.

Domino after domino, I watched my life as I knew it crumble around me.

But through it all, I had football.

Every season started the same, with that feeling of coming home, of the last remnants of summer holding on while fall snuck in on the breeze. It was always my favorite day of the year, the one that filled me with hope and joy like a hot air balloon lifting slowly into a clear blue sky. From my first Pee Wee game, to the first time I ran out onto the North Boston University field with a crowd roaring in the stands, it was a drug, powerful and pure.

But this time... I felt nothing.

Our first game of the season passed like a foggy dream, one where I dressed, ran through warm-up drills and played all four quarters as if I were sleeping through the entire thing. I was there, on the field, next to my defensive brothers as I tackled and sprinted and leapt into the air for an interception that was nearly a pick six. I slapped helmets and chanted cheers, wiped sweat out of my eyes on the sideline, lifted Riley onto my shoulders when the final whistle blew and we won the game, and talked to the line of media like I was the luckiest, happiest kid in the world.

But inside, I was numb.

And as much as I hated to admit it, I knew it was because of Maliyah.

Seeing her warm up on the same field, watching her cheer out of the corner of my eye, trying to ignore the looks she got from not just the guys on the team but those in the stands, too — it was a slow death from sipping poison.

I wished I was stronger. I wished I didn't care. I wished for all the things in my life that could have broken me, this was not the one that finally did.

It was supposed to be us.

It was supposed to be her kissing me before the game, cheering me on as I played, leaping into my arms after a win. It was supposed to be my number painted on her cheek, just like in high school, and my jacket around her shoulders when the fall chill set in.

Last night, I'd almost forgotten the acute pain that resided in my chest when Giana and I had gone out in the Theater District for her first "lesson" in getting Shawn's attention. I was so focused on helping her, on showing her how to play the game that I hadn't had time to even think about Maliyah.

It was a welcome distraction, watching Giana's shock as what I told her to do worked, feeling her tremble and pant beneath me as I teased her in that booth, knowing it was driving Shawn mad to watch it.

I knew, because if I were him, it would have driven *me* mad.

I was surprised how easy it was, how effortless it felt to kiss along her neck, to whisper in her ear and elicit a wave of chills over her skin. It was amusing at first, a permanent smile on my face as I found which buttons I could push to make her gasp, or sigh, or arch into me, or dig her nails into my flesh.

But as the night progressed, that amusement shifted into something primal.

The more I pretended like she was mine to tease like that, the more it felt like she really was.

I soaked up every little mewl that escaped her lips like a hard-fought-for reward. It surprised me how hard it was to peel myself off her when I knew Shawn was about to go on break, and I had to stifle a laugh when I realized I was hard as a rock when I stood up from our booth. I'd had to adjust myself in my pants and stand with my crotch against the bar until I could calm down.

Giana was unexpectedly addicting. Her and her weird books, her unique clothes, her innocence that she tried so hard to cover up with unfaltering sass.

She was... refreshing. And fun.

But not even she could save me from the numbness of today.

"I expect picks like that all season long," Holden said, clapping me on the shoulder once we'd all made it back to the locker room. "Except next time, it better be run in for a touchdown."

"Sir, yes, sir," I shot back with a salute.

Holden smirked, tearing his damp, dirty jersey off and letting it drop to the floor before he tilted his chin at me. "You good?"

"Good."

"Sure?"

I cracked my neck, giving him a look that I hoped told him what I wouldn't voice out loud. No, I wasn't good. Far from it. But I didn't want to talk about it.

He just nodded, lips pressed together as he ran a hand back through his wet hair. "All you can do is focus on what you can control," he said, almost to the ground or himself rather than to me.

I nodded, thankful that he wasn't pushing it.

We finished undressing in silent, both of us dragging our asses to the ice baths before we took showers. By the end of it all, every muscle in my body was screaming in protest — just like it did at the end of every game. Four quarters of putting my muscles and bones and joints through hell never got easier. In fact, the older I got, the more talented I became? The bigger and badder guys I was facing on the field.

I couldn't imagine what it would be like once I was facing off against the tanks in the NFL.

As I finally got re-dressed in my sweats and made my way out of the locker room, I promised the guys I'd see them at the party later tonight. I needed a nap before then, and maybe a few drinks to pre-game.

When I rounded out of the locker room and into the hall, a familiar laugh made me freeze in place.

Maliyah's sing-song giggle floated down the hallway, wrapping itself around me like a warm, esophagus-crushing hug. I followed the sound of it like she was a siren, and I was a helpless sailor on tumultuous seas, only to find her leaning up against the wall a mere twenty yards away.

Kyle Robbins stood in front of her, his arm propped against the wall next to her head as his eyes ran the length of her. He edged in even closer, whispering something in her ear that made her blush and laugh again.

And I saw red.

My fists curled at my sides, jaw clenching so hard I nearly broke a tooth. I dropped my duffle bag to the floor, took two steps toward them with the intent to march right down there and break that motherfucker's nose.

But two steps was as far as I got before Giana sprang into view.

She startled Kyle and Maliyah both when she sprinted past them, her curls bouncing, glasses sliding down the bridge of her nose with every step. But her turquoise eyes were trained on me, and I bent, ready to catch her before she even launched herself off the ground and into my arms.

Just like in the cafeteria, she wrapped her legs around my waist, breath *whooshing* out of her at the contact. Her arms threaded around my neck and my hands caught her ass — her *bare* ass under the skirt she wore. It was apparently something she hadn't thought about before jumping, because shock washed over her, face paling at the feel of my warmth against her.

It lasted only a second, though, because in the next? She was kissing me.

Her mouth collided with mine almost hard enough to draw blood, and she fisted her hands in my hair still damp from the shower, writhing against me. A soft whimper vibrated through her as I held her tighter, and she was breathless when she finally pressed her hand into my chest and broke the kiss.

I heaved a breath, and her chest rose and fell in tandem with mine as I stared at her red, swollen lips. Slowly, my gaze lifted to hers, and those bright eyes shot wider.

"I'm sorry," she whispered, fixing her glasses. "I just, I saw them, and I saw *you*, and I thought—"

I cut off the rest of her words with my hand behind her head, guiding her into me for another bruising kiss. This time, I pinned her against the wall, and she gasped when my abdomen rubbed along her center.

Pressing my forehead to hers, I pulled back, rolling my lips together. "You're picking up on this game quickly, Kitten."

She flushed against a smile. "I've got a good coach."

Someone cleared their throat, and Giana and I turned to find Zeke and Riley walking out of the locker room holding hands. Zeke hiked an eyebrow at where we were locked together, my waist between Giana's thighs, and Riley blushed so hard she had to look down at the ground and away from us.

"See you at the pit?" Zeke asked, a shit-eating grin on his face.

I didn't have to answer. Giana buried her face in my chest and I kissed her hair as Zeke and Riley walked by. Following them allowed my gaze to drift down to Kyle and Maliyah, who were both staring right back at me.

Kyle looked suspicious.

Maliyah looked... *challenged*.

I didn't allow my gaze to linger, pulling it back to Giana and tilting her chin up with my thumb and forefinger. "You're coming, too."

"Coming where?"

"The Snake Pit."

"The do what now?"

I barked out a laugh, carefully dropping her feet to the ground and tucking a stray curl behind her ear. "It's a party house where some of the upperclassmen guys on the team live. When someone who lives there graduates, a new teammate moves in, and it's where we celebrate after every home win." I made a face. "It's kind of disgusting, honestly, but just don't look too closely at the floors or crevices and you'll be fine."

"I don't know," she said, wrinkling her nose. "I was kind of looking forward to a night in after being out so late last night."

"Oh, that's too bad," I said, bending to retrieve my duffle bag and walking toward the exit. "Because someone you want to see will be there."

Giana scrambled to catch up to me, tugging on my sleeve. "Wait, really? *Shawn*?" She shook her head. "Why the hell would he be at a football party?"

"Because I'll invite him," I said. "And he'll shit himself before saying he's in. Probably show up with a bottle of wine as a gift or some shit, too."

Giana rolled her eyes, but an excited smile spread on her lips, a little bounce in her step as we walked.

And right as we passed Maliyah and Kyle, I reached down, threading Giana's small hand in mine.

Chapter 10

GIANA

"**C**hug! Chug! Chug! Chug!"

I ducked out of the way just in time to dodge a beer funnel being lifted up over my head, but didn't move in enough time to escape the driblets that slopped over the edge of it. Beer spritzed into my hair and on my shoulders, and Clay laughed at my expression of horror before grabbing my shoulders and guiding me off to the side.

The Snake Pit, as Clay had called it, was a large house in a surprisingly nice neighborhood that was currently dark, loud, and crawling with NBU students. A DJ spun popular tracks in the main living room, the old couches with torn cushions pushed off to the sides to make way for a giant dance floor. Lights flared and flashed all colors of the rainbow around the scene, girls dancing and guys trying to find a way to join them.

"I love her outfit!" I yelled over the music to Clay, pointing toward a girl in the middle of the dance floor.

She wore a white top that criss-crossed over her slight cleavage, accentuating her toned stomach and paired with shorts that did her already lean legs a favor. Her hair was long and curled down her back, makeup like that of a movie star.

"That's Olivia Bradford," Clay yelled back.

"Bradford?" My eyes shot open. "As in the university president?"

"That's his daughter."

I assessed her again, even *more* impressed with her outfit knowing she had a stern father who ran one of the top universities in New England.

My eyes continued scanning the party, taking in the various games of beer pong and flip cup happening all around the house. There were pods of students laughing and talking, drinking and making out, and — to my surprise — even doing drugs. Though none of the football players were in those specific circles. They'd lose their scholarships and position on the team if they were.

"This is kind of overwhelming," I admitted, but it wasn't anxiety simmering in my gut. It was... *excitement*.

I was at a college football team party.

It felt like something that would happen to a character in one of my favorite new-adult books, and I found myself eager to get into trouble, to try something new, to dance or play beer pong or—

My thoughts were interrupted when Shawn Stetson slipped into my view, a calm, confident smile on his face as he weaved through the crowd. He couldn't make it more than a few steps before a girl was grabbing him by the arm or belt loop. I didn't have to read lips to know they were telling him how much they loved his music, how much they loved *him*. It was all written in the fake-blush he wore, and the way he mouthed *thank you* over and over again.

He wasn't modest. He didn't need to be, not with how hot he was or how uniquely velvet his voice was. It was like Caleb Followill from Kings of Leon had a child with Adele, and they bestowed the best of both their voices onto their bouncing baby boy.

Clay cleared his throat, right up next to my ear so I could actually *hear* it, and I bit my lip against a flush when I turned to find him watching *me* watching Shawn.

"Ready for the game plan?" he asked with a grin.

And just like a football player tugging on their helmet before hitting the field, I nodded, expression serious. "Ready."

Clay pulled me under his arm, so close I felt every inch of his body pressed against mine as he spoke low into my ear. "I'm going to ignore you," he said. "Hang out with my friends, maybe flirt with some other girls. Use that to your advantage. Talk a little shit about me."

I frowned. "What? To Shawn?"

Clay nodded. "Drop hints that you're unhappy, that you're used to being ignored in situations like this."

"That makes you seem terrible."

He shrugged. "So? That's the point. It'll take Shawn's piqued interest and turn it into a burning desire to save you and show you what you deserve."

"That's cliché," I said on a snort. "And ridiculous."

"Have I not proven to you yet that I know what I'm doing?" Clay pulled back enough to hike a brow incredulously. "Just trust me. Oh, and invite him to hang out with you somewhere a little less chaotic. Maybe say you need some air. You can ask about his music, stroke his ego a bit."

I shook my head. "You're a little *too* good at this."

Clay just smiled, glanced back in the direction of Shawn, and then slipped into a more severe persona. It was the wildest thing, to watch how he schooled his features, looking bored and almost a little pissed off as he lifted the red plastic cup in his hand up to his lips. With a long pull of his beer and his eyes nowhere near looking at me, he said, "Good luck," and disappeared through the crowd.

I watched him go, watched as he high-fived a few players he walked by before joining Leo Hernandez in the kitchen. It just so happened to be when Leo was lining up shot glasses, and he poured an extra one for Clay once he joined.

Except, they didn't take the shots out of the glasses.

Instead, Leo cleared the kitchen counter with a sweep of his forearm, littering the sink and floor with plastic cups, discarded lime wedges, and who knew what else. He turned to the girl beside him then — Olivia, I recognized, from the dance floor — and wrapped his hands around her hips before lifting her onto the counter. She laid back, flushed and giggling as he lined her stomach with salt and pooled a healthy amount of tequila in the valley of her abs and belly button.

I watched him do a body shot off her as she squirmed beneath him, and then as soon as she hopped down, another girl crawled up to take her place.

Clay didn't even hesitate.

Leo poured the body shot in just the same fashion, and Clay bit his bottom lip, eyes hooded where they appreciated the girl's ample cleavage heave as the cold liquid met her skin. His massive hands came down to frame either side of her, and he placed a lime wedge in her mouth with a wicked grin as she watched wide-eyed.

I couldn't tear my eyes away as he ran the flat length of his tongue along the salt on her stomach, as his fingertips dug into her skin while he sucked and licked that tequila off her. Then, he was hovering over her face, and he bent slowly and seductively to bite the lime wedge in her mouth.

For only a brief second — then, the lime was gone, and his mouth was on hers.

Pain spiked through my chest like an ice pick, intensified when the girl threaded her manicured nails through his hair. She opened her mouth to let his in, and though the swipe of his tongue against hers was only a split second, it made my neck heat, made my stomach turn, made me...

What, exactly?

I stared and stared at them, trying to dissect what I was feeling, but didn't solve the puzzle before a husky voice was at my ear.

"She doesn't hold a candle to you."

I shivered, the rough lilt of syllables tumbling down the back of my neck and leaving chills in their wake. I angled my head, finding Shawn staring down at me with a playful grin.

I laughed. "Yeah," I said, but without even trying, without having to fake it... my eyes trailed back to Clay. "Sure."

I watched as he helped the girl off the counter, his hands staying at her waist once she was safely on the floor. I knew I'd stared for too long because when I glanced back up at Shawn, he was watching me with his brows folded together, with pity and something like longing in his golden eyes before he leaned close to whisper in my ear.

"Want to get some air?"

While the front yard of the Snake Pit was crawling with students, the back yard was a serene garden, a hidden oasis that it seemed no one bothered to investigate because it was far too quiet to be part of the party. Shawn and I walked by a small pod of people passing around a joint before we found a bench along the stone path, a bubbling bird bath and feeder in front of it along with a rose garden that I was fairly certain had to be landscaped by a paid company.

No way was there a college football player with that green of a thumb.

Shawn gestured to the bench for me to sit first, and once I had, he sat right next to me, his thigh brushing the outside of mine. My cheeks heated at the contact, but he seemed unfazed, simply reclining and widening his stance as he threw an arm along the back of the bench.

"Color me impressed," he mused, eyes trailing over the garden.

I chuckled. "Yeah, not exactly what I expected to find back here. I was assuming it'd be more of a trash-littered patch of dirt."

"Is it your first timc hcrc?"

I tucked my hands under my thighs. "Yes. Although, from the time I've spent in the locker room, I'm pretty used to the noise level. And the smell."

"The locker room?" Shawn frowned.

"I'm the Public Relations Assistant Coordinator for the team," I clarified.

Shawn sat up a little straighter. "No shit?" He shook his head. "You're just full of surprises. Forgive me, but... I can't picture you in that role at all."

"That's part of the reason why I picked it," I said with a smile. "Who *would* look at me and see someone confident enough to boss around ginormous football players?"

"I guess I should expect the unexpected with you, shouldn't I, Giana?"

Shawn offered me a lazy smile, and I bit the inside of my lip, heart picking up its pace inside my chest. I was so used to staring at *him* on a stage. It was unnerving to have him staring back, and so closely.

Talk about his music.

Clay's words snapped me back to the present. "I'm surprised you don't have a gig tonight," I commented.

Shawn relaxed into the bench. "I like to take a Saturday off from time to time. And believe it or not, I'm a pretty big football fan. I wouldn't miss the first game."

"It is kind of hard to believe," I admitted. "That someone so artistic would also be a football junkie."

"What, I can't sing John Mayer songs and also paint the school colors on my chest and scream like a banshee in the stands?"

I chuckled. "Body paint? Now that I'd like to see."

It was a joke, light and effortless when I said it, but Shawn cocked a brow at the insinuation that I wanted to see his body, and I instantly paled.

"Um. I mean, the school spirit, of course. Not the body paint. Or the body. Not that I *wouldn't* like to see your body. I mean, not that I *would—*"

Shawn just smiled, letting me ramble on, no trace of any intention to stop me from embarrassing myself further. So I clamped my mouth shut, burying my face in my hands.

"Sorry," I murmured through them. "It's been a long night."

When I peeked back at him, his smile was gone, concern etched into his features. "Do you want to talk about it?"

I frowned, wondering what he meant, and I was just about to tell him I only meant that I was a little tired after staying out so late *last* night when I realized he was referring to Clay.

Talk a little shit about me.

I folded my arms over my chest, sinking back. "Not really."

I aimed for sad, poor neglected girlfriend as I trained my gaze on my kitten heels, not offering anything further.

"Is he always like that?"

The question was soft, timid, like he wasn't sure he was allowed to ask it.

I shrugged. "He's a football player. It doesn't mean anything. He's just playing the part."

I was surprised how easy that excuse tumbled out of me, and surprised even more when Shawn slid a little closer, one hand coming down to touch my knee gently. He waited until my eyes flashed to his, and I wondered if he could hear the way my heart accelerated at the feel of his hand on me.

"It means something if it hurts you."

I melted at the words, at how sincere his expression was. It was a line straight out of a romance novel, further proving to me that Shawn Stetson was a bonified book hero. My lips parted to answer him, but then his eyes fell to my mouth, and any attempt at speaking failed me.

He stared and stared as I held my breath, and slowly, his eyes crawled back up to mine. That hand on my knee tightened, just a fraction, and he leaned in, just a centimeter, his lips on track for mine...

"There you are, Kitten."

Shawn jumped back, tearing his hand from my knee and scooting a couple feet away on the bench just in time for Clay to round the corner. He wore a threatening grin, one he aimed at Shawn before it turned softer toward me.

"Clay," I breathed, genuinely surprised as I hopped to my feet. I didn't even need to, but I smoothed a hand over my skirt. It was apparently becoming my favorite nervous tic. "Shawn and I were just getting some air."

"I see that," he assessed coolly, and again, his menacing gaze slipped to Shawn. I watched, impressed, as his nose flared a bit, his jaw tight as he gave Shawn a once-over.

Look at him, playing the jealous boyfriend.

"Come on," he said, reaching for my hand. It all but disappeared in his as he tugged me toward the house. "Riley and Zeke want to play pong."

I frowned. "But Zeke doesn't drink."

Clay gave me a look. "Riley will drink double for him." He barely looked at Shawn as he said. "See you around, Steve."

"Shawn," he corrected, his frown just as severe, chest puffed.

Clay didn't entertain him with a response, just threw his arm around me and leaned in to whisper in my ear. "Look back at him while we walk away."

I swallowed, doing as he said, and when my eyes met Shawn's, he was watching me with a mix between gut-wrenching pain and passionate jealousy. He opened his mouth, but I tore my gaze away, back to face forward as Clay weaved us down the stone path toward the house.

"Why did you come get me?" I asked, glancing up at him. "It was going well."

"I can't let you hang out with another guy for *too* long before it gets suspicious," Clay answered easily.

I shook my head. "He looked like he wanted to murder you."

"Then the plan is working."

I laughed, but the sound died in my throat when we slipped back into the loud house only to quite literally smack into Maliyah.

"Oh!" She bounced back in surprise, and Clay's hand shot out to right her before he could even think better of it. I knew, because in the next instant, their eyes locked, both of them swallowing hard.

It was like being in the presence of movie stars, seeing the two of them together. They were both tall, far too gorgeous for their own good, and had the kind of energy that made others in the room revolve around them. I glanced at her and then at him, back and forth, and again found myself wondering how the hell someone like *me* was supposed to make her jealous.

Clay's arm lingered around her, his breath shallow before he finally released her and resumed his grip around me.

"Clay," she said, her doe eyes flicking to me next.

I smiled, thinking she might introduce herself, but instead, her eyes raked over me, brow arching higher as she took in every inch of my outfit.

"Maliyah, let's go dance," a girl I hadn't realized was standing behind her said. She had long, jet black hair and tattoos lining her left arm — which Maliyah threaded her own through before letting the girl tug her away.

She flicked her hair over her shoulder, not looking back, but once she hit the dance floor, her eyes found Clay automatically.

What the fuck?

She clearly knew Clay was frazzled from running into her, and rather than talking to him, she was purposefully dancing while *looking* at him. She wouldn't do that if she didn't care that we were together, if she didn't still want Clay.

But if she wanted him, why wouldn't she just take him? She could do it — right here, right now.

I ground my teeth. "What is *her* game?" I asked, looking up at Clay.

He looked like a sick puppy, face almost green as he watched her in return. "I wish I knew."

I narrowed my eyes, then squared my shoulders, grabbing his hand in mine. "Come on."

I didn't know what my plan was as I dragged him through that crowd, but I made sure to parade right in front of the dance floor before squeezing in on one of the couches lining the wall facing it. I pulled Clay down to sit next to me, and the space was so tight from the other people on it that I was crushed between him and the arm. When I wiggled out of the vise grip, I was half in his lap, tucked under his arm, consumed by every tense inch of him.

"Look at me," I said.

Clay dragged his gaze from where Maliyah was on the dance floor, and I framed his face with my hands.

114

"If you're not playing, you're losing, remember?" I rolled my lips together, swallowing past the knot forming in my throat. "So, let's play."

Clay frowned, tilting his head to the side.

"Use me," I clarified. "Make her remember what you had. Show her what she's missing."

Clay arched a brow, glancing around before his eyes met mine again. "It won't be just her watching."

"I trust you," I breathed, and then I tangled my fingers in the hair at the nape of his neck and pulled him into me.

I should have been used to it.

I should have been struck with the fact that it was fake, all pretend, every time his lips met mine. But it was the same shock of surprise that flitted through me, and my breath caught in my chest, heart plunging off the highest diving board into a pool of white hot fire as he kissed me.

Clay inhaled a deep breath through his nose, one hand winding around the small of my back while the other cradled the back of my head and held me to him. His chest swelled against mine, and then he tilted my chin with the tip of his nose, demanding access to my neck.

My eyes fluttered closed, nipples pebbling under my thin blouse as his large, warm lips caressed the skin stretched over my throat. Each brush of his lips was more firm than the last as he made his way down, and he nipped at my collarbone, eliciting a hiss from me as I twisted my hands in his shirt.

I didn't have to have my eyes open to know we were being watched.

I felt the gazes of not just Maliyah, but every person in close proximity at that party burning into my skin just as fervently as Clay's kisses as he trailed his way back to my mouth. His next kiss was like a brand, demanding and brutal, and for the first time, he slid his tongue against the seam of my lips, requesting access.

And I opened.

I parted my lips and met his tongue with mine, a sharp zip of electricity stunning me at the collision. It was as if his tongue stroked me between my thighs rather than in my mouth, and I squeezed my legs tighter together against the foreign sensation even as I leaned in for more.

Clay moaned, one hand tightening where he held me against him as the other slid down from my face, over my neck, and right over the swell of my heaving chest.

The gasp that slight brush elicited from me was guttural and automatic, so violent that my eyes shot open. But Clay kissed me even more fervently as his hand continued trailing down, his palm warm and confident when it settled over the inside of my thigh.

It was possessive, the way he cradled me, the way he pulled me in tighter, kissed me harder, his hand slowly pushing up under the hem of my skirt.

I gasped, head arching back as Clay moved easily from my mouth to my neck once more.

And again... I opened.

The signal didn't come from my brain, but from a longing so powerful in the very core of who I was that it was impossible to fight against. My legs uncrossed, knees spreading just enough to let him push that hand up under the fabric of my skirt even higher.

My next breath was shaky and shallow, and Clay pressed a feather-light kiss to the skin just beneath my ear.

"Okay?" he asked, simple and soft. That one word seemed to ground me, to bring me back to the room, to reality, to him.

I think I nodded. I think I gave some sort of murmur of affirmation before his tongue licked along my jaw line and back to my mouth. He pressed his forehead against mine, and when my lids flickered open, I found his emerald eyes blazing down at me.

Time stuttered to a stop, the noise of the party dying on a breath. Suddenly, I was acutely aware of where Clay's breath met my mouth, where his chest swelled and fell in rhythm with mine, where his hand crawled achingly slowly up, up, up.

The rough pads of his fingertips slid tenderly along my inner thigh, the skin so beyond sensitive I couldn't do anything but quake and hold onto him for dear life. It was unmarked skin, never touched by anyone but me.

Clay dragged his teeth over his bottom lip, plump from kissing me senseless, and his eyes held mine as he dared to go even higher.

I spread my legs wider, letting him in.

Until he ran the entire length of his index finger right along the soaked cotton of my thong.

I whimpered, a gasp of a moan roaring out of me at the touch, at the feeling of his sure, steady palm against the most private and sensitive part of me. And when he felt my desire, he groaned, his mouth capturing mine just as he retracted his finger only to glide it along that same line of fire with more pressure.

Stars.

No, not stars, a black hole, suffocating and life-ending, was born where he touched me. I gasped, eyes flying open, heart seizing in panic beneath my tight ribcage.

"Meow."

The word was a breathy plea when it slipped unbidden from my lips, and Clay froze, his heart beating hard enough I could feel it through his shirt as I pressed my hand into his chest and forced space between us.

"Meow," I repeated, louder, firmer.

Recognition hit his face, and Clay paled, peeling himself off me with concern laden in his eyes. "Giana," he tried, but I couldn't look at him any longer.

I couldn't be near him, couldn't contain the fire roaring inside me.

I faked a smile, brushed a kiss against his cheek like I was fine just in case Maliyah or anyone else was watching. I stood as slowly and coolly as I could, fixing my hair and righting my skirt before I strolled toward the bathroom.

But as soon as I was out of eyesight, I took a hard left.

And I ran.

Chapter 11

CLAY

My heart was a thunderous march of stallions in my ears as I weaved through the crowded party, eyes trained on Giana's back. Her breaths were more haggard and uneven with every step, and when she disappeared around the edge of the kitchen only to take off in a full run for the door, I let out a curse, pushing past people to follow her.

I'd gone too far.

That safe word was never meant to be used, never meant to be anything more than a joke between us. But I'd pushed, taking advantage of her trust, giving in to my own selfish desire as playing with her in that party became less about Maliyah and more about seeing what noises I could get to come from that pretty mouth of hers.

I hadn't meant to. I'd only intended to kiss her, to peek my eyes open at where I knew Maliyah was watching from the dance floor and show her just how moved on I was. But the more Giana opened for me, the more she writhed under my touch...

The less I was looking at anything or anyone else but her.

It was dizzying, her tongue against mine, the slick desire between her legs that I knew was from me. Like a drug addict, I was greedy for more.

And I didn't think about the consequences.

Giana burst out into the night with me hot on her heels, catching the door before she could even slam it behind her.

"Giana!"

A few students who were gathered on the lawn parted as she sprinted through them, their questioning eyes finding me next as I chased after her.

"G, please, wait," I called, but she kept running, around the front gate and down the sidewalk.

I followed, picking up my pace as my heart hammered like a kick drum in my chest. When I was a few steps behind her, I reached out, catching her by the elbow and slinging her to a stop.

She swung into me, a little gasp of a cry bounding out of her as I caught her and held her steady.

"I'm sorry, I—"

"No, *I'm* sorry," I said, holding her slight arms in mine.

She was sipping shallow breaths, eyes glossing over as she avoided my gaze. It fucking killed me to see her like that.

To know I was the reason.

"Hey," I said, tilting her chin with my knuckle.

I waited until her eyes met mine, and one tear slid silently down the edge of her cheek before she batted it away.

"I'm sorry," I repeated, eyes searching hers. "I'm sorry."

Her breathing slowed, just a bit, one long exhale finding her before she collapsed into me. I caught her in a fierce hug, wrapping her up in my arms like I could shield her from what was hurting her.

Like it wasn't me who was the culprit.

She shook in my arms, sniffing against tears I knew she was angry for shedding. She swiped them away as quickly as they could come, but didn't break from my embrace. She let me hold her, let me smooth my hand along her spine until she calmed, until her breaths were more even and her body was still.

"God, I'm a mess," she said when she finally pulled back, but she didn't put much space between us. She just dipped her face into her hands, shaking her head.

"I went too far."

"No," she tried, but then she sighed, finally meeting my gaze. "Yes. But it's not your fault."

"It is. I got carried away."

"I was playing into it just as much."

I shook my head, ready to argue, but all words died in my throat when Giana beat me to it.

"I'm a virgin."

I blinked, shocked, unsure I heard her correctly. But when she stared up at me unwavering, sorrow and shame coloring her cheeks, I knew I hadn't misheard.

Something feral roared inside me, the teeth of it bared as I clenched my jaw against it threatening to break out of its cage. A long, searing inhale forced it back down.

"I know," Giana said, folding her arms over her chest as she caved in on herself. "It's embarrassing."

I immediately reached for her, lifting her chin until she was looking at me again. "Why would you say that?" I asked, brows bending together as I searched her gaze.

"Because I'm a sophomore in college and I haven't had sex," she answered bluntly.

I shook my head, letting out the breath I'd inhaled before I pulled her into me for another hug. "It's not something to be embarrassed about."

"Well, it feels like it."

"It's not," I reiterated, and then I pulled back, framing her arms in my hands. "Thank you. For telling me."

She nodded, swallowing as her eyes fell to the ground between us.

"I'm sorry I didn't realize."

Giana groaned then, her head lulling back as she rolled her eyes up to the sky. "I don't want it to be a big deal."

"Well, it kind of is," I said with an amused smile. "Especially when I'm pawing you like an animal in a crowded party."

A laugh bubbled out of her, and she pulled her gaze back to mine. "Sometimes I just wish I could just do it with someone and get it over with, you know?"

That feral monster inside me bashed against its cage, and all I could do to stomach it was tuck her under my arm and walk her back toward campus.

"Tell me what happened with Shawn," I said, ignoring her comment, though I knew it would be burned into my brain for the rest of my fucking life.

Giana eyed me like she saw right through my not-so-subtle dodge of the subject, but apparently, she was eager to move on, too, because she sighed, leaning her head against my chest as we walked.

"I don't know how, or *why*, but I did everything you said and he…" She shook her head, laughing a bit as she buried her face before peeking up at me. "I think if you wouldn't have showed up, he would have kissed me."

I laughed despite the way those words made anger flare in my gut. That was a side effect I hadn't been prepared for when we'd entered into this fake relationship, how kissing and touching Giana would blur that line and make me feel like she was actually mine. I didn't have a right to feel any sort of possessiveness over her, so I shoved it down and remembered why we did this in the first place.

For her to get Shawn.

For me to get Maliyah back.

"Let me guess — he said something along the lines of you deserving better than me?"

"Basically," she said. "I'm just… in awe. He went from not even knowing I'm alive to… I don't know… wanting to *save* me from you." She barked out a laugh at the audacity.

I, on the other hand, swallowed against the vitality of his concern.

"So, what's next?" she asked.

When she looked up at me, the tears had dried on her face, and her smile was just as bright and genuine as the one she'd given me when we walked into the party at the beginning of the night. Just like that, she'd bounced back. And even though I'd crossed the line, she watched me with the same unwavering trust in her eyes, looking to me for guidance like I wasn't the devil himself.

"So eager," I teased, smiling as I pulled her under my arm and rubbed my knuckle against her skull.

She shoved me off with a laugh, fixing her hair before launching into other things she'd seen at the party, including a couple hippy kids making mushroom tea, and the garden in the back which I agreed with her was completely bizarre and didn't fit the scene.

I just listened to her, nodding along, and kept my hands in my pockets.

Mostly to keep from reaching for her again.

Chapter 12

GIANA

"**I** want you all to be thinking about your case study," Professor Schneider said on Wednesday morning, a click of her mouse pulling up the requirements on the screen at the head of the class. "It feels like the end of the semester is far away now, but it will sneak up on you, and I will tell you now that I'll *know* if you procrastinated, and your grade will reflect it."

My tired eyes bounced over the text on the screen, though I didn't register much. Social Media as a Mass Communication was the furthest thing from my mind, especially after a late night working on the upcoming team auction.

Charlotte had me cold-calling everyone in the community she could think of who might be willing to sponsor or provide date itineraries for the auction. And as if that wasn't draining enough, she then told me I needed to select the charity for the proceeds to benefit and have it on her desk by morning.

It *could* have been an easy task, if I was lazy and didn't care about every tiny aspect of my job. I could have Googled *charities in Boston* and selected the first one that popped up. But since I was addicted to knowledge and detail, I not only searched charities in the area, but also how much of their funding went toward their goal, how many other national sponsors they had, what their output of help in the local community was, and how their ideals matched up with that of NBU and the team.

I hadn't landed on a decision until well after midnight, and though I passed out as soon as I got home from the stadium, my alarm went off only six hours later.

Early classes were a bitch.

"The quiz on chapters one through five is now live in your online portal. You'll have until Friday to complete it. See you all next week."

With that, textbooks and laptops snapped closed, the shuffling of bags the first sound that filled the room before soft talking followed it. I packed up my own things in silence, glancing at my watch that read ten AM and thinking it would be a two-coffee kind of day.

With my messenger bag lugged over one shoulder, I dragged myself out of the classroom and the College of Communications building, the warm morning defrosting my limbs frozen from the air-conditioning. I was on auto-pilot as I shuffled toward *Rum & Roasters,* pushing through the door just as a yawn stretched my mouth open.

I stood in line like a zombie, ordering a caffè Americano with an extra shot of espresso. I had the life-giver cupped between my palms as I walked toward my usual table.

Only to find it occupied.

Shawn sat bent in my usual chair, one ankle balanced on the opposite knee, guitar in his arms and brow furrowed as he thumbed the strings quietly. His dark hair fell into his eyes slightly, and the way the morning light was streaming through the windows washed him in gold. He looked like the cover of a soft rock album, and when he flicked his hair out of the way and looked up to find me standing in front of him, the sexiest, smoothest smile spread on his dusty pink lips.

"Well, good morning, Angel."

I flushed, glancing over my shoulder as if I wondered if it was me he was talking to. When I looked back at him, he chuckled, setting his guitar to the side.

"You've got a halo right now, the way the light is coming in," he explained.

I smiled. "Hiding the horns holding it up, no doubt."

Shawn gestured to the seat across from him.

I took it hesitantly — mostly because I was debating if I was too tired to even hold a conversation, let alone a flirty one with intention. But one sip from my espresso had me optimistic that I could turn it around.

What would Clay do?

He'd tell me to suck it up and play the game, that's what.

I hadn't seen Shawn since the party on Saturday night, and my stomach flipped the longer he watched me with a curious gaze.

"What?" I asked.

He shook his head. "Nothing. You just... forgive me if this is too forward, but you look beautiful right now."

My cheeks were hot enough to rival my coffee as I looked down at my hands. "I highly doubt that, considering how tired I am at the moment."

"Late night?"

I sighed. "Very. I'm working with my boss on an upcoming charity event for the football team, and it's taking more time and energy than all of my classes combined."

"I still can't get over you being in public relations," he assessed with a smile.

"What would you peg me as, if I hadn't told you otherwise?"

"Librarian."

I laughed. "It's the glasses, huh?"

"Among other things," he said, and his metallic eyes slid down the length of me, brow arching as he took in the eclectic blouse I'd paired with my old jean overalls. They were baggy and hid more than they revealed, but the way his eyes careened each inch, it felt more like I was in a bra and panties.

I cleared my throat, taking a sip of my coffee. "So, do you sleep in the back of the store here, or...?"

He ran a hand back through his long hair, crossing his ankle over his knee again before pulling the guitar back into his lap. "I'm working on a song, and I was a little stunted in my dorm, so I thought a change of scenery could help."

"Has it?"

"Sadly, no," he confessed. "There's something off, but I can't figure out what."

"Play it for me."

His eyes shot open. "Yeah?"

I just smiled, sipping my coffee, pretending like this was *totally chill and cool* and like I wasn't freaking out internally that Shawn Stetson was about to play an unreleased song for me.

He cracked his neck, sitting up a little straighter and clearing his throat before he began.

The intro was soft and slow, smooth chords peppered by brief taps of the heel of his palm against the box of his guitar. It was percussion and strings all in one, the beat seductive and alluring.

I nodded my head in time with it, hips moving subtly in my seat. When Shawn glanced up at me, his eyes froze on that little hip movement, and my neck heated at the lingering gaze.

I couldn't wait to tell Clay.

He'd be so proud of me, how I'd walked right up to Shawn at the table, how cool I'd played the whole thing. I was becoming a natural — or, at the very least, I was leaps and bounds ahead of the girl who couldn't even hold Shawn's gaze across a crowded coffee shop just a few weeks ago.

I was still thinking about how excited I was to tell Clay when Shawn started singing, his voice rough and edgy, smoky like a brush fire.

"I like
the moon
when it bleeds
through the window
and paints your flesh.
I like
your legs
when they're spread
and you're burning
for me, babe."

I nearly choked on my coffee, but somehow managed to cover it up and hold my composure as a smirk creeped up on Shawn's devilish mouth.

"I like
the mountains
of your breasts
when they're swelling
and peaking
and aching for my mouth.
I'll give
you what
you want if you
just open up and say
that magic word."

There was a break in the chords, the heel of his palm beating on the guitar in time with the tap of his fingers in a fluid percussion before he launched into the chorus.

"Beg for me, baby,
scream out my name.
Get on your knees for me, baby,
let desire
erase all the
shame."

Before he could continue, I hopped out of my seat, tilting the last bit of my espresso down my gullet as Shawn abruptly stopped playing.

"Oh God, I'm so sorry. I just realized the time!" I hid my flushed cheeks as I slipped the strap of my bag over one shoulder. "The song is really great. Truly. Very sexy. Can't wait to hear it live."

Shawn set his guitar to the side and stood. "Giana," he tried, but I was already rushing toward the door. I tripped on the leg of a table, windmilling forward before I balanced and did a little spin to keep from running into one of the baristas carrying a tray of dishes.

"So sorry, I'm going to be late if I don't get going. But I'll see you soon!" I threw behind me.

"Wait!"

I stopped, heart thundering, turning with a flush I knew was too furious to hide staining my cheeks.

Shawn ran a hand over his hair. "Can I... would it be possible for me to get your number?"

The blood drained from my hot face.

It was working. *Everything* Clay and I were doing... it was working.

And for the first time, I realized the implications of that.

Swallowing, I held out my hand, typing my phone number in quickly when Shawn pressed his phone into my palm. I gave it back just as quickly, forcing the best smile I could.

"I'll text you," he promised.

I threw a wave over my shoulder as I turned, trying to keep my smile calm and collected. But the way he stood with his hands in his pockets, one brow arched, told me he saw right through the act.

It also told me he *liked* that he'd ruffled me.

When I pushed through the doors and out into the heat growing thicker by the minute, I smacked my palm against my forehead, dragging it down my face with a groan.

I might as well have had *I'm a virgin!* flashing on my face in neon lights.

Embarrassment faded into shame, and just as quickly into panic, as I raced across campus, my pace growing practically to a gallop.

What the hell did I think I was doing?

Here I was playing this... this stupid *game* with someone so far ahead of me it was unreal. Shawn was a musician. A hot, talented, *male* musician. How had it not occurred to me that he'd likely fucked a dozen girls, if not more, by now?

And I?

I hadn't even gone to second base.

I was all but sprinting when I made it to the stadium, the espresso kicking through my pulse like a war drum. I flew through the metal doors, down the hallway, swinging into the cafeteria only to find that the team wasn't there yet. I glanced at my watch again, squinting as I tried to remember Clay's schedule.

Weight room.

A little hop had me switching directions and power walking in the opposite direction. I didn't think about what I would say, or about the consequences of what I was about to ask as I ripped open the weight room doors and hurdled inside.

Loud rap music assaulted me as soon as I did, but it was no match for my heart thundering in my ears as I scoured the room until I found Clay. He was on his back, a bar saddled with heavy weights across his chest as he heaved a breath and pushed it up toward where Holden was spotting him.

With one last deep breath, I made a beeline for him, ignoring the players who arched their brows at me as I passed. Holden helped Clay rack the bar just as I approached, and he'd no sooner sat up on the bench before I was wrapping my hand around his wrist and tugging him off it.

"I need you."

● ● ●

CLAY

Giana's grip was mighty fierce for how small she was, and she all but dragged me through the weight room as my teammates watched curiously. I followed her with an amused smile, shrugging at the players who tilted their chins at me as if to ask, *"What the hell is going on?"*

Coach Dawson slammed a hand hard into my chest before we hit the doors.

"Training isn't over," he said — more to Giana than to me.

"Sorry, Coach. We need Johnson for a quick podcast interview. He'll be back in fifteen minutes or less, I promise."

She held her shoulders back as she said it, though I didn't miss the thick swallow in her throat as she stared up at him. He was at least a foot-and-a-half taller than her, and three times as large. His brow furrowed, a heavy sigh leaving his chest before he took his hand off mine.

"Ten minutes," he conceded. "You'll run laps for every minute after."

I nodded, and then Giana was tugging me out the door.

"So, what podcast is this for?" I teased, knowing damn good and well this had nothing to do with public relations.

Giana ignored me until we walked past a training supply closet, the door of which she wrenched open before shoving me inside.

It was pitch black when the door shut behind us, the silence almost deafening compared to the raucous noise of the weight room down the hall. Giana's breathing was heavy in that quiet, like a caged animal.

"The light should be—"

I went to reach for it, but Giana smacked my arm down, which told me she knew exactly where it was, too.

"Leave it," she said. "I don't know if I'll be able to say this if you're looking at me."

"Say wh—?"

"I want you to fuck me."

The words rode out on a breathy, high-pitched plea that jarred me to the core. It was like a fist to the gut and a mouth around my cock at the same time, both excruciatingly painful and delightfully shocking.

I ignored the beast inside me that fired up at those words, suffocating the wild need for me to grant her wish right now, right here in this fucking closet. A slow inhale and equally slow exhale were all I could manage before I spoke.

"Uh, Kitten, I don't think—"

"No, I mean it," she said, cutting me off. "I want you to take my virginity, Clay."

I was thankful for the pitch black of that closet as I bit my knuckle, stifling a groan at how sinfully sweet it was to hear those words from her lips.

"I'm going to need a little context here," I finally croaked, that monster inside me getting harder and harder to contain.

There was a long sigh, a shuffling of feet followed by a soft curse that told me she probably walked right into something. "Shawn is experienced," she said. "He's probably had sex with more girls than I've even *met* in my lifetime. I mean, he even walks with sexual swagger. He practically *drips* sex appeal."

I wrinkled my nose, again thankful for the dark that covered my not-so-subtle disagreement with every word she just said.

"When I finally get my chance with him — *if* I get my chance — I don't want to be so bad in bed that he laughs or takes pity on me or... or... *walks out completely.*"

Those last words were almost like a shocked cry of realization that that was a possibility.

"He won't walk—"

"You don't know that," she said. "You don't know what it's like to be an almost twenty-year-old virgin because you probably lost your virginity when you were sixteen."

My mouth shut then, because she was right.

"Please, Clay," she said, and I felt her small hands reach for me, wrapping around my forearm and squeezing. "I need your help. Please. *Please.*"

This girl is actually begging *me to take her virginity in a dark supply closet right now.*

"Teach me how to kiss, how to make a man feel good," she whispered. "Teach me how to do it all."

I let out a low hum of a groan on my next exhale because *fuck me,* it wasn't okay how much that turned me on.

My heart picked up its pace, thundering like a dozen stallions as I mulled over what she was asking. Every warning sign and bell and whistle was going off like a chaotic symphony inside me for even considering it. Fake kissing and heavy petting was one thing, but to strip her down, to take her for the first time...

That was an entirely new ball game, one I wasn't sure either of us was equipped to play.

"Clay," she whispered when I didn't answer, and her hands crawled up my chest, fisting in my shirt. "There's no one else I trust. Please."

I closed my eyes at the sound of yet another plea, gut wrenching and chest caving in because I already knew before I answered that I wouldn't deny her.

I couldn't — not when she was asking me for help.

Swallowing, I reached behind her and flicked on the light. We both blinked at the brightness, but then her Caribbean-blue eyes locked on mine, her breath just as shallow as it was when she dragged me in here.

But she didn't waver.

She didn't cower our back down. She didn't shy away. She didn't take it back. She looked me right in the eye and asked again, silently, for me to be the one to take something I knew was more precious to a woman than I would ever understand as a man.

I rolled my lips together.

And then, I nodded.

Her relieved sigh came like her first breath after being underwater for years. She threw her arms around my neck, and I closed my eyes as I caught her, warning zipping down my spine like an electric shock.

"Really?!" she squealed, squeezing me tighter. "Thank you, Clay. Thank you, thank you, *thank you*."

I just buried my face in her neck where I held her, hoping like hell she knew better than I did what we both could handle. It was more disbelief than anything else that washed over me the longer we stood in that embrace.

I'd agreed.

I was going to take her virginity.

Against every obvious red flag telling me this was a bad idea, I couldn't say no.

Somewhere deep inside me, that wild creature I'd tried so hard to tame smiled in victory...

And anticipation.

Chapter 13

CLAY

Our first away game was against the South Vermont University Vikings, and we clobbered them.

The field was a rainy mess from the time we jogged out onto it for warm-ups, our cleats and uniforms both covered completely in mud by the end of the first quarter. My knees ached from sprinting in the conditions, and my left ankle felt worse from all the sliding around than when I'd broken it in the sixth grade.

Still, the entire squad had been on fire, showcasing yet again that we were a team to contend with this season. After our bowl win last year, we had a lot of eyes on us — and now, we were two and zero, and had just defeated a team we barely scraped out a win against last year by more than twenty points.

"Um, excuse me," Riley said, jogging up beside me after a post-game interview on the field. Her hair was soaked, dripping down over her shoulders and in her eyes as she hung her hands on her hips and glared up at me. "Do my three successful field goals not deserve a shoulder ride into the locker room?"

I grinned, reaching for her slight hips and easily helping her climb up. She saddled my shoulders, hands gripping mine as I stood before she lifted them in the air and started chanting one of our team cheers. Player after player filed in around her, joining in, and I ran her through the crowd for high-fives on our way toward the tunnel.

She laughed and squealed with every sliding step I took until I carefully placed her back on the ground once we were inside the stadium. As soon as I did, Zeke swept her up in a hug from behind.

"Nice pick out there, Johnson," he said, and I clapped his hand when he held it up for mine.

"Next time it'll be a touchdown. Mark my words," I promised.

"I have no doubts." He paused, giving Riley a look that apparently told her to get lost, because she made some excuse about needing to talk to Coach before she disappeared down the hall.

Zeke turned back to me.

"So," he said. "How are things going with Giana?"

I smirked. "Nosy much?"

"Like you weren't the same with me and Riley last year," he shot back, deadpan.

"That was different. Giana and I are great. And not denying our feelings for each other like you two were."

Something in my stomach rolled when I said those words, but I ignored it, throwing my arm around Zeke's shoulders.

"Why are you so concerned?"

He sighed. "I don't know, man. Giana is a nice girl. I... don't take this the wrong way... I wanted to make sure she wasn't just some sort of rebound."

I cracked my neck, removing my arm from around him as Holden's warning came back to memory. "Why is everyone assuming that's what she is?"

"Because you were devastated over Maliyah breaking up with you like, a month ago, and now you're making out with Giana every chance you get."

"She's hot. And fun to make out with. And *my girlfriend*," I said. "I'm confused as to why this is such an issue for everyone to accept."

"You're right," Zeke said, holding up his hands in surrender. "I'm sorry, man. I shouldn't have assumed. I'm glad to see you doing so well, honestly. I was worried there at the start of the season."

"You weren't the only one," I confessed, and as we rounded the corner toward the locker room, we were met by a dozen giggling cheerleaders.

Maliyah included.

She was soaked head to toe, every inch of her uniform sticking to her lean body. Water was still gliding down her arms, her abdomen, her legs, more and more of it being released from her hair and adding to the stream.

Her laugh stuttered when she saw me, and her eyes flicked from me to Zeke and back again while all the cheerleaders watched her.

Watched *us*.

"Hey," she finally said.

I swallowed. "Hey."

One of the cheerleaders looped arms with two others and pulled them forward, the rest of the girls following and leaving us alone. Zeke gave me a look, a tilt of his chin his only farewell before he ducked inside the locker room.

Then it was just the two of us.

"That was a great game out there," Maliyah said, and something of a smile bloomed on her lips with the words. "You're even faster than I remember. They don't stand a chance of being open when you're out there."

I sniffed. "Thanks."

It wasn't what I expected, standing there with her, finally alone for the first time since school started. I'd dreamed about having this moment for so long, what I would say, what I would do... but none of it felt like I thought it would.

Part of me longed to hold her, to reach out and pull her into me, to demand answers and ask why she was doing this.

But there was another part of me, louder than it had ever been, that was just... *annoyed*.

"Daddy was watching, too," she said. "He wanted me to tell you how proud he is of you."

That burned me more than I cared to admit.

Cory was the closest thing I'd had to a father figure since my dad left. They'd been close friends when I was younger, and I didn't know if it was because of that or because of Maliyah that he'd taken particular interest in my life. He helped me when school got tough and Mom didn't know what to do, or when I needed to shake off the mental pressure of football. He was a lawyer, calculated — but smart as hell.

His pride was something I wanted, even when I hated to admit it.

"I appreciate that," I said with a little less bite.

Maliyah folded her arms over her chest, eyes a bit sad as she asked, "How are you?"

"How do you think I am, Li?"

My chest ached with the nickname, and I wondered if it did the same for her because she looked down at her shoes, rubbing her arms with her hands like she was cold.

"You seem to be doing fine," she said to the floor, then dragged her eyes back up to meet mine. "With Giana."

Fire sparked in my lungs with the mention of her name, both because of what I'd promised her I'd do, and because I knew just by that assessment alone that Maliyah had noticed us.

And that our little game was working.

"And you with Kyle," I shot back.

"Kyle means nothing to me."

She waited, like she expected me to say the same about Giana, but I knew Maliyah well enough to know that if I gave in too quickly, she'd lose interest just like she had before. I'd loved her for years, and one thing I knew better than anyone was that she loved a challenge.

And she loved to win even more.

When I didn't respond, Maliyah sighed, looking around to make sure we were alone before she uncrossed her arms and stepped into me. Her warmth invaded my space, and she reached out, just the tip of her fingertip trailing my forearm.

"I see the way you still watch me when you're with her," she said, smiling as my skin pebbled under her touch. "What exactly is it you're doing, Clay?"

Her eyes slowly slid up to mine, and she smiled coyly, leaning even more into me until her chest was flush with mine.

And again, I felt myself at war.

The urge to crush her to me and claim her mouth with my own battled with the powerful desire to give her a taste of her own medicine.

And something else... something foreign that I couldn't quite name.

"I'm doing exactly what you wanted me to," I said, angling my mouth for her ear.

She tilted her neck back, hand wrapping around my arm and squeezing tight as her lids fluttered close.

"I'm moving on."

I whispered the words against her neck before abruptly pulling back and peeling her hand off me. I pushed past her and into the locker room, not bothering to turn and revel in seeing her jaw on the floor.

Maliyah wasn't used to being denied.

I kicked the bottom of the locker they'd assigned me in the visitor space, drawing a few looks from my teammates before I forced a ragged breath and peeled off my jersey. Pads came next, and then I hobbled toward the showers, running the water as hot as I could and planting my hands on the cool tile wall as it rained down on me.

It was the first time we'd really talked since everything went down, since she threw me out like old garbage and walked away like it didn't hurt her at all. Even now, I knew she was playing the game, dropping a tempting piece of bait right in my face to see if I'd swipe up and take it, only for her to reel me in and toss me back out again.

It pissed me off.

It broke my heart.

But that wasn't what worried me most.

What made me stay in that hot shower until my fingers pruned and my skin was beet red was the fact that something in the way I felt about her had shifted, transformed into an emotion I didn't recognize.

And now, I wasn't sure what the game even *was* anymore.

Or what I was playing for.

●●●

The bus ride back to Boston was long and rainy, just like the game had been.

Though most of my teammates were rowdy and loud, celebrating our win and making plans to continue that celebration once we made it back to campus, I sat quietly near the front in a seat next to Holden, who seemed content to listen to his headphones and leave me alone.

My mom had texted me after the game, telling me she and Brandon had gone over to Maliyah's parents' house to watch the game on TV. She told me how proud she was of me. She told me how proud *Cory* was of me. She also asked if I was coming home for Thanksgiving.

I can't wait for you to meet Brandon!

I didn't have the energy to answer her, nor to even finish reading the long text my father had sent me not too long after that. It wasn't a surprise to see his name on my missed texts. About the only time I *ever* heard from him was on game days, and usually it was a list of things I could do better, followed by questions on whether I'd found an agent or made my pro plan yet.

I was ready to throw my phone into the nearest river until Giana texted me right as we pulled into the parking lot.

Sorry I didn't get to see you after the game. Field was madness with all the reporters. Are you back on campus yet?

I thumbed back a response confirming we'd just pulled in.

Come over?

My heart stopped before kicking back to life, and I typed back a thumbs up emoji before my sour attitude could talk me out of it. I'd had plans to march straight to my dorm and pass out face down in my mattress, but the truth was I didn't want to be alone.

Not with all the thoughts whirling in my mind like a tornado.

Coach gave a quick speech in the locker room before we were all dismissed, told to enjoy our Sunday and get back here ready to work Monday morning. I flew out of there with my headphones on so no one could ask me to go out to the bars or The Pit.

It was a long walk to Giana's spot off campus. I usually took the train or called for an Uber. But the rain had stopped, and I found myself thankful for the cool night air as I made my way off campus and wound through the Fort Point district. It was busy, locals and tourists alike flocking to restaurants and bars now that the weather had cleared up.

It was almost nine by the time I made it to Giana's, and she buzzed me up, waiting with her door open when I made it to her floor.

"Okay, I figured you were hungry after that *monster* game — that pick was insane, by the way! — but I didn't know what you'd be hungry *for*, exactly," she said, holding the door wider so I could slip inside. As soon as I did, a plethora of aromas assaulted me. "So... I kind of ordered a little of everything."

Her hair was big and frizzy from the rain, piled into a sloppy bun on top of her head with little curls bursting out of the hold and framing her face. She wore her black glasses tonight, the frames wide, and her fluffy, pink house slippers slapped against the wood floor as she walked me toward the kitchen.

She wore a simple white, spaghetti-strap tank top, and it was cropped so that her stomach showed between it and the oversized sweatpants hanging low on her hips. Everything about her screamed cozy, along with the candles burning in every corner of her place.

When we made it to the little kitchen, she bit her lip shyly, gesturing to the spread of food that was entirely too much for two people.

"There's dumplings and rice, and pizza, and some slider burgers from the bar down the street. I got some pretzel bites with beer cheese because *yum*." She rolled her eyes up to the ceiling, patting her stomach like a starved man before she popped a finger up. "Oh! And fries. And donuts. And ice cream in the freezer. I might also have some... chips... up... here," she added, struggling as she reached up onto her tiptoes to open the small cabinet above her stove.

She indeed *did* have chips, two bags of Cheetos — both puffy and crunchy — and she added them to the spread before hanging her hands on her hips in satisfied victory.

"*Bón appétit*," she said. When she finally looked at me, her brows folded in. "Oh God, it's too much, isn't it?"

I tried to smile, shaking my head. "No, it's great."

Her frown only deepened, and she stepped closer, searching my eyes as I swallowed and tore my gaze away from her. I stared at the space between us, my hands tucked firmly in the pockets of my sweatpants.

"You're not okay," she whispered.

Again, I tried to smile, but it wilted like a flower in the desert sun. I lifted my gaze, debating over trying to say I was fine.

But in the end, I just shook my head.

Giana sighed, nodding like she understood without me saying a word. "Okay, *you*," she said, grabbing my arms and marching me toward her bedroom. "Sit," she instructed, pushing me until I sat down on the edge of her bed. "Relax. I'll make us a couple plates. And you pick out the documentary we're going to watch."

"Documentary?" I asked with an arched brow, kicking off my sneakers before I sat back against her headboard.

"Yep. We're going to watch a stupid documentary about something weird and stuff our faces." She thumbed through to Netflix, eyes lighting up a bit when she clicked into the documentary sub-category. "Oh! Look. One on cheerleading."

She gave me a look, waggling her brows.

I swiped the remote out of her hand. "Give me that."

With a smile, she obliged, disappearing into the kitchen. She came back moments later with two plates piled high with a smorgasbord of food, and then she slid onto the mattress next to me.

"*Our Planet*! *Excellent* choice, my friend," she said, popping a Cheeto in her mouth. Then, she grabbed the remote out of my hand, scrolled a few episodes, hit play, and flicked off the lamp next to her side of the bed.

The documentary started, and she kept her eyes on the screen, save for when she reached for something on the two plates between us.

She didn't bug me about what was wrong. She didn't pry.

She was just... *there*.

"Isn't this... *crazy*?" she asked me around a mouthful of Cheetos when we were halfway through the second episode we picked. It was *High Seas*, and glow-in-the-dark creatures that lived far in the depths of the ocean were swimming across the screen. "It *looks* like it's CGI. But it's not. This is real." She paused, waving her Cheeto about like a wand. "I mean... that's *real*. That weird glow-in-the-dark fish that looks like an alien lives right here on the same planet as us."

She popped the chip in her mouth, shaking her head.

"I know aliens are real. I mean, it would be ridiculous for there to be so many universes and not a single other planet has intelligent life on it. But whether we will ever communicate with them? I don't know. But this?" She gestured to the screen. "We have aliens *right here*. We have a whole other galaxy we can't even fully explore because we can't dive that deep. How wild is that?"

I smirked, arching a brow at her as she continued staring at the screen wide-eyed and chomping on the dusty orange chips.

She was so strange, and intelligent, and curious, and full of wonder. She was like a child and a grown ass woman somehow wrapped up in one.

Giana must have sensed me looking at her, because she glanced my way before sucking the crumbs off her fingertips and asking, "Do you want to talk about it?"

I cracked my neck, looking back at the screen. "Not really." I paused. "But... thank you. For this," I added with a nod toward the TV. "It helped."

She smiled, a little shimmy of her shoulders telling me she was proud of that. "Good."

The light from the television battled with the shadows of her room, casting her figure in a soft blue light. I followed the length of it down to her cleavage, the sliver of skin showing above her sweatpants, all the way down to her feet and back up again. I couldn't explain it, but there was something so comfortable about her in that moment, something that begged to be held.

That beast inside me reared its ugly head, rattling against the cage and demanding my attention. And I didn't know if it was for her or for my own selfish desire that I did what I did next.

"So..." I cleared my throat. "Now that you've made me feel better..." I angled myself toward her, propping my chin on the heel of my hand. "Wanna practice?"

Giana frowned. "Practice?" she echoed around a bite of a pretzel dipped in beer cheese.

When she looked at me, I just cocked a brow, hoping the salacious smile spreading on my lips would be answer enough.

Her lips parted, eyes popping open wide before she gulped down the bite in her mouth. "Oh, my God. *Practice!* Yes!"

In a feat of agility and speed, she dropped what was left of the pretzel in her hand and cleared the plates and snacks from the bed between us. She hastily shuffled them into the kitchen before all but skipping back to the bed and jumping into it, landing on her knees and clapping like a little kid.

"Okay. What do we do?"

I smirked, sitting up to join her, but as soon as I did, she gasped and leapt out of the bed.

"Wait!" she exclaimed, and then disappeared into the bathroom. I heard the faucet running and a quick two minutes later she was back. "Sorry. Cheeto breath," she explained.

I barked out a laugh at that. "I'm not worried about your breath. And besides, I've been eating the same shit. Do you want me to go brush my teeth?"

"No. Cheeto breath wouldn't make you disgusting the way it would on me. You'd somehow find a way to make it sexy."

I licked my bottom lip, amused, and Giana rolled her eyes before smacking my chest playfully.

"Come on. Focus. Tell me what to do."

She carefully removed her glasses next, setting them aside before she was tuned back into me. And the way she was perched there, propped up on her knees, her chest swelling and falling, eyes eager... it was the sweetest, most intoxicating sight. She watched me like I had all the answers, like I was her lifeline.

Like she trusted me with everything that she was.

Swallowing, I ignored every voice inside me that warned against what I was about to do, and I moved into her, framing her body with my fists against the mattress as she leaned against the headboard.

"Lie down," I commanded.

A flash of desire pooled in her eyes as she obeyed.

Chapter 14

GIANA

I was consumed.

By the darkness of my room, the incessant pounding of my heart, the towering mass of Clay's body as he lowered me down into my sheets. His rough voice reverberated in my ears, the command low but firm.

"Lie down."

I submitted, and as my back came flush against the mattress, Clay slid on top of me, nestling his thick frame between my thighs. The heat of it sent a chill down my arms, one Clay smiled at before he smoothed his knuckles along my chin.

"Relax," he said. "We're not going all the way tonight."

I frowned, sagging into the sheets as Clay chuckled and tilted my chin. I was ready to protest, to point out the fact that Shawn had my freaking *number* now and I could be alone with him at any moment, completely unprepared. But before I could argue, Clay spoke again.

"Don't look so sad, Kitten," he teased, pressing a kiss light as air to my jaw. "There are many things that come before that, and trust me when I say you won't want to skip them."

An embarrassed smile found my lips before he kissed them, and I sucked in a breath, looping my arms around his neck and asking for more. It felt natural now that we'd done it a few times, almost... *comforting*.

But he broke away all too soon.

"One step at a time, yeah?" he whispered, waiting until I nodded before he descended on me once more.

And with a stroke of his hand along the side of my face, his fingers weaving into the hair at the nape of my neck and holding me still as he kissed me again, I surrendered.

A long, heady breath left me, and I opened my mouth to let Clay slide his tongue inside. Just like at the party, a jolt of electricity shot straight between my legs, something pulsing there like a heartbeat.

I whimpered at the feel of it, and he pulled back from the kiss enough to hear the full sound from my lips.

"Why does that feel so good?" I breathed, my eyes still closed as Clay's tongue lashed out against mine again.

"Do you want the science of it, or the layman's terms?"

I bit my lip against a smile as he kissed down my neck, and his hips rolled between mine, striking me with that hot spark of electricity again.

"Both."

A low rumble of a laugh vibrated at my throat.

"When we kiss, your brain lets off a cocktail of chemicals," he whispered, crawling his kisses back up until he claimed my mouth. "But it's not really about them. It's about what they're telling you."

"Which is?"

He nosed my chin, nipping at my neck. "You tell me."

I let out a breath of a laugh, wriggling beneath him as he sucked the skin at my neck, one hand steadying him while the other trailed down the length of my arm. His fingertips were so gentle, fluid — like ice skaters performing in front of a crowd. They ran all the way down to where I fisted his shirt before they skated back up.

And then he pulled back.

"What?" I breathed, eyes hooded.

"Tell me," he said again.

I flushed. "I can't... I don't know..."

Clay's eyes stayed locked on mine, hand framing my neck once more. But this time, his thumb came to rest on my lower lip, just like it had that night at the club when we went to watch Shawn. His eyes fell to where his thumb rested, and he smoothed the pad of it over my slick lip before dragging it down, pulling my lip along with it.

"Tell me what you feel," he demanded again.

"Excited," I breathed, chest heaving at the admission. "And... *hot*."

"Hot," he echoed with a satisfied grin, and once again that hand of his trailed down, but this time, not over my arm. He slid it along the length of my throat, just the tiniest amount of pressure there before he continued lower, over my collarbone, my chest, and finally, palmed my breast through the thin tank top I wore.

The thin tank top with nothing else underneath it.

My nipple puckered even more at the connection, and Clay groaned his approval, thumbing it through the thin cotton fabric. A pang of white hot shot from that point of contact right between my legs, and I cried out, arching into the touch and pulling away from it both at once.

"That warmth is desire," he explained, rolling his thumb around my nipple again. "You're turned on."

"Yes," I breathed. Then, I rolled my lips together, fighting for the words. "How do I make *you* feel that?"

Clay laughed, the sound low and delicious in my ear. His palm left my breast, cold air sweeping in to take its place as he reached down for my hand. Threading his fingers around mine, he slowly slid my hand along his stomach, and I felt every ridge and valley of his abdomen on the way down.

Until he cupped my hand in his, guiding my palm down to where his thick, solid erection strained against his sweatpants.

"Fuck," I whispered when I felt it, when Clay groaned and flexed into my touch. I couldn't help but wrap around it as best I could with the sweatpants in the way, and Clay dropped his forehead to mine, swallowing.

"There's your answer, Kitten," he husked.

He was turned on. His skin was blistering hot just like mine.

Because of me.

The power of that truth surged through me like a tidal wave, and I tilted my lips up to meet his, to moan into his mouth as I rubbed my palm along his length. It twitched at the contact, and my mouth watered, like I wanted to taste it, like I wanted to know what it felt like going down my throat.

I blame the dirty books.

With a groan, Clay lowered himself, taking his mouth from mine and his cock out of reach with one movement.

I pouted, but he only smiled, shaking his head like I was going to be the death of him. "I need to focus," he explained.

"On wha—"

But I didn't have time to finish, because in the next breath, Clay ran his hand under the hem of my tank top, pushing it up and over the swells of my breasts. It was brute force, the fabric shoved up around my neck and my breasts exposed without warning. The cool air had my nipples peaked, along with the way Clay's eyes swam over them, taking in every inch of them before his palm found me again.

A breathy hiss left me at the touch, at how tightly my thigh muscles clenched when his hand touched me there. I pushed up into the pillows so I could watch, so I could see his thumb swiping over the top of my light mauve bud.

"It's like... sparks," I tried to explain through my panting, and Clay smirked, circling my nipple with his thumb as I whimpered and writhed.

"Some girls like it, some girls don't," he said. "How does it feel?"

"Hot."

He chuckled. "Good hot, or bad hot?"

I considered the question, not really sure. It was a little of both, like touching my tongue to an acidic battery or a copper penny. It shocked me, and felt uncomfortable, but at the same time, I liked it.

At least, I thought.

When I didn't answer, Clay settled lower between my legs, his chest pressed against my aching core now as he balanced on his elbows.

"Close your eyes," he said.

I did, releasing a long breath.

And then, his mouth was on me.

I gasped, the sensation rocking through me violently as his tongue swirled over my nipple.

"Clay," I breathed, and without meaning to, my hands shot for his hair, and I held on like those strands were reins.

"Good or bad?" he asked again.

"Good," I breathed out, wetting my lips. "Very good."

He smiled against my breast, and then his tongue was dancing, circling and flicking as little shots of electricity bolted down between my legs. Then, he sucked my nipple between his teeth, nipping so gently I barely registered it before he released me.

"Is that okay?"

"God, yes," I breathed, hands fisting in his hair, and he kissed a line of sweet, tender kisses across the middle of my chest until he took my other nipple between his teeth, spreading the love.

It felt like hours of that torture, his lips moving from one to the other, tongue never tiring, and when he finally crawled back up to take my mouth with those beautiful lips again, I held him to me, arching into him, wanting to praise him like a saint.

"That was amazing," I breathed. "Now what the hell do I do to you?"

Clay barked out a laugh, but it faded quickly, his Adam's apple bobbing in his throat as he rolled over onto his back. He kept his eyes on me, but I couldn't help but watch his hands where they lowered, thumbs sliding under the band of his sweatpants. He pushed into his heels, lifted his hips, and tugged them down below his knees before kicking them the rest of the way off.

My eyes grew wide, and Clay paused with his thumbs in the band of his briefs next.

"You okay?"

"Take your briefs off, Clay," I said, practically panting as I waited for him to free the beast straining against the black fabric.

A light chuckle left him, and then he did as I asked, and when his erection sprang free, I actually salivated.

I'd never seen one in real life, never known anything other than what I'd glimpsed on raunchy television shows or the occasional porn I indulged in. But I'd read about them. I'd felt my body heating as the authors described the swollen tip, the veiny shaft, the thick base with tufts of hair.

None of it compared.

I reached for him automatically, but his hand snapped out, capturing my wrist and halting me.

"Touch yourself first."

I balked. "Wh-what?"

Clay moved my hand to my stomach, pushing it down under the hem of my sweatpants as my eyes fluttered at the sensation. *He* wasn't even touching me yet. It was my own damn hand.

But his was on top of it.

He lined up his fingers with mine, the pad of his pushing into my nail, and he ran my hand along the length of my vagina, slipping one finger between the folds.

"Are you wet?" he asked.

I nodded, unable to form words.

"Coat yourself in it," he instructed. "Slick your hand with your wetness, and then let me feel it."

My next swallow was rough, like I'd taken too big of a bite — and maybe I had. Maybe I'd bitten off entirely more than I could chew, but *God* did it feel good to have his eyes on me, his hands, his mouth.

I'd debate the consequences later.

I did as he said, and my body heated more and more each time my palm slicked over my clit. Clay helped my hand glide back and forth, drenching my fingers and palm, and then he removed our hands from beneath my pants and moved them over to him.

I leaned up on my elbow, watching as he wrapped my hand around his base.

The second I touched him, he groaned, squeezing his eyes shut and falling back into the pillows.

I ripped my hand away. "Oh, God. Did I hurt you? Did I fuck up?"

"No," he panted, grabbing my hand and moving it back. "It feels good," he breathed, and then a soft curse left his lips as he helped me slide my fist over his shaft. "So fucking good."

I lit up under the praise, mirroring what he'd done. I ran my slick palm up to his mushroom tip, applying light pressure as I slicked it all the way down to his base again. Another moan of satisfaction rewarded me, and he flexed his hips into my touch.

"More."

I squeezed tighter on the next roll down, and he cursed, nodding and flexing into my hand again. He was so thick I could barely get my hand all the way around him, and the thought of taking him inside me both excited and terrified me.

"The tip is really sensitive," he tried to explain through his panting, his chest heaving with every new roll of my hand over him. "You want to touch it, yes, but not too much, not too aggressively."

I nodded, taking mental notes as I slicked his head before moving to his shaft.

"Just like every girl is different, every guy is, too. Some want it slow, some fast, some like light pressure, others like harder."

"What about these?" I asked, dipping my hands down beneath his shaft without warning.

He jumped as I cupped his balls, cursing as his eyes flew open and he rolled, pinning me into the sheets.

"Oh, God. Bad?" I asked, panicked. *Hadn't the books said those were good?*

Clay heaved a laugh, shaking his head before he dropped his forehead to mine. "Good," he breathed. "At least, for me."

"Then why did you stop me?"

"Because I don't want to come before the lesson is over."

I bit my lip, and Clay kissed my shy smile before rolling over to the right of me. He balanced himself on one elbow, the free hand trailing down and drawing a line from one of my hips to the other.

I shivered under the touch, eyes floating up to meet his.

He swallowed, dipping just the tip of his fingers beneath the band of my sweats. "Can I touch you, Giana?" he whispered.

I'd never known such simple words could unravel me.

I nodded, and just like he had, I lifted my hips, using the arm not trapped beneath him to help him push my sweats down. I wasn't wearing anything underneath them, and Clay's nose flared at the sight of me bare before him.

"I didn't... I wasn't sure if I was supposed to like... *shave* or something. Of course, I didn't think we'd be... I usually just have this little strip," I explained, cheeks flooding with heat the longer Clay stared between my legs. I bent my knees together. "I can jump in the shower real quick and—"

"Stop," he told me, catching my knees before they could meet in the middle. He lightly pressed against the inside of my left one until I opened again, and his hand slowly trailed down my inner thigh toward the apex.

He swallowed, pulling his gaze up to meet mine.

"You're perfect," he breathed.

I wasn't allowed the opportunity to refute that claim, not before his attention was back between my legs, and his hand slid farther up.

He cupped me.

Gentle at first, and then firmer, the whole heat of his palm covering me as I gasped for air.

"God, you *are* wet," he husked, gliding his fingers between my lips as I rolled my hips involuntarily. "This is so fucking hot, Kitten."

All I could do was hold onto him, one hand fisting in the back of his shirt while the other twisted in the sheets.

"Has anyone done this to you?" he asked, the heel of his palm rubbing against me lightly as he slipped his middle finger a little deeper between my folds.

"Just me," I breathed.

Clay paused, his eyes finding mine. "Are you sure—"

"Do it," I begged, rolling my hips again. "Please, Clay." I covered his hand with mine just like he'd done with me before, pressing his finger deeper until the tip of it touched my entrance.

We both hissed a breath then, and I pulled my hand back, searching his eyes as he hovered over that spot.

His green irises flared, pupils dilating a bit as they flicked between mine. "Please tell me if it hurts."

I nodded, and Clay took a long, deep breath, his eyes staying locked on mine.

And he pushed.

The tip of him slipped inside me, making my lips part and my breath catch. He withdrew it again, only to slide it in deeper, up to his first knuckle this time.

Slowly, again and again, he withdrew and pushed until I stretched bit by bit for him and let him inside. When he finally pressed all the way in, pushing that thick middle finger inside me and curling into a spot that made me see stars, I cried out his name.

It *did* hurt. But then again, it didn't. It was like picking at a scab, painful but satisfying, and I only wanted more.

My hands found his hair, guiding his mouth down to mine. I needed to kiss him. I needed to feel him encompassing every inch of me.

He obliged.

That torturous tongue of his slipped inside my mouth, a long swipe of it timed just right with his finger gliding inside me and curling again. This time, he left it there, deep inside me, and wiggled it.

"Oh, God," I breathed into his mouth. "I... what is..."

My next gasp for air stole the words, and Clay held me tighter to him as he withdrew and slipped inside me again. This time it felt like... *more*. Full. I was full, and stretched, that bit of pain battling with the pleasure until pleasure won out and consumed my entire being.

I rocked against his touch, even more so when the heel of his hand pressed against my clit and rubbed it in time with his fingers working inside me. That heat that had been building seared white hot and dangerous, like a literal fire was building from the depths of my core.

"Clay," I warned, scared of it, of how it built and built and flooded me and... something... something was happening.

"Let go," he said, capturing his mouth with mine. His fingers worked inside me, pushing and curling, his palm slicking against my sensitive peak.

I shook my head, terrified, but that fear was snuffed out in the next moment by rolling waves of delectation. I whimpered into his mouth, and those little cries turned into moans that grew louder and louder as I shook and writhed and clung to him. It was as if every sense I had was zeroed in on where he touched me, and they all rejoiced at once. I felt and tasted and smelled *everything* and nothing all at once. A black hole of pleasure — that's what it was.

It was violent and all-consuming for what felt like the shortest minute of my life, and then it slowly faded, even as I tried to grapple and hold onto it.

"No," I whimpered as the last of it faded, and Clay laughed against my mouth, kissing me as his fingers stilled within me.

"Don't worry, Kitten," he whispered. "There are plenty more orgasms where that came from."

I gasped. "Is that what that was?"

"Wait," Clay said, pulling back so he could see my eyes. "Was that the first time?"

I flushed. "I mean... I've... you know I've done *that* a few times to myself but... never... never *that*."

Clay's brows bent together, and he shook his head. "Jesus, Giana... I didn't know. I..." He swallowed. "Thank you. For trusting me."

I smiled. "Thank *you* for the lesson."

I leaned up onto my elbows as he carefully removed his fingers from inside me, and I shuddered at the loss.

"Although," I said. "It's not over yet."

I reached for him, paused, and then reached between my own legs, instead, remembering how he'd wanted my hand to be wet before I touched him. I gasped when I felt just *how* wet I was, even more excited to coat him with it and bring him the same pleasure.

But it was almost *too* wet.

I frowned, bringing my fingertips up so the light of the television reflected on them.

And then promptly shrieked in horror.

"Oh, GOD!" I balked, panicking when I realized the same crimson liquid that covered my fingers also covered Clay's.

"Hey, it's okay," he said, holding up that bloody hand as if to soothe me. "It happens. It's natural."

"I *bled on you*," I whisper-shrieked. Immediately, I jumped out of bed and ran to the bathroom. "Oh my *God*."

Frantically, I turned on the faucet and doused my hand, scrubbing it with soap and hot water until the blood was gone. I grabbed a washcloth next, soaking it and turning to run it into the room for Clay, but I slammed into his chest in the process.

His hands framed my arms. "Whoa."

"Here," I said, shoving the warm rag at him as I squeezed my eyes shut. "I'm so sorry. I'm *so* sorry."

"Hey—"

"I'm so embarrassed. You must be so grossed out. *Oh, God.*"

"Kitten," Clay said, firmer, his clean hand tapping under my chin. He waited until I opened my eyes, until he was looking down into them with his piercing green pools. "It's just a little blood. It's not gross. It's natural. It doesn't freak me out. I feel fucking *honored* that you let me be the one to touch you like that for the first time. Okay?"

I closed my lips, swallowing, frowning, freaking the fuck out.

"Okay?" he asked again.

I nodded, though I didn't quite feel it. But it was enough for Clay to release me, to take the wet cloth from my hands. He slipped behind me and quickly washed his hands while I stood there staring like an idiot.

Then, he slowly approached me, like I was a wild animal ready to bolt. His hands found my waist.

My still *bare* waist.

He slid his hands up my ribcage next, catching my tank top, and I lifted my arms for him to slip it over my head.

"Shower with me," he said.

It wasn't a question or a request, but a command.

I turned on the water, waiting until it ran hot before I pulled the plug to turn the water to the shower head. Grabbing two towels, I placed them on the lid of the toilet before stepping in, and Clay slipped in behind me.

The water ran hot down my back as he pulled me into him, the front of him lined up against the back of me, and I could feel how hard he still was, the ridge of his shaft pressing against my ass.

"Clay," I breathed, reaching behind me, but he stopped me before I could reach him.

"Not tonight," he said.

"But I need to learn." I twisted in his arms, and wasn't prepared for the sight that met me. The soft light of the bathroom, the shade from the shower curtain, the water running in rivulets down his arms, his chest, his abdomen...

"I promised I'd teach you, didn't I?" He arched a brow.

I sighed. "Yes."

"Then, I will. But not tonight. Tonight," he said, pulling me into him and bopping my nose with his fingertip. "We celebrate your first orgasm."

I rolled my lips, but the laugh bubbled out of me before I could stop it. I buried my face in his chest, peeking up at him through the steam gathering around us.

"I think orgasms might be my new favorite thing."

"Better than the books?" he asked with a smirk.

I pressed up onto my toes. "So much better," I answered, and then, even though the lesson was over, I wrapped my arms around his neck and pulled his mouth to mine. Sliding my tongue against his lips until he opened, I met his tongue with my own, moaning at how it felt — the hot water and his hot kiss.

Recognition hit me, and my eyes shot open wide before I ripped back.

"Ah... sorry," I said, tucking my hair behind one ear. "Getting greedy."

The joke fell flat, and I cringed at myself as I turned toward the shower head, reaching to the shelf behind it for my body wash.

"I'll let you get cleaned up," he said, and I felt the cool air of the bathroom sweep in as he let himself out.

I internally groaned. I'd quite literally scared him out of the shower with that kiss, one that didn't need to happen. No one was around to witness it. It wasn't a show for anyone. And we were done with tonight's... *lesson*.

I'd done it just because I wanted to.

Embarrassment licked at my neck, but panic rose on its heels at the thought of Clay leaving while I was in the shower. I didn't know why, but I didn't want him to go. Not yet.

"Clay!"

I grabbed the curtain and fisted it back just in time to see him wrapping his lower half in a towel. He turned, running a hand through his damp hair, the vision like a book cover and a Ralph Lauren ad all at once.

"Yeah?"

I swallowed. "Stay?"

A soft smile spread on his lips as he exhaled. "Yeah."

I smiled back, hoping he saw the relief that brought me before I closed the curtain again. I slathered myself with body wash, careful as I cleansed between my legs, and cringing a bit at the red that rinsed down the drain when I did.

But once I was clean, the hot water running down my back, my body completely sated and sore... I covered my mouth with my hand, shaking my head as another smile bloomed like a rose on my swollen lips.

I had my first orgasm.

And all I could think was that I couldn't *wait* for the next one.

Chapter 15

GIANA

The next morning, I hummed quietly to myself as I peeled up the edges of an omelet with my spatula, the first bit of the morning sun streaming through my apartment.

Clay was still asleep, his body comically too large for my bed. I snuck another look over my shoulder at his hair-dusted calf sticking out from under the covers and over the end of the mattress, one arm under his pillow, and bare back golden in the morning light. He was frowning even in his sleep, like he was studying game film.

I smiled to myself as I turned back to the stove, folding the omelet in the skillet.

He'd stayed the night.

We were both exhausted after the rainy game and our *lesson*, so not too long after our shower, we passed out. It was more comforting than I expected, having him there beside me as we both tried to stay awake through another episode of the documentary, but failed miserably. I watched him doze before giving myself permission to do the same.

I was happy he stayed.

I wasn't stupid. I *knew* better than to catch any sort of feelings with Clay, even after all those chemicals were flowing and telling me I should cling to the person who just made me feel that amazing. We had a deal. I'd literally *begged* him to do these things to me, to take my virginity and show me what to do so when it came time with Shawn, so that I wasn't so unprepared I lost him before I even had my chance.

Still, that soft side of me relished in having Clay be the one to do it, in having him stay the night after, like he actually cared about me.

It was better than what most of my friends experienced in high school with *their* first times, that I was sure of.

A loud buzzing on my windowsill in the bedroom sounded over the sizzle of the omelet, and Clay groaned, his gargantuan arm reaching out blindly until he swiped his phone off the ledge. He glanced at the screen, then peeled himself up to sit, frowning at it.

He looked up at me next, but I turned back before his eyes met mine, trying to give him privacy.

I wondered if it was Maliyah.

I also wondered why my stomach did a violent high dive to the floor when I considered if it was.

"Hey, Dad," he answered gruffly, and I peeked over my shoulder again just in time to watch him tug on the last of his shirt. He gave me a tight smile, disappearing into the bathroom.

Something in me relaxed a bit, and I plated the first omelet before starting on the next.

The conversation was a bit muted when he was in the bathroom, especially when he ran the faucet, too. He clearly didn't want me hearing him, so I did my best to ignore it, to focus on cooking and not on the little glimpses I could make out.

Yeah, I miss them, too.

You know, you could all come here for a game.

Right. Busy. I understand.

The faucet and light both clicked off at once before he emerged with a heavy sigh, scrubbing a hand over his face as he rounded the corner into the kitchen. His sweatpants hung low on his hips, his t-shirt wrinkled from being thrown to the floor mid-sleep.

"Mornin'," he said.

"Good morning," I echoed back. "Here. Breakfast," I said, sliding the still-steaming omelet onto the kitchen bar. "Coffee's over there."

He yawned, brushing past me and reaching up for a coffee cup in the cabinet above the maker. It was like he lived here, like he already knew where everything was.

"Do you always make such a lavish breakfast feast?"

I barked out a laugh. "A feast? It's an omelet."

"Better than what I can do in my dorm, I assure you."

I smiled, shrugging as I finished cooking my omelet and plated it. "I don't always cook, but I enjoy it sometimes. My dad used to make omelets every Sunday. I guess the tradition carried over."

Clay's brows folded down, though he still wore somewhat of a smile. "That's cool. You two close?"

"I'm not really *close* with anyone in my family," I admitted, sitting at the kitchen bar. Clay joined me, sitting in front of his omelet as I added pepper to mine.

"But out of all of them, I'd say I'm clos*est* with my dad. He's the only one who really understands me."

"How so?"

I considered the question. "He doesn't push me to be something I'm not. He loves me just how I am, just how I want to be."

Clay nodded. "So what do you mean by 'out of *all* of them'?"

"Mom and Dad, and then all four of my siblings."

His eyes bulged. "*Four?*"

"Yep." The word popped off my lips. "Two older sisters and two younger brothers, with me right smack dab in the middle. It doesn't help that all of them are geniuses and talented in some super specific area. One day, we'll have..." I held up my fingers to count them all off. "A professional athlete, a bio engineer, and two entrepreneurs selling their first business for millions of dollars." I let my fingers drop, reaching for my fork and shoveling a bite of egg into my mouth. "And me."

"You say that like you're not just as amazing."

I snorted. "Uh-huh. The quiet book nerd trying to make it in public relations. Freaking *awesome.*"

I gave him a wry smile, but he just frowned at me.

"You're damn good at what you do," he said, all serious. "It takes someone really strong and confident to boss around a bunch of student athletes — especially the bonehead ones on our team. You run the show and you know it."

Pride swelled in my chest, but I swallowed it down along with another bite of my omelet. "Well... thank you. My mom would argue otherwise. She always wanted me to be like my older sisters — smart, athletic, modest. She hates that I don't go to church anymore." I paused.

"But Dad gets it. He's quiet like me, and he was always content to leave me alone when I'd retreat to my room and get lost in my books. Anytime Mom would start to berate me, he'd steer her toward one of my siblings, refocusing her." I smiled. "We don't really *talk* much, but it's like an unspoken understanding of one another."

"Sometimes those are more powerful than words, anyway."

I nodded my agreement, picking up a rogue piece of avocado and popping it between my lips. "Speaking of family, everything okay with your dad?"

All emotion wiped from Clay's face.

"I just... I heard you a little on the phone. Not much, just that it was him."

He cracked his neck, digging into his omelet. "He's fine."

"Are *you* two close?"

He stilled, fork frozen in the air.

"Come on," I said. "I spilled. Your turn."

He let out a sigh, then took his first bite of the omelet. His face shifted then, and he groaned, turning to me with an incredulous look. "*Thish ish delishush.*"

I laughed. "English, please?"

He swallowed. "This is delicious. What's in it?"

"Egg, basil, mozzarella, avocado, and turkey bacon."

Clay blinked. "You're like a fucking chef."

"Hardly," I said with a laugh. "And stop deflecting. Tell me all your deep, dark daddy issues." I playfully leaned toward him like a reporter, speaking into my fork like a microphone before I angled it toward him.

He rolled his eyes. "Nothing original about them, I promise. He and my mom divorced when I was young.

According to him, she was manipulative and jealous. According to her, he was stepping out on her. Who knows the truth. All I know is he had a new wife less than a year later, and a new family shortly after that."

"New family?"

"I have two half-brothers," he explained. "Both of whom I've spent only a handful of holidays with. They get all Dad's attention, though — save for when I'm playing a football game."

I frowned, pushing the egg around on my plate. "I'm sorry."

He shrugged. "It is what it is. Mom and I are pretty close, though she has her issues, too. One second she's flying high with a new guy in her life, and the next she's..." He paused. "Well, she's not herself."

"What do you mean?"

A shadow of something passed over his face, his eyes on his plate. "She struggles mentally. When things get hard, when she's alone... she turns to things she shouldn't."

He left it at that, letting me put together the missing pieces.

"Seems like you had a lot on your shoulders growing up," I mused.

His eyes met mine, brows unfurling. "Yeah. Yeah, I guess I did." He searched my gaze. "Sounds like you learned to make it on your own pretty young, too."

The corner of my mouth slid up. "I think I prefer it that way."

He met my smile, but then his phone buzzed, and he picked it up quickly, frowning when he saw it was Holden before he sat it back down again.

"Something happened with Maliyah yesterday, didn't it?" I asked.

He cleared his throat, nodding.

"What was it?"

"Ran into her after the game," he said, sniffing. "We talked a bit."

"And?"

He smirked at me. "Nosy."

"Come on! I tell you everything about Shawn."

"Fair," he conceded, sitting back on his barstool. "She asked how I was, pretended like she cared. Tried not-so-sneakily to pry about what was going on with us," he said, waving between me and himself. "I told her I was moving on. It pissed her off and made her jealous."

My stomach flipped and soured at once. "Well... that's good, right?"

"It's something," he agreed, cutting another bite off his omelet. "I definitely think it shocked her that I didn't give in."

"Why didn't you?" I paused. "I mean, that was the plan, right?"

"Yes, but not this soon. I know her well enough to know she's just pulling on the string, seeing if I do what she wants."

I bit down the urge to say how fucked up that was, taking another bite of my breakfast, instead.

"But it shook her up, for sure. Maliyah is like family to me," he said, and the words stung me for some reason I didn't understand. "And her family is like my own. That's been the weirdest part of this, not just losing her, but her parents and sister, too."

I nodded like I understood, even though I didn't.

"If I know anything for sure about her, though, it's that she's a daddy's girl. She wants to be just like him. And he's a lawyer."

I lifted a brow.

"Exactly. She knows me better than almost anyone, and she's not afraid to use what she knows to get what *she* wants. She's used to me bending over backward for her. Same with my dad, which is why he was frustrated I didn't call him after the game like I promised I would." He frowned. "I guess with Mom, too. Maybe with everyone."

"You like to help others," I said easily. "I watched it all last season with Riley and Zeke, and I see it every day in the locker room and on the field and in weight training. You're always pushing everyone around you, guiding them, giving them pointers and tips."

He licked his lip. "Yeah."

"It's not a bad thing."

"It's not always a good thing, either."

I nodded. "Well, how about this," I said, turning to face him in my chair. "From now on, before you do something for someone else, make sure it's something for *you*, too. Deal?"

"That's a lot easier said than done."

"Try."

He smirked. "Okay. Deal."

"Speaking of deals," I said, turning back to the bar. "You're not just helping me with... you know... *things* because you feel obligated to, right?"

"No," he answered easily. "I'm doing it because I like you."

My cheeks warmed.

"And because I can't watch you swoon over Music Boy anymore without getting ill."

"Hey!" I smacked his arm. "I do not *swoon*."

Clay stood, batting his lashes as he clasped his hands by his chin. *"Oh, Shawn! I love that song! Oh, Shawn, what big hands you have! All the better to play that big, bad guitar with. Oh, Shawn!"*

I picked up a piece of bacon that had fallen out of my omelet and flicked it at him before he could continue, loving the roar of a laugh that came from him when I did.

"I've got to run," he said, looking at the time on his phone before he tucked it away. "I'm meeting Holden for some drills."

"It's Sunday. Your day off," I reminded him. "You just played a game yesterday."

He shrugged. "When you want to be the best, there are no days off." Then, he paused. "Are you... okay this morning?"

I flushed, looking down at my plate. "A little sore, but... yes."

"Good."

He opened his mouth like he wanted to say something else, but never did. Instead, he swiped his hoodie off the back of the barstool where he'd left it the night before.

Then, he leaned in and swiftly kissed my cheek.

"Thanks for breakfast, Kitten," he said.

He was gone in the next moment.

And suddenly, my apartment felt a lot more empty.

Chapter 16

CLAY

"**W**atch, watch!" I yelled to Dane at our next game, pointing to where a wide receiver had just jogged from in front of me, down the line, to land in front of him, instead. He nodded affirmatively, and I bent low, fingers wiggling at my sides as I glared at the player across from me through the metal of my helmet.

There were only twenty seconds left on the clock, and we were beating the Philadelphia Lions by three points. But if they got close enough to kick a field goal, we'd be going into overtime.

I was *not* going into overtime.

Especially not on my birthday.

"Shut it down, boys!" someone screamed from the sidelines. It sounded a lot like Zeke, and I sank even lower in my crouch, determination prickling my skin.

The ball was snapped, and the quarterback fell into the pocket with his eyes scanning. They needed at least fifteen more yards to be in a good field goal position, and it was third down — so I knew he would launch it.

His eyes flicked to the receiver who had gone down by Dane, but Dane was on him like white on rice. So the QB kept searching, and when our defensive line started to break through, he panicked, launching the ball down the middle of the field.

I kicked against the turf as hard as I could, juking the receiver I was covering to run toward the tight end who was wide open. Dane caught on a second after I did, but he was too late. Even after he started running, I knew he wouldn't get there in time.

So I dug in deeper, harder, my thighs and calves screaming in protest as I gave it everything I had.

Then, out of nowhere, one of our defensive linemen hopped up from where he'd been pushed back into our zone, and he tipped the ball.

It wobbled, spinning off target, and without hesitation, I leapt into the air and snagged it before the offense could even realize what was happening.

The roar of the crowd assaulted me as I landed, spinning just in time to avoid a tackle, and sprinting the opposite way down the field. My lungs were on fire, ribs aching, but I kept on, glancing behind me to find the opposite team on my tail.

"Go! Go! Go!"

Riley's distinct voice pierced through the noise, and I pushed harder, glancing up to see the clock was about to run out.

And it did.

Right as I crossed over into the end zone.

"TOUCHDOWN REBELS!" the announcer bellowed, and our home team went absolutely insane as I puffed my chest and threw the ball into the stands. I was bombarded by my teammates in the next breath, my helmet being smacked hard enough to concuss me as they hyped me up. Then, before we could get in trouble from the coach or the officials for too much celebrating, we all jogged toward the sideline, only to be encompassed by reporters.

It was madness, and I fielded through each question that was thrown at me until I couldn't take anymore. It was my fucking birthday, and I didn't want to spend all of it answering the same shit over and over, but I also didn't want to be a pain in Giana's ass. So, I politely answered and then politely excused myself and made my way into the locker room.

"Way to end the game, you showboating sonofabitch," Holden said when I dipped inside. He grinned, smacking me with the end of his jersey before he threw it in the dirty laundry basket. "We still would have won if you would have just run out the clock."

I crossed my feet and did a little spin, plucking my jersey off my shoulders. "Yeah, but that wouldn't be as fun to watch on the highlight reels later, would it?"

Holden shook his head, but his smile was wide, hair matted to his forehead after a grueling game. It was at least starting to cool off finally, fall taking over the northeast like it always did this time of year.

"Clay," Leo said, nodding at me as he rounded into the locker room and set his helmet on the bench. "You have a visitor."

He nodded toward the hallway, and a grin split my face as I jogged out, ready to wrap Giana in a sweaty hug whether she wanted one or not. I hadn't seen her outside of us both working at the stadium since last week, me caught up in practice, and her with the upcoming auction.

And every minute since that night, her little whimpers of pleasure were about the only fucking thing I could think of.

It had been so much more than I expected, than I could have ever *imagined*, stripping her, touching her, *tasting* her. I knew she'd asked me to be her first, but I hadn't realized that meant her first *everything*. The girl hadn't even had an orgasm.

Until me.

It was fucking stupid how much that lit me up with pride, how much it made the beast inside me walk with a little more swagger in its step.

It was also fucking stupid how much I had thought about her since.

Every morning I woke up to a text from her — either a simple *good morning* or, more commonly, a random question about sex or how to turn a guy on.

We need to revisit the balls conversation. I want training on how to handle them.

Do guys like red lipstick, or is it just a messy inconvenience?

Tell the truth: do my skirts make me look cute or hot? Because I'm aiming for hot.

When's our next lesson?

Of course, those questions turned into us texting all day, sneaking a minute together whenever we could at the stadium. And every chance I could, I was pulling her in for a kiss.

Even when Maliyah wasn't around.

I told myself it was because it would make it all seem more real. It would convince Maliyah that I wasn't just doing it for show. *It'll get back to her*, I assured my whirring brain, *it'll really make her want you back.*

Those words played on repeat.

That didn't explain why I'd snuck a couple of Giana's books out under my shirt when I'd popped by to bring her dinner in the middle of the week. She'd quickly kicked me out since she was studying for a test. But I took those books and did a little studying of my own.

I memorized what pages she'd dog-eared, or highlighted, which ones had the distinct oil from her fingertips being on them more frequently than others.

And what I found surprised me.

I was eager to test the theories I'd come up with the next time we were alone, and to tease her a little — which was quickly becoming my favorite pastime.

I slung into the hallway, ready to fire off some smartass remark about holding the press when I came face to face with Cory Vail.

My smile dissolved like salt in hot water.

"My boy," he said, smile wide as he held his arms open for a hug. He didn't wait for me to slide into them. Instead, he wrapped me up in a bear hug, clapping me hard on the shoulder as he released me.

I stood there in shock, taking in the father of my ex-girlfriend who had always felt like a father to me, too. He was beaming with pride, his eyes the same brown as Maliyah's. He was as tall as I was, but thicker, like a tree stump of a man. He was dressed to the nines as he always was, from his well-tailored, navy blue suit and silver cufflinks, to the Prada dress shoes on his feet.

Power and confidence — that's what he always exuded.

"That was a hell of a game," he said. "I'm glad I was here to see it."

I blinked, shaking off my surprise. "I am, too."

"Your future is looking brighter and brighter. I know you don't need me to tell you, but I'm proud of you, Clay." He nodded, something cautious in his eyes. "I never got to speak to you after everything happened."

Everything meaning his daughter throwing my heart in a blender.

"I won't pretend to understand my baby girl," he said with a gentle smile. "But I will tell you this — I think it was a mistake. And I hope she realizes that, too."

A knot formed in my throat.

"And I also want you to know that regardless, I'm still here for you. Always. Okay? Anytime you need something — you just pick up the phone and call."

I nodded, biting the inside of my lip as emotion surged through me. I almost wanted to fall into the big man's arms and sob, to thank him for being here, for loving me, for believing in me.

But I also wanted to distance myself.

No matter what I felt growing up with him, he wasn't my family — not then, and certainly not now.

I had to get that through my head sooner or later.

"Thank you, sir. That means a lot to me," I managed.

A nod of understanding was all he was able to offer me before Maliyah swung around the corner, throwing herself into Cory's arms.

"Daddy!"

"Hey, sweetheart. You looked great out there."

She smiled and beamed under his praise just like I did, and my heart ached for a reality where *my* father came to home games and met me in the locker room after.

Maliyah's eyes caught on me, and she swallowed, glancing up at her dad and then back.

"I want to say hello to a friend in the front office," Cory said, and it didn't surprise me that he had friends on the staff.

He had friends *everywhere*.

"Meet me at the car?" he asked, and then he kissed his daughter's cheek without waiting for a response.

When we were alone, Maliyah's eyes searched mine.

And then, without warning, she threw herself into my arms.

"That was *amazing!*" she breathed, holding me tight as I wrapped her up just the same. For a brief moment, I inhaled her scent, inhaled the way it felt to hold her familiar body to my chest.

But in the next, I let her go, stepping back to put space between us.

"You sound surprised," I answered coolly.

"Well, I knew you were good, but... I like being reminded just *how* good."

She offered me a teasing smile, dragging her fingertip down my stomach.

"Some of us are going out," she added. "You should come."

I sniffed, looking down the hall behind her. "We'll see."

"Come on, you *have* to celebrate after that," she pleaded, and then she tucked her finger into the band of my football pants and tugged me into her. Her lips pressed right against the shell of my ear as she pressed up onto her toes. "It is your birthday, after all. I'd like to give you a gift."

I hated that my cock responded to that voice whispering in my ear, that my skin broke out in chills at her touch. She smiled when she pulled back, like she knew she still had that effect on me — like she *loved* it.

And that cooled the fire.

I peeled her hands off me. "I have plans."

Before I could turn, she stopped me, her hand wrapping around my forearm to whip me back around — not that I'd fought it.

"With *her*?" she asked, eyes narrowing.

"That's none of your business."

Maliyah shook her head. "Why are you playing this game, Clay? I *know* you want me." She stepped into me, her cleavage pressing against my lower ribs. Her hand slid down then, cupping me through my pants. "I can feel it."

I shrugged her off so quickly she almost fell. "That's a cup. See you around."

I left her with her jaw on the floor, and once again, I tried to tell myself I did it because I knew it was too early. Her father had pretty much insinuated as much. She'd toss me aside just as quickly if I gave in now.

She just wanted to test me, and this was me passing.

This was all part of the plan.

I was still convincing myself of that when I was showered and dressed, texting Giana that I would meet her in her office.

Ten minutes, she texted back.

And then my phone rang.

Mom's bright smile lit up the screen, her arm around my waist at my high school graduation. I smirked at the sight, knowing when I answered, I'd hear the worst and *loudest* rendition of the Happy Birthday song. It was her favorite thing to do, sing it obnoxiously enough that I hid my face in embarrassment, and that didn't change when I moved across the country.

Last year, she made me put her on speakerphone in the middle of our weight training.

"Mom, before you start, I'm alone. So you don't have an audience if you want to save your vocal chords."

The joke died along with my smile when I was met with a choked-off sob on the other end.

Heat crept into my ears, my heart pounding as I ducked into one of the assistant coach's office that was empty. "What happened?"

For a long time, she just cried, the sobs so loud I pulled my phone from my ear and started looking at flights that I could catch out tonight. I thought she was hurt, or that someone had died. But then she finally spoke.

"He broke up with me."

I closed my eyes on a relieved exhale, but knew I couldn't let on that was my reaction to her. "I'm sorry, Mom."

She sniffed. "He was the one. I thought... I thought he was going to ask me to marry him."

I scratched the back of my neck, thinking of all the things I could say to comfort her. It was a familiar cycle now, one I hoped she hadn't caught on to. "It's his loss."

There was more sobbing on the other end as I gathered my belongings and nodded at a few guys left in the locker room as I made my way into the hall.

"You're an amazing woman, Mom. If he didn't see that, then he's an idiot. There is someone better out there for you."

"There's no one out there for me!"

She screamed the words, crying on the end of them.

"I'm old, and tired, and broke," she choked out. Sniffing, she paused only to add, "I'm... I'm *really* broke, Clay."

The hair on the back of my neck raised. "Did something happen at the restaurant?"

Another long pause met me.

"I... I was going to tell you when you came for Thanksgiving. I quit. A long time ago, actually."

"You *what*?"

"Brandon was taking care of me!" She cried out her defense. "He was taking care of *everything*. He was paying my bills, making plans for me to move in with him, making plans for..." She hiccupped. "He promised. He..."

Her words trailed off as more tears found her, and I cursed, stopping around the corner from the hallway that led to Giana's office.

"They'll take you back," I said. "They always do."

"Not this time." She sniffed. "I tried. They're over it. And I don't blame them. I haven't been a good employee for many, many years."

"That's not true. You're the most charming one there and they know it."

She let out a sarcastic laugh. "My charm ran out along with my beauty years ago."

Inhaling a long, deep breath, I let it out just as slowly before trying to soothe her again. "I know things are hard right now, but it will work out. You can find a new job."

"It's not that easy!"

I closed my eyes as she cried more, wishing I was there to comfort her just as much as I wished I could shake some sense into her.

"Hey, it'll be okay. I can help until you get things sorted."

"Really?" She sniffed.

The instant relief she had from *that* made my stomach sour.

I wanted to help her. I would *always* help the woman who kept me, who cared for me, who raised me when my father walked away.

But the fact that she now *expected* it hurt.

"Oh, Clay. You're too good to me."

"I don't have much," I confessed. "But they give us a little bit of a stipend with our scholarship. I can help with bills until you get on your feet. Just… promise me you'll start looking, Mom."

"I promise."

I nodded. "Alright, well… I gotta go. But I love you."

"I love you, too, sweetie."

"Everything will be okay."

She didn't respond, but I could imagine her nodding, could imagine her hair a wreck and her eyes swollen and puffy and red because I'd seen her that way so many times before.

The line went dead, and I blinked, frowning at my phone when I took it away from my ear. It wasn't that her going through a breakup was surprising.

But the fact that she hadn't wished me a happy birthday was.

I chalked it up to her being upset, thinking of how I was when Maliyah broke up with me. I couldn't be a good friend to anyone during that time. So, I slipped my phone into the pocket of my hoodie and rounded the corner toward the front offices.

And I prayed she wouldn't turn to the bottle or the pills while I figured things out.

I didn't have time to think about how much money Mom would need, how much I could honestly afford to give her, or anything else regarding the breakup because as soon as I pushed through the door to the PR offices, a shower of confetti rained down on me.

"HAPPY BIRTHDAY!"

Giana did a little hop-like dance, blowing a streamer that sounded like a foghorn. A giant, glittery banner hung above her head, and her eyes were wide and joyful in the candlelight coming from the *two* and *zero* candles in a homemade cake on her desk.

"Hurry, before they melt," she said, shoving me toward the candles. "Make a wish!"

I wanted to be happy. I wanted to smile. I wanted to tell her what a nerd she was and how much I adored it.

But all I could do was blow the candles out with a soft breath.

Giana clapped, removing them and setting them aside as she started cutting the cake.

"I had no idea what you liked, but I figured I couldn't go wrong with chocolate. And sprinkles, of course. Everyone loves sprinkles." She handed me a plate with a huge slice on it. "Shawn was at the game today. We talked a little after the media frenzy. He asked if I would be at the coffee shop to watch him at all this week." She waggled her brows at me as she forked off a bite of her own slice of cake. "By the way, you did *not* have to go that hard with the last play, but I am so damn glad you did. That was incredible. The reporters were in a tizzy. You're going to be all over ESPN tonight."

She smiled, handing me a fork, but I couldn't return any of her enthusiasm. And when she realized it, her smile fell.

"What's wrong?"

I swallowed. "My mom."

It was the only answer I could give, but fortunately, Giana didn't press for more. Her brows folded in, and she nodded in understanding, grabbing the cake out of my hand and setting it back on her desk.

"Come on. Let's go somewhere."

"Where?"

"You'll see."

Chapter 17

CLAY

We were the only ones at the university observatory. Because *of course* we were — it was Saturday night and our team had just won a football game against one of our rivals. Everyone else was out partying, whether at The Pit or a bar off campus.

Everyone, that was, except for me and Giana.

She hadn't said a word on the walk over, our steps in time on the quiet sidewalk. We could hear students celebrating all across campus, but it became more and more distant as we got to the outside perimeter, and faded altogether when the off-white dome of the observatory first came into view.

A pimple-faced kid chewing bubble gum too loudly let us in, bored and barely looking up from the game he was playing on his phone.

"Let me know if you need anything," he'd said after running over the rules for the telescopes — and the look he gave us as he left us alone told me that we had better *not* need anything, because he wasn't in the helping mood.

Then, it was just us.

Giana dumped her bag in the corner of the oval-shaped room, eyes bright beneath the reflective lenses of her glasses as she smiled up at the open sky above us. Most of it was covered by the top of the observatory dome, but there was a wide-open gap where the telescope pointed through. When she bent to take her first look through the viewfinder, she gasped, smile widening.

"You have to see this," she breathed, pulling away only to grab my wrist and tug me over to the machine.

There were three different telescopes, but she'd picked the largest one, and when I bent to look in for myself, I understood why.

The sky above Boston typically only gave way to a few stars and maybe a planet or two, the city lights too bright to see much else. But through this lens, the stars came to life, a whole galaxy of them sparkling in the black. But it wasn't *just* black — you could even see the gasses of pink and blue swirling among the darkness.

"Magnificent, isn't it?" Giana asked behind me.

I nodded, pulling away so she could look in again. She carefully adjusted some settings and the area of focus, smiling like a kid in a candy store when she found what she was looking for.

"Saturn," she breathed, and then she tugged me down to look with her.

And I couldn't hide my surprise when I did.

"Whoa," I said, in awe at how clear it was, how we could see the rings spread out around the planet as if it were just a football field away.

"Perfect visibility for it tonight," Giana said. "We should be able to find Mars and Jupiter, too."

I shook my head, pulling back to let her play with the settings again. As she did, I watched her, completely awestruck by how she lit up when she had education at her fingertips. She was antsy the way a drug fiend might be before a hit — bouncing a little on her toes, smiling so wide it made *my* cheeks hurt.

"Saturn is mostly hydrogen," she said as she squinted through the lens and slowly moved the scope with the controls. "It also has *one-hundred-and-fifty* moons. Can you believe that? That planet is in the same solar system as ours and it's mostly gas and moons." She shook her head. "Wild."

The corner of my mouth crept up watching her in her element. Nothing amped her up the way discovering something new did, and I marveled at how curious she was, at how she was like an endless encyclopedia of fun facts, not because she'd studied and committed anything to memory, but because she simply *loved learning* that much.

But as fast as the smile had bloomed, it died again, my chest aching with thoughts of my mom suffering on the other side of the country.

"Found it!" Giana said, and she shoved me toward the scope. "Mars."

I peered through, commenting on what looked like it could be an ice cap before Giana launched into an essay on the powerful snowstorms on Mars. I listened with a distant kind of awareness, leaning against the back wall of the dome and watching her work with the scope.

And I tried to make it work.

I wanted to be distracted by her, by science, by the stars and the universe. But while it should have reminded me how small my problems were, it somehow worked to do the opposite, and I found myself wondering why I'd moved so far away from my mom in the first place.

Maybe it was my fault she was searching so desperately for someone to love and take care of her, because I had been that person, and now I was gone.

My stomach twisted at the thought, even as another one chased right behind it, reminding me that she'd *always* been looking for a partner — ever since Dad left.

But still, I could have been there, I could have been doing *more*.

It was selfish of me to chase my dreams of playing in the NFL when I could have been home with her. I could have a full-time job by now, one with benefits and a decent salary. I could be taking care of her in every way she needs. At the very least, I could have gone to school somewhere close, in California, where she was just a quick drive away.

Instead, I was focused on myself.

All the thoughts and guilt warred inside me, and Giana must have seen, because her brows folded together when she looked over her shoulder at me perched against the wall.

"Come on," she said, gathering her things. "Let's go up to the deck."

I followed her quietly up the stairs, and we were met with a soft, cool breeze when we reached the top of the observation deck. Giana tucked her cardigan around her more for warmth, and I slipped my hands into the front pocket of my hoodie.

There were a few small telescopes along the railing of the dome, but Giana didn't go for any of them. Instead, she tossed her bag down to the side and slid down the outside of the dome to sit on the deck, patting the spot next to her for me to do the same.

"I hate that you're this sad on your birthday," she confessed when I sat next to her, my knees spread, elbows balanced on them, and hands clasped in-between.

I didn't respond.

"Talk to me," she pleaded, angling herself toward me. "Tell me what happened."

I closed my eyes, shaking my head before I opened them again and stared at my sneakers. "Can't," I managed.

"Why not?"

Because it's hard to explain. Because I'm embarrassed. Because I'm ashamed. Because I'm terrified there's nothing I can do. Because I hate that it's my responsibility and feel like an asshole for feeling that way.

All those responses and more rushed through my mind, but I just shook my head again, unable to say a single one of them.

Giana let out a long exhale, then nodded, as if she'd heard what I couldn't dare to say. "Okay," she said. "Then use me."

I frowned, especially when she crawled over to sit between my legs. She sat on her knees in front of me, forcing me to open my stance, to unclasp my hands and let her in. She quite literally forced her way in until I had no choice but to look at her.

I was devastated when I did.

It wasn't her curly hair, a bit frizzy from the game and a long day before that. It wasn't the freckles on her cheeks, or the soft moonlight reflected in her aqua eyes. It wasn't even her brick-red-and-gold plaid skirt, the modest black blouse she'd paired with it, or the knee-high black stockings that drove me mad anytime she wore them.

It was how she looked at me.

It was how she watched me with so much care and reverence that I was fucking speechless, unable to move, unable to do anything but watch her in return.

"Use me to take your mind off whatever it is that's hurting you, to escape." She swallowed. "Give me another lesson."

I let out a shaky breath through my nose, ready to argue that now wasn't the time, but her lips silenced me before I could. She leaned forward, kissing me slowly and confidently, her hands framing my face as mine came to her waist like it was the most natural thing in the world.

"I need you. Show me what's next," she breathed against my mouth, her lips hovering there as she added, "And this time, I want you to go first."

I frowned when she kissed me again, squeezing her hips a little as I pulled back. "What do you mean?"

"I mean that last time you were left without a release," she clarified, and then with all the confidence of a woman who knew everything instead of the shyness of a girl asking me to show her, she climbed into my lap, the heat of her against my abdomen as she settled into place. "Tonight, I want to make you feel good first. I want…" She swallowed, like she was ashamed, but then held her chin a bit higher and looked me right in the eyes. "I want you to show me how to taste you."

Jesus fucking Christ.

I closed my eyes on a dragon exhale to keep from saying that out loud, and I felt the ravenous animal inside me roaring to life. Giana pressed into me, kissing me before I could overthink it, before I could think of any argument to stop her.

"Please," she begged, rolling her hips against me, and I hissed at the contact, at how hard I already was for her.

I couldn't speak, couldn't put into words how much hearing that she needed me was exactly what *I* needed. So, I answered her with a kiss of my own, cradling the back of her neck and holding her to me as I opened my mouth and cued her to do the same. I swept my tongue inside, cherishing the soft whimper of a moan that slipped from Giana when I did. Her hands twisted in my hair until one of them snaked down between us, and she ran her palm along my length straining against my sweatpants.

"Fuck," I cursed, rolling into the touch. I managed to pause, to open my eyes and look at how tentative she was watching me. "Are you sure?"

"Show me."

She answered so quickly, so definitively that my cock twitched under her palm, and she wet her lips, eyes falling down to look at my bulge as she gripped it a little firmer.

Carefully, I hoisted her off my lap, leaving her there on her knees as I stood. I towered over her, nose flaring at the sight of her looking up at me as I went to undo the tie of my sweatpants. As if she'd missed some sort of cue, she pushed up onto her shins, hands reaching out to finish the job.

"Let me."

I paused, internally groaning from just those two words alone. I clenched my jaw so hard it ached as I watched her tenderly loosen the strings, and then she tucked her slender fingertips in the band, tugging them down my hips.

She hesitated when they were a little hard to get off, looking up at me like she was second-guessing. And like a lightbulb in the dark, I remembered her books.

I remembered every scene she highlighted, and I knew without asking what she needed from me.

"Show me you want it," I demanded, voice low and firm.

Her lips parted, chest heaving as she kept her eyes on me and tugged my sweatpants with more force. This time, they slid over my ass and down to my knees. Without hesitation, she grabbed my briefs and did the same with them, freeing my erection.

The air was too cold, and as if she sensed it, her warm hand wrapped around me as soon as my briefs were at my knees. I hissed at the contact, and she looked up at me with worried eyes.

Then, without a word of guidance from me, she pulled her hand away from me, ran her tongue over her palm and along each of her fingers, and then touched me with the wetness.

"Like this, right?" she asked as my eyes rolled back, knees buckling a bit at how it felt to have her warm, wet fist wrap around me.

"Yes," I breathed. "Now, tease me. Get me worked up."

She frowned. "How?"

"Do what feels natural, and listen to how I react." I licked my lips. "You love to study so much, Kitten... study me."

Her eyes were hot with desire, and she ran her thumb over the precum on my tip, swirling it in a small circle. I bit my lip as she rolled her hand down my shaft next, all the way to the base before she loosened her hand enough to bring it to my crown and back down again.

"Just like that," I praised, and like I knew she would, Giana beamed.

Her tentativeness faded, and with more confidence, she rolled her hand over me again, up and down, pressure firm in the right places.

I flexed into her touch. "I love seeing you like this," I husked. "On your knees."

Her eyelids fluttered, and she swallowed, squirming a bit as she continued to work me with her hand.

"It turns you on, too, doesn't it?" I asked.

She blinked up at me. "Y-yes."

The confession made my lips curl. "Touch yourself," I commanded. "Show me how wet you are."

Giana pinned her bottom lip with her teeth, one hand still slowly working me as the other dipped between her thighs. She spread her knees wider to allow better access, and I knew the moment she slipped her fingers under her panties because her breath caught, lips opening.

"Let me see."

Slowly, she withdrew her hand, eyes widening when she saw her glossy fingertips before she offered them up to me.

"Good girl."

She shuddered, grip tightening over my shaft so I knew my words affected her just how I wanted them to. I smiled, stepping closer, and her back hit the dome so that she had no choice but to come face to face with where she gripped me.

"Stick out your tongue."

Hesitating, she loosened her grip on me and did as I asked. And when those eyes crawled back up to mine, I couldn't help but curse out loud at the sight of her — knees still spread, mouth open, tongue out, chest heaving as she waited for my next move.

"Just like our first lesson, every guy will be different," I told her, wrapping a hand around my length and leading it to her tongue. "So tonight, you're going to experiment until you figure out what it is *I* like."

I ran my head over the length of her tongue, groaning at the sensation of her coating me.

"I'll guide you," I promised, noting the worry in her eyes when I put the control in her hands.

Then, I let go, holding my hands at my sides as Giana stared at my length in front of her.

I watched in awe as that same determination slipped over her, and she pressed up onto her knees, grabbing me around the shaft and bringing my crown to her lips. She wet them first, gliding them along my tip before she slowly opened them and sucked me inside.

"*Fuuuccckkk,*" I hissed, closing my eyes and flexing in deeper without meaning to. Giana opened for me, taking in the first inch and a half before she swirled her tongue around me and released.

I looked back down at her with heavy lids, and she held my gaze as she opened up again, this time taking me in even deeper.

"There you go," I whispered, hand coming to cradle the back of her head. I held her on me, sliding her just up to the tip of me before I guided her carefully back down again. "Just like that."

She lit up again, mimicking the movement as I removed my hand and let her take control. Her warm, wet mouth slowly took more and more of me, and each centimeter she enveloped made my toes curl. She closed her eyes, but I snapped my fingers when she did, making her pop them back open.

"Eyes on me," I told her.

My heart galloped in my chest as I thought of what I wanted to say next, what I knew she'd love to hear. If I was wrong, this could go a completely different way.

But I was confident I was right.

So I held her gaze and I said, "Look at me while I fuck that pretty mouth."

She moaned around my shaft, eyes fluttering before she opened them wide and locked them on me. They were heated with even more desire as she took me in again, and this time, she took me so deep she gagged a little.

Shame colored her cheeks as she withdrew, coughing at the sensation.

"It's okay," I assured her, running a hand over her curls. "You've got to breathe with it. In and out through the nose, hold your breath when it gets deep enough to trigger a gag."

She nodded, eyes on my shaft just long enough for her to take hold of it and guide it into her mouth before she was watching me again.

Pleasure churned through me as I watched her suck me in again, over and over until I hit deep once more.

Her eyes watered, and she held her breath through two pumps before she gagged again.

"Fuck, that's hot," I groaned out when she released me, a bit of saliva dripping from her lips.

"It is?"

I nodded, guiding her back to me. "Do it again."

She sat up even more on her knees, taking me in again, and this time, she slicked me three times before taking me as deep as she could. She held her breath, eyes watering and fluttering as she watched me and finally gagged and released.

"God*damn*, Giana," I praised, running the pad of my thumb over her slick bottom lip. "Such a good fucking girl."

Again, my theory was rewarded when desire coated her eyes and she opened her mouth, sucking my thumb between her lips and lashing at it with her tongue. I groaned, cock twitching and aching in jealousy to have that mouth on it instead.

"Now, use your mouth *and* your hand," I told her, guiding her back to me. "Fit them together, roll your hand in a seam with your mouth and go as deep as you can. Find a rhythm." I paused, holding her gaze. "Make me come."

She let out a soft moan as she did what I said, fitting her mouth to me before her hand slipped under it. I helped her at first, telling her when to slow down or give more pressure, but it wasn't long until I couldn't tell her anything anymore because my head was airy, skin prickling as my orgasm built at her touch.

"Fuck yes, Kitten, just like that," I said, hips flexing as I pressed a little deeper into her mouth.

She let me, working me in time with her hand, head bobbing with her eyes still locked on mine. She swirled her tongue around the length of me, making me see stars and want to be deeper.

"I'm close," I warned, the words gritting through me as I tried to speak when I was consumed by how she was making me feel. "You can either pull me out when I'm there, or you can take it in your mouth and swallow me down."

She moaned, intensifying her efforts, and I had no way of knowing what her choice would be until I got there. So I let go, giving up on instructing and reveling in her velvet, slick hand wrapping me up before her wet mouth took its place. Over and over, a little faster each time, she pumped me as a hot fire licked up my spine.

I needed more.

Carefully cradling the back of her neck, I guided her down deeper, a little faster, my eyes squeezing shut as she found just the right pressure and pace to push me over the edge.

"Coming," I managed through my teeth, and I expected her to pull away. I expected to have to pump out the rest of my release on my own and spill onto the fucking wood. But instead, she held her pace.

And to my surprise, she took me even deeper.

"*Fuck*," I cursed, and everything went numb as I released.

I spilled into her throat, the orgasm even stronger when she gagged a little but kept on, squeezing out every last drop of me as I shook and curled my fingers in her hair.

I tried to be quiet, knowing the guide who let us in was still in the front booth and could easily come up to find us. That thought made it even hotter, that she was sucking me knowing we could be caught at any minute, and I stifled a groan as the last of my orgasm spilled into Giana's mouth.

An involuntary shake left me when she kept going after I was spent, and I held her back, slowing her, trembling breaths slipping through my lips.

"It's sensitive after," I told her, and she gently released me, but not before she looked me right in the eyes and swallowed.

Then, she pressed a feather-light kiss to my shaft, and she smiled. "How'd I do?"

I let out a little laugh as another tremble went through me, and I backed up long enough to pull my briefs and sweatpants back up.

"I think you already know the answer."

She flushed, smile brightening.

"But you want to hear it, don't you?" I added, lowering myself down to where she was.

Her eyes widened, smile fading as I invaded her space.

"You want me to tell you how good you made me feel, how hot it was to see you on your knees for me, to watch as I fucked your mouth."

I grabbed her face, tilting her up so I could claim her mouth in a hot, possessive kiss.

"You swallowed my cum," I reminded her, nipping her bottom lip with my teeth as she let out a whimper of a moan. "And you want to know if I liked it as much as you did."

"Yes," she breathed, gasping when I trailed bruising kisses down her neck. I was already unfastening her blouse, already lying her back against the dome wall.

"Let me show you," I whispered into the shell of her ear.

And then I kissed my way down, ready to feast.

GIANA

My heart thundered in my ears as Clay pressed me down against the cool metal of the observatory dome, his hot kisses trailing down the length of my body as I trembled beneath him. I was still breathing heavy from going down on *him*, from the power I felt humming through me at being the one to make him unravel.

He paused at my navel, pressing slow, lingering kisses along each rib as he unfastened every button of my blouse and pulled it from where it was tucked into my skirt. My modest breasts heaved when he peeled the fabric away to reveal them, and he hummed in approval, tracing the cups of my bra over each swell as my skin pebbled under the touch.

"Just like before, you'll have to tell me what you like," he murmured against my skin, kissing the spot above my belly button as one finger dipped under the cup of my bra. It brushed against my nipple in time with a swipe of his tongue over my stomach, and I shivered, hands tightening into fists at my sides. "And what you don't."

I nodded, though my heart was racing so loud I could barely hear him. I just watched in a mixture of fear and anticipation as he trailed his kisses lower, flipping up the hem of my skirt to reveal my white lace panties beneath it.

Clay fixed his eyes on me, then trailed one soft fingertip down the center of the fabric, the sensation so light it was a brutal tease against my aching clit.

"Clay," I cried, my head falling back as my eyes closed.

"*Fuck*, Kitten," he said next, his fingertips playing at the seam of my thong. "You fucking loved that, didn't you? Being on your knees for me. You're soaked."

He slicked a finger through my wetness with the comment, and heat invaded my neck even though I opened for him more. I was as ashamed as I was aroused, and the latter won over.

"Yes," I confessed.

"What did you like?" he teased, running the pad of his thumb over the fabric and back down again. It pressed the harsh lace against me, a burning friction that made me writhe with need. "Did you like how I tasted, how you gagged on my cock?"

"Yes," I breathed, rolling my lips together as I squirmed beneath his touch. "And I loved when you came because of me."

"All because of you," he validated, and that made my nipples peak, made me light up with pride and power.

Clay lowered himself even more, until he was lying on his stomach with his elbows propped under my legs. I had no choice but to set my thighs on his shoulders, and my knees bent inward, because I was suddenly aware that my wet sex was right in his face.

"Don't," he said, stopping me before my knees could touch. He gently tapped the inside of each one until I let them fall back open. "I want to see you, Kitten," he cooed. "I want to taste you."

A breath of a moan fell through my lips as he did just that, keeping his eyes on me as he ran the flat of his tongue over the lace of my panties. He soaked whatever my pussy hadn't already, wetting the fabric and using his tongue to press against it and rub a sweet friction over my clit.

"Oh, *God*," I breathed, head falling back against the dome again. My hands shot out for his hair instinctively, but I tore them away, reaching for my sides, instead.

"Do it," he said, grabbing one hand and moving it back to my hair. "Show me where."

My fingers curled in the soft strands, and he enveloped me with his mouth again, licking from my seam up to my bud in a hot heat. I held him there at my clit, and he grinned against my bucking hips before swirling his tongue over the lace.

I moaned, pushing my hips up and toward him, seeking more.

"There?" he asked, flicking the bud with the tip of his tongue.

I nodded, wetting my lips before I dragged my teeth over the bottom one.

"Let's get this out of the way, shall we?" Clay sat back on his elbows just long enough to tug at my panties, and I lifted my hips, helping him slide them down until he drew them off one leg and then the other.

He paused at my ankle, trailing up my knee-high stocking until he slipped a finger beneath the top of it.

"These drive me insane, you know," he husked, taking his time crawling his hands back up to where I really wanted them. "Every time you wear them, I think of how many ways I could peel them off you."

I knew he was faking. I knew he was just giving me the dirty talk he could clearly see I reacted to. But still, I lit up under those words as if they were the purest truth, as if I really could be sexy enough to drive a man like Clay Johnson to insanity.

He settled back in between my thighs, groaning when he had me open and right in his face. "*Damn*," he breathed. "Such a pretty pussy."

He ran his finger along the outer edges, tracing my lips and the sensitive area between my vagina and ass. I shivered at the touch, and then his hands gripped my thighs and pulled me into him.

His eyes found mine, and he lowered.

The first hot sensation of his mouth enveloping me without a barrier between us sucked me under like a rip current. I was helpless to even try to hold my composure as he did some sort of combination of sucking and licking that *literally* made my knees quake around him.

I let out something between a curse and a moan, something like a breathy prayer, and Clay smiled against my sensitive skin, pressing a lighter kiss to my bud.

"Tell me what you like," he reminded me, and then his fingers gripped into my thighs as he lowered his mouth again.

It lit my entire body on fire, watching as he swayed his head gently, feeling his tongue slicking every centimeter of me. He ran it hot and flat along my seam before tightening it into a hard tip to flick it against my bud. He drew circles and lines, sucked and licked, moaned with a humming vibration that felt like having a vibrator in the best possible spot.

I couldn't speak, couldn't *tell him* anything. Instead, my hands weaved into his hair again, and I tightened my grip any time he paid attention to my clit.

"Mmmm," he hummed against it, and I shook around him, my orgasm building more and more with every lash of his tongue. "What about this?"

He shifted his weight onto one elbow, the free hand trailing up the length of my stomach to rest between my breasts. His palm splayed my ribcage, and then he roughly shoved one cup of my bra up over my breast and palmed it.

I arched into the brute touch, gasping for air as that sensation rivaled with the wet heat of his tongue between my thighs. He massaged my breast as he licked me, then sucked my clit while his fingers tightened over my nipple and gave a gentle, twisting tug.

"*Clay!*"

I cried out his name and I didn't know why. I didn't know what I wanted. I didn't know if I was desperate for him to stop or if I wanted even more. I squirmed beneath him as he held my thigh as steady as he could, continuing his assault on my pussy as his hand worked one breast and then the other.

The combination had me teetering on the edge of ecstasy, but *something* was missing.

"More," I panted. "I need... *more*."

"More," Clay repeated, and his hand trailed down from my breast to between my thighs. He held my stare as that hand disappeared beneath me, and then I felt a fingertip pressing against my entrance. "Here?"

"Yes," I begged.

With a devilish smirk, Clay slipped that finger inside me, all at once and to the very center of me. I cried out, but in the next instant, his mouth was on my clit again, sucking and licking as his finger withdrew and plunged inside me again.

He angled his wrist so he could curl that finger inside me, and as I shook and writhed beneath him, he added another.

It was everything I wanted. I was full, his fingers stretching me as his tongue pressed just the right amount of pressure where I needed it. That along with the sight of him burying his face between my thighs was too much to stay composed under.

"Rub your tits for me, Kitten," he breathed against my skin, the breath cool where I was wet and hot. "Stroke yourself with me. *Come* for me."

I had no choice but to obey, and when my fingers plucked at my pebbled nipple, I whimpered and moaned and squirmed and bucked my hips against his mouth. He met my eager request for more with an increased pressure, the sounds of him sucking and finger-fucking me the last thing that drove me over the edge.

I tumbled, spiraling as my orgasm soared through me. It burned like ice down my spine all the way to my toes, which curled as my legs shook so violently, Clay clamped his grip to hold me still. He never relented, driving his tongue in time with his fingers until the very last of my orgasm spilled through me.

And I collapsed.

Every inch of me fell limp, my breaths erratic, heart a fucking jackhammer in my chest as Clay smiled against my pussy. He softly kissed my bud, but it was so sensitive that I shook with the touch. He continued those sweet kisses on every inch of my body as he carefully made his way up to sit next to me.

Once he was there, he pulled me into him.

I felt like the smallest thing in the world cradled in his arms, my pussy still pulsing between my thighs as I curled into him.

"Lesson complete," he whispered, kissing my hair.

"You are *so fucking good* at that."

He barked out a laugh. "So are you."

"Really?" I peeled back to look at him. "Did I do okay?"

His smile slipped, his eyes skating over my face before he spotted a rogue curl and tucked it behind my ear. "You were amazing."

"Do I need to go deeper? Should I get some lessons on deep throating or something?"

"Jesus, Kitten, are you trying to get me hard again?"

I laughed. "I'm surprised I could even fit you in my mouth."

"Okay seriously, stop talking."

He grabbed himself under his sweats and adjusted, and I flushed, leaning into his chest.

"Thank you for showing me all this."

My chest ached with something I couldn't quite name, like remembering that that's all he was doing hurt for some reason. I was thankful he was showing me. It was what I asked him for.

But he was so good at pretending that sometimes it felt...

I couldn't even finish the thought. I just clamped my mouth shut, closing my eyes and willing the anxiety to fly away.

"Thank you for trusting me," he said, swallowing. "And for letting me escape in you."

I peered up at him. "I'm always here," I promised.

And I didn't mean just while we were fake-dating, or when we were putting on a show for Shawn or Maliyah or whoever else was watching. I meant now, and after... whatever it might look like *after*.

After this was all over, after he had Maliyah back and I had...

Again, the thought raced from me before I could finish it, and I let out a strange noise as I peeled away from him and sat up, collecting my panties from where they rested by his feet.

"We need food," I declared, standing and pulling on my thong without looking back at him. "And probably a shower."

Clay chuckled, taking his time rising to his feet. I could see he was still turned on, the bulge in his sweatpants giving him away. He saw me staring at it and smirked, but then something washed over him, something sad and overpowering.

I didn't know what it was, didn't know what had happened tonight or why he was upset. But whatever I'd done to ease the pain had been temporary, because I watched in slow motion as he became distant again, that lost look in his eyes.

"I think I'm going to head back to the dorm," he said. "Get some sleep."

I nodded, trying not to show my disappointment. "Okay."

"You good?"

I swallowed, then held out my thumb with as big of a smile as I could muster. "Peachy."

Clay frowned, like he wasn't sure if he could believe me, and the smile was getting weaker by the minute, so I turned and grabbed my bag off the ground, slinging it over my shoulder.

I headed for the stairs, Clay on my heels, and when we made it down and out of the observatory, we paused at the fork in the sidewalk — one way leading to his dorm on campus, the other pointing toward my apartment.

"Let me walk you home."

"No," I insisted, shaking my head. "I'm going to get food. Maybe stop by the coffee shop to see Shawn play."

It was a lie, a bold-faced one I tried to seal with an excited smile as if that's all I wanted in the world — to see Shawn Stetson.

The truth was much darker, much more foreign, and much more terrifying.

I was running from a feeling demanding to be felt, a monster with gruesome teeth and sharp claws I knew would maim me if I let it catch up.

Clay didn't let on any emotion when he asked, "He's playing tonight?"

"Yeah. He told me when we ran into each other at the game."

"Oh."

I nodded, adjusting my bag on my shoulder.

"Let me know how it goes," Clay finally said.

"I will," I promised.

And in the most awkward goodbye ever, I offered him a peace sign before scurrying off with the memory of his tongue between my thighs etched into my brain forever.

Chapter 18

CLAY

I stayed away from Giana all week.

It was like refusing myself the pleasure of jumping into a refreshing spring on a hot summer day, like restricting myself from drinking water as I heave from dehydration — but I had to do it.

I was in too deep.

Almost a week ago now, Giana had taken me to the observatory to get my mind off my mom, even though she didn't know the full extent of what had happened. She'd somehow known enough to not push me when I said I couldn't talk about it, and she'd somehow *cared* enough to not leave me alone — even when every sign I gave off was cold.

She knew, without me having to say a word, that I needed something.

She knew *what* I needed.

And she let me lose myself in her.

It had haunted me all week, how it felt to come apart for her, to have her come apart for me. It was all under the guise of a lesson, but I knew if I was being honest with myself, that wasn't what it was for me.

I wanted her.

I wanted her so badly my chest had a gaping hole in it whenever I wasn't with her.

I wasn't even thinking about Maliyah anymore, and maybe I hadn't been for a while now. I couldn't put my finger on when it changed, when my focus shifted, but I knew the shift was fundamental. I knew every time I wanted to reach for Giana now, it wasn't because I gave a rat's ass about someone watching us and reporting back to my ex.

It was because I wanted to touch her, to hold her, to taste her.

But that wasn't what *she* wanted.

I'd starved myself of her attention all week long to remind myself, to hammer into my thick skull that she wanted another man — and I was just the foolish punk who agreed to help her get him.

No, whose *idea* this whole thing had been.

Frustration battled with gratitude inside my soul all week long, no matter how I tried to work through it in the weight room or on the field. I was consumed by overanalyzing each moment we'd spent together, wondering how it'd taken me so long to really see it, to really understand what I was feeling.

And I didn't know which emotion I felt more.

I was angry with myself, with her, with Shawn and Maliyah both. I was gutted by the situation, by even the *thought* of Shawn touching her the way I had been.

And yet, if this was it, if this was the only way I could ever have her... I was thankful.

I'd take every stolen moment, every fake kiss, every *lesson* she'd let me teach her. I'd ground myself down to sand and let her leave me behind in the end if it meant I got to soak up everything that she was right now.

A fool, that's what I was.

A fool who wouldn't stop playing the game he knew he'd lose.

The contrast between Giana and Maliyah ran through my head like a PowerPoint presentation all week, too. I couldn't help but compare them, where one was soft and the other a sharp razor. Maliyah got off on manipulating me, on knocking me down a peg or two, on reminding me just how lucky I was to have her, and how easily I could lose her — just like I *had* lost her. I used to get off on that, how confident she was, the games she loved to play. It was a thrill, a chase.

But Giana was the opposite.

She knew before I even realized it was an issue that I put others before myself more than I should, that I let Maliyah and even my own family walk all over me because that's what I've always been expected to do. She reminded me every chance she could that I was worthy, that I was good, that I was going somewhere.

My stomach rolled as I adjusted my tie in the dirty mirror of my dorm room, knowing I wouldn't be able to avoid her tonight. It had been hard enough through the week to ignore texts or tell her I was busy, to not look her way every time she was on the field or in the cafeteria, to adjust my schedule so I wasn't in the same place with her for too long.

But tonight was the team auction.

It was *her* event.

And I knew it'd gut me to see her, to be around her, to even be in the same *room*.

It would kill me.

And yet I craved it.

It was sick and toxic, and I couldn't discern good from bad anymore, not as I turned to each side and watched my reflection in the mirror, smoothing my hands over the all-black tux I'd rented for the night. I was as much of a mess as I had been when I'd left her at the observatory last week as I turned out the light and made my way out of the dorm, telling my roommate and teammate that I'd meet him at the stadium.

I needed to walk alone.

Fall greeted me as I strolled through campus, ignoring the looks I got from various groups of girls as I passed them. I kept my hands in my pockets, listening to the breeze through the trees and watching as more and more of the colorful leaves fell to the ground.

I would have been lying if I tried to tell myself, or anyone else, that my mom's situation wasn't adding to my stress. I'd talked to her every night, and it had been the same every time. She was wasting her days away drinking or doing God knew what else, her words always slurred and garbled through tears when we spoke.

And for the first time in my life, I not only recognized that I needed help.

I was prepared to ask for it.

Still, my chest was on fire as I pulled my phone from my pocket, thumbing through to Dad's name. I tapped it before I could talk myself out of it, pausing at a bench by the campus fountain as the line rang.

"Son," he greeted, his deep voice familiar in the aching kind of way. "Good to hear from you. Ready for the big game tomorrow?"

I paused, thrown off by his joy, by how unbothered and peaceful he was. He'd been that way ever since he left Mom.

Since he left us.

A whole new life greeted him on the other side of that divorce, one where I wasn't sure I fit anywhere anymore. He had his window office in Atlanta, his giant house in the suburbs, his perfect lawn and perfect kids and perfect wife. Outside of football, we had nothing in common.

He didn't know a single thing about me, not anymore.

"Providence is tough," he continued when I didn't answer, mistaking my silence for nerves about the game. "That offense is quick and crafty. But you're a beast. You'll give them hell. Be aggressive and don't get lazy in the second half — that's where they typically do the most damage."

"I'm not worried about the game," I finally said.

"Good. You shouldn't be. You—"

"Mom needs help."

I was surprised by the depth of my own voice, by how steady the words came from my throat. I knew it surprised my father, too, because he grew silent, clearing his throat after a long pause.

"Your mother is no concern of mine anymore."

"Yeah, I know. You left her and your first son behind years ago."

"Clay," he warned, like I was out of line. That deep rumble of his voice made me pause, made the hair on the back of my neck stand up the way it always did before I tried something risky — like a new play on the field.

"It's true and you know it. And you know what? It's fine. Honestly, it is. I've gone on without you. We both have."

"Without me?" he interjected. "Just who do you think helped pay for you to get out there to college in Boston? Who got your laptop and your moving truck and—"

"And who only calls me after a game? Who has nothing to talk to me about *other* than football? Who knows everything about my half-brothers and absolutely nothing about me?"

"Don't be ridiculous. I—"

"Name *one thing* you know about me other than my position on the field. One. I'll wait."

My nose flared as I bit back the urge to keep going, as I fought to be silent enough to let my point sink in. And it did. I knew it did, because my father didn't say another word.

"I don't begrudge you," I finally said, calmer. "I love you. I understand. I know how Mom can be... a lot," I confessed. "And I know she wasn't the right woman for you. But she needs help, Dad, and I can't do it on my own."

He blew out a sigh. "Let me guess — her fling of the week left her and now she's a mess."

"They were dating for months," I clarified. "But yes. And he was taking care of her, and now she has no job and is surviving off what little money I can afford to send home."

"Well, whose fault is that? She did this to herself."

I shook my head. "She never knew this would be her life, Dad. It was supposed to be *you* taking care of her. You knew when you met her that she didn't even graduate from high school. She never wanted a career. She wanted a family." I paused. "She wanted *you*."

"What she wanted was to gaslight me and control me and belittle me until I lost myself," he barked at me. "Something you should know a little bit about after dating Maliyah, I'd imagine."

My jaw tightened. "Don't talk about her like you know her."

"I might not have been there through everything, but I know that girl. I know her father. And I know enough to tell you that you're a momma's boy through and through, because you were even looking for her in the girl you wanted to marry." He scoffed. "Thank God you dodged that bullet."

Something about his words stung, not because they were an insult, but because there was truth in them — truth I didn't want to see or admit to.

"At least Maliyah has a father who actively participates in her life," I spat back. "In *my* life. You know, he flew across the country to watch me play. He was here for the last home game. And guess who can't say the same?"

My nose flared, and I ignored the part of my brain that reminded me that he hadn't *technically* come for me. He'd come for Maliyah, and I was just there.

But Dad didn't need to know that.

"I wish you were more like Cory," I said, voice low.

Dad almost laughed. "I don't want to be *anything* like that man."

"Yeah. I can tell."

There was a frustrated breath on the other end, and I pinched the bridge of my nose, shaking my head.

"Mom is broke," I ground through my teeth, getting back to the reason I called. "I have sent all that I can. Dad, please. I'm begging you. Please help her. Just until she can get back on her feet."

"She never will if she gets a handout from me or you or anyone else, Clay."

I scrubbed a hand over my face. "Unbelievable."

"Look, you can call me an asshole and think I'm evil if that's the picture you want to paint. But let me tell you the truth, son — she is an addict. She has been for years. She finds a man who can take care of her and give her all the drugs she wants and she's happy. The second he's gone, she's destructive. She doesn't have it in her to work for herself."

"Like hell she doesn't!" I screamed. "She raised me! *She* raised me — not you. She was there, every night, cooking dinner for me using whatever we had in the pantry even when it wasn't much, all after working all day — sometimes double shifts."

"And how do you think she had the energy to do that, hmm? Why do you think there was barely any food in the house, yet she always had money for what *she* needed to get by?"

I ignored the insinuation, even though my throat stung with the possibility that he was right. "You're a monster," I breathed. "You're selfish and you can't think of anyone but yourself. You never have."

"I used to be just like you," he shouted over me. "I used to bend over backward for her and everyone else in my life. But one day, it was too much. I didn't want to be the fucking rug everyone stepped on anymore. And trust me, you'll get there, too. Or, at least, I hope you do.

Because living a life where what you put in isn't reciprocated is no life at all."

I shook my head, tuning out most of his lecture. "So, you won't help." It wasn't a question. It was a fact, one I knew before I made the call.

"It wouldn't be help. It would be enabling. And no, I won't do that."

I swallowed the knives in my throat, nose flaring. "So what am I supposed to do?"

"*You* are supposed to play football," he said, his voice calmer now. "And get your degree. Date pretty girls and get into trouble with your friends. Be a *kid,* for Christ's sake. Your mom is a grown woman. She can take care of herself."

"Clearly."

He paused, a long sigh meeting me on the other end. "Life is hard, Clay. I know you already understand that, but you're only beginning to peel back the layers of just how hard it can be. Your mom will figure it out. She will. And if she doesn't? She only has herself to blame."

It baffled me, how he could find relief in that, how he could say those words and believe them wholeheartedly.

"I don't know how you came to be so self-centered, but I hope I can *never* stomach turning my back on my family the way you have."

I hung up as soon as the words were off my lips, fisting my phone so hard the screen cracked in my hands before I shoved it into my pocket.

The rest of my walk across campus was fast-paced, a sheen of sweat on my forehead when I blew through the stadium doors. I was still seeing red, still fuming from the conversation, and I debated ducking into the weight room to hammer out a quick set just to burn off the steam.

But as soon as I rounded the corner and slipped into the hallway, I saw her.

The entryway to what was usually a club for our most influential benefactors had been transformed, lights and music thumping from inside while a giant banner hung over the double glass doors. Giana stood in front of them, a photo booth background with the team's logo behind her and a dozen cameras in her face as she spoke into the microphone at the podium.

She was a vision, draped in a floor-length dress that glittered like starlight against her pale skin. The dress was sleeveless on one arm but wrapped all the way down to her wrist on the other, the neckline elegant and refined where it slanted her chest. I knew even without her turning around that it was a low back, the slivers of her ribcage visible from my viewpoint giving it away.

Her curls were tamed, brushed back into a high, sleek bun that transformed her from a young woman into a timeless movie star. She smiled with her rose-painted lips, gray-blue eyes sparkling under the lights of the cameras as she spoke with confidence, her chin lifted, shoulders squared.

I was speechless.

I was *mesmerized*.

And I was rooted to the spot until the moment her eyes flashed behind the cameraman in front of her and landed on me.

She dismissed herself from the media frenzy, pulling Kyle Robbins up to the podium to take her place. He launched into his interview easily, and Giana watched only for a moment before slipping away, the hem of her black dress gliding along the tile as she floated to me.

"Wow," she breathed, letting out a low whistle as her eyes ran the length of me. "I knew you could clean up, but I don't think I've ever seen a black tux look this good."

She smiled with the compliment, all light and easy and playful like we'd always been. It set my heart on fire, but I masked it as best I could by the time she found my gaze again, knowing those were feelings I would need to bury alive if necessary.

"And I didn't know slits could go this high," I mused, arching a brow at her exposed thigh. "No glasses?"

"Contacts," she answered easy, but then, she frowned. "Does it... do I look okay?"

"You look..." I bit my lip against everything I wanted to say, landing on a quiet, "breathtaking."

She blushed, stepping next to me and slipping her arm around mine. "Come on, let's get you mingling so you can steal some poor rich woman's money and make me look good on that auction stage."

"Is that my job tonight?" I asked. "Make you look good?"

"And raise a lot of money for charity," she added.

Her smile slipped a bit when we passed through the entryway, not even needing to do more than nod to the volunteers taking tickets. They knew who I was.

I marveled at how the club had been transformed, the uplighting and dance floor, the champagne fountain and various waiters walking around with appetizers and hors d'oeuvres. Every member of the team had cleaned up for the occasion, and even Holden looked relaxed where he drank water as a group of older women fawned over him.

"Maliyah is already here," Giana said quietly when we made our way into the space. "She looks beautiful. And I... I overheard something."

I just swallowed, looking down at where she still clung to my arm.

"I think she really misses you, Clay. I think... I think our plan is working." Her eyes searched mine. "She told a group of the cheerleaders in the bathroom that she wants you back."

I blinked at her reveal of information, waiting for it to hit me, to strike me in the chest, to fill me up with hope or the sense of pride I felt after winning a game.

But I felt nothing.

Two months ago — hell, even *one* month ago, I would have leapt for joy, or perhaps even cried. I would have run to Maliyah. I would have held her in my arms and begged her to take me back, to believe in us, to see the future I had always seen.

But now, that future was nothing but a foggy, distant dream — one I couldn't see clearly anymore.

One I had no desire to ever chase again.

I didn't know what to say, but I tried to pretend to be happy, to fake like that was the news I'd been waiting for.

"Well," I said, grinning as best I could. "She can eat her heart out when she sees you on my arm tonight."

Giana tried to return my smile, but there was a bend to her brows that tainted it, and before either of us could say anything else, Charlotte Banks strolled up to us.

"Giana, it's time," she said, offering me a small smile before she pulled Giana off my arm. "We've got the first five teammates lined up next to the stage and ready to go."

Giana looked over her shoulder at me as her boss pulled her away.

Her eyes were as mysterious as the ocean depths.

● ● ●

GIANA

From the moment I was pulled away from Clay and shoved onto the auction stage quite unwillingly, the night flew.

I blacked out for most of it, nerves rattling my bones as I somehow managed to stand at the podium, to speak loud and clear, to introduce each teammate and their date before accepting bids from the audience.

I wasn't a natural. I didn't crack well-timed jokes or charm the room with my dazzling personality the way I'd watched my mother and sisters do all my life. But I did speak clearly, with my chin held high, and with enough confidence to fool the room into thinking this wasn't so entirely out of my comfort zone that I was certain I'd vomit the moment I stepped off stage.

"Alright, ladies and gentlemen," I spoke into the microphone, a warm smile touching my lips when I saw who was next on the list. "Refill your champagne and get those paddles ready, because this next date is one you won't want to lose. Please help me welcome to the stage, Clay Johnson!"

Polite cheers rang out just like they had all through the auction, but there were also some whistles and little screams of excitement that pierced through the air. Bidders really couldn't go wrong with *any* of the date auctions tonight, but where some of the players were won by affluent older women in the community who would donate the money for the cause without taking the actual date, others were fought over by NBU students. They weren't here just for charity — they were here for a husband.

And they were out for blood when it came to the top players.

Clay approached the stage from the stairs behind me, his hand brushing the small of my back as he passed. I flushed, though I didn't look back at him, not even when chills raced from where he'd touched me all the way up to my ears.

"Safety Clay Johnson is six foot four and two-hundred-and-fifteen pounds of pure muscle," I read from the script, chuckling when the room echoed with cat calls. "He's a Cali boy with a love for the beach and reggae music. When we asked his teammates what word best describes Clay, they answered easily and in unison with..." I paused, smiling at the word before I said it. "Loyal."

I glanced back at Clay then, loving the humble smirk that found his lips as I did.

"His date has been graciously donated by Picnics & Posies," I said, turning back to the microphone. "Join Clay for a romantic picnic in Boston Common, complete with a bottle of sparkling grape juice, or champagne for those old enough to legally drink, as well as a charcuterie board and local pastries from the North End."

The room was buzzing with whispered conversations, everyone preparing to make their bids.

"We'll start the bidding at one-hundred dollars."

Paddles shot up into the air all over the room, which made everyone laugh and start screaming out random dollar amounts they were willing to pay to win.

"Five hundred," I jumped, surprised at how many numbers still stayed in the air. "A thousand!"

We lost quite a few with that one, but there were still a dozen holding strong.

"Fifteen hundred," I tried, and I laughed in true disbelief as I ran straight to, "Two thousand."

That dropped all but three.

I beamed at the remaining contenders, one I recognized from the board of a local advertising agency, one who was sporting a Zeta Tau Alpha jersey and conversing with her sisters like they were all throwing in money for the bid, and...

Maliyah.

My eyes caught on her, and hers narrowed into slits before she held her paddle even higher, as if I didn't already see it.

"Twenty-five hundred," I said, though my voice wasn't quite as loud this time.

The Zeta pouted, looking to her sisters who shook their heads before she let the paddle drop.

"Three," I said, not needing to say the thousand, and Maliyah glanced over at the lovely older woman whom I *wished* would win, only to immediately hate myself for wishing it.

Clay would want Maliyah to take the highest bid.

This is what we'd been working for, what we'd been parading our fake relationship around campus for months to achieve.

Maliyah wanted him back — and she proved it with a victorious smile as the other woman nodded her congratulations and lowered her paddle.

My sandpaper tongue wouldn't work, wouldn't swallow or let me speak as I banged my gavel against the wooden podium. "Sold, to number two-eighty-one," I finally croaked.

Maliyah arched a brow at me, and I wished I could have schooled my expression, that I could have refused her the satisfaction of thinking she'd gotten to me. But I was a pale, frozen ghost as I watched her in return.

And I didn't even have to fake it.

Clay was ushered off stage by one of the volunteers, and I tore my eyes off Maliyah where she darted through the crowd to meet him at the other end of it as the next player was brought up to take Clay's place.

The show had to go on, and I was the conductor.

Three more players were auctioned before we took an intermission, one I needed so desperately that I all but sprinted from the podium once the band began playing again. I stumbled down the steps of the stage, swiping a bottle of water offered to me out of someone's hands before I even recognized who it was.

"Breathe," Riley said when I'd guzzled half of it.

I came back to the room with a dozen blinks, only to have her gently take me by the arm and guide me over to a less crowded part of the room. She was a total knock-out in the red number she'd worn for the occasion, and she offered smiles to everyone we passed along the way until she had me tucked behind a table in the corner.

"You okay?"

"I'm great," I said, trying to seal that lie with a smile.

Riley arched a brow. "That was a low blow from Maliyah."

I shrugged. "It was generous. It's a great donation for a wonderful cause."

"Cut the shit, Giana. She bid on her ex-boyfriend. On *your* current boyfriend. And she did it to be a bitch."

Riley shook her head, glancing over her shoulder at where Maliyah was gathered with the rest of the cheer-leading squad on the dance floor. They moved their hips in time with the beat, laughing and tossing their hands up in the air without a care in the world. "I've watched enough *Breaking Bad* that I think I could help you get rid of the body."

The laugh that escaped me brought my first real breath in what felt like hours, and Riley offered me a genuine, sympathetic smile as she turned back to me.

"It's okay, really," I assured her. "It was hard to watch, but I'm not threatened by her." I swallowed down the lie, eyes flicking to where Maliyah was on the dance floor. "After all, it's me he's with. Not her."

Acid bubbled at the base of my throat, and as if I cued her, Maliyah's eyes slid to mine.

A snake-like smile curled on her red lips before she flipped her hair over one shoulder and turned back to her friends, and her body language was much more con-vincing than my words.

It didn't matter if she believed we'd been dating, or if she thought Clay might actually have feelings for me.

She knew, regardless, that he was *hers*.

"Damn straight," Riley said, tossing her arm around my shoulder as best she could for being three inches smaller than me. "Now, you should go find your man and remind her of that fact. Oh! Never mind," she added with a coy smile. "Looks like he beat you to it."

I followed her gaze to where Clay easily split the crowd, everyone parting for him as he moved purpose-fully across the floor and toward me. He walked with the swagger of a professional athlete, the tux he wore perfectly fitted, eyes heating more and more as he closed the gap between us.

"Make that twat cry into her pillow tonight," Riley whispered, kissing my cheek and releasing me just as Clay made it to the table. She gave him a knowing look before dipping behind him, and Zeke pulled her onto the dance floor before she could make it more than a few steps.

When she was gone, my eyes slowly trailed up to meet Clay's.

Those green wells were darker than I'd ever seen them, shadowed by something that seemed to be weighing down on every inch of him as he stood there in front of me. He swallowed, and without a word, extended his hand for mine.

I tried to aim for nonchalant and casual as I slipped my hand in his, letting him lead me through the curious crowd out to the dance floor. We made it just in time for the band to slow things down, soft melodies and a harmony of voices singing a rendition of "Without You" by The Kid LAROI.

Clay pulled me to the very center of the floor, then tugged me into him, his hands finding my waist easily. My own slipped up his chest, and he looked down the bridge of his nose at me, his jaw tight with words unspoken as we began to sway.

Just like any time Clay had his arms around me, we garnered attention from every set of eyes in the room. I felt the heat of them burning into the bare skin of my back exposed by my low-cut dress, and as if he could sense it, Clay smoothed his thumb over the very spot I ached.

"You look—" he started to say at the same time I blurted out, "Well, looks like it's working."

Clay frowned, tilting his head a bit.

"With you know who," I said, making a very subtle tilt of my chin in the direction of where Maliyah was now gathered with her squad on the side of the dance floor. I didn't want to say her name just in case she was watching us.

And I knew she was.

"We won't have to put up the charade much longer," I added, forcing a smile, hoping the words came out as light and happy as I wanted them to. And I did. I wanted so, *so* badly to be happy for Clay, to feel nothing but unbridled joy in my heart that he'd gotten exactly what he wanted.

Maliyah wanted him back.

And I'd helped him *get* her back.

It should have filled me with pride, the kind you get only after being a great friend to someone you love. Instead, it soured my gut, and I dropped my head to Clay's chest to avoid looking at him any longer for fear I'd crack and reveal the truth.

Which was... *what*, exactly?

I felt Clay's hands tighten where they held me, felt his heart pick up speed in his chest where my ear was pressed against it. He stopped swaying, pulling back until his hands were framing my arms and his eyes were pinned on mine.

"Giana, I—"

But before he could speak another word, the band stopped playing, applause rang out so loud it drowned out the rest of what he was going to say, and within seconds, Charlotte was speaking into the mic that it was time for bidding to begin again.

"Meet me at my place after," I breathed.

And then I reluctantly slipped out of his grasp.

Chapter 19

CLAY

It was cold and windy as I waited on the steps outside Giana's building after the auction. I'd dipped out long before the event actually ended, unable to stand the charade or Maliyah's not-so-subtle gazes across the room for any longer than I already had.

Can't wait for our date, she'd said seductively after I'd walked off the stage. I still felt the chill from her fingernail dragging down the length of my arm, could still see the promise in her eyes.

It had worked.

Just like I knew it would, seeing me with Giana had driven her mad, had made her realize that she still wanted ed me.

But now...

The soft sound of heels clicking on the dark sidewalk brought me out of my haze, and I jumped to my feet just as Giana met me at the bottom of the stairs. She looked frazzled, her hair falling from the bun she'd fixed it in thanks to the wind, and her makeup was a bit smeared, the night too long and involved for it to survive unscathed.

Without a word, she slipped past me, unlocking the door to her building and holding it open for me to pass through first. We walked silently up the stairs to her apartment, and once we were inside, she was on me.

I was just about to tuck my hands into my pockets when she dropped her keys and her purse, barely peeling off her coat before she launched herself at me, her mouth on mine in pure desperation and need.

I caught her with surprise, but also with a groan that echoed deep in my chest as she pressed every inch of her supple body against me in that dangerous, thin dress she wore.

"Tonight," she whispered against my mouth before claiming it in another needy kiss. "I want you to do it tonight."

My eyes shot open, but I couldn't respond, not when she was kissing me with fervor, backing me up toward her bedroom while kicking out of her heels on the way. Every muscle in my body tensed, heart galloping and mind racing alongside it.

Tonight.

She wanted me to take her virginity *tonight*.

"Giana," I tried, but she slammed her mouth onto mine before I could finish the sentence.

"Please, Clay," she begged. "I need you."

I closed my eyes at her words, at how they lit me up from the inside, how every molecule that made up who I was beamed at the truth I knew she said them with.

She slipped out of my arms, stepping back with only the light from the lamp on her bedside table illuminating her. With one gentle pull of a zipper lining her side, the dress gaped, and she slipped it off her shoulder, letting it fall to a sparkling pool at her feet.

She was completely bare beneath it.

"Jesus Christ, Kitten," I groaned, swallowing as I stepped into her. I reached out to brush against her ribcage with the back of my knuckles, loving how she peaked and arched like she wanted more. "You're so fucking perfect."

Her breath caught as I dragged my knuckles up higher, over the swell of her breast and up to trace her collarbone before my palm flattened against her chest. I backed her up with small, calculated steps, the beast inside me taking over until I had her flush against the wall.

"Are you already wet for me?" I asked against the shell of her ear, palm sliding up to wrap around her throat.

Giana pressed into the touch, like she wanted me to grip her harder, to choke the life out of her as she answered on a breath. "Yes."

"Show me," I rasped.

Her hand dipped between her thighs, and then she held her shiny, wet fingers up in evidence.

Then, to both our surprise, she pressed those fingertips against my bottom lip.

I sucked her fingers into my mouth without question, tasting her arousal which fired up my own. Her moan when I sucked her digits had my cock aching for relief, and I squeezed her throat where I held her, giving her the pressure she wanted.

Then, she was pure, beautiful chaos.

Her hands blindly ripped at my tux, pulling at my bowtie before she tore at the lapels and wrangled the jacket off me. I released my grip on her long enough to let her strip me, watching with proud amusement as she unfastened every button of my white dress shirt before sliding it over my shoulders and down the length of each arm. She left them bunched at my wrists behind me like handcuffs as her hands moved to my belt.

She was less steady then, her breaths coming harder as she struggled with the metal and leather before finally freeing the restraint. And when she pressed up onto her toes to kiss me as her fingertips pushed the button of my pants through the slit and she peeled the zipper down, it shocked me like a Taser.

I froze.

I panicked.

And I tamed the animal inside me long enough to remember all the reasons this couldn't happen.

"Giana, wait," I managed on a breath, struggling to get my shirt back over my shoulders so I could stop her. My hands wrapped around her wrists, and I held her there, pinned against the wall with her labored breaths meeting mine in the dark space between us.

"I'm okay. I'm ready," she assured me, even as she shook, even as her heart beat loud enough for us both to hear.

And maybe she was telling the truth.

Maybe she was ready.

But I wasn't.

I dropped my forehead to hers, swallowing past the fiery breath that expelled from me next. "I... I *can't*," I croaked. "Not like this."

Giana's breaths came harder and harder until they caught on an inhale, one she held as her eyes slowly crawled up to mine.

I didn't know how to tell her. I didn't know how to form the right words to explain that I didn't want to take her virginity for the purpose of her having sex with another man, that I couldn't bear to show her how to find pleasure, only to know it would be Shawn she really craved it from. It killed me to admit it, and I wanted so badly to push all my fucking feelings aside to give her what *she* needed in that moment.

But I couldn't.

"Oh," she finally answered.

And then she shut down.

She pulled away from my grasp, slipping under my arm that pinned her against the wall and bending for her dress. She haphazardly brought it up to cover herself as she stared at the floor. "I… um… I understand."

I swallowed, heart breaking at the sight of her, at how I knew she felt rejected when that was the furthest thing from my mind.

Tell her. Tell her something, anything.

I begged myself, but I was frozen, standing there in her bedroom half-naked, wondering if I'd lost my damn mind.

After a long pause, I bent to retrieve my jacket, shrugging it on over my open dress shirt before I fastened my pants and redid the belt. I stood there a moment longer once I was half-dressed again, watching Giana and breaking with every second that I did.

I approached her slowly, sliding my hand against her cheek until she closed her eyes and let out a long exhale.

"I'm not breaking my promise," I told her, waiting until her eyes opened again and found mine.

And I believed it. I believed in the very center of who I was that I still *would* take her virginity and show her the map of every way to achieve pleasure in bed.

But I wouldn't do it under the guise of it being fake.

I needed to clear my head, to sift through every fucked-up thought and emotion that had been haunting me all week so I could tell her what I was feeling.

And then, I had to pray it wasn't one-sided.

Pressing a soft kiss against her temple, I released her, bolting for her front door before the beast inside me could overturn my control.

And on my walk home, I started making a plan.

Chapter 20

GIANA

"**H**ow's my little mouse?"

It was ridiculous, how those four words from my father nearly made me burst into tears. They filled my eyes without warning as I walked across campus two days later, tucking my coat more around me to shield from the brutal wind.

"I'm good, Dad," I lied, but couldn't stop myself from sniffing to keep the tears at bay, as well as the snot running from the sudden onslaught of emotions.

"Mmm," he responded, and we both knew he was well aware that I was *not* okay. "Did you hear that Laura is receiving an award for the research she did last semester?"

"Really?" Instantly, my emotions stabled — which was likely why Dad had changed the subject. He knew when I wanted to talk and when I wanted to hermit. "That's incredible."

"Your mother and I are going to visit for the ceremony next month. I thought maybe we could come visit you, too. It's when you have a home game against the Hawks. We'd love to see you in action out there on the field."

I let out a bit of a laugh on my next breath because he and I *both* knew that it was *I*, not we, that belonged in that sentence.

"You know I don't suit up and play football, right?"

"And *you* know that I see you working hard on the sidelines every game, right?"

I stopped mid-stride, emotion strangling me once again. "You do?"

"Of course, I do, my little mouse. And I watched every interview you did for the auction Friday night, too. You're very well-spoken, young lady. I was highly impressed."

The compliment mixed with the pride I heard in his voice made me smile, but it slipped quickly when I remembered the auction I'd been trying to forget. Yesterday was easy. It was game day, full of reporters and wrangling the team. But today was Sunday, a day of rest, a day where I didn't have class *or* anything with the team to keep me busy.

And so I was drowning in my thoughts.

Clay had rejected me.

There was no way to sugarcoat it, to explain it or make an excuse for the way he'd walked away from me when I was literally stripped bare for him. It was the most vulnerable I'd ever been with him, with *anyone*, and he'd turned me down.

As much as my stomach curled in on itself with that feeling of dismissal, another emotion battled with it, one that reminded me of the desperation with which I'd launched myself at Clay without warning. I hadn't told him that was the night, hadn't prepared him for anything.

But that was exactly what I'd felt — *desperation.*

I was losing him, losing *us*, and so I tried to cling to him even as Maliyah slipped her arms around him and pulled him from me. Of course, he wouldn't want to have sex with me when Maliyah literally paid thousands of dollars to prove she wanted him back now.

This was what was always supposed to happen.

And yet now that it was, I was thrashing.

"Save me a father-daughter dinner when we come?" Dad asked, breaking the silence I'd left him with.

I let out a slow exhale. "I'd love that."

"Me, too. Until then, promise me you'll take care of yourself?"

"Promise," I managed, though my voice was weak.

"I love you, Giana. Remember everything is temporary."

Those words, though well-intentioned, made my nose sting with another wave of nausea. He meant to assure me that no matter what I was going through, it wouldn't last forever, that everything would eventually be okay.

But he only reminded me of what was causing the pain in the first place.

Everything is temporary.

First and foremost, whatever relationship I had with Clay.

"Love you, Dad," I whispered, and then I pulled out my phone, ending the call and tugging my earbuds out of my ears. I tucked them back into my pocket along with my phone before heaving myself onto the nearest bench, one that overlooked a small pond on campus.

The bitter wind swept over my already-chilled face, making my eyes water as a hundred more colorful leaves were swept from tree limbs and blown across the park. It was quiet on campus, between it being a weekend day and the freezing temperature, most students were in their dorms resting or boozing it up in one of the many favorite brunch places.

Hearing from my dad should have brought me peace and comfort, but it somehow did the opposite. I found myself wishing I'd taken the time to make more friends when I moved to NBU, that I hadn't spent all my time either with my books or my internship. I thought about calling Riley, but knew she'd be spending the day after a game win celebrating or resting with Zeke — as she should.

The one person I wanted to call, to be with, hadn't talked to me since he walked out of my apartment after I threw myself at him.

I was alone.

So alone I felt like I didn't exist.

"Well, there's a pretty face I haven't seen in far too long."

I blinked out of my haze, looking up to find Shawn strolling toward me. He wore a dark, forest green pea-coat and a pecan brown scarf wrapped around his neck. His nose was pink, breath coming in little white puffs from his lips as he took the seat next to me.

Right next to me.

His body heat enveloped me as his thigh pressed against mine. "It's fucking brutal out here today, eh?" He shook his head, looking over the pond before his eyes flashed down to where my hands were clasped in my lap. "Jesus, you don't have gloves on?"

Before I could respond — to *any* of his greetings — he pulled his glove-covered hands from his pockets and reached for me, pulling my hands into his.

He smoothed the warm fabric over my icy digits, and then, carefully, he pulled my hands up toward his mouth, blowing hot breath on them before he rubbed them between his palms once more.

And I must have been about to start my period because my eyes flooded with tears when he did.

"Hey," he said, frowning, his grip tightening on my hands. "What's wrong?"

I shook my head, pulling my bottom lip between my teeth in an attempt to keep my shit together as I stared down at our hands, vision blurring and fogging up my glasses. Just a few weeks ago, I would have had a stomach full of butterflies seeing that, feeling him holding me in such an intimate manner.

But now, all I could do was think of another pair of hands, larger and rougher and so familiar with me now that they felt like my own.

"Come here," Shawn said when I didn't answer, and he tucked me under his arm, wrapping me in a warm embrace and shielding me from the wind. He was quiet for a long while before he finally asked, "It's Clay, isn't it?"

I buried my face in his chest more, heart squeezing just from the sound of his name.

Shawn let out a long, slow breath, and for the longest time, he just held me, his hands smoothing over my arms to warm me through my jacket that was doing a poor job. After a while, he gently pulled back, still hold-ing me but waiting until I lifted my gaze to meet his.

"I hate to leave you like this, but I'm playing at the coffee shop. My set starts in twenty minutes. Do you want to come?"

I shook my head immediately, but couldn't find the word to tell him I wasn't up for *anything* right now, least of all a crowded café.

He nodded in understanding. "Look, I don't want to overstep, Giana, but... do you think..." He paused, swal-lowing. "Could we maybe hang out Friday night?"

I blanched. "What?"

"Is that all I had to do to get you to speak? Ask you on a date?" Shawn smirked.

I couldn't help the genuine chuckle that left me then, and I wiped the wrist of my jacket against my nose. "I have a boyfriend," I reminded him, though my convic-tion was weak.

"To be honest?" Shawn dipped his gaze until I was looking at him again. "I don't care. Not when he treats you like this."

My brows bent inward, heart squeezing in my chest at the insinuation that Clay treated me any way but with respect. But this was the picture we'd painted for Shawn, that Clay was a cocky athlete, that he neglected me, that I couldn't see that I deserved better.

This had been the plan for *me*.

While we'd played the game to get Maliyah back in his life, we'd also weaved the perfect story to get Shawn in mine.

And *both* had worked.

This was what I'd wanted. This was what Clay had offered to help with, what I'd asked him to prepare me for in more ways than he originally signed up for.

Shawn Stetson was asking me out.

So why was my throat shutting down at the thought of saying yes?

"Hey, I'll behave," he promised, smiling when he saw the worry in my eyes. "Just friends. We can hang out as just friends, right?"

I let out a long breath. "I don't see why not."

His smile widened. "Great. I actually have a Friday night without a gig for once. What do you say we keep it low key... you come over to my place? We can talk, get to know each other, maybe watch a movie?"

My cheeks warmed with that last part, because we all knew what *watch a movie* meant in college.

But this was what I'd been planning for, what I so *painstakingly* wished for. Even now, the thought of Shawn leaning in to close what little distance was still between us, the idea of him kissing me? It was intoxicating.

Maybe I was just reading too much into everything with Clay. Maybe I'd let my feelings get caught up in something we both agreed to keep feelings out of.

Everything we'd done, it was all fake.

The public appearances, the hand holding, the kissing, even the nights he'd shown me how to please myself, how to please *him*... it had all been a ruse.

Clay had Maliyah now. He'd proven Friday night when he'd walked away from me that that was what he wanted.

He wasn't caught up in feelings for me.

I was a fool to stay tangled up in mine for him.

"I'd love that," I finally answered, holding my chin higher. "I really would."

And just like that, I had a date with Shawn Stetson.

● ● ●

CLAY

I looked like an absolute idiot as I walked across campus, the bouquet of flowers in my hand blowing precariously in the wind. More and more petals blew off and joined the decaying leaves rapidly covering the grass, and try as I did, I couldn't shield them enough to save them.

"Giana, I know I don't deserve it, but I want to explain why I left Friday night," I mumbled to myself, reciting the words I'd planned out in my head. "It wasn't because I didn't want you. Trust me," I breathed. "I wanted you so fucking badly I could barely breathe when I left."

My chest stung with that, the memory of leaving her, of her wide eyes and quivering lip when I turned my back and walked out of her apartment. It wasn't my brightest move, but then again, I *knew* if I stayed, I would have taken her. I wouldn't have been able to resist her, not with her bare before me and begging me to have my way.

It had hit me like a sledgehammer to the head, my feelings for Giana, and it had taken me all weekend to untangle them.

Yesterday, football was my focus. It *had* to be. As a student athlete on scholarship, I had one job to do, and for the hours that stretched before the game until I was showering after the game last night, that was where my head was. We secured another win, steering us closer and closer to another bowl game.

This year, we wanted *the* bowl game, the one that would lead us to the championship.

If it was possible, we were on fire even more so than last season. We'd had a lot of new blood, myself included, and had to learn how each other worked, how to jell. This season, we were becoming more and more comfortable, running plays like we knew them better than the back of our hands.

It was all falling into place.

But the second the game was over, my mind shifted gears, and all thoughts were wrapped up in Giana.

Or should I say, ninety percent of them — the other ten were reserved for Mom, especially when I applied for a student loan late last night. It hadn't been something I'd needed up until this point. My scholarship covered my tuition, books, dorm, and fees, and even gave me enough to live on — especially considering most of my meals were at the stadium.

But I had drained my savings helping Mom pay bills and get by, and rent was due next week.

It was a small loan, one I hoped I could pay off easily once I was drafted with a signing bonus. Still, my ribcage ached when I hit the submit button, when I got the automatic approval and realized I was in debt for the first time in my life.

It was so easy to do, and now, I understood why so many people were crushed beneath the weight of it.

"Don't worry," I'd told Mom after the loan was secured. "I will take care of you."

"You always have," was her response.

I still wasn't over my anger with my father, either. I couldn't understand how he could so easily turn his back on his family when we needed him.

But then again, we weren't his family — not his primary one, anyway. We were a past life, one he clearly wanted to leave behind.

I sniffed against the fierce wind, a cool resolve sinking over me along with it. We didn't need him. We would be just fine.

It had been a tornado of emotions over the last week, especially over the last seventy-two hours, and I couldn't contain the hope that bubbled in my heart at the thought of telling Giana how I felt about her and having her reciprocate it.

I could see it already, her eyes watering as I pulled her into me. I could feel her lips on mine, her body melting as I held her, could taste her tongue and hear the sweet moans she saved only for me.

But there was a niggling fear tickling at my stomach as I approached her building, because I knew the *other* way this could go, too.

The truth was I didn't know where her head was at, where her *heart* was at.

And the only way to find out was to put my own on the line.

I lifted my hand to ring the buzzer for her apartment, but before I could, I heard my name behind me.

"Clay?"

I turned, finding Giana shivering in a jacket I knew couldn't be keeping her warm in this cold front that had swept in over the city.

Her eyes were dark, underlined with a deep purple that told me she hadn't slept, her face red and blotchy like she'd been crying. Or maybe it was just the wind. Either way, she looked how I felt — emotionally drained.

She blinked at me, then at what was left of the flowers in my hand. She swallowed when she saw them, then held her chin higher, and I swore I saw her slip on a mask of indifference right in front of me.

"I was just about to text you once I got home," she said, plastering on a smile as she shimmied past me and unlocked the door. We both ushered inside, the warmth welcome after being in the blistering wind. "You're never going to believe what happened."

I followed her up the stairs to her apartment as she peeled off her scarf and coat, and my heart hammered harder and harder in my chest with every step knowing the words I would say once we were inside her apartment.

"So, I was walking around campus, just…" She paused, eyeing me over her shoulder before she hit the top stair and unlocked her apartment door. "Enjoying the weather," she finally said. "And who do I run into?"

She pushed the door open, slipping in first before I followed and shut the door behind us.

"Shawn."

She whipped around as she said the name, her turquoise eyes catching mine just as her rosy cheeks lifted with the wide spread of her lips.

That blooming smile formed a knot in my throat, one I couldn't swallow past as Giana hung up her coat and scarf before reaching for the flowers in my hand.

"Oh, yeah, I… I got these for you," I said lamely, cringing a bit when she took them and surveyed the broken stems and ragged petals still holding on. "They looked a lot better before my walk."

Giana smiled, though it was weak, a flash of something in her eyes as she looked at the flowers, then at me, then turned for her kitchen. She pulled a small vase from under the sink and began snipping the flower stems and arranging the ones that had survived.

"Anyway, so we talked a bit and..." She bit her lip, doing a little bounce when she looked up at me again. "He asked me on a date!"

Rage simmered in my chest. "He *what*?"

"I know, right?!" Giana mistook my question for pleasant surprise rather than the anger that it was. "It's crazy. You really know what you're doing," she added with a wink.

"That motherfucker asked you on a date when you have a boyfriend?"

"Well, *technically* he just asked to hang out. As *friends*," she said with a knowing grin. "To *watch a movie*."

My hands curled into fists at my side, and I gritted my teeth together to keep from roaring at the bastard's audacity. "What a disrespectful creep."

Giana rolled her eyes, leveling her gaze at me before she snipped the stem of an orange daisy-looking flower and plopped it into the vase. "Oh, come on, this is what we've been goading him to do this whole time. Remember? It was your idea to play the part of neglectful boyfriend."

She said the words so playfully, like nothing had happened between us Friday night, like everything was completely normal and we were still faking a relationship.

Like we were nothing but *friends*.

"I just can't believe it worked," she almost whispered, shaking her head with a dazed smile as she finished the last of the flowers. She shook her head then. "Anyway, I need your help. What do I wear? And what do I *do*? I mean, we both know what *watch a movie* means."

She waggled her brows with that, turning to press onto her tiptoes and reach for something on top of her fridge just before my fury made an appearance. I tried my best to school it before she turned around, tea kettle in her hand.

"Want some?" she asked.

I think I nodded. Or maybe I shook my head. I couldn't be sure, because I was rounding into the kitchen with one thing on my mind. "So, wait, you're just going to go over to his place and hang out?"

"Yes."

I blinked. "You realize what that means, right?"

"Yes," she said on a grin, almost like she was exhausted. "That's what I was trying to say. I mean... what if he wants to... you know."

I couldn't fucking breathe.

"You don't have to move fast."

"What if I want to?"

The words shot from her lips, all smiles gone as she pursed them and leaned a hip against the stove. She folded her arms over her chest, lifting her chin a bit as I stared back at her.

"I'm ready," she said. "I've *been* ready. I want it."

My eyelids fluttered at hearing those words from her, desperation surging over me.

"I want to know what it feels like, what *all* of it feels like," she whispered, her eyes falling to rest somewhere on the ground between us. She smiled, dazed, and then looked at me again. "Especially after the previews you've given me."

She said it as a joke, even punctuating it with a little laugh as she took the kettle to the sink and filled it with water before setting it on the stove top and flicking on the burner.

"I just need to know what to wear. I mean, I want to be casual, comfortable, but also *cute*. Like, I know what to wear to a dinner date, but what do you wear when you're just going to someone's dorm?"

She bit her lip, and then rambled on, something about maybe she could wear her gray joggers and a tank top, something that would show her cleavage. Or maybe I made that part up. Maybe I was driving myself mad with my worst nightmare, with imagining Shawn peeling those sweatpants off her the way I had the first night she'd let me touch her.

I blacked out as she continued talking, not registering a word of it. My entire plan blew up in a nuclear fashion right before my eyes.

I was too late.

I'd missed my one shot to tell her how I felt.

Just two nights ago, she was naked and clinging to me, kissing me desperately, *begging* for me.

Now, I knew I'd never touch her again.

Shawn had seen his opportunity, and he'd made his move.

Then again, if she'd so willingly agreed, did I really ever have a shot with her in the first place? Was it all really fake to her, void of feelings?

Was I just a friend in her eyes?

Thought after thought pummeled me like relentless waves crashing against a jagged shoreline until it was too much to bear the weight of. Between my father, my mother, Maliyah, and now this? I couldn't swim anymore. I couldn't fight to keep my head above water.

So, I took one last breath, one last longing look at Giana as she lit up talking about what her date would be like with another man.

Then, I let myself sink down to the bottom, and I sat there, vision blurring through the salty water, slowly drowning, but not struggling to save myself.

This whole thing had been *my* plan, my idea.

And now, I had no choice but to lie in the watery bed I'd made.

Chapter 21

GIANA

The week dragged by like dead weight in quicksand, each day seeming to last longer than the one before it.

Even though I felt like I'd extended an olive branch and cleared the awkward air between me and Clay after the whole *sorry I walked out on you naked, here are some flowers* debacle, he was still acting weird. Or maybe he was just focused on the upcoming game against the number two seed in our conference. Or maybe he was spending all his time with Maliyah. I had no way of knowing, because other than him stopping by my apartment on Sunday, I hadn't heard from him.

I didn't know what we were doing, didn't know if we were just letting the fake thing between us slowly fizzle out, or if we were unintentionally planting seeds for our fake breakup. Riley asked me about what was going on halfway through the week, but I just shrugged, told her things were fine and tried to seal the lie with a convincing smile.

Meanwhile, Shawn had been blowing up my phone, texting me first thing in the morning and well into the night. He texted me funny memes, interesting news articles, songs that he wanted to know if I'd heard before, and even pictures of him throughout various sections of his day. The only time his name *wasn't* on my phone screen was when he was in class or at a gig, and I marveled at how I'd gone from being invisible to him, to feeling like I was the center of his attention.

And I liked it.

I *liked* that he was thinking of me, and that he was making an effort to let me know that he was. I liked that he called me things like *beautiful* and said *good morning, gorgeous* every single day.

Still, something was off, something deep inside me that I couldn't put my finger on — not directly, anyway.

I was in a book funk, unable to read more than a page or two before I'd huff and close the book, shelving it in an attempt to try another one. Even my tried and true favorites to re-read weren't doing the trick, and so I spent whatever time I wasn't in class or at the stadium lying on my bed and staring up at my ceiling.

I talked to my sisters and brothers on a group sibling video call, listening to them catch me up on their lives as I was silent as usual. Only Laura asked me how my job was, one time, and after a short but satisfying answer for them, the conversation shifted back to our brothers' current business venture.

Eventually, Friday came, and though they weren't the familiar ones I remembered when I was trying to pick out an outfit for that night Clay took me to see Shawn play downtown, I still had butterflies as I dressed in my joggers and a tank top. I styled my hair to make it look like I hadn't tried, applying light makeup and throwing on an oversized hoodie before I walked the few blocks to Shawn's place.

He lived a little off campus just like I did, though his building was newer, with a lobby that had a twenty-four-seven attendant at the desk. She called Shawn when I arrived, getting his approval before letting me into the bank of elevators and pushing the number for his floor.

My stomach twisted as the numbers ticked higher and higher, and then I stepped out into the hallway, immediately seeing Shawn standing in his open doorway at the end of it.

Those strange butterflies fluttered into a tizzy at the sight of him.

He leaned against the frame, arms and ankles crossed casually as he watched me walk every step of the way toward him. He didn't hide his gaze as it traveled the length of me, and I couldn't hide the blush that warmed my cheeks at his unyielding stare.

"Hey," he said easily when I was close, and then he pushed off from where he'd been leaning and wrapped me in a tight hug.

That hug was warm and cozy, like we'd known each other for years, like he was welcoming home a long-time friend he'd missed dreadfully. He smelled of some sort of herb, patchouli, maybe. He offered me a lazy smile when he pulled back, his eyes sort of glossed as he held out a hand to usher me inside.

"I hope you don't mind takeout," he said when he shut the door behind us. "I was too exhausted to cook anything."

I didn't answer, mostly because I was too busy gaping at the scene that waited for me inside. His dark studio was faintly lit by warm candles, their flickering flames casting shadows on the walls and over the dinner spread in the center of the room. He'd covered a coffee table with a cream silk tablecloth, a dozen roses right in the center along with more candles. Pillows piled up on either side made up the makeshift chairs, and he'd set the table for two, with Italian takeout I recognized from a nearby restaurant offering everything from chicken and pasta to lamb and bruschetta.

Soft music poured over the scene, jazzy and smooth, and my eyes traveled over the dinner spread to take in the minimalist dorm as a whole. A keyboard sat facing the windows, his guitar propped next to it, and his laptop sat open with some sort of music engineering software on the screen. He had one small couch, brown leather like the boots he always wore, and a box spring and mattress on the floor hugged the corner wall.

It was a bedroom, kitchen, living room and music studio all in one, and with the vinyl playing on the Crosley in the corner, and the myriad of posters hanging on the wall, it had an almost grunge-like romantic appeal, like something straight out of a 90's movie.

"Wow," I breathed, taking it all in.

"I hope it's not too much," Shawn said, scrubbing a hand back through his shaggy hair. "I like candles."

"It's beautiful," I assured him, even with my voice thick in my throat. I took his lead then, taking a seat on the pillows opposite the side of the table he'd sat on.

"Wine?" he asked, tilting the bottle toward my glass before I'd even answered. "It's Moscato. I haven't really developed a taste for anything deeper."

I chuckled. "Well, since you're nineteen, I guess I'll let it slide."

"Twenty," he corrected after filling our glasses, then he held his up. "To you, Giana," he said, his eyes sparkling in the candlelight. "And to the music that fills our souls."

I smiled, clinking my glass against his before I took a sip. The wine was almost *too* sweet, tasting more like grape juice than like anything that had alcohol in it. But I liked the bubbles dancing on my tongue as I looked around.

"I've missed you at my shows," Shawn said, plating a pesto pasta onto his dish before passing the container to me.

"I'm surprised you ever realized I was there in the first place."

"Why would that surprise you?" he asked genuinely. "*Look* at you."

I arched a brow, looking down at my sloppy, large sweatshirt and joggers. "Yeah. A total babe."

Shawn laughed. "You are. And you're unique. You stand out in a way I've never seen any other girl do."

Something about that wrinkled my nose — mostly because I absolutely *loathed* the *you're not like other girls* line. It felt divisive and like more of an insult to womanhood than a compliment to me.

"You never seemed to notice before that night I saw you downtown," I commented.

"I noticed every time."

His words came swiftly, and he paused where he was plating a chicken cutlet.

"I saw you at the café all last year, watched as you sang along to every song — even my originals."

I flushed.

"I watched you drink the same coffee order, some sort of large espresso foamy thing," he added with a laugh. "Every evening when I was there. And I always wondered if you'd ever stick around, or come up and say hi, but you never did."

I balked, unable to believe that he ever paid attention to me, but even more so that he was waiting for *me* to make a move. "You could have been the one to come break that barrier, you know," I told him.

"Maybe," he agreed. "But every time my set ended, you would bolt. And when I had intermission, you would pick up your book." He leveled his gaze with mine. "Do you *know* how intimidating it is to approach a girl when she's reading a book? That's like trying to pet a cat's belly. It might work out great, but more than likely you'll get claws to the face for assuming they wanted anything to do with you."

The laugh that shot out of me surprised me, and the snort that followed brought a wide grin to Shawn's face.

"Fair enough," I said through my laughter, and then I sipped the sweet wine before taking my first bite of pasta.

"Can I ask you something?" Shawn inquired.

I nodded, and he paused a long moment with his fork hovering over his plate before he finally spoke again.

"Why are you dating Clay Johnson?"

I froze, a painful chill washing over me for more reasons than I could keep up with. The sound of Clay's name, the memory of what had happened between us, the reminder that I *wasn't* dating him — not really — all hit me at once.

I swallowed. "Why does it matter?"

"Because I can't figure it out," Shawn answered honestly. "Not for the life of me. You know, I thought he was cool, but then I've watched the way he's treated you. That night in the club when he was basically molesting you for everyone to see? And then at The Pit, when he took that body shot off another girl?"

Fake. All of it was fake.

"She didn't mean anything to him," I whispered.

"Well, do *you*?"

I frowned, looking up to find Shawn watching me like I was poor, pathetic girl who didn't realize I was being abused.

But he didn't know what happened when no one was looking.

"You deserve to be happy, Giana," Shawn said. "And you deserve a man who treats you like the princess you are."

I couldn't hide my face twisting at that.

Princess? Ew.

I somehow smiled through it, though. "Well, thank you," I said. "And thank you for this. It's... honestly? The most romantic thing anyone has ever done for me."

Shawn sat up straighter, shoulders square. "Good. I'm happy to have that title."

The conversation was easy after that. Fortunately, Shawn dropped anything related to Clay and focused on getting to know me, on telling me more about *him*. I smiled as I listened to him tell me about growing up in a van with his hippy parents, how he'd been to more music festivals at the age of ten than most people went to in their entire lives. And he leaned over the table, completely enraptured as I told him about my siblings, and my love for smutty books.

Before I knew it, dinner was done, and we moved over to the small sofa. For a long time we continued talking, but then Shawn flicked through his Netflix and turned on a documentary that I, miraculously, hadn't seen yet. He said he knew I'd love it, if I loved nerding out about space.

And I did.

We sank back into the leather cushions, Shawn offering one of his blankets to me and covering up with another. But as the documentary went on, I felt him moving closer and closer, the distance between us narrowing until his arm was somehow around the back of the couch and thus *me*, too.

My heart hammered in my ears, and I was acutely aware of every breath he took, every centimeter his arm traveled until it was resting around me. I couldn't pay attention to anything, least of all the monotone man listing out how infinite the galaxy was.

My galaxy was currently revolving around Shawn Stetson.

I dared to look at him, and he angled his face toward me, his eyes searching mine in the low light from the candles and television. He reached out, sweeping my hair behind one ear, though it was a tentative, unsure touch.

"You've smiled so much tonight," he commented.

He cued another one with that. "It's been a great night."

"You should smile like this all the time. You should have a boyfriend who makes you happy, Giana."

I swallowed, and without warning, tears glossed my eyes.

Shawn moved in, closing the space between us as his eyes flicked to my lips. "Let me be the one to make you happy," he whispered.

And then, he kissed me.

A little flash of excitement and desire shot through me at the first contact, and I sucked in a breath, meeting his gentle kiss with one of equal measure.

But in the next moment, I felt...

Weird.

He smelled wrong, *tasted* wrong. His lips were too soft, his hands too weak where they held me. He didn't possess me, didn't wrap me up in all that he was with that kiss. I didn't *feel* anything, other than curious over what the difference was.

Maybe I just wasn't focused.

I mentally dragged my full attention to him, kissing him with more earnest. That made him groan, and I smiled in victory as he pressed into me a little harder, leaning me back until my head hit the arm of his couch and he settled in on top of me.

He was hard.

I felt it against my thigh, but again, I couldn't focus on anything other than that it didn't feel right.

Stop comparing to Clay, I warned myself, wrapping my arms around Shawn's neck and pulling him in for a deeper kiss.

I wanted this. I *wanted* Shawn. He had been my obsession all last year. I'd *dreamed* of this, of what it would be like to have him want me, to have him kiss me and hold me.

But now that I had it...

I tried and tried to make my brain shut off, to chase away every comparison that flew at me. But it was useless. Every kiss was lacking, cold and awkward compared to the heated ones I'd shared with Clay. Every touch was wrong, every roll of his hips against me made me wince in pain more than writhe in need.

Emotion strangled my throat as I tried with desperate kisses to *feel* something, anything, other than a longing sadness for what I'd lost. But it was useless.

I didn't want Shawn.

I didn't want *anyone* who wasn't Clay.

I sniffed against a sob, pressing my hands into Shawn's chest and stopping him before he could trail kisses down my neck. "Shawn, wait."

"We've both waited long enough," he rasped, kissing my fingertips. "I've got you, Giana. You're safe with me."

I almost rolled my eyes at how hard he missed the point.

"I should go."

But Shawn kept kissing, trying to lower himself down my body before I abruptly shoved his chest until he was off me.

"I have a boyfriend."

That sobered him, and he sat back on his heels, chest heaving and eyes wild as he tried to calm himself. I could see his erection straining through his sweatpants, but he nodded, running a hand back through his hair before giving me more space.

"Yeah," he said. "Yeah, I... I'm sorry."

I reached out to touch his hand. "Don't be. I... I wanted you to kiss me."

He smiled at that.

"But," I added quickly. "I'm not yours to kiss."

It was easier than telling him that once he *had* kissed me, I hadn't liked it.

He frowned, but nodded. "I understand."

A moment of awkward silence passed between us before I stood, swiping my phone off the table and tucking it in the pocket of my hoodie. "I'll text you," I promised.

And then before he could say anything else, I left.

● ● ●

I was numb as I walked the few blocks back to my place, unable to even shiver against the cool fog that had settled over the city. Groups of students laughing and going out for the night stumbled past me like I was invisible, and that was exactly how I felt.

How I'd *always* felt.

It was a pathetic sentiment, one that wasn't warranted after having a very hot, very desired musician practically throw himself at me. I should have felt honored, should have been reveling in how badly he wanted me, in how he would have taken me if I'd only let him.

But the fact remained that he wasn't who I *wanted* to want me.

To Clay, I was just a tool, a ploy in his plot to get Maliyah back. And I couldn't even be mad at him, because I'd jumped headfirst into his offer to help me get Shawn because Clay wasn't even on my radar then. *Shawn* was all I'd wanted, all I'd fantasized about.

How foolish of me to not remember that when Clay was holding me, when he was touching me, *kissing* me.

I was an absolute idiot, acting like I was the main character in some stupid romance novel instead of remembering that I was just the weird, nerdy girl trying to fake it.

Trying to fake *everything*.

I faked that I was confident enough to be a public relations associate, faked that I was Clay's girlfriend, faked that I didn't feel anything when he undressed me, when his mouth and hands brought me pleasure I'd never known in my life.

I faked that I didn't care about him, that I wanted Maliyah to come back into his life, that I wanted to *help* that happen.

I had been living one giant lie for months.

And now, I had no idea who I was.

I dragged my feet as I rounded the last corner that led to my block, digging in my pocket for my key. I was too busy staring at the sidewalk that I didn't notice that I wasn't alone until I was at the edge of my stoop.

And a large pair of white Allbird sneakers came into view.

My heart stopped in my chest at the sight of them, at the dark gray joggers that cuffed at the ankle of legs I could draw blind, I knew them so well now. I clutched my key in my hand as my eyes trailed up those sweats, the NBU Football sweater, and finally, to Clay's face.

His miserable, tortured face.

I couldn't speak, couldn't do anything other than watch where his knee bounced, his clasped hands balancing over it wrung together like he was a man on the edge of breaking. His nose flared, red eyes taking in the length of me like he was looking for something he couldn't find even with a magnifying glass.

"How did it go?"

His question surprised me, especially with how slow and achingly it came from his lips. It was barely a croak, like the words had burned his esophagus on the way out.

"Honestly?" I asked on a slow breath. "Awful."

Clay didn't show any emotional response to that.

"I mean, he tried," I clarified. "I... I got what I wanted, I guess. But I just..." I paused, stomach rolling painfully at the truth I wasn't brave enough to say. "It felt off. It felt... wrong."

I stared at my shoes, at Clay's, at his hands that were still white-knuckled.

After a long moment, I managed a swallow, pulling my gaze to meet his. "Why are you here?" I whispered.

I swore I saw a world war raging behind his eyes, heard gunshots and bombs exploding as he battled with whatever was on his mind. It was like he was on the precipice of deciding whether he wanted to say it or keep it inside forever.

And then, he looked at me, Adam's apple bobbing hard in his throat before he dared to push forward.

"I couldn't eat," he started, knee still bouncing. "Couldn't train, couldn't sleep, couldn't do anything other than make myself *sick* thinking about him touching you."

My breath caught at the need, at the pure, desperate possession that rolled off his tongue along with those words.

"I tried to pull my head out of my ass, to remind myself that this was what you wanted, what we *both* have been playing this game for." Clay shook his head. "But it was useless."

He dropped his gaze from mine, staring somewhere at the ground between us, instead.

"I have thought of nothing and no one but you since that night on the observatory tower."

His words were just a whisper, and emotion wrapped its hands around my throat, gripping tight as I held onto every word he said.

"I want you to be happy, Giana," he continued, voice ragged. "Maybe more than I've wanted anything in my life. And if he's what makes you happy? I'll leave. Right now." His gaze snapped to mine. "We can publicly break up and you can have what you want. I will walk away. I will leave you be. I will sincerely, with all my heart, wish nothing but the very best for you as I let you go."

I struggled with my next breath at the thought, at all of it being over.

Clay stood then, slowly, his eyes never leaving mine as he did.

"But that's not what I want," he continued, testing the space between us. "And it hasn't been for a while now, no matter how I tried to fight it."

The bitter breeze did nothing to cool my steaming cheeks as Clay took another tentative step toward me, but he didn't close all the space. He didn't reach for me, didn't touch me, didn't dare take the control he was granting to me.

"I want you," he declared, and the admission must have pained him as much as it elated me. His brows bent together, nose flaring like he was laying himself down at my feet and handing me a sword, not knowing if I'd ask him to stand again or cut his head off. "I want *you*," he repeated on a raspy breath. "And I don't want to pretend anymore."

I nearly sobbed when those words danced into the shell of my ear, when I realized every aching rip of my heart was one he'd felt, too.

It was real.

All of it was real.

And the only way I knew how to tell him that was with my hands sliding up his chest, arms wrapping around his neck, and toes pressing against the sidewalk until I could meld my mouth with his.

"I'm yours," I whispered.

And then I was raked into his arms.

Chapter 22

GIANA

My back was slammed against my front door the second it closed behind us.

Clay pushed into me with everything that he was, the entirety of his body covering mine. His hips pinned me against the wood, my legs wrapping around him, heels digging into his ass and begging for more. His hands gripped my hips hard as he kissed me, lips soft and warm and somehow tender in their demand.

I opened for him, softening with every touch, releasing every bit of tension that had weaved itself into my bones since the night he walked away from me. And as if he could sense that was where my head had gone, he intertwined his hands with mine, holding them beside my head as he pressed his chest hard against my own.

"This was why I left last week," he whispered into the space between us, his forehead to mine, our breaths labored between. "I walked away from you even when everything in my body begged me to stay. Because when I took you for the first time, I didn't want it to be under the guise of any of this between us being fake."

He squeezed my hands in his own, kissing my chin until I tipped it up and allowed him access to my neck.

"This isn't fake," he swore against my skin, kissing and nipping it along the way. "Nothing between us has ever been fake."

His mouth was on mine in the next breath, and then I was being carried through my apartment — mostly blindly as I hadn't had time to even turn a light on. The only one was from above my stove, and it just barely lit up the space, darkness battling with the light in every corner.

Clay was careful as he lowered me onto the bed, and I sat at the edge of it as he backed away from me, taking his heat with him.

With his eyes watching me, he reached for the back of his hoodie and tore it over his head, flinging it to the side before he did the same with the t-shirt underneath. I reached out, my fingertips just barely getting a taste of his abdomen before he peeled them away and sat them at my sides again.

"Strip for me."

His words were hot, confident, and sealed with intention as he stepped even farther away and kicked off his sneakers before carefully ridding himself of his sweatpants.

He was a masterpiece there in nothing but his black boxer briefs, briefs that were strained as they held back his thickening erection. Clay's eyes heated more when I grabbed the wrist of my hoodie, tugging it off one arm and then the other before I peeled it overhead.

My nipples were peaked under my tank top, the thin fabric easily disposed of in the next second. I snapped my gaze to meet his when my chest was bare, and his eyes dropped to take me in, a low groan rolling from his throat at the sight.

His hand slid down his abdomen and beneath the band of his briefs, stroking himself as his eyes trailed to where my sweatpants were still fastened around my hips. I reclined back onto the comforter, using my heels on the floor to push my hips up and slide the thick fabric down my thighs, my knees, until the pants pooled at my feet.

"Stop right there."

Clay advanced on me, taking only a moment to slip out of his briefs before he was towering over me at the edge of the bed. I rested on the heels of my hands, panting, *throbbing* for him as he raked his gaze over every bare inch of me.

"Up," he said, grabbing my wrist to help me. And once I was standing, he spun me, gathering my hair in one massive hand and pulling it to the side so he could whisper his next words against my neck. "Wanna know why you didn't feel anything with him?"

His question was lost on me, because his hand released my hair, trailing down my ribs and hips until his fingertips hooked in the cotton of my boy shorts. One swift pull had them over my ass, and another freed them from around my thighs until they dropped to my ankles to join my sweatpants.

"I've been reading your books," he continued, tongue lashing out to taste my earlobe before he nibbled it. The sound of his breath in my ear combined with that little bite sent chills racing down my legs, and I arched into him, my ass meeting his firm erection that slid between my warm cheeks.

He groaned at the contact, but kept on with his slow torture, hands crawling up my abdomen until he was softly plucking at each nipple.

"I know what you want," he rasped. "What you *don't* want."

He twisted my nipple between his finger and thumb, a small snap of pain quickly covered by a roll of pleasure as he massaged my full breast in the next breath.

"You don't want soft, sweet, tender," he told me, punctuating each word with a kiss against the back of my neck. He trailed those kisses down until his teeth were sinking into the flesh at my shoulder, and I hissed before a guttural moan I'd never heard myself release before filled the space around us.

Clay grinned, kissing the spot he'd just bitten.

"You want possession," he continued, one hand sliding down, down, down as the other traveled up over my breasts. "You want someone to take control, to *ravage* you."

He cupped me between the legs at the same time his other hand wrapped around my throat, and the double sensation made me shudder violently, collapsing into him in the most sincere surrender.

"Shawn is an artist, a musician," he whispered against my ear, his grip on my neck tightening a bit. It made my next breath a little harder to grasp.

And I fucking *loved it.*

"But you're in control of so much in your life — the team, your job, school..." His middle finger slid between my labia, gliding into the wetness pooled there for him before he dragged it back out and circled my clit. I trembled at the feel of it, but he held me steady as he continued. "So in the bedroom, you want that duty to be on someone else."

I couldn't verbalize my agreement — mostly because I hadn't realized it until that moment that he pointed it out, though every sentiment he spoke rang so true, I wanted to throw my hands up and scream *amen*. But also, because every ounce of my awakening was tapped into his hands, the one around my throat and the one between my legs, each claiming me in equal measure.

"You don't want to be someone's muse," Clay rasped. "You want to be someone's undoing. And let me tell you, Kitten..." His voice rumbled against my ear before he sucked the lobe between his teeth. "You're mine."

I whimpered at the admission, at the knowledge that *I* could be the undoing of such a powerful, explosive man. Then, all at once, all his warmth left me, hands and mouth disappearing, all but the pressure to spin me around to face him again. I nearly fell with how my ankles were still tied up by my pants, but Clay steadied me.

We were heaving chest to heaving chest, Clay's emerald eyes sparking a fire low in my belly as he dragged the tip of his nose along the bridge of mine.

"You read my books," I breathed, a question and a disbelief all at once.

"Fuck yeah, I did."

"Why?"

Clay swallowed, brushing his knuckles along the side of my cheek. "I told myself it was to help you get Shawn," he said. "But in truth, it was to help *me* please *you*."

I shivered as those words rolled over me, my nipples hardening at the cold air and the delicious warmth of that sentiment.

He wants to please me.

He read my fucking *books*.

"Now," he said, running one hand roughly up the front of me. His fingers dove up between my breasts, thumb sliding over my nipple on the way up to my neck. He gripped it for only a second before his hand was framing my jaw, tilting my chin, his thumb sliding to cover my mouth. He circled my lips with the pad of it, dragging the bottom one down slowly until it popped free. "Get on your knees for me, Kitten."

I dropped so fast Clay smirked, and then he wrapped his hand around his length, guiding it to my lips. I lapped up the precum rolling off his tip like a drop of dew, moaning at the taste of him before I took his full crown along my tongue.

He bit out a curse, eyes rolling back before he let his head drop, too. His hand cradled my head, fingertips curling in my hair as he helped me suck him. I knew just what to do after our lesson, how to roll my tongue along his shaft and hold him deep in my throat before releasing him with a little gag. And Clay took every stroke I gave him with pure adoration and appreciation, his eyes crawling over me or casting up toward the ceiling when it became too much.

It wasn't long enough that I was down there for him before he was hiking me back up, helping me out of the clothes still restraining my ankles before he laid me back into the bed. He grabbed his sweatpants then, reaching into the pocket for something that he sat on the bedside table before he was crawling on top of me.

"That made you so wet last time," he mused, trailing hot, peppery kisses down my ribs and across my hips. "Let's see if it had the same effect tonight."

He settled between my thighs, taking each one on his shoulders before he dipped his nose between them. He teased my clit with that brush before his tongue dragged soft and slow over my folds, and I trembled at how badly I wanted him to separate them, to dip inside and give me the connection I needed.

"Fucking soaked," he confirmed, and he sucked my clit with tender care before one hand slid under his mouth and tested the wetness at my entrance. "Absolutely drenched for me, Kitten."

I loved how he talked to me, how every dirty word made me arch and pant and *ache* for him. I wanted to do it, too, to talk back to him and make him feel the same. But I was shocked silent by every touch, every kiss, every warm lash of his tongue against my bud as he used his fingers to slowly spread my lips and toy with my entrance.

"Show me how you want it," he whispered against the sensitive flesh. "Use my hand to fuck yourself."

I mewled, chest heaving, and I watched through hooded lids as Clay guided my hand to his before dipping between my legs once more. He hovered there at my entrance until I pressed his fingers inside me, my desire so thick he slid in without much resistance, and we both moaned as he filled me.

"God, I love feeling that tight pussy stretch open for me," he rasped, and I shook around his fingers as he withdrew them and pumped them in again at my grip's request.

Slow and steady, he worked me open, licking at my clit in time with his fingers — though *I* controlled those. He went at the pace my hand around his directed him to, and it wasn't long before I was writhing under his tongue and fingers, so close to coming I could feel the fire catching at the end of every nerve of my body.

"Clay," I begged, and he knew what I needed without another word. He took control, his fingers pumping in and out of me in the same sort of rhythm I'd directed before they slowly picked up pace. His tongue kept time, and my fists twisted in the sheets just in time for me to come, my body shaking and heart racing far too fast as I exploded into a million little stars.

I'd only had a few, but every time seemed better than the last, like my body was learning more and more how to come undone and take full advantage of the pleasure Clay was determined to bring me.

I cried out with the last of it, trembling in his grip before I fell completely lax.

"That's my girl," Clay praised, and he licked up my release like it was his only meal before slowly crawling up my body. "I hope you know that's just the first one tonight."

I smiled, laughing a bit as my breath steadied. But then I was seeking him again, hands wrapping around his neck and pulling him into me for a deep kiss.

"I'm ready."

Clay swallowed, meeting my warm kisses with his own before he reached blindly for whatever he'd put on the bedside table. When I heard the foil tear, I realized what it was.

My heart hammered to a gallop in my chest, beating so loud and hard I could hear it in my ears. I imagined Clay could hear it, too, because he paused with the condom in his hand, using the other to brush the hair from my eyes.

"We can wait," he offered.

"No."

I reached for the condom, plucking it from his fingers and kissing him as I blindly felt for his erection between us. When I gripped him, slowly rolling the condom over his length, he moaned into my mouth, hips flexing into the rubber as I continued stretching it over him.

"I need you inside me," I whispered, rolling my hips to meet his. "I want you to be the first one to fill me, Clay. I want you to be the first one I feel like this."

He growled, biting my bottom lip as he reached between us for my wrists. He pinned both by my head, leaning up a bit to take in the length of me as I panted and writhed beneath him.

"You want me to be the *only* one," he corrected me, and fuck if I didn't gasp out a weak *yes* in affirmation.

Clay's eyelids fluttered at the word, and his jaw was tight as he reached between us and adjusted himself at my entrance. I kept my hands where he'd placed them, even with his grip gone, twisting my fingertips into the pillow at my head as I held on for dear life.

His crown slipped between my lips, and he ran it up through my wetness before sliding it down to my entrance. He paused then, his eyes finding mine, and then he tested it, flexing forward just enough to stretch me open for him.

I gasped, that same familiar cocktail of pleasure and pain surfacing from the first time he fingered me.

The dominance faded from his face, brows folding together as he lowered himself down to his elbows and brought his lips to mine.

"Okay?" he asked softly.

I nodded, wrapping my arms around him and sliding my fingers into his hair. I gripped him to me, kissing him harder as I tucked my hips just enough to help him slide a centimeter more.

We both inhaled a stiff breath at the feel of it, and then Clay took control again, withdrawing that small bit of his tip before he flexed forward and filled me even more.

The pain intensified, but it was smoothed quickly as he kissed me and took his time, each roll of his hips stretching me open just a little more. Over and over, again and again, inch by blissful inch — he opened me, sliding in deeper and deeper as he kissed me reverently, his thundering heart matching the beat of my own.

And then, with a hiss and a moan, he filled me.

We both shuddered when he was fully inside, and I clung to him, nails digging into the flesh of his back as he softly kissed where his head was buried in my neck.

"God*damn*, Kitten," he groaned, withdrawing only to flex fully inside me again. "You feel so fucking incredible."

I couldn't speak to tell him he felt the same, because too fast for it to be normal, another orgasm built heavy and hot in my gut.

"I... I..."

I tried to say it, tried to bring the words out that would let him know what I was feeling. Whether he knew or not, I couldn't be sure, but he gave me just what I needed. He slipped out of me only to slide back in, finding a rhythm as he kissed my neck and massaged my breast in his large, warm hand.

The sensations battled for my attention, and I spread my thighs even wider for him, needing *more*.

Clay pressed up onto the palms of his hands, towering over me, and I watched the sensuous roll of his body as he fucked me. It was the most gorgeous, most hedonistic sight I'd ever seen in my life. His abs contracted and released with every roll, his heavy eyes locked on mine as he drove me closer to the edge.

"Clay," I whispered, as scared as I was excited for the feeling building inside me.

"Take it," he demanded.

My hand shot down between my legs, and it took only the softest roll of my fingertips over my clit in time with him pumping in and out of me to find my release.

I quaked and cried out, this one even more powerful than the last, more powerful than *any* I'd ever experienced before in my life. My walls tightened around him as he kept pace, and I shook and writhed in the sheets, reaching out to drag my nails down the valleys and peaks of his abdomen.

"*Fuck,* Giana," he groaned, and just as my orgasm was fading out, his pace quickened.

He was close.

I pressed up onto my own palms, heels of my feet finding the bed so I could meet his thrusts with my own.

"Oh *shit,*" he cursed, watching my breasts bounce wildly as I met his eager pumps, and I captured his mouth with my own just as he groaned out his release.

I felt it, felt him twitching inside me as his seed spilled into the condom. I was so sensitive I could feel every rivulet as it expended from him, and my mouth watered with the desire to taste him like I had that night at the observatory.

It was the fiercest rush I'd known in my life, to make Clay come, to feel him release inside me and know it was *me* who'd brought him that pleasure.

He collapsed onto me, forcing me to sink into the sheets as one of his hands painfully gripped my hip and he pumped out the last of his orgasm. He trembled when he was spent, forehead dropping to mine as we both panted, our slick skin dampening each other and the sheets.

And as fiercely as he had taken control, he surrendered it back to me.

"Are you okay?" he asked softly, searching my gaze before he pressed a gentle kiss to my nose.

"I'm fucking amazing."

He smiled, one brow arching up as he flexed his softening member inside me. "That makes two of us." He paused. "Come. Let's shower."

Carefully, he removed himself from inside me, disposing of the condom before he helped me stand. I didn't realize I *needed* help until I tried to walk on my shaky legs, thighs aching in protest from how I'd flexed every muscle in my body chasing both of my releases.

Clay ran the shower warm before helping me step inside, and he came in right behind me, closing the curtain and enveloping us in a warm, dark enclave.

His arms wrapped me up as the water washed down my back, and I sighed at the contentment that spread over me, the pure ecstasy of that moment.

Clay held me like that for a long while before he pulled back, swallowing as his eyes flicked back and forth between mine. He grabbed my face in his hands, thumbs against my jaw forcing me to look at him as he said, "Thank you for trusting me with that, for letting me be your first."

I bit against my smile, shaking my head. "You really are like a book boyfriend, you know?"

At that, he chuckled, tucking me into his chest against before pressing a kiss against my wet hair. "I'll be even better," he said. "Just wait and see."

And I had absolutely zero doubts that was a promise he wouldn't break.

Chapter 23

CLAY

I'd never felt so whole.

Not with a football in my hands, not with my mom's arm around me in pride on my graduation day, not in *any* of the moments I'd ever shared with Maliyah.

Nothing had ever filled me up, all the way to the brim, the way waking up next to Giana did.

Her dark curls were an absolute mess, frizzy and sticking this way and that, the golden highlights in the midst of brown like a chaotic halo around her head on the pillow. Her mouth was open, shallow snores slipping through her pink lips as a little drool slid through the corner.

I smiled, letting my eyes trace over the beams of light streaking in through her blinds and casting her in a golden glow. And suddenly, I realized how very differently last night could have gone, how differently this morning would be had I made a different decision — had I not said *fuck it* and gone after the girl.

My chest ached.

One choice. One moment where I'd decided I couldn't stay silent anymore, no matter what kind of pain it would bring to her or to me for me to speak the truth. It was nearly a week I let my pride sit on top of me, holding me down with its weight and the stinging reminder that her date with Shawn was what she wanted, what I'd promised to get her.

But when Coach let us go last night and told us to get some rest for the game today, I knew rest would be the last thing I'd find until I told her how I felt.

Part of me wished I'd been wise enough to do this *last* week, when I had her in my arms ready for me to take her. But it wasn't right, the timing of it, the *feeling* of it. And maybe the last seven agonizing days were what made last night so sweet.

She felt the same.

She wanted me, too.

God, just *thinking* of how she'd whispered that she was mine on her front stoop made my chest squeeze in a mixture of possession and elation.

It was enough to drive a sane man out of his mind, to have a girl like Giana open up for me, let me in, trust me with everything that she was, and give herself to me in every way that she could.

I wouldn't take a second of it for granted.

A garbage truck squeaking to a stop outside stirred Giana awake, and she blinked a few times, smacking her lips together before her tongue slid out to wet them. Her eyes widened when she found me staring back at her.

"Good morning," I said.

She blinked, and then instantly covered her head with the comforter. "Oh my God, look away. Close your eyes so I can make an escape to the bathroom."

The words were muffled under the covers, and I chuckled, ripping them off her head before I pulled her into me and kissed her — long, slow, and with every intent to do it all morning.

"You're beautiful," I told her.

"Not at seven AM, I'm not."

"Especially then," I argued, kissing her nose, but I still held her in my arms. "How are you feeling?"

Her resistance faded, and she melted into my embrace, watching her fingernails as they drew lines over my bicep. "Amazing," she whispered, a blush tingeing her cheeks. "Sore, and dehydrated," she added with a laugh. "But... amazing."

I intertwined her hand in mine, pulling her to my lips so I could kiss each of her fingertips. She watched me as I did, brows furrowing even as a smile bloomed on her lips.

"This is real," I said, hoping I could soothe whatever anxiety was already creeping into her mind in the daylight. "You and me, we're real."

She let out a long sigh. "So, it wasn't a dream."

"Like your imagination could cook up something *that* hot."

She snorted, rolling her eyes before she climbed on top of me. I let her maneuver us until I was on my back, she on her knees and settled into my lap.

"So, what does this mean for us now?"

"What do you want it to mean?" I countered.

Giana considered, her hands interlaced with mine and floating in the space between us as she pulled her mouth to one side in thought.

"Well," she started. "I guess not much has to change, does it? Everyone already thinks we're dating."

"Correction — a *lot* will change. Because as if it wasn't hard enough for me to keep my hands off you when we were pretending, it's going to be fucking impossible now."

I trailed my eyes over her breasts, visible through the sheer white tank top she'd thrown on after our shower last night. Her sleep shorts were so small they barely covered her ass, and I broke my grip with her hands so I could palm that behind and roll her against my hardening shaft.

She bit her lip, rolling her body to give me the friction I desired. "Promises, promises," she teased.

I groaned when the middle of her ran along my hard length, pulling her down so I could wrap my arms fully around her and feel the warmth of her pressed against me. "As much as I want to watch you ride me in the morning light," I said, flexing my hips to show just *how much* I wanted that. "You need to rest after last night."

She pouted, sagging in my arms.

"Trust me," I assured her. "You're going to be more sore there than you realize."

"I'm fine," she said.

I gave her a look, but then, in a move of both selfish need and stubborn persistence to prove I was right, I snaked my fingers up the inside of her thigh and under the fabric of her sleep shorts. Giana trembled when I ran the pad of my thumb against her seam, and when I pushed *just* the slightest bit against her entrance, she hissed, pulling away from the touch.

"See?" I arched a brow.

Giana conceded with a sigh.

"Besides," I added, holding her in my lap. "I need to get down to the stadium. Bus leaves in an hour."

Giana blinked as if coming out of a hypnosis. "Oh, *shit*. It's game day!"

She hopped off me in an instant, scrambling to her closet with only a quick glance at the time on her phone.

"I don't even have a bag packed."

"It's one night."

"I'm supposed to be down there already. We have to pack up all the gear."

"Charlotte will manage," I promised her, but she kept sifting through her clothes until I got up and physically hauled her into my arms, her back to my chest, sinking us both back down into the bed with her on my lap.

"You brute," she teased, smacking my chest.

"You love it."

"Another tip you picked up from my books?"

"Those things are like a treasure map. Just follow the tabs and highlights to find the pot of gold."

My fingers walked along her thigh until I could cup her, and she rolled into the touch, sighing as her head fell back against my chest. For a moment, she rested there, and then she pivoted in my arms to straddle me again.

"It was awful last night," she said, brows bending together. "With Shawn. I mean, it was fine, like if I wasn't in my head about *you,* I'm sure it would have been a great date. But I was so sick," she admitted, shaking her head. "When he kissed me, I—"

"He kissed you?"

The ice in my words knocked her silent. "Y-yes."

I gritted my teeth. "I'll murder him."

"Hey, this *was* our plan, technically. I don't think we can kill him for doing exactly what we wanted him to."

I arched a brow in my beg to differ, but Giana smoothed her thumb over it before leaning in for a long, slow kiss.

"I don't want him," she said against my lips. "You've had me since the first fake kiss."

I let out a deeper exhale with that, wrapping her up. "That kiss was *not* fake."

Giana buried her head in my chest for only a moment before she hopped off my lap altogether, grabbing me by the wrists and tugging me up, too.

"Come on. We have a game to win," she said, tossing me my t-shirt. I caught her wrist when she did and pulled her back into me.

"I think we already won."

She smiled against my kiss, letting me dip her back before she shoved me off again.

"Shirt. Now," she said, snapping her fingers and pointing at the cloth in my hand. "You can try another tabbed scene on me later."

"Oh, trust me. I plan to. The ones you highlighted in *Sated Love...*"

Her cheeks burned bright red before she was smacking me in the chest and shoving me toward the front door.

"Get your own breakfast, you book stealer," she barked.

But that didn't stop her from melting into me when I pulled her in for one last kiss on my way out.

"COME ON, BOYS! HOLD 'EM!"

Coach Sanders's voice rang out over the roar of the crowd, almost thirty-thousand people in the stands —

most of them wearing the other team's colors. The Waterville University Bandits were the largest in the state, and they drowned out the NBU students who had dedicated themselves enough to make the drive from Boston to cheer us on.

It had been like that all four quarters.

Rain assaulted us yet again this game, only this time, it was cold enough to turn to sleet, a nasty mixture of rain and snow that made the playing conditions absolutely horrendous. I was already so sore and tired that I thought my body would revolt when I bent into position for the next play, training my mind on our one goal.

Stop the Bandits offense from getting the first down.

They were only up by three points, and with a little over a minute left to play, that was enough time for us to get the ball down the field far enough for Riley to kick and tie the game for overtime. But if they got even one more first down here, they'd be in field goal range — and that would put us down by a touchdown.

The ball was snapped, and I fired off the line, chasing after the wide receiver I was covering. I had him, no matter how he tried to juke and break away. The quarterback's wild eyes as he frantically searched the backfield told me my teammates were doing their jobs well.

There was nowhere for him to throw, and the poor sucker ran out of time.

One of our defenders blasted through the line, wrapping the quarterback up and taking him down in a sack that made the stadium go quiet, save for the roaring little corner of it that was filled with NBU students.

We celebrated on our way back to the sideline, the loss so big we knew they wouldn't dare a field goal. And as our special teams jogged out for the kick reception,

I guzzled down water and tried to preserve what little energy I had left for what was still to come.

It took every ounce of effort I had to keep my mind on the game and off Giana.

That was new for me. Football had had my full attention since I was a kid. Even when I was with Maliyah, the girl I thought I'd end up marrying, she faded easily to the back of my mind when it was game time.

It was different with Giana.

She was on the sideline, too, fielding reporters and camera crew with a cool, steel reserve. It shouldn't have made sense, how well she handled professionals at least five years older than her, some more than that. She also wrangled us as student athletes, which was akin to herding cats. But somehow over the last year and a half, she'd found her voice, her confidence. She spoke clearer and louder, knew what she was doing, and had the ability to look as cool as a cucumber while she did it.

It was hard not to watch, to admire — especially when I *also* knew how to unravel that well-put-together woman when it was just the two of us.

Zeke catching the ball down at the ten snapped me back to the present, and I watched him zoom almost thirty yards before he was taken down. I kept my focus on the field as Holden ran out with the offense next, leading them in a myriad of plays that got us well within field goal range.

But we didn't need it.

Leo Hernandez took a snap that should have just been a short run, but he found an opening and bolted, juking every defender who caught up too slowly to do anything but watch him fly past them.

And just like that, we scored a touchdown with mere seconds left on the clock.

It was just enough time for Riley to kick the extra point, and for the Bandits to get one Hail Mary play in that resulted in nothing.

We won.

And I was convinced we were fucking unstoppable.

●━●━●

Even a long, piping hot shower couldn't thaw my bones after a freezing cold game in the sleet, but I felt marginally better once I was dressed in my sweats. The team was jovial as we showered and dressed and got ready to get on the bus, one that would take us to our hotel for the night. I had no doubt the team would be going out to celebrate.

I, on the other hand, had much different plans.

"So, what shithole bar are we hitting tonight?" Leo asked, towel around his neck as he waggled his brows at me.

"I found one called *The Looney Bin*," Riley answered, showing her phone with the reviews she'd been reading. "College bar. Apparently pretty strict on fakes, but that's never stopped us before."

"Look at Novo getting in the spirit," Leo praised.

"After a win like that?" Riley threw a thumb over her shoulder. "We're essentially guaranteed a bowl."

"Not just a bowl game," Zeke added, tossing his arm around her before he kissed her temple. "*The* bowl game."

I started bobbing my head, drumming out a beat on the lockers as I did. "*Ship. Ship. Ship. Ship.*"

I chanted and danced until the rest of the team joined in, and before long, there were hollers and screams ringing out, guys standing on the benches or literally hanging from the rafters. It was absolute chaos in the most incredible way — the way only a team on the brink of greatness truly understood.

I was wrapped up in watching it all unfold when a pair of cool hands covered my eyes.

I smiled, ready to whip around and drag Giana into me for a kiss that I'd been dying to give her since the beginning of the game. But it wasn't her voice that cooed, "Guess who?"

It was Maliyah's.

I stiffened, peeling her fingers off me before I turned with a bored expression on my face.

She was freshly showered, her long blonde hair in a wet, messy bun on top of her head, and oversized cheer sweats covering her from neck to toe. Despite my non-enthusiastic greeting, she held a wide smile, bouncing on her toes a bit.

"Great game, babe."

I grimaced at the nickname, but chose to ignore it as I turned back to my locker and began packing up my bag. "Thanks."

"So, when do I get that date?" she asked, leaning between me and the locker to block me from grabbing my cleats. I frowned at first, confused before I remembered the stupid fucking team auction.

"You do realize it's not a real date, right?"

"That's what I paid for," she argued as I politely scooted her to the side so I could finish getting my shit together. "Besides, we haven't had any real time together since I got to NBU."

"And whose fault is that?"

Her expression flattened, but she shook it off, forcing a smile. "I've missed you. It would be good for us to have some alone time. Time to talk."

"I don't have anything to talk to you about."

"Clay—"

"Look, you can have the picnic voucher and take someone who actually gives a fuck about you," I said, slamming my locker shut before I shrugged my bag over one shoulder. "Or you can take me and we can sit there in silence. Your choice."

I didn't know why anger was licking its way so fiercely up my spine. Maybe it was my father's voice in my ear, how he pointed out the manipulative tactics I never realized she used against me. Or maybe it was Giana, how she made me promise to put myself first and not be shy about it.

Either way, I had zero interest in playing this game any longer with my ex.

"I highly doubt we'd sit there in silence," Maliyah countered, still trying to laugh it off. I saw in her eyes that she was about to reach out and touch me, but before she could, I ducked away and headed for the door.

She was hot on my heels.

"What the fuck is your problem?" she demanded, catching me by the arm and turning me to face her. I could have easily shrugged her off if I wanted to, but maybe part of me was ready for the fight.

"My *problem*?" I asked incredulously, and I didn't care if half the guys left in the locker room had stopped celebrating now and were very tuned in to our conversation. I stepped into her, towering over her as she sank away. "I'm happy, Li."

I paused, letting those words sink in as I breathed over her. Her narrowed eyes softened, something like pain flashing in those blue irises.

"Can you accept that and just... fucking *let me be happy*?"

I waited for only a moment to see if she had anything to say to that, and when she didn't utter a word, I just shook my head and turned, leaving her and the rest of the team behind as I headed for the bus.

●●●

I waited until most of the team had gone out, until all the coaches had retired to their rooms and put Holden in charge of letting them know if anything went wrong. I almost felt bad for our QB, our captain, our most responsible leader. He wore a lot of weight on his shoulders.

But he wore it proudly.

"You sure you don't want to come?" he asked me at the door of our hotel room, and I knew he was asking less because he wanted me to party, and more because he didn't want to be alone with the motley crew we called a team — especially after such a win.

I smiled. "Sorry, man. I've got other plans."

Holden smirked at that, but he didn't make to head out. He just watched me, his eyes assessing.

"What?"

He shrugged. "Nothing. I just... I'm sorry, about what I said earlier this season. About Giana being a rebound. I can tell she's much more than that for you."

I grabbed the back of my neck. "Well, honestly... you weren't wrong. At least, not at first. But now?" I shook my head. "I'm so far gone for that girl it's fucking terrifying."

Holden laughed. "Yeah, well, I wouldn't know what that feels like. But I trust you. And I'm happy for you." He pointed at me then. "Just stay focused on the season, okay? And don't let your grades slip. You can spend all spring doting on her, but I need you for a few more months."

"Aye, aye, captain," I said with a salute. "You really have never been like this with a girl?"

"Come on, Johnson," he said, thumping his chest. "You know football is the only love of my life."

I arched a brow. "Yeah... we'll see how long that lasts."

He just smiled on his way out the door, and as soon as he was gone, I texted Giana to make sure the coast was clear.

Fortunately, she didn't have to share a hotel room the way the guys on the team did — she and Riley were the only ones afforded that luxury. Even when Charlotte came, she was too bougie to share a room with an employee. But she hadn't come to this game at all, leaving it completely in Giana's hands while she attended a friend's wedding on the other side of the country.

That, alone should have told Giana and everyone else how good she was at her job.

I snuck quietly down the hall to the elevator, taking it two floors up to where Giana's room was. She opened the door before I could even knock, pulling me inside and immediately melting into my arms.

Her scent invaded me, hair freshly shampooed and smelling like raspberries as she kissed me deep and long. I inhaled that kiss, that woman, wrapping her up as tightly as I could as I blindly walked us inside her room.

"I've missed you," she breathed against my lips.

"You saw me this morning. And all game."

"Shut up and tell me you've missed me, too."

I chuckled, still kissing her as I laid her in the bed, and everything about her was comfortable and pure. Her wet hair, her warm skin, her oversized t-shirt and tiny sleep shorts that I loved so much — it all felt like home.

She felt like home.

"I've missed you, too," I murmured, sliding between her legs and framing her with my biceps on the bed. "I've missed your smile," I said, kissing her lips. "And your laugh." Another kiss as she laughed to appease me. "And the feel of you wrapped around me."

She took the cue, ankles hooking behind my ass as she pulled me down for a deeper kiss. Her tongue was eager, meeting mine on the heels of a soft whimper as she rolled her body against mine.

I groaned, pinning her hips against the bed to stop her. "Woman," I warned.

"I'm fine," she protested, fighting against my hold. "It'll hurt for a second, yes, but I want it. I want *you*."

Jesus Christ.

How any man could deny Giana Jones was beyond me.

I certainly wasn't the man to try, not with her gripping me and pulling me into her and demanding that I give her more.

It was different than last night, our moves slower and softer as we took turns undressing one another. I peppered kisses down her abdomen when her shirt was gone, helping her out of her sleep shorts before I settled between her thighs ready to feast.

It was an addiction, how my body hummed to life at the sound of her pleasure. I reveled in the fact that it was me giving it to her, that she twisted her hands in the sheets more and more with every swipe of my tongue over her.

I took my time, kissing and licking and sucking until her pussy was soaked and swollen and aching for relief. I wanted her nice and warm and ready for me to help combat the soreness I knew she was experiencing after her first time.

When she started spreading her legs wider, eyes squeezing shut as she chased her release, I slowed, kissing my way back up to her mouth.

"No," she mewled, and I laughed against her lips before rolling us so she was on top.

"So impatient," I teased.

She straddled my waist, her slick lips gliding along my shaft without a barrier between us. We both hissed at the sensation, and before I could stop her, Giana rolled her hips to do it again, to feel me slip between her lips and tease her entrance.

She sank, just an inch, just enough to fit my crown at the tight opening of her.

Enough for both of us to see stars.

I gripped her hips hard, halting her as I groaned through every urge that beast inside me was signaling to slam her down on my cock and fill her up, raw and without restraint. Somehow, I managed a breath, managed to reach over for the condom I'd sat on the nightstand and roll it over me.

Then, Giana's hands found my chest, and I held myself steady for her as she slowly lowered down.

When the tip of me sank inside her, we both moaned, her nails digging into my flesh as I gripped her ass in equal measure. I helped lift her, just a little before she sank down even more.

"Oh God," she breathed, rolling her hips as she repeated the motion. "It feels so fucking good like this."

I loosened my grip on her, letting her take control and letting *myself* appreciate the full fucking beauty of her naked body as she rode me. She rolled it as she found her rhythm, sinking a bit more each time until finally, she took all of me inside her.

She gasped, and I bit back a groan at the feeling of her walls clenching around me. "Fucking *Christ*, Kitten," I cursed, my words rasped as she pressed up onto her knees, coming all the way off before she sank down again in one fluid motion.

"Yes," she breathed, eyes fluttering shut. "More."

Balancing her in my lap, I maneuvered until I was sitting up, my back against the headboard as I shoved pillows out of our way and took her fully in my lap. In the new position, I could open my thighs, could take the weight of her as she rode and meet her with thrusts that drove me even deeper inside her.

She trembled at the depth, wrapping her arms around me and kissing me hard as she wound and rolled and ground her clit against my pelvis with every thrust.

"I fucking love when you ride my cock," I husked, sliding my hand up between her heaving breasts. Up and up it went until my fingers could curl around her throat, my palm hot against her esophagus as I claimed her gasp for my own. "You love it, too, don't you, Kitten?"

"Yes," she whimpered.

"Show me how much you love it," I commanded, gripping her a little tighter as my other hand helped her ride. "Ride my cock until you come so hard you scream my fucking name."

It was almost too brutal for only her second time having sex, but just like she had last night, she bloomed for me under the filthy instruction, panting and moaning more and more with every dirty word I whispered in her ear.

She loved it like this, rough and raw and possessive — and I'd give her exactly what she wanted for as long as I had the pleasure.

The more she rode, the faster her movements became, the harder it was for me to focus on *anything* other than her pussy hugging my cock. But I stayed focused, sucking her nipple in my mouth as her movements became more wild and chaotic. Eventually, she was trying to move so fast that she wasn't moving at all, and I took control, holding her to me as I pounded into her at the pace she needed for her release.

And she found it.

Her cries built more and more until she was full-on screaming, so loudly that I clamped a hand over her mouth to drown them out. I didn't miss how my name sounded in those muffled cries against my palm, and I ate that shit up, fucking her hard and fast until she fell completely limp in my arms.

"Oh... my... *God*," she breathed when I released my grip.

I smirked, kissing her hair and half-expecting her to stop then. I knew she was spent, knew she *had* to be sore, and with her orgasm no longer something she could chase against the pain, I wouldn't have faulted her for wanting to stop.

But slowly, she began riding me again.

Her hips rolled, soft moans escaping from her lips as she adjusted to me again. Her pussy was even tighter somehow, swollen from release, and I savored the way it felt to plunge into her each and every time.

"Roll over," I demanded, and before she could obey, I did it for her — flipping her off me and onto her stomach before I was straddling her from behind. I hiked her hips up to meet my pelvis, positioning myself at her entrance before I drove all the way in.

"*Fuuuuck,*" she hissed, arching her back. I took the cue to grab a fistful of her damp hair, holding onto it tightly and restricting her from moving her neck back to neutral. I kept her arched, her eyes cast up to the ceiling as I pumped into her.

It was sensational, the way she felt, the way she *looked* — completely sated and yet entirely focused on making sure I found the same release. Her hungry eyes looked back over her shoulder when I finally released her hair, both hands gripping her hips, instead, as I watched the lips of her pussy suction to my cock each time I withdrew.

"I wish you could see this view," I told her, slowing down and taking my time with every new thrust. "The way you're stretching open for me, how your tight little pussy hugs my cock every time I pull out."

"Clay," she moaned, and then in a move I was *not* expecting, she lowered her chest down to the bed and reached through her legs, through *mine*, until her fingertips gently caressed my balls.

The noise that came from me was one I didn't recognize, and I saw a whole universe of stars as she did the move again. I could barely keep pace, barely focus on anything with her touching me there, and with more confidence when I didn't tell her to stop, she rolled them in her palm, squeezing with just the right amount of pressure to drive me over the edge.

"Oh fuck, Giana. I... I..."

I couldn't even warn her, couldn't say a fucking word as my release spilled violently from me, taking every ounce of awareness I had and focusing on that one euphoric feeling. I pounded into her, savoring every thrust of my release like it was the sweetest drug.

And it was.

She was.

It was the longest orgasm I'd ever had, one that continued to assault me with wave after wave even when I was sure it was over. I didn't know if it was her hands on my balls or just *her*, period, but I was so fucking spent by the time I stopped coming, it was all I could do to carefully pull out of her and roll to the side, my chest heaving, lungs burning from the exercise.

"Holy shit," Giana said, crawling over until she was lying on my chest. "Is it... is it always like this?"

"Never," I answered honestly, and I cocked a brow at her before we both erupted in laughter.

I pulled her into me then, our legs tangling together as we held onto each other and traced lines on our bare skin as our breathing slowly calmed.

Eventually, our breaths evened out, the room growing quieter, more still. I ran my fingers through her hair, pressing a soft kiss to her forehead as something achingly foreign pulled at my heart.

"I'm yours," she whispered, as if she knew where my spiral was taking me, how I was picturing a day when she'd decide I wasn't enough for her, a day when she'd walk away and leave me in her dust.

I swallowed against the tightness that built in my throat at the nightmarish thought, choosing to find comfort in her words instead of questioning the truth of them.

"And I'm yours," I whispered back.

Her arms tightened around me, and for one night, everything was perfect.

We should have known it could never stay that way.

Chapter 24

GIANA

In all my favorite movies, and in all my favorite books, there's this moment that I like to call *the cotton candy cloud* moment.

It's usually at the beginning, but sometimes a little toward the end, when everything is working out perfectly for the main character. They're high on life, everything going their way, and they bear an impenetrable smile as they seemingly float through every day on a cloud of fluffy pink and purple sugar. It usually happens right before everything crashes down.

That was me.

I was having my cotton candy cloud moment.

And there was no crash in sight.

Charlotte was so impressed after the auction and especially by me handling our away game in Maine that she offered to extend my contract through next season — and with that came a signing bonus and a raise. I was shocked to silence when she first told me, but she'd only smiled and arched a brow.

"Your determination to prove everyone wrong about you worked," she said. "But now, I want you to ask yourself what it is you really want from this. And then, I want you to take it."

Her belief in me had stoked a fire, making me consider all the ways my career could pan out. It was intoxicating to think about.

But nothing was as intoxicating as Clay.

I woke up with him in my bed almost every morning, and on the ones I didn't, he would be at my door within seconds of me waking. Classes dragged by, practice always seemed too long, and even happy as I was in my job, I couldn't wait for the work day to be done, for the interviews and publicity events to end.

I couldn't wait to be back in his arms.

Every moment he spent unraveling me was ecstasy, my body singing like never before under his symphonic conduction. Just when I thought I'd found my favorite way to have him touch me or fill me, he'd find a new way, something to excite me and surprise me and bring me pleasure not even my books could rival.

And that wasn't even the best part.

The *best* moments were when we were wrapped together in the early hours of the morning, talking and laughing and discovering one another more than just physically. Or when we'd have a whole conversation across the crowded practice field with just one single glance. Or when anxiety would start to creep in for one of us, and the other would quickly soothe it with just the right words and a kiss to seal the promise.

"What would you think about coming home with me for Christmas?"

I blanched at Clay's question one morning, the first words he spoke in the early light.

"To California?"

He nodded.

My heart burst at how he looked at me, with reverence and a tinge of fear. I held onto that gaze as I curled into him, wrapping my arms around his waist and lying my head on his chest.

"On two conditions."

"Name them."

"One, you meet my dad when he comes in a couple weeks for my sister's award ceremony."

"Done."

I smiled into his chest.

"And two?"

"Two," I said, drawing a circle on his stomach with my finger. "You have to teach me how to surf."

"I can't surf."

"Then we can both learn."

"It'll be freezing."

I peeked up at him. "I bet we can find ways to warm up after."

His sleepy grin matched mine, and then he kissed me, and I was the happiest girl in the world.

Every day was a gift, shinier and more promising than the last, and I floated on my little cotton candy cloud in pure, unbreakable bliss.

Even when Maliyah tried to rip me off and throw me to the cold hard earth.

I was in the stadium bathroom about a week after our win against the Bandits, wiping under my eyes from where my mascara had run. It had been a long day, especially with Kyle Robbins signing yet *another* deal that meant I was committed to helping him through a photoshoot for a sports drink. Honestly, I couldn't fault him.

If I could make a couple hundred-thousand dollars for a photoshoot, I'd do it, too.

As I reapplied my lipstick and tried to give my hair back some of the volume that the humid cold had brought, Maliyah whipped through the door.

She paused at the sight of me, swallowing as her eyes trailed me from head to toe. I expected her to go into one of the stalls, but instead, she walked straight toward the sinks, flicking on the water as she began to wash her hands.

"Long day?" she asked, arching a brow but not really looking at me.

I swallowed, but kept my focus on my reflection. "Seems like they're all that way during the season."

"Tell me about it. I long for the day when I can sleep in past six again."

She smiled with the comment, and I had to actively fight to keep the confusion off my face.

Was she actually trying to have a conversation with me?

As she dried her hands, she leaned a hip against the bathroom counter, facing me. "So... things with you and Clay seem pretty serious."

Oh, God.

Here it comes.

I didn't know how to respond, so I just smiled.

"He's a good man," she said, her voice softer, brows folding together. "I didn't realize that until it was too late."

"He is," I agreed.

"And he deserves to be happy," she added. "It... well, quite frankly, it infuriates me that you do that. That you weren't just a rebound like a lot of us thought."

I couldn't tell if she wanted to make me upset with that last comment, but the truth was all I could do was smile to myself at all the missing pieces she'd never know.

That *no one* would ever know.

"Anyway, I just want to apologize if I've come off a little... bitchy," she said after a moment. "I was threatened by you."

I couldn't help the laugh that bubbled out of me. "I can't imagine why."

"Neither could I at first," she said, unflinchingly. "But look who got the guy."

I pressed my lips together.

Maliyah watched me for far too long, long enough that I considered saying goodbye and pushing past her. But before I could, she took a step toward me, lowering her voice.

"But let me just be clear," she said, looking down her nose at me. "I want him to be happy. I'll leave him alone. But the *second* you slip up, I'll be here, waiting." She smiled, the curl of her lips making my stomach drop. "And I promise, if I get him back?" Her eyebrow hiked as she eyed me. "He won't remember your name, let alone why he ever wanted you."

My jaw tightened, heart spiking with the kind of fight-or-flight response I imagine my ancestors used to feel when getting chased by a predator.

But I reminded myself that I wasn't defenseless.

I had a fucking sword of a tongue.

"And I promise *you*," I said, stepping up to her just as much. "That you won't get the chance."

I smiled sweetly, patting her on the shoulder as I pushed past her.

Every molecule in me wanted to jump and thrust my fist into the air in victory when I swung out of that bathroom, but I kept my cool, walking slowly and calmly all the way back to my office.

No one could knock me off my cloud.

⬤ ⬤ ⬤

I was practically prancing across campus on the first Monday of November, the bitter chill of the air not enough to wipe the smile from my face as I ducked into the coffee shop and ordered my usual. When I had the steaming latte in hand, I turned for the door.

And ran right into Shawn.

"Whoa," he said, grabbing my upper arms to steady me with a grin. "Easy there, you're going to knock someone out with all the sunshine you're bouncing around with."

I laughed on a breath, tucking my curls behind my ear as I righted myself. "Hi," I said, and instantly, my cheeks flushed — not because of the warmth of the coffee shop or my latte, but from the way Shawn watched me, from how I'd completely blown him off after the night at his apartment without so much as a text to explain why.

He looked like a mix between a dog that had been kicked, and the poor sucker who'd kicked it and then regretted it.

"Hi," he replied.

He slid his hands into his pockets, eyes washing over me as his brows bent together.

"You look great," he said after a moment. "Happy."

"I am," I said easily, a genuine smile finding my lips. "I really am."

"Good." Shawn nodded, rolling his lips together against what he wanted to say before it burst free. "Are you... did you and Clay break up?"

"What?" I frowned, shaking my head. "No."

"No," Shawn repeated, deadpan. "What do you mean, *no*?"

"I mean, no, we didn't break up. We're still together and..." I smiled, shaking my head. "We're amazing."

Shawn looked like I'd just punched him in the stomach.

"Giana, come on... you're not stupid. Please tell me you don't believe what you just said."

My brows shot up into my hairline, and I stared at him incredulously for one moment before I turned on my heels. "Wow. Goodbye, Shawn."

He followed me despite the farewell and my attempt to shut the glass door behind me before he could catch it.

"He isn't good for you, he isn't good *period*."

I spun to face him. "You don't even know him."

"I know how he treats you," he said, his nose flaring, chest puffing like he was my shining knight riding in to save me. "That's enough."

I fought the urge to laugh, letting out a long, slow sigh. "Shawn, I promise — it's not all that I made it seem. You don't—"

"Don't tell me I don't understand. I saw how he made you cry, how he made you feel worthless and disrespected with his mouth on another girl's body right in front of you."

I battled with the decision on whether to tell him about the whole ruse, but decided it wasn't for him — or anyone else — to know.

"We've worked through things," I landed on, reaching out to squeeze Shawn's forearm. "And I'm sorry I brought you into the situation. I shouldn't have. It was wrong of me, and selfish. But... we're okay now. We're *better* than okay."

Shawn shook his head. "Don't you see? This is how guys like him work. They'll push and push you until you're on the edge of leaving, and then they'll do whatever it takes to lure you back in. It's *him* who's the selfish one."

My defenses shot up, more for Clay than for myself. "I'm done having this conversation. You don't know him. You don't know *me,* for that matter."

"That's not for my lack of trying."

I blew out a breath, though I couldn't deny how his words stung. It wasn't like me to play games with people, and though I hadn't really intended to — that was exactly what I'd done with him.

"I have to go," I said. "Take care, okay?"

Before he could say another word, I turned, heading toward the stadium and leaving him on the sidewalk outside the café. I felt bad for him, for the game we'd played that had worked so well. We'd fooled him and Maliyah and everyone else around us, too.

But I shook it off, deciding it was better to leave all that in the past.

And I continued floating on, basking in my sugary, pastel paradise.

Chapter 25

CLAY

I'd forgotten about her.

Perhaps that was the wrong way to phrase it, because it sounded like I never thought about my mom — and I did. I thought about how I couldn't wait to introduce her to Giana, how delighted she'd be when I told her we were coming home for Christmas. I thought about her cooking in the kitchen with G, teaching her how to make our favorite salmon croquets, and pulling out old photo albums of me as a kid while I pretended to be embarrassed.

But I'd forgotten about her quitting her job because she thought her ex would take care of her.

I'd forgotten how beat up she was mentally and emotionally, how she was having trouble doing more than getting out of bed, let alone looking for a job. I'd forgotten about her using, about the way I could tell by her words slurring over the phone.

Maybe it was because she hadn't called after the last time, when I took out a student loan and sent her enough money to get through at least a month, if not two. Maybe it was because I wanted to assume the best, that she was okay, that she was working on getting a job and finding herself. Maybe it was because I was so caught up in Giana that I simply hadn't thought about anything else.

Regardless, the fact that I'd forgotten about her struck me like a frying pan to the head when her face lit up my screen after practice on a Thursday afternoon in early November.

My stomach dropped, veins running icy cold as I stared at the word *Mom* and felt the phone vibrating in my hand. It was selfish, how I didn't want to answer because I didn't want to face her misery, her pain, her tears.

And the fact that once again, I'd have to find a way to help her.

I was running out of ideas.

My heart was heavy, a sandpaper knot in my throat as I slid my thumb across the bottom of the screen and plugged my headphones in, setting my pace toward my dorm room.

"Hey, Mom," I answered. "You okay?"

"Oh, sweetie," she answered on a sniff, the words garbled by crying.

I braced myself.

"I'm *more* than okay."

Something more like confusion, rather than relief, found my next exhale, especially as Mom continued to cry as I waited for her to explain.

"We've been blessed with a miracle," she said. "The Lord has shined his almighty light upon us."

I stopped walking. "Holy shit, did you win the lottery?"

"Language!" She chastised with a laugh. "And I guess you could say I did."

"Mom, what's going on?"

I continued walking, hiking my bag up over my shoulder.

"It's Cory."

I frowned, and though I had no reason to be anxious, something inside me was on high alert. "Cory? As in Maliyah's dad?"

"The very one," she confirmed. "I don't know what happened. I mean, Maliyah called me last night to catch up — which was *so nice*, by the way. I haven't really talked to her since you two split up, and it was just so lovely to hear from her."

My lips flattened. "Mm-hmm."

"Anyway, so we were talking, and you know how close we are. She's always given me such great advice when it comes to men." She paused. "Should be the other way around, ages considered."

"Mom," I said, dragging her back to the point.

"Well, I was telling her about the restaurant, and about... about Brandon." Her voice cracked a little with his name. "And she was just so sweet, listening to me being all heartbroken." She sniffed. "And I guess she must have told her dad about the whole thing, because he called me earlier today."

I waited, heart picking up pace in my chest like it knew well before I did that something was wrong.

"He's going to help us, baby," she said, all joy through her tears. "He came by this afternoon with a check for ten-thousand dollars."

"He *what*?!"

"I know! I know," she said, like I was excited when the truth was I was fucking appalled. "He wanted us to have enough to get through the holidays, so I could focus on getting better instead of getting a job. Oh, I can't tell you the relief it brought me. I feel... I feel... *loved*."

She choked on the word, all while I tried to force a calming breath.

"He's a good man. A good father," she added. "Much better than your own. If I'd have been a smarter woman, I would have gone on a date with *him* when they all came into my diner that night."

"Mom."

"Oh, I'm only teasing," she said, and I could picture her waving me off even as we both knew she wasn't joking, not even a little bit.

"I don't understand," I said. "What... *why* did he do this?"

"Because he's a good, Christian man," she said, almost defensively. "And because he saw someone who needed help, and he happens to be in the position of helping."

I swallowed.

Cory *was* a good man. Hadn't I just argued that point to my father? Hadn't I wished the very same thing Mom had, that it was Cory in our life instead of Dad?

So why was my stomach curdling like bad milk?

"This is a good thing, sweetheart. And I can pay you back for what you sent, so you can pay off that loan before it even has time to accrue interest. It's all working out, don't you see?"

But I couldn't see anything but red.

Because I knew that while Cory had the means to help many people, he rarely ever did without wanting something in return.

"Mom, I need to go."

"Okay, honey. I love you. It's all good now. I'll be sending you a check, okay?"

I couldn't even manage to acknowledge her further before I was hanging up with shaking hands, and immediately thumbing through my contacts for Maliyah's number. I typed out a text.

We need to talk. Now.

The bubbles bounced on the screen, then went away.

I gritted my teeth as I marched the rest of the way across campus, and I'd just swung through my dorm room door when my phone buzzed.

I have class until six. Meet after?

I only responded with a thumbs up emoji and my dorm number, although I was pretty sure she already knew it, and then I promptly threw my phone down, dragging my hands back through my hair as I tried to figure out what the hell was going on. It was only four now, and I was going to drive myself insane trying to piece this all together in the time I had until Maliyah could meet.

I was just about to hop in the shower — a cold one — when my phone rang.

Cory Vail was the name staring back at me.

My throat thickened, and I forced a breath before answering. "Hello?"

"Hello, son," his deep voice echoed back. "How are you?"

The emotions that warred inside me then were too much to bear, a cross between familial pride and the wariness of a cornered animal.

"I'm having an interesting afternoon," I answered, leaving the ball in his court.

He chuckled. "I imagine so. Your mom said she called and told you."

"She did."

The line was silent.

I cleared my throat. "Thank you, sir, for... for helping her."

"You don't sound particularly happy that I did."

I sighed, sinking into the old couch from 1972 that was assigned to each athletic dorm room. "I am. Truly, I am. I just..."

"You're wondering why I did it."

"Frankly? Yes."

"You're a smart boy," he assessed. "Smart man, soon to be. You know nothing really comes for free."

The hair on my neck prickled.

"Here's the truth of it, son — Maliyah has been miserable this last month or so. I know you can tell. I know you know as well as I do that it's because she misses you."

"She broke up with me," I ground out.

"I realize that," Cory replied, calm as ever. "But young women do a lot of things they regret. And as she's my daughter, it's my job as her dad to try to help her undo those wrongs if I can."

I shook my head. "I don't understand."

"It's simple. I take care of your mom," he said. "And you take care of my girl. It's as easy as that."

"No."

"No?" Cory's question back to me was incredulous.

"It's not easy, for more reasons than one. I don't want to take care of Maliyah anymore," I answered honestly. "And she made it clear that she doesn't want me."

"And clearly, she lied."

"Well, that's on her. I've moved on. I'm with someone else now."

"I think whoever it is you're with can't possibly have as much of a connection as you and Li now," he said, laughing like I was a child trying to explain something I knew nothing about. "You two grew up together. You were in a relationship for years. You can't have been with this new person for more than, what... a few months?"

"What Giana and I have is none of your business, respectfully."

My neck burned with anger, but I held my voice steady and as calm as I could.

"Fair enough," he said after a moment. "Well, my boy, the choice is yours. But if I were in your shoes, I know what mine would be." There was the sound of papers shuffling before he continued. "You can take my offer, or you can continue putting yourself into debt to haphazardly patch up a hole in the boat without actually fixing the problem."

I frowned.

"She needs rehab, Clay," he said, his voice lower, more serious.

I closed my eyes against the tears that seared my eyes at his words, at the truth in them that I'd hoped to deny until my dying day. My next inhale was stiff and full of fire.

"I don't expect you to know about this at your age. Hell, I don't *want* you to know about it. I don't want you to have to think about it — which is why I'm trying to..." He paused, like he caught himself rambling. "She's a functioning addict, son, and she needs real help. I can get her that. *We* can get her that."

I shook my head, even though he couldn't see me, *no one* could see me. But I had to non-verbally communicate to the fucking universe that I couldn't do this.

"I know it's not fair. I know it's hard. You're too young to have to make decisions like this. But trust me when I say this is just the start of hard choices that will line your life. And what you decide to do with this first one will define you as a man."

I choked on something between a laugh and a cry for help.

"Don't turn your back on your mom, Clay," he continued, his words hitting their intended target as my chest cracked open. "I watched your father do it, and I can't watch you do it, too. She needs you. And this is as easy as it's going to get to help her while also being able to keep what you want." He paused. "Football."

I swallowed, eyes glossing over as I stared at the floor.

"She hasn't cashed the check yet," he said quietly. "I just want to remind you of that."

Ice seared my veins. "So, you're blackmailing me."

"I'm making you a fair offer," he countered. "One you should take."

My nose flared.

After a long pause, Cory continued. "Think on it. I'll give you the night. Oh, and let's not tell Maliyah about this, okay? No need to involve the women we love in how the sausage gets made. We can handle it. Yes?"

I didn't answer, but he took my silence as affirmation.

"That's my boy. Alright, I need to run. We'll talk in the morning."

With that, the line went dead, and I collapsed into a heap, mind racing with everything that had just unfolded in the last hour.

And in that quiet dorm room, the weight of responsibility crushed me like a boulder.

He was right.

In so many ways, he was right.

I couldn't turn my back on my mother, but I also knew there wasn't much more I could do to help her. I wasn't there to help her get clean the way I had many times in high school, nourishing her as she went through all the ugly stages of withdrawal before finally feeling more like herself.

And I didn't have the financial means to help her, either.

I wasn't pro yet. I didn't have a job, didn't have *time* to get a job. And without the help from my dad, taking out more loans was the only answer — if I could even get approved for them.

Panic seized my chest, but it was a muted stress, like I was already dying and someone just told me as if I didn't already know. I felt eerily calm inside that overwhelm, as if I deserved this punishment, as if it was my own fault that Mom was an addict, that she was in the trouble she was in.

Even if I could convince myself it wasn't my fault, I couldn't do that if I walked away from her now, if I turned my back on the opportunity to quite literally save her life.

I closed my eyes, heart squeezing so painfully I doubled over as the cost of this weighed in on me.

Giana.

It would be *her* on the other end of this fake relationship, now — one I would never be able to tell her about. Maliyah would never know it wasn't real, either.

To her, to Giana, to *everyone*, it would be real — it would be me getting back together with my ex just like they thought I'd do all along.

Like *I* once thought I'd do.

Now, it made me sick to even think about.

I longed to have my own father there, to have him tell me what to do and actually be able to trust it. But he wasn't a man I admired, a man I wanted to be like.

Cory was.

My head spun, heart cracking more and more with each devastating blow.

I had no choice.

This was my mother. My *mother*. The woman who stayed with me, who kept me in the face of every odd, who provided for me and supported me and believed in me and *loved me*.

I couldn't leave her to fend for herself.

It didn't matter if Giana would never understand, if *no one* would. This was the choice I had to make not only as a man, but as a son.

She depended on me.

And unlike my father, I wouldn't let her down.

No matter the pain and hell it would cause me.

Chapter 26

GIANA

I had *entirely* too much hair to be whipping it around in such a passionate show of head banging, but I didn't care.

My curls bounced and flew around me as I danced and sang to Lizzo on the Friday night before our home game against the Hawks, glasses sliding down the bridge of my nose with every pump of my hips. The spatula in my hand was the microphone, the fuzzy socks on my feet serving as perfect twirling material when I sashayed from the stove to the sink to drain the angel hair pasta.

My phone buzzed with the number that automatically rang when someone hit the button next to my apartment number outside, letting me know Clay was here. I tapped the code to let him in and felt my smile growing wider without me even willing it to. I texted him right after.

Door's unlocked.

The homemade vodka sauce I'd put together bubbled precariously on the stove, so I turned the heat down before bending to check on the cheesy garlic bread toasting in the oven. The sausage was already done, covered in foil in the microwave to keep it warm. My entire apartment smelled like an Italian heaven, and my stomach grumbled just as my front door slowly creaked open.

Clay didn't even stand a chance of a normal greeting, not before I skipped over to him and grabbed his wrists, pulling him the rest of the way through the door and kicking it closed with my foot behind us.

I mouthed the words to the song just as my favorite part came on, and I even made a little *hang ten* gesture with my hand as I pretended it was a shot I was throwing back in time with the lyrics. The beat was intoxicating, and I pulled Clay to the middle of my living room floor, doing a little spin under his hand before I let him go altogether and turned around just in time to drop it down in a twerk for him.

He should have laughed.

He should have been dancing with me, being a silly fool like we always were together.

At the very least, he should have had his hands on me after that twerk situation, because I *knew* my ass looked good in these sweatpants.

Instead, he watched me with a long, expressionless face, his eyes far off and distant.

And my heart bottomed out at the sight.

"Shit," I said, running over to my phone to pause the song and pull the vodka sauce off the burner. I took the bread out of the oven before rushing back to him. "What's wrong? Did something happen at practice?" My eyes shot open wider when I thought of the next possi-bility. "Oh God, are you hurt? Did you get injured?"

I grabbed him by the arms, taking in the full length of him in search of anything that might be bandaged or bleeding. When I didn't find anything, I let my gaze find his again.

And the misery staring back at me stole my next breath.

"Clay..." I warned. "What is it? You're scaring me."

I saw every ounce of effort he put into trying to keep his face straight, into trying to remain emotionless. But slowly, little by little, he gave himself away. His eye-brows bent, nostrils flaring, bottom lip quivering just once before he blew out a breath and pulled out of my grip.

I stood there in his absence, feeling the cool wind of him brushing past me. When I turned, he was facing the kitchen, his back to me, hands clasped on top of his head as his back muscles flexed with every haggard breath.

"Clay," I tried, fear prickling my nerves.

He stood there silent for so long, I almost said his name again. But then finally, his hands fell to his side, and he pulled his shoulders back, holding his chin high as he turned to face me once more.

"It's over, G."

I frowned, confusion sparring with the anxiety nig-gling at my belly. "What's over?"

His throat constricted. "Us."

I laughed. It was automatic, even as I frowned and shook my head and felt tears burning behind my eyes. "What? Don't be ridiculous. What are you talking about?"

When he didn't answer, all laughter ceased.

"Clay, what are you saying right now? What are you... What..."

Everything I tried to ask was cut off by the absolute refusal of me to accept what he was saying. I shook my head, over and over, crossing my arms over myself as I stared at him and took in all the pain he was clearly feeling.

"It was all a game to me," he said, his voice stoic and unmoved, eyes glossed over. "I'm sorry I used you, that I pretended like I wanted to be with you. I had to do what it took to get Maliyah back."

A single tear fell over my cheek, so fast I couldn't catch it with the swipe of my hand that came too late. "Get Maliyah back?" I echoed.

"She came over last night," he said, and the coldness in his voice made me shiver like a tree in a storm. "We talked, and she wants to be together again. It's what I want, too. I'm just sorry I pulled you into this."

My face warped with betrayal and emotion, stomach turning so violently I doubled over a bit with the pain. But then I stood again, staring at him through my blurred vision.

And again, his façade slipped.

His bottom lip trembled so bad he wiped his hand over his face to cover it, and then he hung his hands on his hips and turned away from me again to hide the rest.

I narrowed my eyes in suspicion.

And then I charged.

"Bullshit," I seethed, shoving him from behind. He stumbled forward before turning to face me just in time for me to push him again. "This is all bullshit and I know it. Why are you doing this? What the fuck is going on, Clay?"

"I just told you what's going on. This has been my plan all along," he said, voice louder, and I watched as he willed himself with all his might to be angry, to glare down at me — but he failed pathetically, and tears filled his eyes, falling over his cheeks as my heart broke with the sight.

I reached out for him, swiping the wetness from his face before I held his cheeks in my hands.

"Don't do this," I begged. "I don't know what's going on, but please, *don't* do this."

His face twisted in grief, and he turned away from me but leaned into my palm, closing his eyes and releasing another wave of tears before he peeled my hands off him.

"I have to go," he whispered, brushing past me.

But before he could reach the door, I ripped him back.

"Stop!" I screamed. "Stop this right now. Look at me," I begged, grabbing his chin in my hands and forcing him. "Look at *yourself*. You don't mean this. You don't mean any of it." I shook my head. "You don't."

"Please," he pleaded, and as more tears filled his eyes, he tried to pull away from me. I didn't know if it was shame from crying, or shame from what he was saying, or both. "I can't."

"You can't *what*?" I asked desperately, trying to read between the lines.

He shook his head, freeing my hands from him before he kissed my fingertips and let them go completely. "You deserve to be happy, Giana. I want you to be happy. Just... move on. Go be with Shawn and—"

"I DON'T WANT TO BE WITH SHAWN," I cried, pressing back into his space. I pushed up onto my toes, wrapped my arms around his neck and refused to leave any distance between us when I whispered, "I want to be with *you*."

He cracked, a sob breaking through his veneer as I slammed my mouth over his, tasting the fresh tears there. His arms wrapped fully around me, and he kissed me like he fucking *hated* me, like I was the absolute bane of his existence.

And then, he pushed me back.

"I have to go," he said, voice cracking as he went for the door.

"Whatever it is, *who*ever it is you think you're helping, you're breaking the promise you made to me," I said to his back, and I knew I was right, knew I'd struck a nerve when he stopped abruptly, his back heaving with every breath.

Carefully, I moved around him, bending to catch his gaze.

"The promise you made to *yourself*," I reminded him.

He closed his eyes, letting out a long, hot exhale. "I have to."

"Have to *what*? What are you doing, exactly?"

But he wouldn't answer me. He just shook his head, all his effort going toward strangling the emotion desperately trying to break free.

And in an instant, in a snap of a band I didn't realized was stretched so thin, I went from sad and hurt to all-encompassing anger.

"You're a coward, Clay Johnson," I whispered.

His eyes snapped to mine, pain laden in them, but I didn't care.

He was hurting me, too.

"You're a coward, and a fool, and this isn't what you want, and I *know* it." I shook my head. "Let me in. Tell me what happened. Tell me and we can fix it *together*."

Clay just stared at me, his nostrils flaring as his eyes wandered over the length of my face like he was savoring every inch of it and storing it in his memory.

Like he'd never see me again.

And that broke me.

"Fine!" I screamed, and in a move that surprised both of us, I punched him straight in the chest with both of my fists. "Go! Leave!"

Clay took every hit, his eyes fluttering shut, not so much of a flinch each time my little hands rained down on him.

"Go be with Maliyah. Go pretend like none of this mattered, like *I* don't matter."

He shook his head at that, reaching for me, but I swatted him away.

"No. No, don't try to take it back now."

"Kitten," he whispered in a pained breath.

"GET OUT!" I screamed, hitting him again and again as I shoved him toward the door. "I hate you! I never want to see you again! I *hate you!*"

The words came out more desperate and garbled with every breath as sobs ripped free from my chest, echoing off every wall of my apartment.

"I'm sorry," he whispered against another flood of tears, trying to hold onto me as I pushed and pushed.

"You…" I stopped, melting into his arms as he wrapped me up tight. I shook and cried and he did the same. "You broke my fucking heart."

Silence fell over us, one long, still moment.

"I broke mine, too," he whispered.

And then he released me.

I gasped at the loss, but didn't have time to do more than reach for his back as he pulled my front door open and flew out of it without looking back at me.

A mangled cry fell from my lips when he was gone, and I sank down to the floor, bones collapsing in a heap before I hugged my knees to my chcst like that was the only way to keep myself together.

Just like that, my cotton candy cloud moment was over.

And no matter how I braced for it, I knew I'd never survive the crash to the ground.

Chapter 27

CLAY

I dragged my ass into the locker room after our loss against the Hawks the next day, wondering why I didn't feel the same emotion as my teammates.

Zeke threw his helmet into his locker with more force than necessary, the clang of it echoing off the walls of the room. Riley tried to soothe him, but the way she shook her head and hung it between her shoulders told me she was just as upset. Kyle sat mutely on the bench in front of his locker, no phone in sight, no bragging on social media or dancing in celebration. And even Holden's jaw was tight as he stood in the middle of the locker room and thought of what to say to rally us.

It was a brutal beating, a poor showing on all our parts against a team we should have easily defeated.

My team was angry. They were disappointed.

I, on the other hand, was just fucking numb.

It should have been something I was used to, the hollowness in my chest. After my breakup with Maliyah,

I thought I'd felt the worst emotional pain of my life, thought I had survived the worst heartbreak I'd ever experience.

I wanted to laugh at that now, but I couldn't muster up anything that even resembled joy — no matter how sarcastic.

This wasn't just pain. It wasn't just heartbreak. It wasn't just missing someone and being mercilessly reminded of them everywhere you looked by memories that would haunt you for what seemed like eternity — although all those things were present.

This was the kind of torture only those who put someone they cared about through hell knowingly could understand.

It was guilt, and failure, and recognition that I was the villain. It was someone else's blood on my hands. It was the cry that I had to do it, that there was no other way, weak as it left my lips.

My mom was the happiest she'd been, not just since Brandon split, but since Dad had. Cory was putting her up in a five-star rehab center in Northern California that frequently housed the rich and famous, and she was tickled pink, not just at the chance of running into one of them, but at really changing.

I'm going to be a better woman, she'd told me on the phone last night, though I'd been too fucked up to really listen. *A better mom for you.*

She was packing her bags, getting ready to leave tomorrow, a check to repay the loan I'd taken out, and then some, already in the mail and on its way to me.

And even though it was my money, even though it was me who'd loaned it to her and therefore deserved it coming back to me — it felt like dirty money, like it had blood on it, too.

You're doing the right thing, son.

Those were the words Cory said over the phone yesterday morning when I'd agreed to his deal after not having slept or ate or done anything but stare at the wall of my bedroom. I could almost imagine him clapping me on the shoulder with pride.

And I hoped he was right. I hoped this would be what was best for my mom, that I could finally give her even an ounce of all that she'd given me over my life. She had sacrificed so much for me — her youth, her body, her time and energy. I'd never seen her buy something for herself, not in all the years she raised me, because every dollar she had either went to bills or to me — mostly so I could play football.

And so, I would sacrifice for her. Over and over again, no matter how much it took.

But it didn't make any of it hurt any less.

Maliyah lit up like fireworks on the Fourth of July when I told her I wanted to try again, and she confessed to me how heartbreaking it had been to watch me with Giana. I told her it was all just a ruse to get her back, and she had smiled with the satisfaction of knowing she'd won.

It was an awful, disgusting lie — one I couldn't seal with anything more than a hug, which I was surprised didn't make Maliyah suspicious. I told her I wanted to take it slow.

The truth was that I couldn't imagine ever kissing anyone who wasn't Giana ever again.

So, Mom was happy, and Maliyah, and Cory, too.

But I was miserable.

And so was Giana.

That was enough for me to wonder if I'd made the right decision, after all.

When I closed my eyes to try to sleep last night, nightmarish visions of Giana beating on my chest kept me awake. I could hear her cries, see the tears staining her cheeks as she begged me not to break her heart.

And she knew, even without me saying a word — she *knew* it wasn't me in that moment.

How she knew, I'd never understand. But even as I stared at her unwavering and told her we were finished, she somehow fought through her own pain to try to shake me awake, to try to make me put myself first.

That was what fucked me up the most, the fact that even at my worst, she somehow saw through it all to my true heart.

But what she didn't understand was that this wasn't about sticking up for myself against Maliyah, or even my father. This was about caring for the one person who had cared for me.

It wasn't the time to put myself first.

And one day, I hoped there would come a time where I could tell her everything, make her understand.

Until then, I was committed to my misery.

"...next game. That's where our focus needs to be. We're not out of this race — not even close. We're all but guaranteed a bowl game at this point," Holden said as I came to, realizing I'd missed the first half of his speech. "Mark your mistakes, fix them, and come back hungry for more. We all have our jobs to do. Win as a team, lose as a team," he said, pausing. "And *fight* as a team."

Coach Sanders watched the speech unfold in the corner of the locker room, his arms folded. He clearly wasn't happy with how the game played out, either, but he let his captain take full control.

All around the locker room, players nodded their heads, fierce determination etched in their brows as they gathered around where Holden had extended his hand. They covered it with theirs, and Holden's eyes met mine, the signal for me to take over and yell out one of our team chants.

But I didn't have it in me.

I sniffed, looking down at my hand at the top of the pile.

"Fight on three," Holden said. "One, two—"

"*Fight!*"

The team's response echoed around us for only a moment before the gentle murmur of talking and packing up filled the space, some heading toward the training rooms or showers, while others opted to just go home.

Holden was at my side before I could so much as untie my cleats.

"Let's take a walk," he said, and he didn't wait for me to confirm before he was sauntering out of the locker room.

I begrudgingly followed him, and since the field was still covered in fans, players from the other team, and the media circus, he steered me toward the weight room.

"Sit," he said, pointing at a bench. When I did, he hung his hands on his hips, staring at the ground for a moment before he looked at me. "What happened?"

"I don't—"

"I don't care if you don't want to talk about it. You're a part of this team, and you're a big reason why we pulled an L today. You were shit in coverage, and giving us twenty percent of your all, at best."

I was ashamed at how spot on that assessment was.

"So, as captain, it's my job to figure out what's going on whether you want me to or not. You can either tell me now, or I can make your life a living hell every practice until you do."

I flattened my lips. "What, you going to make me run laps?"

"If that's what it takes."

I shook my head, balancing my elbows on my knees as my shoulders drooped. "It's family shit. Nothing I want to share with anyone — no offense."

"Did someone die?"

I frowned at him. "What? No. And that was a little harsh, Cap."

"I need to know how serious this is."

"Why, so you can replace me?"

He gave me a look that echoed his earlier sentiment. *If that's what it takes.*

I ran a hand back through my hair, sitting up straight again. "I broke up with Giana. I'm back with Maliyah. My mom is going to rehab. My dad is a piece of shit who couldn't care less about any of it, and if you push me off my spot, I swear to God, I'll kill you, Holden, because you'd be ripping away the only source of joy I have. Football is my lifeline," I said, surprised at the way my throat tightened with the words. "It's... it's all I have left."

I met his gaze then, chest heaving, and something softer washed over his expression as he watched me in return.

"You're back with Maliyah," he said, choosing to ignore the rest.

I sniffed, looking at the ground again. "Yeah."

"And that's what you want?"

"Yep," I lied, standing. "Can I go now, sergeant, or are you throwing me in the brig?"

Holden gave me a look that told me he clearly wasn't amused by the joke, but still, he seemed satisfied enough to stop torturing me — at least for the day.

"Go," he said, waving me off. "Get your head right before Monday."

I nodded, but before I could reach the door, he called out again.

"And don't forget we're not just your team," he said, halting me.

I waited, but didn't turn.

"We're your friends. We're family. I know you're always the one lending the hand, Clay, but we can help you, too." He paused. "You just have to be willing to let us."

Something about that sentiment pierced me like a hot blade between the ribs, so I simply nodded to let him know I'd heard him and then ducked out the door, heading for the locker room.

As soon as I turned the corner, she was there.

Giana was dimly lit at the other end of the hall, her hair in a frazzled mess of a bun on top of her head as she fumbled with the keys to her office while balancing an iPad tucked under her arm. Even from a distance, I could see the bags under her eyes that mirrored mine, the slump in her shoulders that reminded me of the pain I'd caused her.

When the door clicked open, she sighed, and glanced down the hall.

She froze when she saw me.

The burning pain in my chest was like experiencing every tackle I'd ever been victim of all at once. It was bone-crushing and soul-stealing, and yet I took every horrendous second of it so I could stare at her a little longer.

She opened her mouth and took a minute step toward me, but then stopped, clamping her lips together again.

And then she ducked into the office, slamming the door behind her.

●　●　●

GIANA

"You know I hate to see you like this," Dad said, sipping his bourbon as I used my fork to push the salad around on my plate. I thought by at least moving it a little, it would look like I'd eaten some, but the heap of soggy arugula staring up at me begged to differ.

I released my grip on the utensil, sitting back in my booth on a defeated sigh. "I know. I'm sorry, Dad."

"I don't want you to be sorry about what you're feeling. I want you to talk to me about it so we can figure out if there's a way to fix what's hurting you."

"There isn't," I told him.

The corner of his mouth lifted a bit even as his brows inched together, his black wire-framed glasses shifting with the movement. He swirled his glass, taking another sip before he sat it down and leaned forward.

My own aqua eyes stared back at me, only his were darker, as was his skin and hair. But anyone who passed the table could see we were related, could see how much I favored him over my mom.

"Out of your control, huh?"

I nodded, picking up my fork again just so I could have something to do with my hands.

Dad thumbed a beat on the table. "Well, you're at an age where life is going to start coming at you fast. This is likely the first of many things you'll encounter that are out of your control."

"It drives me crazy," I admitted. "And it... hurts."

I said that last part softly, wincing as my heart ached with that same fierce pain it had been randomly assaulting me with since Clay broke up with me.

He broke up with me.

I still couldn't believe it.

I'd always thought the stages of grief went in order, but I found myself bouncing around between them like a pinball, knocking into denial only to swing over to anger on my way down to depression. I still hadn't hit acceptance yet, though.

Part of me hoped I never would, because accepting it would mean it was real.

It still felt like a nightmare, like something happening to someone else. I kept staring at my phone, willing him to call it, willing *myself* to pick it up and text him. And when I wasn't wishing to run into him at the stadium, I was debating if I should hand in my resignation so I could get out of there and *never* have to run into him again.

It had been relatively easy on game day to keep busy. Even with the loss, I had a lot of reporters to field. But when I made it through the circus and dragged myself back to my office, I expected him to be gone already, or at the very least, back in the locker room.

But of course, he was right there, staring at me from the other side of the hall as if it was *me* who'd broken *him*.

I wanted to run to him as much as I wanted to curse him out and spit in his eye.

I was a mess.

And what hurt me more than anything wasn't what he did, but rather that I *knew* there was more to it than he was telling me. It was like having the first three-hundred dred pages of a thriller, only to have the end ripped out, to never know what secrets the main character was keeping from you all this time.

Even though I knew he was hurting as badly as I was, he wouldn't let me in.

What more could I do?

"This wouldn't have anything to do with the nice young man you were so excited to introduce me to today, would it? The one who suddenly came down with the flu?"

I didn't answer.

Dad reached over, grabbing my wrist and waiting until I dropped the fork before he pulled my hands into his. "I can't help if you don't talk to me, little mouse."

I shook my head. "I just... I don't even know where to start."

"The beginning usually works out nicely."

I tried to mirror his smile, but it fell flat.

"You have to forget I'm your daughter for, like, the next ten minutes."

Dad lifted a brow. "Okay, now you're not leaving until you tell me everything."

And so I did.

I didn't realize how badly I *needed* to confide in someone about what happened between me and Clay until the words were spilling from me like an avalanche, faster and faster until the dust was so thick I couldn't speak through it. I told him about Shawn, about the deal, about how Clay wanted Maliyah back. I left out the gritty details of exactly *how* we played our little game, but I didn't hold back on how close we'd become, on how much I knew he cared about me.

How much I cared about *him*.

When I finished, Dad let out a low whistle, tapping my hand in his. "Well, I can't say I don't want to kill the kid for hurting my baby girl."

"Dad."

"I also can't say that I understand why you would ever agree to *fake date* someone," he added. "Although, some of your book titles make more sense now. *My Fake Bodyguard.*"

I smiled a little at that.

"But," he continued. "I have to agree with you that something doesn't add up here."

"Right?" I leaned forward as if my father and I were cracking open the case together. "I mean, I think I could admit it if I'd judged his character wrong, if I'd misread the signs and just let some asshole jock take advantage of me."

Dad arched a brow that made me flush and look away, choosing not to elaborate on that.

"But I know him. I know him maybe better than any of his teammates. And I just... I can't believe that suddenly, out of nowhere, he decided he wanted to be with Maliyah again. I mean, Dad... he was *crying* when he broke up with me."

"Guys cry, too, you know," he said with a smirk.

"Yes, but... it takes a lot," I pointed out. "No?"

Dad nodded. "Yes, usually. But maybe he was just crying because he knew he was hurting you. He could very well want to end the relationship, but not want to bring you pain in the process."

I frowned, deflating as I realized that was a possibility. "I guess I hadn't thought of that."

Dad patted my hand. "I know this is hard, little mouse. Believe it or not, I dated a few girls pretty seriously before I found your mom. I know what it's like to have a heart broken."

I folded in on myself, my heart squeezing painfully tight in my chest as if cued.

"But if Bonnie Raitt taught me anything, it's that you can't make someone love you if they don't."

"Wait," I said. "That's an Adele song."

"She covered it."

"Bonnie Raitt did?"

Dad blinked. "I'm going to choose to ignore the fact that my daughter doesn't know who Bonnie Raitt is and get back to the matter at hand, which is this," he said, leaning in closer. His blue eyes flashed with warmth, a sympathetic smile on the lips that mine were mirrored after. "At this point, it doesn't matter what you *think* you know about what *might* be going on behind the scenes for this boy. All you have to go off is what *actually* happened, what he told you, and what you do know for certain." He paused. "He looked you right in the eyes and told you it's over."

My bottom lip trembled, and Dad squeezed my hand.

"At some point, you have to accept that and move forward. I'm not saying you need to sprint, or that it's not going to hurt every step of the way. But that's what life is, sometimes. It's just getting up, getting dressed, and putting one foot in front of the other until one day... the pain fades. And you know what else?"

"What?" I whispered.

"Life has a funny way of surprising us and bringing us something even *better* down the line."

I swallowed, nodding, trying to find solace in his words. "I... I think I love him, Dad."

My words broke at the end of the confession, tears blurring my eyes as I glanced up at my father who looked like I'd just fallen off a cliff right in front of his eyes.

"Oh, sweetheart," he said, and in a flash, he was up out of his side of the booth and dipping into mine.

He wrapped me up in a fierce hug, one I felt all the way to my bones as I clung to him and let myself cry.

"It's okay to love him."

"Even if he doesn't love me back?"

"That's the thing about love," he said, kissing my hair. "It doesn't need to be reciprocated to be real."

I couldn't be sure how long we sat there, Dad holding me while I fell apart in a hole-in-the-wall restaurant full of rowdy college students, but I savored every moment of that comfort he brought me.

And the next morning, I woke up with the same excruciating agony that had plagued me since Clay broke my heart. But this time, I didn't surrender to it. I didn't overanalyze every word he'd said to me, or replay all the moments we spent in my bed. I didn't cling to the memory of his laugh, or how I could still close my eyes and feel his hands on my face, his lips on my lips.

This time, I got dressed.

I put on my shoes.

And one slow step at a time, I moved forward.

Chapter 28

GIANA

A week later, I waited on the bench outside *Rum &
Roasters,* tucking my peacoat tight around me
against the chilly breeze. It was a poor choice to wear
my tights and skirt today, but I missed skirt season. I
was tired of wearing sweaters and pants, and I wanted
to break out the whiskers skirt.

For reasons I probably would never admit to anyone, myself included.

So, I rubbed my legs through the thin fabric to try to
bring a little warmth, eyes scanning the students walking by for Shawn. As soon as he got here, we could dip
inside the coffee shop so I could defrost.

I didn't know exactly *why* I had felt the need to
call him, to ask him to meet up — but something about
coming clean about everything felt like it would give me
a little closure. I certainly wasn't going to get anything
close to closure from Clay, so maybe this was my heart's

desperate attempt to take back some of the control that had been stolen from me.

My phone buzzed in my coat pocket, and I sighed at the text on it when I pulled it out.

Sorry, running a little late. Be there soon.

I thumbed out a reply, but before I could send it, someone's shadow swept over me.

"Cute skirt, but I don't know how the hell you're not freezing your tits off right now."

I frowned, angling my head up and squinting through the sun to find a smirking Riley staring down at me.

I smiled, looking down at the whiskers on my lap. "Maybe it's because I don't have any tits to freeze off?"

Riley laughed. "Scoot over."

I did, and Riley took the seat next to me, looping her arm through mine and instantly warming me with her body heat through the much more comfortable athletic sweats she was wearing. I gave a small sigh of content, both at the heat and at the comfort she brought.

"What are you doing sitting in the cold, weirdo?"

I chuckled. "Waiting for someone."

"Clay?"

His name sucked the smile off my face like a vacuum. "No," I said, swallowing. "Just a friend."

Riley nodded, quiet for a moment before asking, "You ever going to tell me what happened between you two?"

"I would if I knew."

She frowned. "What does that mean?"

"It means he's back with Maliyah, but I... I just know that's not what he actually wants."

"How do you know?"

I let out a breath, eyeing her for a moment before I turned to face her fully, and because I knew how big of a deal they were to her, I held out my pinky. "Pinky promise you won't tell a soul what I'm about to tell you?"

Her eyes lit up, complete seriousness washing over her as she hooked her digit around mine. "My lips are sealed."

And with that promise, I spilled everything.

Not just the version I'd told my dad, which had been sugarcoated and left out *many* details, but the full story. I told her about our agreement, how it had been fake at first — to which she perked up and declared *I knew it!* I told her that somehow along the way, things changed. My cheeks tinged red when I admitted that I was a virgin, and how Shawn singing his stupid steamy song had made me panic and beg Clay to help me *not* be anymore.

Everything.

The observatory, the auction, the days and nights we'd spent wrapped up in each other.

The break.

I couldn't fight back my tears when I told her that part, and she squeezed my hand in hers, nodding like she knew exactly what I was feeling. After what happened between her and Zeke last semester, I had no doubt she really did.

"So, like I said, I'd tell you what happened if I understood it myself, but I don't. He just... ended it. And I don't care what he says about being back with Maliyah, I know it's not what he wants. I just don't know *why* he's doing this."

"Do you think he felt bad for hurting her? Or maybe she has something on him!" Riley bounced. "Oh my God, maybe she's a sneaky cheerleader drug dealer and he got caught up in her web, and now she has him by the balls and he has no choice!"

I blinked. "Okay, I read mafia romance books for fun, and not even *my* brain went there."

Riley shrugged. "Could be possible. Just saying."

I smiled, but it fell quickly as I shook my head, still trying to process what had been plaguing me since he left my apartment that night. "I don't know. But my Dad gave me some pretty sage advice last week. He told me I might never get the answers I need," I said. "And that I needed to move on."

Riley frowned. "Why does that make me want to cry?"

"Because it's awful and unfair," I answered. "But... he's right. I don't know what Clay's keeping from me, why he did this, but all that really matters is that he did it. He broke up with me." I shrugged. "As much as it kills me, I have to just accept that and figure out a way to keep going."

Riley shook her head. "You're stronger than I am."

"Tell that to the ice cream-stained pajamas and mountains of tissue littering my bedroom right now."

Riley leaned her head on my shoulder, slipping her arm through mine again. "You love him," she whispered.

My throat constricted. "I do."

"Isn't it the worst?"

I choked on a laugh at that. "Yes," I agreed. "It really, truly is."

She was quiet for a long moment, and then she squeezed my arm. "I'm really sorry. And also, *really* mad at you for not telling me any of this. We're friends, G."

"I'm not really used to having friends," I admitted.

"Well, *get* used to it. Especially because if you ever have a secret pleasure-fest where a man acts out your dirtiest book fantasies again, I want every sordid detail as it unfolds."

I laughed at that, but then an acute sadness pierced my lungs. "God, that really was the most romantic thing anyone has ever done for me."

"He's one of a kind, that boy," Riley said softly, and for a moment, we were both silent. Then, she sat up, nudging me. "But so are you. And you're going to be okay, no matter what happens next."

"Thank you, Riley."

She smiled, and then her eyes flashed somewhere behind me. "Your guest is here."

She stood as I turned to find Shawn heading our way, his guitar case slung over his right shoulder. He gave me a tentative wave when he saw me, and I stood to join Riley.

"Thank you for telling me," she said, and then with a nod at Shawn, she added, "And good luck."

With a fierce hug, she was gone — just in time for Shawn to stop at the edge of the bench.

I smiled, gesturing toward the café. "Shall we?"

It was an awkward quiet as we stood in line and got coffee, and Shawn found an empty table right in the center of the shop once we had our drinks in hand. He sat first, angling his guitar against the table, and I took the seat across from him.

"Thanks for meeting me."

He nodded. "How are you?"

"I'm…" I paused. "Awful, honestly," I admitted, but it was with a smile. "But I'll be okay. Eventually."

"Is that why you called me? To talk?"

"Yes, but not really about me. Well, kind of." I shook my head. "I just... there's something I want you to know. Something you deserve to know."

Shawn cocked a brow, and with one last sip of my coffee and a deep breath, I told him about the deal I'd made with Clay in this very coffee shop, about the part Shawn played in our whole relationship. I left out the details I'd told Riley, even some that I'd told my dad, focusing instead on apologizing for playing a game with him that he wasn't even aware of.

It hurt the worst to tell him out of everyone, especially as I watched a cold resolve wash over him when he realized everything between us had been carefully construed. When I finished, I lifted my coffee to my lips, waiting for him to process.

He sighed, running a hand over his hair. "Well," he finally said. "I won't lie and say I don't wish I would have noticed you *before* Clay fake dated you and then consequently swept you off your feet."

I smiled.

"But," he continued, "I'm glad to know you now."

His eyes danced in the low light of the coffee shop as he said it, and I felt a wave of relief wash over me. "Really?"

"Really," he said. "Maybe we could start over."

Panic seized me, my face reddening. I hadn't thought of this as a possibility, him still wanting to date me. In fact, I thought he'd be pissed. I thought he'd curse me out and call me a psycho before storming out of the café.

"Um..."

"As friends," he clarified, leaning forward on a smirk.

He smiled even more when I let out a breath of relief, and then he stood, holding his arms open for a hug.

I stood, too, and slipped into his grasp, squeezing him just as tightly when he wrapped me in his embrace.

"Friends," I agreed.

I looked up at him when we pulled back, and he shook his head, arching a brow. "I can't believe you played me like a damn fiddle."

"I can't believe you were trying to hook up with someone who had a boyfriend."

"Hey, in my defense, you made him seem like a pretty shit boyfriend."

"Fair," I conceded, and he slowly released me, both of us taking our seats again.

"Speaking of which... I'm sorry. About the break-up."

I nodded, lungs squeezing painfully tight in my chest. "Thank you. So am I."

And with the truth sitting out in the open between us, I felt a marginal scrap of closure wrap itself around my bleeding heart. Dad was right. It wasn't going to happen overnight. I wasn't going to stop hurting or stop missing Clay, not for a long, long time.

But I was still here. I was still breathing, still living.

And I didn't want to shy away from the pain as I moved forward.

It reminded me of all that was, all the powerful emotions I'd felt with Clay in the time our lives were tangled together. I never wanted to lose those stinging lashes of pain, never wanted to forget how it felt to be held by him, touched by him, kissed by him.

Loved by him.

Maybe I didn't get to have him forever.

But I'd hold on to every little piece of him that he gave me for the rest of my life.

And after, too.

● ● ●

CLAY

I was so fucking tired of Boston winter.

And technically, it wasn't even winter yet. We were smack dab in the middle of fall, but the sleety mixture of rain and snow piercing my skin like tiny branding irons didn't feel like fall to me.

In California, fall meant crisp evenings and warm days. It meant sunshine and clear blue skies. We rarely ever had nights below fifty degrees, and most days hovered somewhere in the seventies.

That was football weather to me.

But the masochists who grew up here in New England? They *loved* playing in this shit. It was written all over their faces as we practiced — Zeke sticking out his tongue with a victorious smile after a big return, Riley doing a little dance after knocking in a thirty-three-yard field goal. As for me? I grumbled through every minute of it until we were all jogging into the locker room to shower, all the while longing for the hot shower that waited inside.

My stride slowed when I saw Giana.

She was too focused on rounding up a few of the players for the Instagram Live she had scheduled to notice me, so I took advantage of the moment, watching her curls bounce as if in slow motion as she pointed and directed and bossed everyone around. Her skin was brighter, eyes still tired but not lined with red the way they had been. Her head was held high, focus locked in on the task at hand like she didn't have anything else on her mind.

She looked better than she had in weeks.

And I knew it was because of Shawn.

My next inhale burned as I recalled the memory that would be etched into my brain for the rest of my life. Last Sunday, I'd been cramming for a test in my anatomy class and had barely been able to keep my eyes open — thanks mostly to my tossing and turning all night, which was my normal sleep routine now. So, in a desperate attempt to wrangle my focus, I'd jogged over to *Rum & Roasters.*

But I'd never made it inside.

Through the windows of the shop, foggy from the warmth inside combatting the bitter cold outside, I'd seen her.

In Shawn's arms.

My heart bottomed out at the sight, at how she held him tight before looking up at him with a smile that used to belong to only me. He'd said something to make her laugh, and that was all I could stomach before I had to tear my gaze away and jog past.

She'd moved on.

God, how I wanted to be happy that she had. I wanted to feel relief that I hadn't broken her complete-ly, that Shawn was there for her to pick up the pieces I'd left behind. I wanted to find solace in the knowledge that she was going to be okay, that he was going to take care of her.

But it only made me sick with possession and dizzy with rage.

It was a betrayal, one I felt like a sword through my stomach — which I promptly emptied after I stumbled away from the coffee shop and found a trash can off the sidewalk path that circled campus.

It was a beating I deserved, one I shouldn't have been even a little surprised or upset by.

But it fucking killed me.

"Hey," Maliyah said, jarring me from my memory and snapping my attention from Giana to her. She slid her arms around my waist, pressing up on her toes to peck a kiss to my lips before I could pull away. "Great practice. Let's get inside. I'm freezing."

I swallowed, nodding as I tucked her under my arm with that same familiar nausea rolling through me.

And I caught Giana's gaze on our way in, holding it as she looked from me to Maliyah and back again. Those Caribbean-blue eyes burned a hole through me even from yards away, and I wanted to memorize them, to stare so long I wouldn't forget the exact shape and color of them for as long as I lived.

But she turned away, back to what she was doing — all without a single ounce of emotion showing that she cared.

Maybe I hated the weather because it matched my mood so well. Maybe I longed for sunshine and clear skies because I thought they could act as some kind of miracle drug that would snap me out of my pathetic haze.

"Let's get sushi," Maliyah said when we made it to the locker room, releasing me so she could continue down the hall to the one for the cheerleaders. "Shower, change, meet back here?"

"Sure."

She smiled, but something in her eyes was sad as she took me in. She would have had to have been blind not to see how miserable I was, no matter how I attempted to fake like I was okay for her, and for my mom, and for Cory.

"You okay?"

I managed a nod. "Just cold. And tired."

Her mouth twisted to the side. "You can talk to me, you know. I... I know we have a lot still to work through. I know I hurt you, that I betrayed your trust. But... I know you. Probably better than anyone else."

I wanted to roll my eyes at how wrong she was about that.

"I can tell when you're not okay."

"I just have a lot on my mind."

"Well, we can talk about it. Over dinner."

Again, a little nod was all I offered.

She opened her mouth like she wanted to say something else, but thought better of it. Then, she turned, making her way down the hall as I slipped into the locker room.

The team was used to my sour attitude by now. They'd stopped giving me hell about it, stopped trying to pry information out of me, too. Now, they just sort of avoided me, like I was a flu they didn't want to catch.

I quietly undressed, leaving my Under Armour briefs on until I made it to the shower, mostly just for Riley's sake. When it was just me and a few guys, I stripped the rest of the way down, sighing heavily as the first bit of steaming hot water rained down on me.

My skin burned in protest before it adjusted, and then my muscles all relaxed at once, and I stood there under the showerhead content to be that way for hours.

I ran my face under the water, squeezing my eyes shut as the warmth enveloped me.

Until, very suddenly, the water ran cold.

"What the fuck!"

I reached out blindly for the faucet, but was met with a wet t-shirt instead. Then, in my blind disorientation, the water shut off, I was thrown a towel, and all but shoved down until I was on my ass with my back against the cold tile wall.

"Cover your anaconda," Zeke said, his voice one I'd recognize anywhere. I used the towel to wipe my eyes clean before I laid it over my lap and looked up to find him and Holden standing over me.

"Out," Holden said, snapping his fingers to the two other guys who had been in the showers with me. They gave me a look that said *thoughts and prayers* before dipping out at our captain's orders.

"What the hell is going on?" I asked.

"Riley," Zeke called, ignoring me, and where the two guys had just disappeared, she peeked around the corner, making sure I was covered before she walked all the way in.

"Sorry for the barbarian ambush," Riley said, crossing her arms as she joined the other two standing over me. "But we didn't know what else to do to get you to talk."

"Talk?"

"We want to know what's going on," Holden said, filling in the gaps. "And not the bullshit lie or half-truth you've been spitting when someone is brave enough to press you. You're not okay. And if being with Maliyah was really what you wanted, you'd be over the fucking moon instead of a human version of Eeyore."

I sighed. "I do want to be with Maliyah."

As soon as the words were off my lips, Riley gave the guys a look, and they both stepped back just in time for her to turn the faucet and make icy cold water rain down on me.

"Riley! What the fuck!"

I held up my arms to shield myself from it — not that I really could — until she turned it off again. The towel over my lap was soaked now, and cold.

"You're getting an ice bath every time you say some stupid shit like that," she warned. "So I'd try again if I were you."

I growled. "This is bullshit, I'm not—"

I tried to stand, but Zeke met my chest with a firm hand, pushing me back against the wall.

"Stop trying to handle whatever is going on alone," he said, his voice loud and firm. "Goddamnit, Clay — can't you see your friends are worried about you? You've been there for every single one of us at one point or another," he continued, and I looked behind him at where Riley and Holden nodded in agreement before my eyes met Zeke's again. "Let us help *you* now."

Something raw and emotional snagged in my throat, and I tore my gaze from them, looking at the empty shower hall as I swallowed down whatever it was that was choking me. I was silent for a long while, shaking my head, intent to come back with some sort of argument.

But I didn't have one.

Instead, I finally relented, sighing and letting my head fall back against the tile.

"It's a long story," I croaked.

Riley carefully lowered herself down onto the wet

tile next to me, not a care in the world that it was going to soak her shorts when she did. She reached over and grabbed my forearm.

"We have time."

Zeke and Holden sat down, too.

"We could move somewhere that *isn't* the shower," I suggested.

"Not a chance," Riley said. "I need that faucet threat hanging over you. Literally."

I smirked, then blew out a breath, and told them everything.

I was shocked at how easily the words came once I started, beginning with the deal I'd struck with Giana and ending with the nightmarish scene at her apartment — which was the last time we'd spoken.

All three of them leaned in, listening intently, and at the end of it all, they exchanged looks before Holden shook his head and said, "So, you did all this for your mom?"

I nodded. "I know it might not make sense to you, but she's... she's done so much for me, *given up* so much..."

"I understand more than you'd think," Holden said, his stare severe where it held mine. But he didn't elaborate before he added, "I get it. She's your mom. She raised you. But, man... she's the parent. She's *supposed* to do that."

I frowned. "Okay... so?"

"So, you're the kid. You're her son. And as much as you love her and want to help her, she's an adult who needs to first help herself."

"But she can't. Not without me."

"Yes, she can," Riley said. "Your mom made a lot of choices that got her here. And I know you feel like you need to fix it for her, but if she doesn't have to do the work herself?" Riley shrugged. "How is she ever really going to learn the lesson and grow?"

"This is not your battle," Zeke added. "We are all for you helping your mom if rehab is what she needs, and we'll figure out a way to get her there. But this? Accepting money from Cory in exchange for giving up the girl who's made you happier than we've ever seen you?" He shook his head. "That's not the answer."

"But what else can I do?" I asked, throwing my hands up. "I already took out a loan. I can't just keep doing that. My dad won't help. And I don't want to enter the draft early."

"That's not happening," Holden said, as if it wasn't even an option to consider. Zeke's equally stern glare told me he felt the same.

"We will figure it out. Just give us some time to think," Riley said. "And until then, your mom is an adult. She can take care of herself — the catch is, you have to *let* her. You have to take the crutch away and show her that she doesn't need it. She can walk on her own."

"And if she doesn't? If she falls?"

Zeke looked at Riley and then back at me. "She'll get back up. That's what we all do — we get back up, and we try again."

I shook my head, even as their words started to clear the fog in my head. "I already accepted that check from Cory. Mom cashed it. She's in rehab on *his* dime. And he... he cares about us," I said, not realizing how much that hurt until the words were out. "In his own fucked-up way, this is him showing that."

"This is him getting what he wants," Riley argued. Zeke gave her a pointed look that made her zip her lips shut, though I could tell by how red her cheeks were that it was an effort to keep from saying more.

"Tell him you appreciate his help and his offer, but that you've changed your mind," Holden said calmly. "And if he takes the money back and she has to go back home? Again, we'll figure it out."

"And by the way, I know she hurt you in the past, but *none* of this is fair to Maliyah," Riley added, unable to stay quiet any longer. "You and Cory are a lot alike, I can see that just from what you've told us. You both want to help people you love. But this isn't the way to do it." She shrugged. "Your mom is hurting. So is Maliyah. They're probably regretting decisions they've made that led to where they are now. But that doesn't mean you take it on *you* to fix it all and make everything better — because that only leaves them feeling emptier."

"So what am I supposed to do then?" I challenged.

"Just *be there* for her," Riley said, shaking her head as a smile curled on her lips. "Tell your mom you love her and you understand. Listen to her when she needs it. Support her when she asks for your advice. When she decides what she wants to do next, offer whatever help you can *within* your physical, emotional, mental, and financial means."

"Love her through the hard time while reminding her it won't last forever," Holden added, and again, there was something so solemn in his gaze that I wondered if he was speaking from experience, from a lesson he'd learned himself.

"You have a right to be happy, Clay," Riley said softly. "And you do not have to bear everyone else's burdens. You've done enough of that."

I swallowed, head falling back as I looked up at the showerhead. "I don't want to hurt her."

"She's your mom," Zeke said instantly. "If anything, she will be proud of you for setting boundaries. She wants the best for *you*, too. And she *will* be okay, man. I promise."

I closed my eyes, shaking my head, not because I was refusing to listen, but because I hated how much everything they said made sense. Maybe it was something I'd known all along, something that swam under the surface of my need to be the one to fix everything for my mom, for Maliyah, for anyone in my life who was in trouble.

"Where was all this sage advice two weeks ago?" I whispered on a sad laugh.

"Right here. You were just too damn prideful to come to your friends and ask for help," Riley said.

"Fair," I admitted on a sigh. Then, I looked at each of them. "I hear you. And I... I know you're right."

"How badly did that hurt?" Zeke teased with a smirk.

I tried to smile, too, but it fell flat as I considered everything. "I'll talk to Cory. And I'll call my mom, explain everything. Maliyah wants to get sushi right after this, so I guess I can face her first. She deserves to know the truth."

My stomach curled at the thought. It would be back-to-back disappointment from each person, but I knew I had no choice but to face the mess I'd created.

"And Giana?" Riley pressed.

My chest ached. "She's moved on."

Riley frowned. "Okay, I love you, Clay, but how stupid *are* you?" She shook her head. "That girl is *far* from moved on. She…" Riley inhaled a breath that stopped her next word. "You need to talk to her."

"She's with Shawn," I said, the words nearly killing me as I croaked them out. "I'm too late."

"What are you talking about?" Riley asked.

"I saw them together on Sunday. They were at the coffee shop." I swallowed. "He was hugging her, and she was staring up at him, laughing." I paused. "As she should be. I want her to be happy."

"Oh, cut the shit," Riley said, abruptly standing. "She's not *with* Shawn, you dummy. She met up with him to tell him everything that happened. She needed some sort of closure — and she knew it wasn't coming from you."

Zeke and Holden stood with her as I shook my head, confused. "How do you know this?"

She tilted her chin. "Don't worry about how I know it. What *you* need to worry about now is how you fix this."

My head was spinning, and I stood to join them, carefully maneuvering the towel so it stayed covering me until I could tie it around my waist.

"I… I *can't*." I said. "I fucked this up beyond repair."

"Ugh, you are infuriating," Riley said, hanging her hands on her hips. She looked at Zeke next. "Were you this stupid, too, when we were broken up?"

"Worse," he answered.

Riley rolled her eyes, then turned her focus back to me. "You read her books, didn't you?"

I narrowed my gaze. "How do you know *that*?"

"Answer the question."

"Yes, I read her books."

"Okay, well, did you only pay attention to the sex scenes, or did you read the end?" She threw her hand

out at me, as if the answer was floating in the air between us. "She's waiting on you. She's waiting for you
to tell her the truth — which is that you fucked up, that
you love her, that you're stupid and you're sorry and
you can't live without her." She smiled. "This is the part
where you get the girl, you idiot."

"The grand gesture," Zeke added, and my eyebrows
shot up as he shrugged me off. "What? I know how to
romance," he said in defense.

I shook my head, running a hand back through my
hair as hope flitted dangerously in my chest. I wanted to
snuff it out like a flame not meant to be started, but it
grew and grew, raging into a full-on forest fire as an idea
bloomed under the smoke.

"Your wheels are turning, aren't they?" Holden
asked on a smirk.

I looked at him, at Riley, at Zeke — at my friends,
who had essentially run into a burning building to save
me. And the amount of gratitude I felt was too much to
hold, too much to speak into life — but I hoped they saw
it. I hoped they knew.

"What do you have in mind?" Zeke asked.

"And more importantly," Riley added. "How can we
help?"

Chapter 29

GIANA

"Leo, I need you in the press room — now," I said, tugging him by his grass-stained jersey.

He made a joke that I didn't quite hear, because our intern was screaming into her headpiece about how Holden was being surrounded on the field and couldn't break loose.

"I'm on it," I said into my mic, and then I released Leo, hoping he would make it the rest of the way down the hall to where we'd set up our press box before I was jogging out onto the field.

It was complete madness, the kind only a Thanksgiving Day game can bring.

The kind only a bowl-clutching game can bring.

It was like we'd already won the championship, how confetti of our school's gold and brick red colors littered the field. I weaved through the still-buzzing crowd on my way out to the fifty-yard line, where an extensive group of cameras and reporters were gathered around Holden.

"Yeah, we're just staying focused and keeping our eyes on the next game," he answered as I pushed through the wall.

"You're not thinking about the playoff bowl game against the Huskies?" a reporter asked, shoving the microphone back in Holden's face.

"We'll worry about that when we get there. For now, it's on to North Carolina."

I stepped in-between him and the crew. "If you can all please make your way to the press room, we will have full interviews with the players, including Leo Hernandez who is setting up now. Holden will be in later. Thank you."

I didn't wait for them to start shouting more questions *despite* me telling them we were done on the field before I was ushering Holden away — which was comical, since he towered over me and was at least twice my mass.

"Thank you," he uttered as we moved through the crowd.

"You know, you're bigger than me. You could have stopped that way before I did."

"I don't want to be rude. I'm captain. If anyone needs to field the rabid reporters, it's me."

I smiled. "You're too good for the world, Holden Moore."

When we finally got to the tunnel that led into the stadium, security warded off anyone not on or with the team. Holden ambled toward the locker room while I set straight for the press room.

It was only *maybe* sixty seconds, that walk of quiet, but it was just enough to let my mind drift to Clay.

A month.

It'd been almost a *month* since we broke up, and I still couldn't think of him without my entire body curling in on itself. I wasn't lying around broken and pathetic, but I was certainly far from moved on, far from forgetting him or even so much as thinking about trying to date someone else.

Every time I saw him out on the field, my heart warmed with the desire to cheer him on, to be the one he ran to after the game, the one he swept into his arms. Then, I'd hate myself for it, and do everything I could to avoid him — only to be sick when I *didn't* see him even more than when I did.

I pretended like I didn't notice him when my every sense was tuned into him, so much so that I had more than a few questions burning into my brain. One of the most pressing was why I hadn't seen him with Maliyah in over a week now. She no longer hung onto him after every practice, or tried to suck his face off after a game.

They seemed friendly, cordial, but... *not* romantic.

Why I was so engrossed in the details, I didn't know. Masochism was something I was becoming well-suited for, I supposed.

But today, it had been especially impossible to ignore him.

He'd had quite possibly the most monster game of his career. He had not one interception, not two, but *three* — and one of them he ran back for a touchdown. He was on fire, and I knew the reporters would be clamoring to talk to him after that.

I just didn't know how I would find enough professionalism to talk to him without bursting into tears.

I shook my head, deciding I could deal with it later. Right now, I had Leo to wrangle, and then an exclusive interview with Riley and Zeke that they'd promised me if we won today.

"Oh, perfect," I said as I rounded the corner into the press room, finding Zeke and Riley already standing back behind the logo wall we'd erected. I could hear Leo answering questions, making the entire room laugh as always. "Now I don't have to hunt you two down. Are you both ready to go on next?"

"Born ready," Riley said, and she and Zeke exchanged a look that made my smile slip.

"What was that?"

"What?" Zeke asked.

I pointed between them. "That... *look* you just gave each other." I balked. "Oh, my God. You're not about to drop some crazy bomb on live television, are you? Are you engaged or something?" My heart dropped as I looked at Riley. "Fuck, are you pregnant?"

Even though I whispered that last bit, Riley's eyes went wide as saucers before she socked me in the arm.

"Ow," I said, rubbing the spot.

"Don't be ridiculous," she said. "We're giving you the exclusive about our relationship like we promised we would all season. We just wanted to make sure we were focused and could secure this game first. And don't even whisper about things like *that*," she added, not even daring to speak the word *pregnant* out loud again. "You'll start a whole rumor chain."

I frowned, still rubbing my arm as I surveyed them, but didn't have the time to pry deeper into whatever they were hiding before Charlotte gave Leo the last question sign from beside the podium stage.

"Okay, you're up," I told them, and as soon as Leo stepped off the platform, Riley and Zeke took his place.

Cameras flashed like mad.

Everyone spoke over each other, trying to get the couple's attention for the first question as Zeke held out Riley's chair for her to sit before he did the same. They shared an adoring look, Zeke grabbing Riley's hand and holding it on top of the low table as a hundred more flashes assaulted them.

"Joe," Zeke called out first, nodding toward a well-known reporter from the local sports station. We always liked to show him favor when we could — mostly because the local station covered all the university sports, and because Joe was actually a nice reporter focused more on football than gossip.

"Riley, you missed your first field goal attempt in the second quarter, but ended up kicking your longest one yet in the third. How did you come back from that first kick and re-center?"

"I've learned over the years to not let one kick get under my skin and to just focus on staying consistent. Everyone has bad kicks, bad throws, missed catches — but it doesn't have to define the game." She shared a knowing look with Zeke then. "Besides, when Zeke had that sixty-two-yard return at beginning of the second half, I knew I had to bring my game to show him up or I'd never hear the end of it."

The room lit up with laughter, and then Riley called on the next reporter.

I watched, amazed, from the side of the stage as they fielded each question — and of course, they started steering more toward their relationship than the game after a while. They handled it all like pros, giving a little

detail on how dating while playing on the same team had
been without going into too much mush. They cracked
jokes, illustrated their respect for each other and the
team, and when the timing was right, one of them would
deliver the perfect sweet line that had the whole room
smiling at their young love.

Even me.

Even while my stomach coiled and chest ached with
the kind of pain that can only come from having once
had what they did and lost it just as fast.

Charlotte ate up every minute of their interview,
too. She leaned in, speaking softly so the mics wouldn't
pick her up. "I don't know how you managed to get this
interview from them, but great fucking job, Jones."

I beamed as Charlotte gave Zeke the signal to take
one more question.

He looked out over the hands raised, the people
calling out his name, and then pointed to someone near
the back.

"Clay Johnson," he said.

And my heart stopped.

Murmurs fell over the crowd as every head snapped
in the direction of where Clay was in the back of the
room. I peeked at him from beside the stage, my view
mostly blocked, but I could spot his towering figure, his
solemn face as he grabbed a nearby chair and climbed to
stand on top of it.

He was still in his uniform, the white jersey stained
with dirt and grass and sweat. His hair was matted with
sweat, too, and the eye black he'd lined under his eyes
before the game was smeared now.

But he was still breathtakingly handsome, rugged
and intoxicating in the most effortless way.

"Uh, yeah, I was just wondering," he said when he was standing on top of the chair fully, and he yelled out the words over the crowd. "Have either of you either done something really stupid that almost ended your relationship?"

A golf ball-sized knot formed in my throat at the question, at the way my heart raced with the words.

Zeke and Riley smiled at each other. "Both of us have made mistakes," Riley answered. "But we admit when we were wrong. And we always come back to each other."

The room shifted back to them, a few pictures snapped as more hands went up, confused as to whether that was really the last question or not.

"I appreciate you sharing that answer," Clay said, and heads swiveled again, confusion washing over everyone trying to figure out what the hell was going on.

Me included.

"And you guys have a really great story."

"Aw, thanks Clay," Riley said, giving Zeke googly eyes as she leaned into him.

"But ours is better."

My heart stumbled, stopping altogether for a long breath as Clay's eyes snapped to mine.

"Wait... *ours*?" someone asked, and there was a brief pause before the madness, before every camera turned toward Clay and reporters struggled to find mics they could hold out toward him, since all the press ones were focused on Riley and Zeke at the podium.

"Yes, ours," Clay confirmed. "Mine and Giana Jones' story."

"Oh, my God," I whispered, covering my mouth with shaking hands.

"Oh, my God," Charlotte repeated, though her voice was firmer, and filled with the disdain of a PR agent whose client had gone rogue.

"You probably don't know Giana Jones, at least — not by name. But she's the gorgeous girl who's always wrangling us, who gets you your interviews and podcast exclusives and commercial spots." The side of his mouth tilted up as he faced each camera. "And she's my girlfriend. At least, she was — before I screwed it all up."

Charlotte snapped her fingers, waking me from my haze. "*Go fix this,*" she hissed.

I nodded, bolting from behind the stage and squeezing through the crowd that grew thicker and thicker around Clay.

Clay, who was now holding up a small book for everyone to see.

"*Blind Side,*" he said, showcasing the simple black cover. "The story of how I fake-dated the girl of my dreams and then lost her from being an idiot."

There was a mixture of laughter and the buzz of questions as the crowd leaned in, making it even harder for me to shove through.

"Excuse me, excuse me," I muttered, shoving as politely as I could.

Clay opened the book, holding it up and showing the godawful stick figures drawn inside it along with the large text like it was a children's book.

"Once upon a time, there was a beautiful PR princess named Giana," he said, showing the stick figure with glasses and curly hair with a headpiece on. He licked his thumb and flipped the page. "And a dumb safety named Clay."

The crowd laughed at the next drawing, which was a stick figure with beefy arms in a too-tight jersey.

"Excuse me," I said, shoving through the last bit of the crowd. When they parted, someone murmured, "I think that's her," and before I could stop them, cameras turned.

Toward me.

Panic zipped through me as I finally reached Clay just as he turned the next page.

"Clay and Giana made a deal — he would help her get the attention of the Prince of Rum & Roasters, and she would help him make his ex-girlfriend jealous. How? By agreeing to fake date each other." He turned the page, showing the two stick figures locked in a hug as people watched. "Except, there was nothing fake about what they felt for each other."

My heart squeezed, and as much as I wanted to hear the rest of whatever was in that poor excuse for a book, I reached out for his jersey and tugged.

"Clay, stop."

He looked down at me. "No."

"Clay," I whisper-threatened through my teeth, trying to remain as professional as I could. I turned toward the crowd. "If you all want to take a quick break, we'll have Holden Moore in here in ten minutes to answer more questions," I tried.

No one budged.

Least of all Clay.

"No," he said again, hopping off the chair and down to the floor in front of me. My breath caught as his scent enveloped me, as he stepped closer and closer until we were chest to chest.

Or rather, chest to abdomen.

"No, I won't stop. I *can't* stop, Giana. I can't hide or pretend anymore. I can't let my pride keep me from being honest and admitting that I fuuu—"

He paused, an awkward smile on his lips as he amended his language.

"Messed up. Bad."

I swallowed, ribs squeezing painfully tight around my lungs.

"I hurt you. I know I did. And I also know that I don't deserve the chance to explain everything to you, to admit my wrongs and ask for your forgiveness." His brows folded together. "But I'm going to anyway. Because I love you, Giana Jones."

The room was aflutter, cameras flashing and microphones being shoved as close to us as they could manage as Clay moved in closer, one hand moving up to sweep my hair out of my face.

"I love you," he repeated, quieter this time, as if he only wanted me to hear. "I love your smutty books, and your weird documentaries, and your obsession with orange, processed snacks."

I choked on something between a laugh and a sob.

"I love the way you dress, and the way you light up when you talk about the universe, and the way you saw through every wall I tried to put between me and the rest of the world and knew who I was even when I didn't."

He shook his head, licking his lips before he continued.

"I love how you believe in me, and how you burn to prove everyone wrong when they size you up too quickly. I love that you challenge yourself." He paused. "I love that you challenge *me*."

I leaned into his palm, bottom lip quivering before I bit down to hold it still.

"I love everything about you — big and small, silly and serious. And I'm sorry I was an idiot and tried to end our story before it even had the chance to begin."

I closed my eyes, not even realizing the tears that had flooded my eyes until that motion released them and two rivulets ran silently down my cheeks.

Clay thumbed each away.

"I know I have a lot to explain, and I promise I'll tell you everything. But right now, I just need you to know that I might have been good at pretending a lot in our time together, but I never faked the way I felt about you." His thumb slid across my jaw. "You have owned my heart since the first fake kiss, Kitten."

Something of a laugh left me as I opened my eyes again, and Clay waited until I looked at him before he held up the book in his hands.

"This baby needs some revision," he said, trying to smile, though it fell quickly as his eyes searched mine, the same pain I felt reflected in them. "So, what do you say? Want to rewrite it together?"

A few more tears slipped quietly down my cheeks, Clay wiping them away before they had the chance to even hit my jaw line as I shook my head. My eyes bounced between his, heart swelling with the hope he'd restored.

I sniffed, grabbing the book and turning it over in my hands as I surveyed the horrid cover and font.

"Only if we start completely over," I whispered, smiling as I peeked up at him. "Because this is the ugliest thing I have ever seen in my life."

The room burst into laughter at that, and I had almost forgotten about the crowd until that moment. But I didn't have time to even blush before Clay took the book out of my hand and dropped it to the ground.

"Deal," he breathed.

And then he kissed me.

His arms wrapped me up in a fierce embrace, sweeping me off my feet until just my toes touched the ground. I snaked my arms around his neck just the same, holding on tight as he kissed me breathless in the flashing lights of a dozen cameras.

"Atta boy!" I heard Zeke yell, and the room erupted into applause.

That brought me back to the moment, and I flushed, breaking our kiss and ducking my head into Clay's chest as he grinned and tucked me into his side.

"Alright, alright," he said, holding up his other hand. "No more questions. You can read all about it in our book." He looked down at me then. "If we ever stop kissing long enough to write it."

Riley blew out a loud whistle as Clay swept me up in his arms, kissing me to another bellow of applause before he was carrying me through the crowd and out the door. Cameras and crew tried to follow us, but Riley and Zeke held them off — along with Charlotte, who turned and crossed her arms once we'd shut the door that led into the team hallway.

"Oh God," I said, scrambling out of Clay's arms. "Charlotte, I'm so sorry. I—"

"Sorry?" she asked, severe, and then a slow smile spread on her face. "For what? Making us the headline?"

I blinked. "I...uh..."

"It's fine," she said, begrudgingly, before she turned and pointed at Clay. "But don't *ever* pull that shit again. And you both owe me an interview with the reporter of my choosing. A long one."

"Yes, ma'am," Clay answered.

Charlotte smirked, waving a hand at me as she clicked by in her high heels. "Go get a room, you two, before you make us all sick."

I hid my face in Clay's chest again, and then he used his knuckles to tilt my chin, wrapping me in his arms before he turned to face Zeke and Riley.

"Thanks for helping me pull my head out of my ass," he said.

Zeke put his arm around Riley. "Anytime, bro."

"You two were in on this?" I asked, pointing between them.

"Duh," Riley answered. "Although, don't blame those stick figures on me. I offered to help sketch and he refused."

"My stick figures are a masterpiece," Clay said, holding his head high.

Riley and I exchanged looks before all four of us burst into laughter.

"I can't believe you did that," I said, shaking my head as I looked up at Clay. My heart beat faster when I did, when I realized his arms were around me and we were together.

Together.

"I can't believe you're giving me the chance to explain," he countered.

"Speaking of which, we'll leave you to it," Zeke said, and he and Riley gave a wave of their fingers before disappearing down the hall, leaving me and Clay alone.

I turned in his arms, fingers crawling up his chest before I hooked them behind his neck. "Is this real?" I asked, chest pained at the thought that I was dreaming.

Clay swallowed, nodded, and pulled me into him. "I'm sorry I ever made you doubt my feelings for you. I'm sorry I hurt you the way I did."

"I knew you didn't want to."

"I know," he said, shaking his head. "Which is crazy, by the way. *How* did you know?"

"Because I know you," I said simply, searching his eyes. "Because I love you, too."

Clay blew out a breath, his forehead bending to meet mine. "Fuck, it feels good to hear you say that."

I smiled, pressing up on my toes to kiss him. We both inhaled deeply at the contact, savoring the way that kiss felt as Clay swept his tongue in to taste mine.

"I want to know everything," I whispered. "But first, I want you to take me home."

Chapter 30

GIANA

"That is... a lot," I confessed after Clay told me everything that had happened, head on his chest as he idly drew circles on my bare back with his fingertip. Each new spiral sent chills down to my toes, and I curled into him like a sated cat, still sore between my thighs from him ravishing me as soon as we pushed through my apartment door.

I couldn't stop touching him. I couldn't stop holding onto him and pressing soft kisses to his skin and inhaling his scent to convince myself that this was real, that he was here, that we were together.

"I know," he said, fingertip trailing over my shoulder. "I'm sorry I didn't let you in. You probably would have been like Riley, Zeke, and Holden and been able to talk some sense into me."

I frowned. "I don't know. Honestly, I might have just cried more and clung to you as long as I could before I had to let you go."

"Let me go?"

I leaned up onto my elbow, looking down at him. "I understand, Clay. What your mom has done for you is precious, and I don't fault you for wanting to pay her back for that, for wanting to give her everything — regardless of whatever demons she might be fighting. You love her," I said on a shrug. "And Mommas come before girlfriends."

His smile was sad, brows furrowing. "I don't want anyone or anything to come between us. And I think that's what I forgot. I can give to the ones I love without sacrificing everything that brings me joy in the process." He made a face. "Although, I have no idea what I'm going to do for her now."

"Is she home?"

He nodded. "She was more than understanding when I told her everything. In fact, I saw the Momma Bear come out in her," he added with a smirk. "She wanted to kill Cory. But I told her I had it handled, and she trusted me." He paused. "Or Cory's dead right now and we just don't know yet."

I chuckled.

"Either way, she's home, and looking for jobs. She's proud of me, and loves me, and understands. But..." He shook his head. "I know she's still not okay, Giana. I know she needs help. She might be fine for a while — find a job, find a guy. But the cycle always repeats."

I stared at my hand on his chest. "What if there was a way," I whispered.

"A way to what?"

"To help your mom the way she really needs it."

Clay's brows perked up.

"What if you could cover the bills for a while, and still send her to rehab — maybe not one as fancy, but a nice one."

"I think that would be amazing," Clay said, thumbing my cheek. "But I also think it's impossible, unless I'm willing to take out a pretty sizable loan."

"Not necessarily."

Clay eyes me curiously as I sat up fully, crossing my legs under me. He slid up until his back was to the headboard, waiting.

"We had a sponsor reach out to us, and they're looking to do a big campaign leading up to the bowl games and championship."

The curiosity on his face vanished, replaced by hard stone. "No."

"Hear me out," I said, putting up my hands. "It won't be like a Kyle Robbins situation."

"How would it be different?"

"Because you don't want it for the same reasons," I explained easily. "And it wouldn't be an ongoing commitment."

"I need to be focused on the field right now. We're only a month away from bowl season."

"And you can be. Look," I said, pulling his hands into mine. "One commercial. One event where you sign some sneakers. You'd probably have to wear them exclusively for a while, but it wouldn't be forever. I can work out the terms to be whatever you're comfortable with."

Clay frowned, considering. "It can be like that?"

"When you're the best safety in the nation?" I arched a brow. "It can be like anything you demand."

He smirked, leaning his head back against the headboard as he studied me. "You're sounding like my agent now, Kitten."

"Maybe I will be one day."

"Is that something you'd want to do?"

I shrugged. "I don't know. Maybe. Charlotte said something to me when she extended my contract. She said I'd already succeeded in proving people wrong about me, but now she wanted me to ask myself what I actually want from this so I can reach out and take it."

Clay sat up. "I'm not kidding, if you wanted to be my agent, I'd take you in a heartbeat. I bet Zeke, Riley, and Holden all would, too. Maybe even Leo — if the showboating sonofabitch doesn't try to represent himself."

My heart zipped in my chest at the thought, but I waved him off. "We can talk about that later. Right now, let's focus on getting your mom the help she needs."

Clay sighed, pulling on my hands until I was collapsing into his arms as he laid back against the headboard again. "You're too good to me."

"No, you're just not used to being in a relationship where the love and care is reciprocated."

"It's going to take some getting used to."

"Good thing we have all the time in the world."

He smiled, kissing my hair.

"Is... is Maliyah okay?"

Clay shook his head. "Only *you* would ask if my ex-girlfriend is okay."

"I mean, you told her everything, right?" I frowned. "That wouldn't be easy for anyone to hear."

"It wasn't," he agreed, his gaze lost between us. "She cried, a lot, and I held her and tried to soothe her as best I could. In the end, though, she said she understood. She said she'd hurt me just as badly — which isn't wrong. I think she was most upset by her dad," I admitted. "And I know *he* isn't happy that I told her what happened."

"Well, I'm glad you did. She deserved the truth."

"She did. And, weirdly... I feel like we could maybe be friends now. Not close friends," he amended quickly. "But... friendly. Cordial. I don't know that I could say the same for Cory, though. I think his days of acting as my stand-in dad are over."

I smoothed a hand over his bicep. "What about your real dad?"

He blew out a breath. "*That* I haven't even begun to tackle yet. But... I owe him an apology. I see now better than I did when I went off on him that he was just trying to help me."

"To be fair, he could show up a little more."

"He could," Clay agreed. "Maybe now... he will."

I smiled, nodding as I watched where my fingertips drew lines on his skin.

"I am a little pissed off at you, though," I admitted after a moment.

"As you should be."

"Not for this whole mess," I said, waving a hand as if it was on the foot of my bed. "But you've known for almost *two weeks* that you messed up, that you wanted me back, and you waited to tell me?"

"Hey," he said, popping up long enough to lean over and grab his book off my nightstand. "It takes time to write and print a book, okay? Even one this shitty."

I snatched it out of his hands, smiling as I flipped through. "It really is horrendous."

"I know."

"But you didn't need the book to tell me how you felt," I pointed out, peeking up at him.

"I needed a grand gesture," he argued. "I couldn't just show up here with my tail between my legs."

"You could have."

"It wouldn't have been nearly as romantic."

"Or public," I said with a laugh.

"Now everyone knows you're mine." Clay grabbed the book out of my hands and tossed it aside before pinning me in the sheets, kissing all up and down my neck as I laughed and wriggled under the ticklish touch.

After a moment, he stopped, balancing on his elbows above me. His jade eyes scanned my own, and he swallowed, shaking his head.

"What?" I asked.

"I just... I thought I'd lost you. Forever. I thought I'd never get to be here again, holding you like this, touching you, kissing you." His face crumpled in pain. "I was miserable without you."

"I don't want to talk about how many bags of Cheetos I ate."

He smirked, brushing my hair out of my face before he gently removed my glasses and set them aside. Then, he pulled me into him, lips pressing against mine with tender warmth.

My body sparked to life under that kiss, under his massive hands as they pinned my hips beneath him, and he rolled into me. He was already growing hard beneath his briefs, and I whimpered at the feel of him, nails digging into his back.

All conversation ceased as those kisses ran deeper and deeper, until we were panting and moaning and stripping what little clothing we had put on since our first round. When we were fully bare, Clay rolled onto his back, helping me climb onto his lap.

Except then, he pulled me up higher.

"What are you doing?" I breathed.

"I want you to ride my face."

I balked, but I didn't have the chance to scurry away or argue against him before he yanked me up, positioning the back of my thighs against his shoulders, my pussy hovering right over his face. He slid his hands down my ribcage, gripping my ass in both palms as he pulled me to him.

And I had no choice but to hold on.

My hands flew out to find the headboard, and I gripped hard as he not only rolled his tongue against me, but used his hands on my ass to roll my hips against *him*, too. Back and forth, I ground against his mouth as he swirled and flicked and sucked and licked.

It was dizzying in the best way, and I was almost embarrassed at how fast I came for him, at how he stayed right there and lapped up every last second of my release. Only when I was fully sated and trembling did he carefully help me dismount, and then he rolled me over onto my stomach, kissing all along my back before he disappeared for the amount of time it took him to grab a condom.

I saw stars when he slid inside me from behind, and he hooked my hips, hiking me up to arch for him as he withdrew before plummeting inside me again. I was desperate to be close to him, so I pressed up onto my knees, one hand reaching back to hook around his neck while the other reached behind for his ass.

He groaned when I squeezed him, pulling him deeper into me as I pressed my ass back and begged for more. He trailed kisses along my neck, sucking my earlobe between his teeth as I moaned and ground against him.

"You're mine, Giana Jones," he growled into my ear, hand crawling over my chest until it clamped down over my throat. I arched into it, gasping in pleasure. "And I'm never letting you go."

Our first time reconnecting when we'd come back to my apartment was fast — desperate and rabid and over before either of us had the chance to take a real breath. But this time, Clay was slow and purposeful with every thrust. Just when I thought he was ready to release, he'd pull out, kissing me long and deep as he switched us into a new position.

It was on the heels of another orgasm for me that he finally came, too, my ankles on his shoulders as he pumped out every rivulet of his release. And when he carried me into the shower, my legs too weak to move on their own, he sank down under the streaming hot water and cradled me to his chest.

"I love you," he whispered, tilting my chin up.

"I love you," I echoed, threading my fingers through the wet hair at the nape of his neck.

And then he kissed me, and for the first time in my life, I felt like the main character.

This was my happy ever after.

Chapter 31

ONE MONTH LATER
CLAY

We all stared at Coach Sanders for a full twenty seconds without anyone saying a word.

And then, it was fucking chaos.

"What?!"

"You can't *leave*."

"We just lost a bowl game. And now this shit?"

"*Literally* just lost."

"We're on fire. Why would you leave?"

"We can't do this without you!"

I just watched the calamity unfold, my heart stuck in my throat even as I attempted to swallow it down. One glance at Holden standing quiet and calm in the corner told me he was still processing, too — and likely trying to decide how a leader should react to this news.

Our head coach was leaving us.

We were on the cusp of *greatness*, and he was taking a job in the NFL.

I couldn't fault him. Hell, I knew that when it came down to it, *none* of us could. It was a dream for almost all of us to play in the League, and nearly every college coach dreamed of the day they were invited up.

But we'd just lost the playoff bowl game against one of the top schools in the nation. We were beat up from it, down — but not out. If anything, that loss only made us want it more.

Now, we'd have a new coach to guide this pack of hungry wolves.

After the noise erupted to an unbearable level, Coach Sanders held out his hands, swallowing as he waited for us to calm down.

"I know this isn't easy news," he said. "And believe me when I say it wasn't an easy choice for me, either. I have been here with you every step of the way. I'm proud of what I've built here — of what *we* have built together. And I have absolutely no doubt in my mind that it will be you holding up that championship trophy next year. It guts me that I won't be there holding it up with you."

My eyes watered, and I sniffed, internally cursing as I hid my face from the team.

"You don't need me."

There were several shouts of disagreement, but Coach held up his hands again.

"You don't. You can do this — whether it's with me or another coach or on your own. You're strong. You're diligent. You're dedicated. And you're talented." He nodded, looking each of us in the eye. "Never forget that. Never stop fighting. And never forget that even across the country, I'm in your corner, and I believe in you."

The sadness in the locker room was so palpable, I could taste it. We'd just dragged our asses off the field after a bowl loss, and now, even worse news hit us upside the head unexpectedly.

We looked pathetic.

After a long, silent moment, Holden stood, quietly making his way to stand next to Coach. He clapped him on the shoulder, the two of them exchanging a nod of respect before Holden turned to face the team.

"Coach is right," he said, his eyes determined as they scanned the room.

I swore I saw him step into even *more* of a leadership role, if it was possible. It was as if the ship was going down and the captain took the only lifeboat, so the first mate took the wheel, doing all he could to steady us in the storm.

"This isn't the end for us. We showed the entire nation this season that we are *the* team they should all be afraid of. We nearly went undefeated, and we showed real grit and heart out there against the top team in the nation tonight," he added, pointing behind him like we were still on the field.

It was true. We hadn't gotten our asses handed to us in the loss. It had been by only three points — a field goal that was scored too late in the last quarter for us to do anything about it, though we tried.

"Our victory may not be tonight," Holden said, nodding as he looked around. "But it still exists. Our championship is waiting. Now, are you going to turn your back on it because we're losing some of our family? Our brothers," he said, gesturing to a couple of our seniors. He smirked then, arching a brow back at Coach. "Our Pops."

He somehow made us all chuckle, even in the darkest hour, and Coach socked him across the arm — but he was smiling, too.

"Do you think they'd want us to give up?"

One of the seniors stood, pointing his gargantuan finger at all of us. "If you don't win next year, I'll fly back from wherever I am in the country and kick every single one of your asses."

Another senior popped up to join him. "I'll help."

"See?" Holden said, gesturing to them. "Today, this loss? It stings. It hurts like hell. It feels unfair, like our one shot was stolen. But that's just it — this isn't our last bullet. We have another in the chamber." He paused, letting that sink in. "So, are we going to throw in the towel? Or are we going to fight?"

"Fight!" Leo said, jumping up from where he was seated in front of a locker.

"Fight!" Zeke echoed, jumping up, too.

One after the other, every member of our team stood, thrusting their fists in the air with their brows bent, a new fire lit.

I stood last, crouched over as I bobbed my head and sifted through the crowd like a creature of the night. I walked to the rhythm of a song not playing, but Kyle caught on, and he started drumming out a beat on the nearest locker.

"Who are we?!"

"*NBU!*"

Their response was so loud it nearly knocked me on my ass.

"What do we want?!"

"*What all champs do!*"

Anyone walking past that locker room would have thought we were insane. We just *lost* the bowl game — and here we were changing like we'd won it.

"How do we win?"

"Fight with class!"

"And if all else fails?"

"KICK THEIR ASS!"

That last part was garbled and riddled with what sounded like war cries from everyone in the room. Helmets hit against lockers, cleats stomped on the floor, and my teammates beat their chests like warriors.

I glanced at Holden through the madness, who wore a slight tilt of his mouth as he nodded at me — my captain, and I, his new first mate.

It didn't matter that Coach was leaving.

It would be *our* season next year.

And no one would take it from us.

●●●

GIANA

New Year's Eve was a mixture of sadness and loss, of celebration and renewal — a juxtaposition of a cocktail that dizzied me the more I tried to figure it out.

I leaned my back against Clay's chest on the rooftop bar, his giant arms wrapped around me and doing more to warm me than my oversized coat. He was quiet after the bowl game loss, after the news of Coach Sanders heading to the NFL.

"Are your thoughts eating you alive in there?" I asked, smoothing my hands over his forearms where he held me. Our eyes were trained on the lights of Dallas flickering before us, fireworks already going off even though there were still a few minutes until midnight.

Clay let out a long breath, squeezing me tighter. "Everything is changing," he said softly.

"That's not necessarily a bad thing."

"No," he agreed. "But it makes me feel unsteady."

I turned in his arms, wrapping mine around his neck and pulling his gaze from the city down to me. "You are the steadiest man I know," I said truthfully. "And with Holden by your side, I know you two can hold the team together and face what comes next. Zeke and Riley will be there, too. And Leo." I paused. "Hell, even Kyle seemed fired up tonight."

Clay scoffed. "He just hopes the new coach is a pushover so he can bring his phone on the field again. Coach Sanders wouldn't have it."

"I'm sure the new coach won't either."

Clay sighed, shaking his head. "I'm nervous," he admitted. "But you're right. It's nothing we can't handle."

I nodded, playing with the hair at the nape of his neck as I pressed up on my toes, needing more contact. "You know... I've been thinking about what you said. About me being an agent."

He cocked a brow. "Yeah?"

"Yeah... and... I think I want to try."

Clay smirked, the first real light coming back to his eyes since Coach's news. "Wait, really? Holy shit, Kitten — that's epic."

"Don't get too excited just yet," I told him — mostly because it was dangerous for *me* to get too excited. "I talked to Charlotte about it. She said she'd help me, introduce me to some people, and let me take over leading our guys who have current NIL deals."

"That's huge!" Clay said, ignoring my request not to get too excited. He lifted me up, spinning me around as some of his teammates backed away so as not to be hit by my kitten heels. When he put me back down, he grabbed my face in his hands. "I'm so fucking proud of you."

I flushed, leaning into his palm. "We'll see what happens."

"Oh, I already know what will happen."

"Do tell."

"We're going to win the championship next year. And then the year after that, I'll get drafted in the first round, and you'll be my agent — negotiating the sickest signing bonus anyone has ever seen."

I let out a breath of a laugh. "And what about now?"

He frowned, confused.

"What happens before all that?"

Clay inhaled a long breath, his green eyes searching mine as he thumbed a curl behind my ear. That thumb traced my jaw next, and he framed my face, pulling me closer.

"Now, I spend the entire off-season spoiling my girl," he said easily, and as the crowd around us began to countdown from ten, he leaned in closer. "Starting with giving her her first New Year's Eve kiss."

Three... two... one!

With a tilt of my chin up to meet him, Clay's mouth claimed my own, and my heart floated off on the wings of a million butterflies as fireworks splayed overhead, their booms echoing in my heart.

Epilogue

HOLDEN

The locker room was completely silent on the first day of spring training.

My teammates sat in front of their lockers or leaned against training equipment, eyes on the floor as we waited.

I wanted to pump them up, to have some grand speech that would soothe all their worry.

But the truth was, I was worried, too.

Despite how I'd somehow managed to redirect their energy after our bowl game loss, I knew as much as everyone else in this room how much a new coach would change things. A new coach meant new drills, new ways of doing things, new plays and tactics and — possibly — new starters.

That was what scared everyone in this room the most.

All eyes snapped to the doorway that led into the hall when Coach Dawson, our defensive end coordinator, swung through it. On his heels was our special teams coach, our offensive coordinator, and our trainer staff.

And then, at the very end of the line, Coach Carson Lee.

Coach Lee shared a few similarities with our last coach. He was brutal in his training camps when he coached down south, he had a zero-tolerance attitude when it came to any of his players stepping out of line, and he expected greatness.

But he was different from Coach Sanders in many ways, too.

For starters, he was twenty years his senior, which somehow made me respect him even more just because he'd been coaching ball before I was even born. He also had a bit more of a radical approach, one that got him headlines for doing things like making his team run half the length of the Florida Panhandle one weekend after a loss to a team they were expected to beat easily.

We all stood when he entered, like soldiers coming to attention for their sergeant.

He swept into the room with purpose, talking to our new assistant coach whom he'd brought with him. I watched the two of them conversing as they moved toward the center of the locker room.

That was, until she walked in.

I almost thought it was Riley at first — because she and Giana Jones were the girls we ever really saw in the locker room. But the girl who swung through the door behind Coach was no one I'd ever seen before.

Her long, leather-brown hair flowed over her shoulders like chocolate waves — and that was the only thing soft about her. Every inch of her face was etched into severe precision, her jaw set, bow-shaped lips flattened into a tight line. In a red crop tank top and black track pants, I could tell she was fit, her toned, golden stomach peeking through the gap between the two. She was slight, narrow hips and lean arms, which made her ample bust stand out even more.

In every possible way, she was a complete knockout.

But it wasn't her body that held me captive.

It wasn't her hair, or the graceful line of her neck, or the arrogant indifference with which she strode into the room.

It was her eyes.

Warm, endlessly deep brown, framed by thick lashes that swept across her cheeks with every blink.

"At ease, gentlemen," Coach Lee said with a smirk, holding out his hands and signaling us to sit once he was in the center of the room. "And lady," he added with a pointed look at Riley.

The rest of the coaches lined the wall behind him, giving him our full attention.

"I know I've already met a few of you during my tours here, but I'm excited to finally get real time with each and every one of you. I won't pretend like I'm blind to how uncomfortable and uneasy this all must be for you. I'm not just a new player, I'm a new coach — and I know how that can shake things up more than anything else."

I swallowed.

"But I want you to know, I'm not here to change everything. Obviously, a lot of what you have going here has been working. It's an honor to be walking onto this team." He paused, hanging his hands on his hips. "It'll be even more of an honor to give you the last push to the finish line, to be there when they crown us champs at the end of the season."

That made several players exchange looks of determination and delight, that fire that I'd stoked at the end of last season just one good poke away from roaring again.

"It's the first day of spring training, and I don't want to use this precious time babbling on about myself. We'll get to know each other as the season progresses. For now, I want to introduce you to Coach Hoover," he said, gesturing for the man who'd walked in next to him to come up. "Hoover is my right-hand man, and will probably become your favorite person in the world because if anyone can talk me out of making a team run laps, it's him."

Coach Hoover smirked as Coach Lee clapped him on the back.

"And this," he said, waving a hand behind him. "Is my daughter — Julep."

Hesitantly, she stepped up to his side, though she didn't smile or show any ounce of emotion other than a slight raise of two fingers from where she'd folded her arms across her chest.

"Julep is a junior, and for some reason, loves me enough to transfer from our last university and finish out her degree here. She's majoring in sports medicine, and she'll be interning under the training staff on the team."

My heart rate spiked at the thought of her being around all the time, at the mere inference that she might be the one to stretch or massage me before a game.

Coach paused, something more severe washing over his expression as his jaw hardened, eyes narrowing.

"And let me be *extremely* clear," he said, scanning the room. "If any of you even so much as *thinks* about flirting with Julep, let alone having the balls to ask her on a date, you will have me to answer to. She's not here for you to ogle over. She's here to work — just like you. I imagine since you have Riley Novo as a teammate, I don't need to lecture any further than this about respecting females in the athletic industry."

Riley smiled a little at that, obviously impressed, and Julep rolled her eyes like she hated that this was a conversation that even needed to happen at all.

All the while, I was burning from the inside out.

Because all my life, football had been my one and only focus. It was all I cared about. It was my reason for waking up in the morning, and the only thought that consumed me when I laid my head down at night. It was my lifeline, my muse, the center of my attention.

But in one fatal moment, that focus shifted.

Julep Lee was the coach's daughter. She was completely off limits.

And yet, I knew right then and there that I had to have her.

What happens when the role model quarterback has his morals tested with the head coach's rebellious daughter? Find out this fall in Quarterback Sneak! *Pre-order now.* (https://amzn.to/3NgA5AM)

◆ ◆ ◆

What's worse than hating your brother's best friend? Rooming with him. Read Riley and Zeke's story in *Fair Catch* – FREE in Kindle Unlimited! (https://amzn.to/3wZPq1p)

MORE FROM KANDI STEINER

The Becker Brothers Series
On the Rocks
Neat (book 2)
Manhattan (book 3)
Old Fashioned (book 4)
Four brothers finding love in a small Tennessee town that revolves around a whiskey distillery with a dark past — including the mysterious death of their father.

The Best Kept Secrets Series
(AN AMAZON TOP 10 BESTSELLER)
What He Doesn't Know (book 1)
What He Always Knew (book 2)
What He Never Knew (book 3)
Charlie's marriage is dying. She's perfectly content to go down in the flames, until her first love shows back up and reminds her the other way love can burn.

Close Quarters
A summer yachting the Mediterranean sounded like heaven to Jasmine after finishing her undergrad degree. But her boyfriend's billionaire boss always gets what he wants. And this time, he wants her.

Make Me Hate You
Jasmine has been avoiding her best friend's brother for years, but when they're both in the same house for a wedding, she can't resist him — no matter how she tries.

The Wrong Game
(AN AMAZON TOP 10 BESTSELLER)
Gemma's plan is simple: invite a new guy to each home game using her season tickets for the Chicago Bears. It's the perfect way to avoid getting emotionally attached and also get some action. But after Zach gets his chance to be her practice round, he decides one game just isn't enough. A sexy, fun sports romance.

The Right Player
She's avoiding love at all costs. He wants nothing more than to lock her down. Sexy, hilarious and swoon-worthy, The Right Player is the perfect read for sports romance lovers.

On the Way to You
It was only supposed to be a road trip, but when Cooper discovers the journal of the boy driving the getaway car, everything changes. An emotional, angsty road trip romance.

A Love Letter to Whiskey
(AN AMAZON TOP 10 BESTSELLER)
An angsty, emotional romance between two lovers fighting the curse of bad timing.
Read Love, Whiskey – Jamie's side of the story and an extended epilogue – in the new Fifth Anniversary Edition!

Weightless
Young Natalie finds self-love and romance with her personal trainer, along with a slew of secrets that tie them together in ways she never thought possible.

Revelry
Recently divorced, Wren searches for clarity in a summer cabin outside of Seattle, where she makes an unforgettable connection with the broody, small town recluse next door.

Say Yes
Harley is studying art abroad in Florence, Italy. Trying to break free of her perfectionism, she steps outside one night determined to Say Yes to anything that comes her way. Of course, she didn't expect to run into Liam Benson...

Washed Up
Gregory Weston, the boy I once knew as my son's best friend, now a man I don't know at all. No, not just a man. A doctor. And he wants me...

The Christmas Blanket
Stuck in a cabin with my ex-husband waiting out a blizzard? Not exactly what I had pictured when I planned a surprise visit home for the holidays...

Black Number Four
A college, Greek-life romance of a hot young poker star and the boy sent to take her down.

The Palm South University Series
Rush (book 1) FREE if you sign up for my newsletter!
Anchor, PSU #2
Pledge, PSU #3
Legacy, PSU #4
Ritual, PSU #5

Hazed, PSU #6

Greek, PSU #7

#1 NYT Bestselling Author Rachel Van Dyken says, "If Gossip Girl and Riverdale had a love child, it would be PSU." This angsty college series will be your next guilty addiction.

Tag Chaser

She made a bet that she could stop chasing military men, which seemed easy — until her knight in shining armor and latest client at work showed up in Army ACUs.

Song Chaser

Tanner and Kellee are perfect for each other. They frequent the same bars, love the same music, and have the same desire to rip each other's clothes off. Only problem? Tanner is still in love with his best friend.

ACKNOWLEDGEMENTS

To my almost husband (!!!), Jack, thank you for answering all my questions while writing this series. We both know I'm more of an NFL girl myself, so the college rules confuse me every time. Thanks for setting me straight, and for always being there at the end of each day with a kiss. I love you.

Momma Von, thank you for being such a football nut while I was growing up that you made me become obsessed, too. And for always supporting my dreams.

To my alpha readers: Lily Turner, Frances O'Brien, Kellee Fabre, Trish QUEEN Mintness, and Monique Boone — thank you for letting me take you on this ride and for understanding when it kept growing and growing. I just couldn't get enough of Giana and Clay! Your feedback this time around was absolutely crucial, and I can't thank you enough for your help.

My beta team is always fundamental in my process, but this time around, y'all really came through with some editing notes that completely changed the feeling of this book — in the best way! Carly Wilson, Sarah Green, and Janett Corona, thank you for giving me your time and attention.

Elaine York of Allusion Publishing — there are no words for how much I love and appreciate you. Thank you for always working with me moving my timelines around and for never tiring of fixing my use of "further" versus "farther" because let's face it — I'll never get it right.

To Ren Saliba, thank you for the jaw-dropping cover photo that brought Clay to life. I'll never get tired of staring at that eyebrow and smolder.

To my dear friend Tina Stokes — THANK YOU for loving me and never saying no to a new adventure. And thank you for letting me obsess over Clay and Giana on our Virginia trip. I love you.

A big shout out to my friends at Valentine PR for spreading the word about this series and helping others fall in love with it. And to our blogger community (that includes you, Bookstagrammers and Booktokers). No one would even know I WRITE books if it weren't for you. You're the backbone of what we do, and I thank you.

Finally, to YOU, the reader. You are the reason I am able to do what I do! Thank you for reading indie and for shouting to the rooftops about books you love. A special shout out to those of you in Kandiland (http://facebook.com/groups/kandilandks) and who engage with me on social media. You make this even more fun every day and I can't wait for many more adventures together!

ABOUT THE AUTHOR

Kandi Steiner is an Amazon Top 5 bestselling author and whiskey connoisseur living in Tampa, FL. Best known for writing "emotional rollercoaster" stories, she loves bringing flawed characters to life and writing about real, raw romance — in all its forms. No two Kandi Steiner books are the same, and if you're a lover of angsty, emotional, and inspirational reads, she's your gal.

An alumna of the University of Central Florida, Kandi graduated with a double major in Creative Writing and Advertising/PR with a minor in Women's Studies. She started writing back in the 4th grade after reading the first Harry Potter installment. In 6th grade, she wrote and edited her own newspaper and distributed to her classmates. Eventually, the principal caught on and the newspaper was quickly halted, though Kandi tried fighting for her "freedom of press."

She took particular interest in writing romance after college, as she has always been a die hard hopeless romantic, and likes to highlight all the challenges of love as well as the triumphs.

When Kandi isn't writing, you can find her reading books of all kinds, planning her next adventure, or pole dancing (yes, you read that right). She enjoys live music, traveling, playing with her fur babies and soaking up the sweetness of life.

CONNECT WITH KANDI:
NEWSLETTER: kandisteiner.com/newsletter
FACEBOOK: facebook.com/kandisteiner
FACEBOOK READER GROUP (Kandiland):
facebook.com/groups/kandilandks
INSTAGRAM: Instagram.com/kandisteiner
TIKTOK: tiktok.com/@authorkandisteiner
TWITTER: twitter.com/kandisteiner
PINTEREST: pinterest.com/authorkandisteiner
WEBSITE: www.kandisteiner.com

Kandi Steiner may be coming to a city near you! Check out her "events" tab to see all the signings she's attending in the near future:
www.kandisteiner.com/events

Ingram Content Group UK Ltd.
Milton Keynes UK
UKHW040620250723
425738UK00004B/140